FORGING DARKNESS

FALLEN LEGACIES BOOK 2

FORGING DARKNESS

JULIE HALL

USA TODAY BESTSELLING AUTHOR

Forging Darkness (Fallen Legacies Book 2)

Published by Julie Hall

ISBN (paperback): 978-0-9989867-9-1

ISBN (hardcover): 978-1-954510-00-5

Julie Hall

www.JulieHallAuthor.com

Developmental and Line Editing by Rebecca Faith Editorial.

Proofreading by Janelle Leonard.

Cover design by Mirela Barbu.

Interior artwork by Salome Totladze and Kalynne Pratt.

AWARDS

Finalist, Speculative Fiction
Huntress
2018 ACFW Carol Awards

Young Adult Book of the Year
Huntress
2018 Christian Indie Awards

Gold Medal Winner
Huntress
2018 Illumination Awards

First Place Winner, Religion
Huntress
2018 IndieReader Discovery Awards

Christian Fiction Finalist
Huntress
2018 Next Generation Indie Book Awards

Alliance Award (Reader's Choice)
Warfare
2018 Realm Makers Awards

Parable Award Finalist
Logan
2018 Realm Makers Awards

Gold Medal Winner
Huntress
2017 The Wishing Shelf Book Awards

Best Inspirational Novel / Best Debut Author
Huntress / Julie Hall
2017 Ozarks Indie Book Festival

Second Place Winner
Huntress
2017 ReadFree.ly Indie Book of the Year

First Place Winner
Huntress
2012 Women of Faith Writing Contest

USA TODAY Bestselling Author
August 17, 2017 & June 21, 2018

Embers will enthrall fans of Cassandra Clare and Sarah J. Maas, or anyone who loves beautifully written urban fantasy with a sizzling-hot dose of romantic tension. Prepare to become addicted!

Audrey Grey

USA Today bestselling author of the *Kingdom of Runes* series

---

This delightful read was everything I wanted in a book and more. Author Julie Hall kept me turning pages far into the night, and I wanted the next book in the series the moment this one was over. Stealing Embers just may be one of the best books I've ever read. Well done!

Michele Israel Harper

award-winning editor and author of the *Beast Hunter* series

Crazy-talented Julie Hall has leapt onto my auto-buy-author list! Stealing Embers is an enthralling story, that easily ensnared me with its compelling characters and quintessential Nephilim concept! I need the next book—NOW!

Ronie Kendig

award-winning author of the *Droseran Saga*

PROLOGUE
STEEL

Freezing rain pelts me as I fly down the highway on my Ducati. My hands are numb despite my leather gloves, but that doesn't stop me from picking up speed during the straightaways. The desolate countryside I ride through has plenty of those.

I haven't seen so much as a single exit in miles and nothing that even hints at civilization in more than thirty minutes. I'm in Wyoming. Or maybe I've already hit Montana? Hard to tell when only a quarter of my brain is actually focused on the ride.

I fled Seraph Academy without having any real idea of where to go. I headed east toward Denver and then cut up north to get out of the state.

My body is stretched to its limits, wound like an over-strained rubber band. When I finally snap, I want to be as far away from that place as possible.

Water sluices in twin rivulets on either side of my front tire as it cuts through the downpour of rain and ice. If I was smart, I would have gotten off the road hours ago. Riding a motorcycle in weather like this would be suicide for a human, but my angel-born senses are sharper and more focused, downgrading the danger level from "absolute insanity" to "mildly stupid."

My headlight reflects off a sign in the distance: *Welcome to Montana.* That solves that mystery.

I drive another thirty minutes before finding a motel. It's early morning when I pull my bike into a parking spot and cut the engine. Despite my iron will to forge ahead through the night, my body aches with exhaustion. An hour of sleep is all I'll allow myself. It should be enough to keep my edge.

Yanking off my helmet, I notice the rain has stopped, but ice is crusted on my clothes. Shards of frozen water crack off the leather of my jacket as I tug my belongings from the saddlebags on either side of my ride.

Shoving through the front doors of the shabby motel, the glass door bangs against the wall, startling the clerk awake where she was dozing behind the front desk. She yelps and teeters on her stool. Grabbing the tabletop in front of her to right herself, she knocks over a cup, scattering pens across the shiny surface.

"Shoot." Her hands run back and forth, collecting the fallen objects. It's not until I'm standing right in front of her that she glances up. Her eyes grow in size as she takes me in, pupils dilating even as she clears her throat and leans away.

Slight enough that a strong breeze would knock her over, she hunches, subconsciously trying to make herself appear smaller, but it's too late to hide—I already have her in my sights.

Nephilim may be tasked with protecting humanity, but I'm still a hunter by nature—doubly so as a shifter—and have to tamp down the desire to attack when something cowers in front of me. It's that innate nature that makes humans wary of Nephilim. We may look like them, but we are a different species with lifetimes of violence bred into our very DNA.

"One night. Paying with cash." My voice is extra deep from lack of use for the last half day.

I plunk a hundred dollar bill on the counter and wait for her to take it. She doesn't move, hardly breathes. Like a deer in headlights, she remains motionless until I remember to break eye contact.

Being fully immersed in the human world is going to take some getting used to.

I scan the motel lobby, curling my upper lip in disgust. I'll be staying in roadside dumps like this for the foreseeable future. I can't use a credit card and there are only so many places I can rent a room with cash. But it can't be helped. My parents will be on me in a heartbeat if I leave an electronic trail, and I need the rest of my family to stay out of this. It's my mess, and I'm going to clean it up myself.

"Here you go." The girl's voice is soft as she pushes the bills across the counter. "Check-out is at eleven and the Wi-Fi password is on a card in the room. You're in 104 on the first floor."

Fisting the money, I shove the change in my pocket and palm the key card with only a slight tick of my chin to acknowledge I heard her.

I'm about to stalk off to my rented room—dang, I'm tired—when she slides another piece of paper toward me. I blink at the set of numbers scribbled across the small square and glance at the girl with a raised eyebrow.

"In case you need anything while you're here, you can

reach me on this number." Pink stains her high cheekbones as she tucks her long brown hair behind an ear.

Interesting. This one is braver than I guessed. Most people consider lions majestic, but not many would seek to tangle with one.

I cock my head and stare into her watered-down blue eyes. Blue is the right color, but the shade I'm partial to is the midnight version—dark enough to appear black at night and rich as the deep ocean in the light of day.

The corners of the girl's mouth lift in a tentative smile as I continue to observe her. Perhaps I'm confusing bravery with stupidity.

"This is my *personal* cell number," she emphasizes unnecessarily.

The chuckle I release is dry and rusty. I shake my head, turning my back on the stupidly brave girl, and stride away.

Doesn't she know the devil comes disguised in a pretty package?

*M*oist air caresses my neck, and the bed shakes rhythmically with each heavy heave from the large animal behind me. My tank top is plastered to my skin, and my cheek rests on something damp.

Turning my head, I'm face-to-face with a black and white Great Dane snuggled up against me. Its hind legs stretch over my hip and waist, and its tongue lolls on my pillow. A drool stain the size of the massive dog's head spreads across the pillowcase.

Nasty.

I'm gonna kill Tinkle. The idiot likes to shift into large animals and cuddle with me at night.

My pillow buzzes. I reach underneath it and grab my cell —the first phone I've ever had. Aside from the occasional group text, and the random gifs Sterling likes to send me, I hardly ever use it. It's basically a glorified alarm clock.

The screen lights up with one word: Unknown.

My heart starts to beat double-time. This is the fifth unknown call this month. Most of them have come through in the early morning or middle of the night. When I answer, I'm only ever met with silence—total serial killer stuff—but my gut tells me who is on the other line.

Maneuvering out from under the dog sprawled across my comforter, I pad to the bathroom, making sure Ash is still asleep. She's a lump under the covers, slowly inflating and deflating with her even breaths. Only a few clusters of ringlets peek out from under her blankets.

Shutting the door as gently as possible, I scurry to the far end of the small room, anxious to answer the call before my voicemail picks up.

I hit the green button on the screen and hold it to my ear for several ticks before saying anything.

"Hello?" The word passes my lips as barely more than a whisper.

As usual, I'm greeted by silence.

My stomach bottoms out in disappointment.

Is he ever going to talk to me? If not, why does he even bother calling?

I slide down the wall until my butt settles on the chilled tiled floor, pulling my knees to my chest.

"Steel?"

I know it's him. I haven't told anyone about these calls, mostly because there's nothing to tell since he never talks. Also, I don't want to explain how I know it's him. With every call, there's a tug on my heart that only ever happens when he's around.

Audible breathing on the other end of the line should probably be creepy, but it's not. It's a connection to Steel I'm desperate to hang on to. The last two months he's been gone have been . . . hard.

I'll only admit it to myself, and under duress I'll deny it to my dying breath, but I miss him.

The frustrating part is that I can't put my finger on what exactly I miss. Steel was a grade-A jerk to me ninety-five percent of the time. He pushed me and aggravated me and didn't let me get away with anything. He never took it easy when we trained, and the tender moments we shared were few and far between. But since he left, I feel the hollowness inside more acutely. I'm over trying to figure out why.

My grip on the phone goes white-knuckle as the silence continues.

"If you're not going to talk to me, please check in with your family. They're worried sick about you."

His parents and siblings haven't heard from him since the day he rode off. The youngest twins seem to be taking Steel's absence the hardest. They've practically adopted me as a surrogate sibling. I've even found them hiding in my dorm room a few times. They claimed they were making sure I hadn't been devoured by monsters, but I knew better. They missed their older brother and were looking for some sort of connection to him. Unfortunately, they weren't going to get what they needed fighting the dust bunnies under my bed.

Even though Steel and I had buried the hatchet—kinda . . . sorta—he probably wouldn't be okay with them seeking me out. When it comes to his siblings, his protective instincts run deep, and who's to say I don't still have a target on my back?

"Steel, at least tell me if you're okay," I say. I don't hold out much hope that he'll respond, so when he does, my heart stutters.

"Em . . . I found her."

I stop breathing.

There's no mistaking who he's talking about: Silver, his twin sister, thought to be deceased up until we learned she orchestrated the youngest Durands' kidnapping to lure me into a trap. It didn't work, but it was a close call. I still don't know what the Forsaken want with me, but if the Nephilim from Seraph Academy hadn't tracked us down that day, I have no doubt I'd be dead now.

Steel has been hunting her since the day he found out she was alive.

My lungs start to burn, reminding me I need oxygen. I drag in a ragged breath. "Tell me where you are, Steel. I'll talk to Sable and she'll send help. Please don't do this alone."

Steady, Emberly. He spooks easily.

I press a hand to the floor beneath me. The thought of Steel going up against his sister sends earthquakes of trepidation rolling through my body.

Silver isn't your average Forsaken. She's cunning and strong and somehow seems to have retained part of herself even after being possessed by a Fallen. She's dangerous in a way I don't fully understand.

Steel doesn't want to admit it, but he needs help.

My fingers curl as the silence stretches and pulls. My nails scrape across the porcelain tiles as if dragged against a chalkboard.

"I have to." And then the line goes dead.

I lower the phone from my ear, but my grip tightens until it snaps. I've broken the glass screen. A long fissure splinters its way from the bottom corner to the top.

I tap the screen and only feel a mild sense of relief that it's still working. What I really want to do is yell in frustration, but I don't want to wake Ash, so instead I simply squeeze my eyes shut and let my head fall back and bump into the wall.

Relief that Steel is still alive and safe wars with fury at his refusal to accept help. And although I'm glad he's at least checking in with someone, he's put me in an impossible position.

Now that I know he's actually found Silver, I don't know if I can keep this secret anymore.

The room brightens behind my shut lids, and I blink them open. Ash stands in the doorway, rubbing her eyes. The pink eye-mask she wears is pushed up on her head, keeping her hair off her forehead.

The girl gets epic bedhead when she's too lazy to wrap her hair before sleeping, like tonight. The curls on one side of her head are squished flat against her scalp, while those on the other are fanned out in an afro. She's rocking a half-mohawk that's going to be a nightmare for her in the morning.

After shuffling a few steps forward into the bathroom, Ash catches sight of me folded in the corner. She tilts her head and draws her eyebrows together.

"You okay?" she croaks, her voice heavy with sleep.

Pressing my lips together, I shake my head before pushing to my feet. This weight is too heavy for me to bear alone.

"We need to talk."

2

"*H*e just breathes into the phone? That's very Stalker 101. He's going to tarnish the family name with courting skills like that."

"Something to share with the class, Mr. Durand?"

"Oh snap, bro. He just 'Mr. Durand-ed' you. You're in trouble."

Greyson levels his twin with a harsh glare before apologizing to Seth for interrupting his demonstration. But as soon as Seth goes back to showing the benefits of defensive sparring, Greyson's interrogation resumes.

How long have we been communicating? Did Steel tell me not to tell them he was calling? Did I know where he was? How heavy was his breathing?

What made me think combat class was the perfect time to tell the twins about my midnight phone liaisons? Oh right, Ash wouldn't let me keep the secret for a moment longer and forced my hand as soon as we ran into the brothers, which happened to be during mid-day training.

I scowl at her before quietly trying to answer Greyson's

questions. She returns my glare with narrowed eyes. She wasn't happy I'd kept Steel's calls a secret and had been very vocal about her opinions last night. I felt berated as well as defensive.

"He's only spoken once," I whisper-hiss back at Greyson, worried I'll get called out as well. I hate having a class full of eyes on me. Greyson doesn't share the same concerns.

"If he only talked once, how do you even know it was him?"

That was the question I was hoping to avoid, but knew I wouldn't be able to.

"I could just . . . tell."

Greyson's mouth puckers and twists to the side as he considers my weak explanation. His gaze bounces around my face as if he'll learn some truth in one of its contours. After a beat, he moves on without pressing me further on the subject. I hold in my sigh of relief.

"And when he did speak, he only said, 'I found her'?"

"Yeah."

"And you're sure he meant Silver?"

"Who else could he have meant?" I mean, really?

"Maybe he meant 'her' as in 'the one,'" Sterling suggests with raised eyebrows. "Maybe he fell in love and wanted you to be the first to know."

My heart skips a beat before resuming its normal pace. That doesn't even make sense. Sterling needs to lay off the romance novels.

Ash discretely elbows Sterling in the ribs.

I shoot Sterling a deadpan stare. "Get real."

Greyson is quiet for a blessed moment, his brow creasing as he thinks. "The only choice we have is to find him. He's going to need our help."

"You four!" Seth stands at the front of the class, pointing in our direction. "Out of the gym. If you're not going to pay attention, I don't want you in my class."

Hunching my shoulders, I shrink down as far as possible, properly scolded in front of a class full of peers. This is shaping up to be a great day.

Sterling pops up off the mat. "Thanks, man." He salutes Seth as if he's just done him a solid.

With downcast eyes, I follow the others out, feeling the stares of my classmates as we make the never-ending walk past the different training sectors.

In the locker room, I skip a shower since we didn't get a chance to spar before being kicked out of class. Greyson and Sterling finish changing before Ash and me, and we find them both leaned up against the wall in the hallway, waiting. Greyson's head is down, and he's typing out something on his phone. It's a moment before he looks up.

"Let's go somewhere we can talk." He tilts his head to indicate the direction and starts off. The rest of us follow.

"So why do you think he's only called you? It's not like he doesn't have his brothers' numbers. In fact, he would have had to do some research to find yours. You didn't get a phone until after he left." Sterling speaks the other question I didn't want to be asked.

Looking into Sterling's blue-green eyes, I take the coward's way out and shrug. "Your guess is as good as mine."

We're about to round a corner when the sound of shoes beating against the stone floor echoes off the corridor in front of us. We all pause. A mischievous round of laughter rings out a heartbeat before Blaze and Aurora careen around the bend, crashing into Greyson.

He catches them both, one in each arm, miraculously keeping them all on their feet.

Aurora's face is flushed red. A sheen of sweat makes her face glow and her eyes bright. Her long mane is ruffled in a few spots and fine hairs stick to her forehead.

Blaze is equally disheveled. His gaze darts behind him as if he's expecting someone to appear in pursuit any moment.

"What have you hellions been up to?" Greyson asks.

"Nothing." Blaze's response comes too quickly. Paired with the fervent glances he keeps lobbing over his shoulder, it's obviously a lie.

"Emmy!" Aurora wiggles out of Greyson's hold and jumps at me. I absorb her weight with an "oomph" and return the hug. It's impossible not to fall in love with her. She pulls back and peers up at me, the very picture of innocence. "Blaze and I need to lie low for a bit."

Uh-oh.

"So you've been up to no good." A grin spreads across Sterling's face. "I approve." Holding up a hand, Blaze slaps him a high five.

"What trick did you play today?" Greyson asks, a touch of weariness permeating his words. In Steel's absence he's the one who keeps having to talk to the teachers when the twins pull something on the staff or another student.

"It's not our fault he doesn't have a sense of humor. And really, what do they expect in a student science lab? We need to be free to learn and explore."

This ought to be good. I do my best to plaster a neutral expression on my face, wanting to support Greyson, but I'm not sure I'll be able to hold it together.

"What *exactly* did you do?" Greyson presses.

Aurora snuggles into my side, using my arm as a partial

shield and leaving her twin to face the firing squad on his own. He shoots her a quick look that screams *traitor*. Toeing at an invisible scuff on the ground, he opens his mouth to confess, when someone shouts the twins' names from down the hall.

"Whoops, gotta go!" Blaze says and grabs Aurora's hand, pulling her from my side. With a half-wave they dash off, disappearing around the bend only a half-second before Eric, the younger grades' science teacher, appears around another corner, his eyes wild and covered from head to toe in a moss green substance.

"Where did they go?" he asks our group.

Sterling immediately points in the opposite direction from the one his siblings went, and Eric takes off. The putrid stench of rotten eggs and skunk wafts off him as he passes us. It's bad enough that I slap a hand over my face, pinching my nose and breathing in and out of my mouth, waiting for it to dissipate.

"I couldn't be prouder of those two," Sterling announces, the grin on his face a picture of brotherly affection.

Greyson shakes his head, but I don't miss the ghost of a smile on his face. "Let's get out of here. We have some serious things to discuss."

After all the weeks I've spent at the academy, I've never visited the boys' dormitory, but it looks pretty much the same as the girls'. Girls on the boys' side and vice versa isn't forbidden during daylight hours, but it isn't encouraged either. This time of day, the hallways are barren. Greyson opens a non-descript wooden door halfway down the hall.

"It's about time," Nova snaps when we walk into the room. She's sitting on one of the beds, her back against the headboard and shoe-clad feet propped up on the dark comforter beneath her, while Tinkle, in the form of a hummingbird, flits around her head. The Celestial has taken a shine to Nova and spends just as much time with her as he does me. I'm not sad about it. The little dude has a lot of energy. "What kept you guys?"

"I texted her," Greyson offers by way of explanation.

Sterling pushes past his brother. "Could you have at least taken off your shoes?"

Nova lifts a perfectly shaped eyebrow. "I want to have as many layers of protection between me and your bedding as possible." She shudders theatrically.

Is Sterling . . . blushing?

"I clean my stuff," he grumbles under his breath. "If you're not going to take your shoes off, get off my bed."

Nova gives Sterling a one-shoulder shrug, but slides off his bed. Kicking off her heels, she climbs on Greyson's bed, crisscrossing her legs under her.

"Oh, so *that's* how it is," Sterling grouses. The pink on his cheeks deepens, but it isn't embarrassment reddening his face now.

He receives another one-shoulder shrug from Nova. A sly smirk dances on her lips. She's a cat playing with a mouse, thoroughly enjoying the game.

"All right you two, playtime's over." Greyson pins Sterling with a pointed look. "Ash, Em, feel free to sit wherever you want."

Spying what looks to be a jock strap sticking out from under Greyson's bed, I quickly avert my gaze and sit gingerly at the foot of the bed. There are just some things I don't want to know about my friends. Ash eyes Sterling's bed with disdain before plopping down next to me.

As Sterling flops into his desk chair, my eyes bulge at the command center behind him.

Sterling has five monitors.

Five.

Three sit on top of his desk, and two more hover above those on dedicated shelves bolted to the wall. He has two keyboards and three laptops docked below the monitors. An open bag of licorice sags out of the top desk drawer, and empty cans of Red Bull litter the little space he has left.

Sterling snags a red candy rope and starts chewing on one end. He lifts up one of the energy drink cans and gives it a little shake to check for liquid. "Score," he says before bringing it to his mouth and chugging whatever contents remain.

"He has a massive sugar tooth," Greyson offers.

Yeah, no doubt.

"It helps me concentrate."

Nova rolls her eyes. "Caffeine and sugar don't affect our supercharged bodies like humans. But if it makes you feel better to think that, go on shoving that junk in your mouth. It's going to show up on your gut eventually."

Sterling looks down and lifts his shirt to check out his stomach. He's sporting a perfectly sculpted six-pack. I resist the urge to fan myself. These angel-born boys are nothing like the scrawny human high schoolers I used to go to school with. Tracking his gaze to Nova, a broad smile grows on his face. "I think I'm good."

Red and blue sparks rain down on us as Tinkle flits around the room.

"What's up with him?" I ask. He seems a bit more spastic than usual.

Nova sighs. "He wanted to try some of Sterling's Red

Bull. He's been flying around like that for the last ten minutes."

"See. It does give you wings!" Sterling picks up and shakes a few more cans, looking for dregs, but comes up empty.

Chuckling under his breath, Greyson snags the other desk chair in the room. "All right, we need a game plan." He props his elbows on his knees and glances at each of us. "Now that we know Steel's found Silver, what are we going to do about it?"

I don't dare turn my face to see Nova's reaction. I already don't like discussing Steel, but talking about him with her is downright awkward. Maybe it's my imagination, but I feel her regard like a heater against my skin whenever his name is brought up.

"I think—" Ash only gets two words out before Tinkle drops from the air, landing on Sterling's bed with a soft thud.

"Sweet nectar," he mumbles before falling asleep.

Ash clears her throat, garnering our attention once again. "As I was saying, I think Steel is going to need help. It's dangerous to be out there on his own, hunting Forsaken. We need to decide if we're going to be the ones to help him, or if we're going to petition someone else to do it. Either way, we obviously have to do something."

Greyson's head bobs as Ash speaks. "I agree. It was foolish of him to go off alone. He needs help. I can understand why he did it—Silver is . . . was my sister as well, but Steel can't take on the world alone, even though he thinks that's written into his job description."

"Are we sure the Nephilim will do anything if we give them the information?" I ask. "Will they even use the resources to track him down? They haven't yet, so why start now?" My questions are met with silence and lowered brows as the group considers. The Nephilim have known about Silver since the battle all those weeks ago. They refused to send anyone after her when Steel asked, and then when he left, they made no move to retrieve him. Why would now be any different?

"If Sable knew he'd found Silver, she'd have to send help," Ash says. Around me, no one looks certain of that—not even Ash.

"First things first. We need to find Steel," Nova says. "Until then, this conversation is premature."

Greyson exchanges a look with his twin. An unspoken conversation passes between them. With a whoop, Sterling spins in his chair and starts typing away on one of the keyboards. The screens in front of him come to life. Random characters, letters, and numbers fill most of the monitors. Maybe code or computer language? Is that the same thing? I have no idea.

Did Sterling just enter the Matrix?

"What's he doing?" I ask Greyson.

"He's going to look for Steel by back-tracking your calls."

"Just like that?" I snap my fingers. "This isn't a movie."

"That's right. The movies make it look way harder than it actually is," Sterling says. "As long as you're not opposed to breaking a few laws, which of course I'm not, it's actually quite easy. I just need to figure out which cell towers he's using when he calls you, and then we'll know approximately where he is." Glancing over his shoulder, Sterling's gaze lands on his brother. "He's probably using an analog phone and blocking his number, thinking that's going to protect him."

"That would be my guess. As if having his number displayed as 'unknown' is going to shield him."

"He was never the brightest one in the family, was he?"

Greyson smirks. "It depends on who you ask."

"Pfft." Sterling scoffs. "As if anyone believes Steel is more intelligent than me."

The four of us exchange looks. Noticing our silence, Sterling tips back in his seat and shoots us an upside-down glare. It would pack more of a punch if a strand of red licorice wasn't hanging out the side of his mouth.

Righting himself, Sterling interlocks his fingers, cracks his knuckles, and renews pounding on the keys. "Oh ye of little faith. Just you wait. Before the end of this adventure you'll all be singing ballads about my giant—"

"Sterling!" Nova launches a pillow at his head, which bounces harmlessly to the floor.

"Brain," he finishes with a chuckle.

"We should check the network, too. You know he wasn't able to track Silver down on his own. It's not like we're blood hounds."

"Already on it."

Greyson shoves off the bed to stand beside his twin. His gaze slides over the gibberish on the screen like he actually knows what's going on. Maybe he does. Catching sight of my quizzical look, he starts to explain. "The Keepers are a team of people devoted to monitoring the human world. They collect whatever data they feel might be of use to us and store it in a super-protected cloud network. It's like the Neph version of The Dark Web, and a lot of angel-born don't even believe it exists. Sterling thinks it's a game to try to hack into their system without getting detected."

"Sable mentioned a group of investigators that had been monitoring me while I was in foster care."

"That would be the Keepers. They horde information and are extremely savvy at tracking down people and Forsaken—a group of true tech geniuses who know how to slip in and out of all sorts of interesting digital places. There's a good chance Steel's been relying on a Keeper friend for help if he's been able to successfully track Silver."

"Gotta be Jem," Sterling pipes up.

"Or Vivian," Greyson offers.

"Or maybe Izzy?"

I crack my neck. All right, we get it. Steel has a million female friends who are Keepers.

"I'm in!" Sterling announces. He holds his fist up and waits for his brother to tap it.

"You're getting faster."

"Practice makes perfect. Now, let me work my own brand of magic."

It takes Sterling thirty minutes to finally admit he can't hack his way into locating Steel.

"If we're going to track him through his janky cell phone, I'm going to need access to Emberly's phone while Steel is on it. At least two minutes of talk time," he explains.

"Which means we can't just keep the cell phone with us. If we pick it up, he'll hang up right away," Greyson adds, running a hand along his jaw. "You're just going to have to stick close to Emberly."

"How is that going to work?" I ask. "Steel always calls at inconvenient hours. I'll most likely be in my room—and sleeping—when or if he calls again."

"Isn't it obvious," Nova pipes in with an amused gleam in her eye. "Sterling is going to have to sleep in your room."

There's a strangled sound, and I tilt my head to see Ash choking on air. She holds a finger up while she regains control of her breathing. "That—" Cough. "Presents a bit of a problem."

"Don't worry. I don't snore," Sterling announces. "I'll even wear clothes at night if that'll make you feel better."

There's nothing to do but shake my head.

"You're not allowed to spend the night in our room."

"It's not like I'm going to announce it. And besides, it's only going to be until Steel calls again. How many nights could that really be?"

3

*I*t's a miracle.

A single trickle of sweat treks down the side of Deacon's face. Hugging his brow, it slips to his chin before dropping to the ground.

"Victory!" I punch the air and wiggle my legs in an imitation of a bad end-zone dance.

"What is happening right now?"

Deacon's face looks . . . well . . . pretty much like it always does: devoid of emotion. The slight arch to his left eyebrow is the only indication of confusion.

Since Steel's departure, Deacon has taken his place as my sparring partner. I always limp away from our sessions a hot sweaty mess, while Deacon remains fresh as a daisy. I'd resent him for that if I didn't like him so much.

"Dude, you are perspiring." I point to his forehead with both index fingers, still shimmying my shoulders. Sleep deprivation makes me a tad slap happy, so I can't seem to stop wiggling. Sterling totally lied about not being a snorer. "I did that. I finally made you work up a sweat."

A slight shine glosses his hairline. Lifting his forearm, he swipes it across his temple.

"This isn't sweating. I prefer to think of it as a healthy glow." His words are dry enough to mask sarcasm as sincerity, but I know better.

"Admit it," I demand. "I'm getting better."

"I never denied it. Of course you're improving. I am, after all, your teacher. I wouldn't waste my time otherwise."

"Did you just call me a waste of your time?"

"No, Emberly. I said that if you weren't improving, *that* would be a waste of my time."

I knew perfectly well what he meant, but I get a kick out of listening to him calmly explain himself.

"I think we should go tell Sable the good news," I say, bouncing on the balls of my feet. "I'm sure she'd appreciate the check-in."

Sable and Deacon are a pet project of mine. It's hard to miss the change in Sable whenever Deacon is around. I caught her giggling at something he said last week.

Giggling.

She's been known to blush a time or two in his presence as well. I have this irresistible urge to shove the two of them together whenever I can.

Deacon stops himself from grabbing his gym bag to shoot me a stern look.

Busted.

Clasping my hands in front of me, I do my best impression of Sterling's "Who, me?" look. He's the Jedi master of sliding out of sticky situations. I'm barely an apprentice.

Shaking his head, Deacon slings his gym bag over his shoulder and walks past, pausing at the door. "Remember,

I'm out on a mission for the next several days, but I should be back before the break."

Right. Mid-winter break is a week and a half away. The academy students will head home to spend the holidays with their families. Everyone except me. They don't know what to do with me yet.

"See ya." I wave.

Sable asked me to drop by, and I've been avoiding it all day. Since we learned my father might be a full-fledged seraph, I've been under Sable's microscope more than usual. In the past it never ended well when an adult paid too much attention to me, and despite Sable's good intentions, old habits die hard.

Shoving my gym shoes into my bag, I heft it on my shoulder and head in the direction of Sable's office—slowly. When I reach her door, I knock once, and then like a coward, take off when there isn't an immediate response.

I'm only three steps from her door when she calls out, "Come on in."

Hanging my head, I turn back.

"Emberly. I'm so glad it's you. Take a seat." Sable stands when I enter, lowering herself when I settle in a seat across from her.

"So, how are you doing?" Her hands steeple on the desk in front of her. She has her headmistress hat on. I'm not getting out of this with a simple answer, but that's still what I give her.

"Fine." The answer isn't false, but she's hoping for specifics.

"I'm glad to hear that. Deacon says training is going well."

I nod because there's not much to say about that.

"And things are going well with your friends?"

Another nod.

"Classes going smoothly?"

Third nod.

She clears her throat, the only indication that my non-verbal answers annoy her. She didn't get to be the head-mistress of one of the nine angel-born academies without a seemingly unending pool of patience. There's a reason she called me in here, and I just want to get to the point. Beating around the bush wastes both of our time.

"Well." She shifts in her seat, and her gaze levels on the empty desk in front of her before volleying back to me. She straightens her posture, but not fast enough to hide the wave of apprehension that rolls over her.

Strange.

I squirm in my seat in response to the vibe Sable throws off, already anticipating hating whatever words move past her lips.

"As you know it's part of my job—part of my duty, really —to inform the Council of Elders on the progress of all the students here at Seraph Academy."

No surprise there. I'm aware that Sable reports to the Elders—the closest thing to a ruling body that Nephilim have. It makes me twitchy, but she isn't divisive or sneaky about it, which I appreciate.

"And, as such, you know I have been required to deliver regular reports on your progress.

Saying you are of great interest to us isn't an understate-ment. Finding a Nephilim that isn't already a part of our community is extremely rare, but with the differences you present . . . Well, all to say, we'd like to find out as much about you as possible."

I nod, wishing she'd just get to the point.

Up until now, the Council has only requested that I continue training, which I'm also thankful for, but I worry that it's only a matter of time before they require something of me I don't want to give. That's why I have contingency plans in place in case things go south. Not even Ash knows about the bugout bag I stashed under my bed, or that I learned where the keys to the academy vehicles are kept in case I need to nick one.

"A Nephilim of seraph descent isn't just unusual, it's unheard of."

"My parentage hasn't been proven yet," I point out.

My friends, along with Sable and Deacon, are the only people at Seraph Academy who know the suspicions about Camiel. So far, all we have to go off of is Tinkle's word. And although I don't think the Celestial would outright lie, he does have his moments of confusion and purposeful misdirection. Anything short of the great and mighty Camiel dropping from the sky and declaring me his daughter is going to be hard for me to believe. It's the main reason why I think finding him should be a priority.

Sable tips her head in acknowledgement. "And because of that, the Council feels like the best way to move forward with this situation is for them to meet you."

Boom, there it is.

I'm not exactly jumping up and down at the idea of meeting the oldest Neph in each angel line, but worse things have happened to me.

Sable shifts again, and clears her throat for the second time.

"Is that all?" I prod. "They just . . . want to meet me? What exactly do they think that will accomplish?"

"Yes, they want to meet you. You are extraordinary in ways we don't fully understand. And from what Deacon tells me, you've only begun to tap into your abilities. I can't fully speak for the Council members, but I believe they're searching for some understanding of your powers and limitations."

"Limitations?" A snake of unease slithers in my belly. Sable didn't say anything unreasonable, but even so . . . "When will they be coming?"

"They aren't coming here. You'll be traveling to their compound to meet them."

The bottom of my stomach drops out.

"You're sending me away?"

"No, no. It's not like that at all." Sable waves a hand through the air, dismissing the idea. "It will be a quick visit. I'll be coming with you, and we'll return to the academy together after the holiday break. I think this will be a good thing for you. You'll get a chance to see more of our world, get a better understanding of where you come from. And maybe after meeting them, some of your fears about the Council can be put to rest."

Standing, she rounds her desk and leans back against it. I have to tip my chin upward to hold eye contact.

"I'm not going to lie to you, Emberly. We're at a bit of a dead end. We haven't been able to uncover any of the mysteries surrounding your heritage. Tinkle has certainly been helpful, but the information he provides us is sporadic at best, and unverifiable."

"Any luck tracking down dear ol' dad?"

Sable shakes her head. She's told me more than once Nephilim don't have a way to communicate with angels, but that shouldn't stop us from trying.

"If your father truly is a seraph angel rather than a Fallen or Nephilim from one of the other represented lines, you'll have your own spot on the Council. That alone should give you an incentive to want to meet them. And we still have a big question mark when it comes to your mother. None of the reported fatalities around the time you were abandoned were female angel-borns who had recently given birth or were even reported as pregnant before their deaths."

Pushing off her desk, Sable crouches in front of me and takes my cold hands in hers. "I think it's a good idea to shake things up a bit and see if we can find any new leads. I told you we'd do our best to try and learn about your history, and I meant it. I believe this is the natural next step.

"The Elders have millennia of experience under their belts. They've seen things the rest of us haven't. I'm hoping that if they see you transform, it might trigger something in their memories. If the information Tinkle provided us proves untrue, perhaps our original conclusion has some merit and you are actually a descendant of the angel line. And maybe there are more of your kind out there. Maybe you aren't the only one after all."

I'm glad Tinkle isn't here to hear his word questioned. He'd probably take it as some sort of challenge and transform into a unicorn in Sable's office.

"Have any of the Council members ever met a Nephilim from the angel line?"

The corners of Sable's lips pull down in a frown. "Those Nephilim were said to be a very protective group. Even before their line went extinct, they kept to themselves."

Disappointment saturates my body and leaks through my voice. "Why were they declared extinct if they were always a private group? Maybe they just went into hiding or something?"

"Their village was found over two thousand years ago. It was a massacre. Not a single angel-born was found alive. Declaring their line extinct was a fair assumption to make at the time, but it may very well have been an incorrect one."

"That's a big 'oopsie.'"

"You're not wrong. Since your discovery, the Council has shoveled resources into searching for the lost branch of angel-born."

A spark of hope starts to warm my chest. I'm much more comfortable being a regular Nephilim descended from a previously-believed-to-be-extinct line than the only living Nephilim to have been sired by a full-fledged angel.

"But I wouldn't get too excited about it. If they do exist, they've gone to a lot of trouble to remain hidden. Saying it's going to be difficult to find them is an understatement."

The flickering hope immediately snuffs out.

"But you won't regret this trip. I promise."

The look on Sable's face is so earnest, I do my best to smile back, hoping she's right. I live with enough burdens—I'm not looking to add regret to the pile.

When I leave her office, I pull out my phone and type out a short message to the group. *We need to talk.*

4

*S*terling slams his hands against the library table. I jolt back, the front two legs of my seat lifting off the ground as several students shoot curious or annoyed glances our way.

"You absolutely can't go."

"Don't hold back. Tell me how you really feel."

"I'm serious, Emberly. If you go, you may never come back."

"Geez, Sterl. Dramatic much? She said Sable was going with her." Nova files her nails, looking completely bored. I didn't even realize she'd been listening. Tinkle is who-knows-where. Probably napping. "The Council of Elders is not the Illuminati."

"Are you sure about that? Do you remember Jude? Here one day, gone the next."

"Because he transferred to another academy."

"That's what they want you to believe."

Nova shakes her head and goes back to her nails.

Sterling's reaction to my Council announcement makes

me want to burst out laughing as much as it makes me want to run and hide. Anything that could possibly lead to the loss of my freedom makes me twitchy. I trust Sable, but . . .

"Stop, Sterling." Ash leans forward and points a finger in the twin's direction. "You're going to freak her out. We all know Sable has been sending them updates about Emberly since Blaze and Aurora were kidnapped. They've had weeks now, months really, to pull Emberly out of the academy and ship her to an undisclosed location, and they haven't. That has to count for something."

I offer Ash a weak smile. She's trying to reassure me, but that wasn't the strongest argument. Just because they haven't tried kidnapping me—again—doesn't mean they won't. I don't have the best track record when it comes to authority figures. Granted, up until I learned I was a Nephilim, all the adults in my life had been humans who were genetically predisposed to be wary of me, but still, when you find out someone is trying to have you committed, that'll do a number on you.

I can't rely on Sable's protection alone. At the very least, she'll be outnumbered if the Council tries to pull something. For all his boasting of unparalleled cosmic powers, as far as I can tell, Tinkle's main ability is shading me from Fallen and Forsaken . . . and shooting sparks out of his butt.

"I think," Greyson starts, the last of our group to speak up. He waits until it's clear he has our attention. "We're missing the obvious opportunity this presents. If we manage to track down Steel, we can use Emberly's trip as a cover. We could slip away to help him *and* go with her to Egypt as backup."

Sterling leans forward, obviously intrigued. "How do you figure?"

"Sable wants to take you to the Council's compound over break, right?" I nod. "So we campaign to go with you, but ask if we can spend a few days with our family in New York first. We tell our parents we're going straight to Egypt and tell Sable to pick us up in New York at a set date. Boom, we've just created a window of time to be wherever we want to be. With a bit of luck, we'll be able to help Steel and make it back to New York before anyone knows we were gone." Greyson makes it sound so simple, but I doubt it will be.

The table is silent for a beat while his suggestion sinks in. It's Sterling who reacts first, by whooping and jumping to his feet. He pounds his fist in the air and starts chanting "road trip" over and over again. Someone throws a balled up piece of paper at him.

"Sit down," Ash orders. "You're in a library, you putz. And also, the Council resides in the Middle East. You can't road trip over the Atlantic Ocean."

"Same difference."

"Not really."

"You guys can't come," I cut in. "This is one of your only yearly breaks. You should be with your families to celebrate the holidays."

"I could swing it." Nova's still working on her nails. I think she's filing them all to points. "My parents won't miss me," she says with a shrug.

I don't have parents and even *I* know that's sad. My features must soften because Nova snaps, "Stop giving me Bambi eyes. My parents and I are solid. We're just not big on traditions. I come from a long line of powers. We're not the most touchy-feely bunch. If I tell them I can't make it home for Christmas, they're just going to use the time to pick up an extra mission somewhere, and I'll see them next break. Angel-born are incredibly long-lived, you know. What's one holiday in the grand scheme of things? Not to mention having an audience with the Council is considered an honor—"

Sterling snorts.

"—for some," she finishes.

I suppose that makes sense. I'm sure there are lots of different dynamics within families. No two are alike and all that business.

"I think Sterling and I could make it happen as well. Otherwise I wouldn't have brought it up."

"I was just thinking Mom will have a fit if we don't come home over the holidays. You really think she'd go for it? I feel like we might have to pull some next-level deception to get away with it." The look on Sterling's face says that the idea of using trickery is even more exciting than getting permission.

"If she knew we were petitioning for help to find Steel, I'm pretty sure she'd be on board. She was pretty chill about him going off for the first month, but she's been freaking out the last few weeks. Who we really need to worry about are Blaze and Aurora. They're going to make us pay for missing Christmas. You know it's their favorite holiday after their birthday. We're probably going to be picking fire ants out of our underwear for the next year."

"But worth it, right?"

The grin that works its way onto Greyson's face makes him look even more like his brother. "Absolutely."

Ash chews on her lip, looking uncertain. If powers aren't known for being touchy-feely, the same can't be said for dominions—Ash's angel-born line. They're a tight-knit group that's big on loyalty, friendships, and family. In a lot of ways, rulers are the glue that keep the angel-born factions held together. That's Ash to a tee.

I can make this easier for her.

"You guys, as touched as I am that you would sacrifice your holiday and time with your families for me, that's not something I can ask you to do."

"We're your friends. You don't have to ask. Besides, families extend further than blood. You're part of ours now." The sincerity in Ash's eyes causes my chest to tighten.

Who are these people? Yes, we've had an intense few months together, but I've never experienced acceptance like this before. And I don't know exactly what to do with it. There's security in being part of a group. Feeling included, accepted, and adopted by these angel-borns is what the buried part of myself has always longed for. But my flight instinct is so overdeveloped that there's also a part of me that wants to shove them away and run in the opposite direction.

The emotions percolating inside my gut are itchy and prickly and wholly unfamiliar. Warmth spreads from my center outward, making my blood buzz. Utterly overwhelmed by their care and concern, my fingers tingle and feet go numb.

I start to collect my few belongings. Shoving my Book of Seraph in my bag, I almost eye-roll myself. Did I really think I'd get any studying done with this bunch? Maybe if Sterling hadn't been there.

"I think maybe it would be best—"

"If we came along with you. Yes, we totally agree. It's decided. I've always wanted to see the compound where the Council of Elders chills. I hear they have a kickin' training center. Their VR is supposed to be superior to ours."

"Seriously, Sterling?" Unlike me, Ash doesn't hold back her eye-roll. "You were just claiming the Council was going to experiment on Emberly, and now you're excited about their training center?"

"What?" Sterling holds up his hands, palms facing the ceiling. "If they don't try to kill her, it could be a really cool trip."

"Come on, bro. Let's go rip off the Band-Aid and call Mom."

"Good call. Ash. Em. I'll see you ladies tonight," Sterling says with an eyebrow wiggle. I hold in my groan. Tonight is day five million three hundred and twenty-seven of our sleepover with Sterling. If Steel doesn't call soon, I may never get another uninterrupted night of sleep.

Pushing out of his seat, Greyson heads toward the exit with Sterling in tow, asking if he thinks there will be any hot chicks who like younger men at the compound. They're out the door before I can hear Greyson's response.

"So, I guess this is happening," I say. Despite myself, I feel a level of relief knowing I'll have backup on this trip.

"You okay?" Ash asks. Nova simply regards me over the top of her nail file.

"Yeah, this will be . . ." Scary? Horrific? A giant cluster? "Fun."

CHAPTER FIVE
STEEL

Silver-blonde strands slip through my fingers. Soft as corn silk, each piece a delicate thread of tinsel sliding over my palm. Following the metallic length up, I bury my hand in the mass and draw her closer. Her scent is heavenly. Not flowery like some girls, but sweet, like a sugary treat.

Like always, some of her facial features are obscured by light. It's the reason I didn't recognize her immediately outside the dreamscape where we currently exist. But I can still see the slope of her nose, the curve of her cheek, and the endless blue ocean of her eyes.

I've experienced enough of these dreams to recognize them for what they are, but it doesn't stop me from tipping my face and pressing a kiss to her neck. Her skin is rose-petal soft, and I take the opportunity to run my nose up her throat and plant another kiss behind her ear. She shivers under my touch, and the corners of my mouth rise in satisfaction.

If I ever see the real Emberly again, I want to know if she'll have the same reaction.

"—listening to me?"

The phantom in front of me is saying something, but her words go in and out. Her hands push at my shoulders, and I draw back but slide my grip to her waist, refusing to concede too much space.

I squint against the light surrounding us. Her brow is pinched in concern and her mouth is moving, but I can't make out the words. She lays a hand on my cheek and I lean into it, closing my eyes and dreading what comes next.

"Steel! It's not—have—figure out—kill her."

The words get swallowed, as if she's shouting them into the wind. Around us, the world darkens to a putrid shade of green. Pea soup mist curls around our feet and slithers its way up our calves.

I don't know how the dagger appears in my hands, but there it is, same as always. Ruby blood already drips from the curved blade. The metal hilt burns my palm, yet I can't seem to release my hold. Panic balloons in my chest as I see the liquid bubble from her gut. It pours down her gilded armor in macabre rivers, covering the bottom half of her breastplate and the front of her legs in seconds.

She reaches for me with bloodstained hands but I jerk out of the way, terrified her touch will trigger another stabbing.

I'm lost in a realm where fiction is reality.

The atmosphere darkens to shadows, the shine from her blood-drenched armor the only brightness.

Masculine arms wrap around her from behind.

Standing a head taller than her, a man holds her close. His light hair is pulled back away from his face. His hands press against her wound, trying to stop the deluge, but the thick red liquid seeps between his fingers. He presses his mouth to her ear, whispering, but she shakes her head and reaches for me. Casting a glare in my direction, he bares his teeth and yanks her away.

With a roar of fury I lunge forward, intent on ripping her from his grasp, but the dagger in my palm finds its way past her armor to bury in her gut another time. I try to pull the blade away but my arm is locked, the weapon fused to my hand.

A tear drops from the corner of her eye. Shadows obscure part of her face, but there's a question in her gaze I don't know how to answer: *Why?*

Anguish rolls over me in unrelenting waves.

And then she's hauled back. The dagger slides out of her, and I'm finally able to release my hold. As the knife falls and she disappears into the shadows, I hear her tortured shout.

"Steel, kill me!"

When I wake, I don't make it to the bathroom before vomiting. Falling to the floor, I grab the trashcan by the nightstand and empty the contents of my stomach into it. When there's nothing left, I cough bile into the bin until the retching finally stops.

Tremors wrack my body for several minutes after the puking ceases. I don't know why I bother with clothes at night anymore. They always end up drenched in sweat after one of these dreams.

My phone lies on the ground by my knees—likely pushed off the nightstand by my thrashing. My hand itches to grab it and call her, but I tell myself not to. If I can get through my cleanup routine, the urge will pass.

I huff out a self-deprecating laugh. This happens frequently enough that I have a routine.

Wake up. Vomit. Shower. Brush teeth. Dress. Get back to work.

No matter the time of night I wake up from the dream, or vision, or whatever it is, I don't ever go back to sleep. Depriving myself of rest is a small penance to pay for the atrocities I visit upon her—even if only in my mind.

Lumbering to my feet, I strip off my shirt and briefs as I stagger to the bathroom. It isn't until the ice-cold spray hits my body that I remember the new portion of my recurring dream.

The man clutching Emberly.

The thought of him makes my fists and teeth clench. The muscles in my back become so tight I can't order them to loosen. It's only when the water warms that they slacken a fraction.

As with all dreams, the details are fuzzy, but I remember he was a fully-formed person rather than the shadowed figure he's always been before. His height and build matched a typical angel-born, but his coloring—much like Emberly's—was off. His skin and hair were pale. I can't recall the shade of his eyes, but I'm not in the habit of checking dudes' eyes so I doubt I even looked.

He could be another angel-born, perhaps like Emberly in some way. Or maybe he's only a figment of my imagination. With the lack of sleep, and Silver leading me on a wild goose chase, perhaps my mind is playing tricks on me.

I punch the shower wall hard enough to crack the porcelain. I'm going to have to leave some extra cash to cover the damage, but I hardly care at the moment.

Why are these dreams dogging me? What do they mean?

Are they premonitions, warnings? Or simply subconscious conjurings of an overactive and obsessive mind?

I sink my hands into my wet hair and fist the strands, wishing I could rip the meaning of my nighttime terrors out of my brain as easily as I could yank the hair from my scalp.

Releasing a breath, I let my arms drop to my sides. The water pounding my back scalds, but I don't adjust the temperature. When my fingers prune, I finally set about washing myself.

Turning the water off, I shake my head, splashing droplets on the shower curtain. I grab a towel but wince when I catch an eye-full of myself in the cloudy mirror. I wipe away the condensation clinging to the glass surface. The circles under my eyes are dark enough to be shiners. The hollows of my cheeks are more pronounced, and I'm in need of a proper haircut. And when was the last time I even shaved? My regular five o'clock shadow is turning into a full beard.

"Haggard" is the word that comes to mind.

Leaving the bathroom, I snatch the clothes from the day before off the ground, sniffing my crumpled t-shirt. I yank my head back with a slight grimace, but shrug a beat later. Could be worse. Good thing I don't want anyone coming near me anyway.

I tug on my ripe clothing and scan the room. My computer is here somewhere. I spot it on the tiny desk in the corner and next to it, the small flip phone I use for calls I don't want tracked.

The impulse to punch in Emberly's number rides me. Hard. My fingers twitch in anticipation.

I shouldn't do it. I can't do it. I called her less than a week ago and am still kicking myself over it. And I couldn't keep my mouth shut. I had to tell someone I'd finally spotted my prey, and the craving to have Emberly be that someone overwhelmed my better sensibilities.

The wooden chair groans in protest as I settle my oversized frame onto it. For all the noise it makes I half expect it to break in half just out of spite.

These dumps are getting old. If only I could use my platinum AMEX card rather than cash. I'd be living it up at the Four Seasons.

Okay, probably not. But I'd at least pick a hotel with decent Wi-Fi.

I open my computer, clicking to a piece of footage I've already watched over and over, hoping in vain I'll catch a detail I missed before.

On the screen, a willowy, dark-haired figure pushes through glass doors. She struts forward, wearing a long wool coat that hits mid-thigh over dark, close-fitting clothing and a ridiculous set of heels that no one could fight in.

Even at nine years old, Silver had had a thing for shoes.

But this isn't Silver, it's a monster wearing her face. It is purely coincidental they have similar tastes.

Pausing under the awning, Silver waits for the valet to bring her car around.

"Where are you going?"

I've asked the screen the same question before, but never received an answer. This time is no different.

When her car arrives, she tips the valet and opens the driver's side door. Right before she slips into the seat of a chrome-wrapped Lotus Evora, she pauses and tilts her head so she's staring directly into the camera lens.

An oily smile slides onto her face as she blows a kiss. Sliding into her seat, she guns the engine and takes off.

There's nothing subtle about that car or the look she shot me.

She's luring me.

I know it. She knows it. And we both know I'm going to take the bait.

Slapping the lid of my computer shut, I crack my neck. Like a siren's song, my gaze is dragged back to the crappy phone. A phantom breeze brushes my face, and I swear I can smell Emberly on it. I close my eyes, and as if it has a mind of its own, my hand grabs the phone and dials her number.

It's easier to live with myself if I pretend I didn't give the command.

The phone is pressed up against my ear before I even open my eyes. It rings twice, and I tell myself I'll hang up when she answers. I only really need to check to make sure she's all right. Hearing her utter a single word will be enough for me.

Yeah, right, Steel.

I don't even believe my own lies anymore.

The phone rings for the fifth time, and I begin to get nervous. It's never taken her this long to answer. Maybe this is the time something truly is wrong.

My heartbeat gets caught in my throat.

The sixth ring is cut off mid-chime, and my heart starts thumping again, double-time.

"Steel?" The word comes out breathy, like she's been exercising. I check the clock and do the proper time zone adjustments and realize it's 2 AM for her. What, besides sleeping, could she possibly be doing at this time of night?

Just like always, my mind takes me to dark places. I want to ask her what's wrong, but smash my lips together to keep from uttering a word.

"Steel, please talk to me," she urges.

Hanging my head, I rub my forehead with my palm. What am I doing?

I start to pull the phone away from my ear, prepared to hit End, when her next comment stops me.

"I know who my father is. Or rather, who he might be. Would you like to know?" Her words are soft, but they resonate like a bass drum, thumping around my head and making me second-guess if I even heard her correctly.

Her father? Yes. Yes, I definitely want to know. But I can't say anything because once I do my resolve will shatter. I almost didn't hang up the last time we spoke.

"His name is Camiel. At least that's what I was told by . . . by someone who would know."

Who would know who her father is? What am I supposed to make of that hitch in her sentence?

I clutch the phone like a lifeline. I have to order my hand to loosen or I'll be left with a pile of plastic and wiring good for nothing but the garbage—and this call really will be over before it begins.

"There's actually quite a bit that's happened in the last few weeks. I've wanted to tell you, but I was hoping to be able to say it to your face. But since I don't know when I'll see you again, well, I suppose this will have to do. See, we might have exposed some of my origin story." She laughs gently. "I like to call it that because I can pretend I'm a superhero. Would you like to know more?"

Tell me, I mentally order, but not even a breath passes my lips.

"I'm going to take that as a yes. So this, um, person who knows my father also knows what angel line he's from." Her words come out in a rush, as if she's worried I'll slip away before she can finish. "And it actually turns out—I can't believe I'm even saying this—

but there's a chance I might be descended from a seraph."

I lean back, and the wooden chair underneath me screams and splinters. I end up sprawled on my butt and back.

"Steel? Are you okay? What just happened?"

I wouldn't tell you even if I was talking, I think to myself.

I get up and only just stop myself from kicking the remaining lump of wood into the drywall as punishment for interrupting Emberly's revelation.

A seraph Neph. Is that even possible? There's never been one before. I blow out a breath and start pacing as I contemplate the implications. Nephilim pretend to know everything, but Emberly is living proof that they don't.

"Well, I can hear you breathing, so I'm going to assume you're still alive and kicking. I know it's probably a shock. I wouldn't blame you if you didn't believe me."

I believe you. I'll always believe you, I want to shout, but I remain silent.

"I've had a hard time believing it myself." She laughs again, quietly so as not to wake Ash I presume, and the sound washes over me like a warm breeze. "Part of me still doesn't, if I'm being honest. If it is true, what if it means . . ."

What? What do you think it means?

"I have to go," she says, rather than finishing her thought. I open my mouth to stop her from hanging up on me, but it's too late. She already has.

*S*terling spins in my desk chair and whoops, "I got you, Sucker! Score one for the middle sib!"

"Sterling!" I whisper-hiss. "Why don't you announce it to the whole girls' dorm?"

Grimacing, he ducks his head and shoots me a guilty look, then continues a silent victory dance which includes a full-body gyration that would make any female popstar proud.

Under normal circumstances I'd have trouble masking my amusement, but my conversation with Steel hangs at the forefront of my thoughts, pressing down on my mood.

I avoid Ash's gaze even as I feel it bounce over my face. She heard every word, including the bit where I almost confessed how isolating it feels to know I might be the only seraph angel-born. At some point during our one-sided confessional, I'd forgotten about the other people in the room. It wasn't until Sterling turned to me with a giant grin and two thumbs-up—the signal that he'd tracked Steel's location successfully—that I jarred back to reality. After that, I'd gotten off the phone as quickly as possible. Steel's hung up on me so many times I didn't feel at all guilty doing the same to him.

Rather than face Ash's knowing eyes, I turn to Tinkle and chuck a pillow at his furry head. Currently in the form of a monkey, he scampers out of the way and onto the bookshelf.

"What the heck? I almost missed the call."

When the phone rang, Tinkle snatched it and started bouncing around the room like a caffeinated . . . well, like a caffeinated monkey. Ash and I chased him until she managed to tackle him to the ground so I could pluck the phone from his spindle-like fingers. By that time, the phone had already rung five times and I wasn't sure Steel would still be on the line when I answered.

"What?" Tinkle cocks his head. "I thought we were playing keep-away."

"Why in the world—" Stopping myself, I take a long drag of air in through my nose before exhaling out my mouth. It's a breathing technique I've picked up since Tinkle dropped into my life. "Okay, Sterling. Let's hear it. Where is he?"

"Right." Spinning back to his computer, his fingers run over the keys. A moment later all three of our cell phones ding.

When I unlock the screen, I see Sterling has sent a group text. Except instead of "Sterling" where his name should be, it reads "#HotStuff."

I glare at him. "Stop hacking into my phone and changing your name in my contacts." Last week it was "Ironman," and the week before that, "The Most Attractive Durand Sibling."

"It's not hacking when your passcode is one-two-three-four."

"He has a point," Ash says.

I bite my tongue and read the message.

#HotStuff

Busted. Steel's in Michigan.

"That's . . . random," Ash says. I nod in agreement.

Even though it's the middle of the night, the first reply comes through barely a minute later.

Nova

Detroit?

#HotStuff

A suburb north of Detroit. Pontiac.

Greyson

Never heard of it.

Nova

What's Steel doing in the mid-west?

Greyson

Better question is, what's Silver doing there?

The chat goes silent.

"Don't Forsaken usually keep to the larger cities?" When I was on my own, I'd convinced myself there was safety in numbers. Turns out, living on the streets in Denver was the wrong move. I should have holed up in a ghost town somewhere. Hindsight is twenty-twenty.

"Usually," Ash answers.

#HotStuff

I guess that's what we'll ask Steel when we see him. If anyone knows why Silver's holed up there, it would be him.

"This is really happening, isn't it?"

"You bet it is," Sterling says.

"And not a moment too soon," Ash adds. "This is cutting it close."

We're scheduled to leave for the Elders' compound in three days. I'd been nervous Steel wouldn't call before then —and six nights of dealing with Sterling hiding out in our room was plenty. If Steel hadn't called, our plans would have burned to ash. Over the last several days, we've been weaving an intricate web of lies. Everyone's parents think we're headed to the compound in Egypt later this week, except Nova's. I don't even know what story she fed her mom and dad—she simply told us, "It's taken care of." For all I know, she told them the truth and has their stamp of approval.

But it wasn't only the parents that had to be fooled— there was Sable as well. Greyson could do an eerily accurate impersonation of his father and had convinced Sable that Laurent was going to pick the three of us up and take us to their family penthouse in New York for two days before traveling to the Council's compound. That's our three-day window to find and help Steel without a horde of Nephilim looking for us. We even gave Sable a different address to pick us up at in New York so the Durands don't find out we weren't in the Middle East the whole time.

Greyson

We have our destination. You guys know what comes next.

Something settles into my gut. I want to tell myself it's apprehension; we only have two and a half days to modify our plans and keep all the adults in the dark. If even one thing goes wrong, our plans will fold faster than a house of cards. But the truth of the matter is that it feels a lot like anticipation instead.

"I can't believe that worked." It's the fifth time since crossing the Colorado border that Ash has woodenly uttered the words. I agree, but keep my mouth shut.

We barrel down I-80 at exactly sixty-five miles per hour, not a mile over or under the speed limit. Greyson has been fastidious about going the exact speed limit since we slid through the gates of Seraph Academy in our stolen vehicle and weaved our way down the mountain and onto the interstate.

"I never had a doubt," Sterling announces from the seat beside her. Greyson and I exchange a look in the front of the car. "The White Whale wasn't going to let us down."

White Whale is what Sterling named the van we nicked from the academy. We were fairly confident it wasn't going to be missed, parked as it was in the underground lot next to sixteen other white vans. It's identical to the one Sable and Steel used to abscond with me this past fall. I overlooked that because it easily fit all five of us. Well, six if you counted Tinkle—currently shifted into a Koala, and fast asleep on the back bench seat next to Nova. His snores carry all the way up front.

"We're just lucky Blaze and Aurora traded their assistance for the truth. There's no way we'd have been able to keep Sable and Dad from each other if the twins didn't run interference for us." Greyson tips his chin in my direction. "Good idea to include them. It might also mean that their retribution for us missing Christmas this year will be lighter than what they'd already planned."

"I wouldn't hold your breath."

"Yeah, you're right. We're going to get it either way. Now

that they've staked their claim on you, you'll be getting an equal portion of that torture. Buckle up."

Shoot. I hadn't considered that.

I check the clock on the dash for probably the thousandth time. Eleven AM. The seventy-eight hour timer until Sable tries to collect us in New York started the moment we snuck off campus. We've eaten up over four hours already and have another fourteen to go until we reach Pontiac. That means once we hit ground zero, we'll only have sixty hours to find Steel, defeat Silver, and get all our butts over to New York City before Sable and the Durand parents realize we're in the wind.

But no pressure.

The chances of us getting away with this without anyone discovering what we've done are slim—we all know that. But at the very least we're hoping for the full seventy-plus hours without a contingent of angel-born breathing down our necks. Our recently adopted motto is "Ask for forgiveness, not permission."

Sterling leans forward and grabs the back of my seat. His face appears in the space between me and Greyson. "Yo, Em. How did you snag the keys to this sweet ride anyway?"

The smile I shoot him is all teeth. "Wouldn't you like to know?"

His head tips in confusion. "Um, yeah. That's why I asked."

I'm not keen on letting him and everyone else know that my exit strategy—which includes stealing a ride from the academy van pool—has been mapped out for the past several months. I did a lot of poking around under the guise of not knowing the layout of the school to gather information.

Like I said, old habits die hard.

"Come on, dude. I lived on the streets for the better part of a year. My brain is hardwired for stuff like this." I force out a light laugh, which I hope sounds convincing.

Sterling's face is pinched in consternation, but just as he opens his mouth to speak, Greyson twists the knob on the radio and a twangy country song fills the van. Covering his ears, Sterling yells at his brother to change the station. The argument between the two lasts for at least ten minutes, until they finally agree on neutral territory . . . which ends up being a contemporary station that plays hits from the last several decades.

Sterling settles back in his seat, singing along to Britney Spears' "Hit Me Baby One More Time."

Greyson's gaze slides to me.

"Thanks," I mouth.

The corner of his lip tips up in a half-smile, and he nods once before training his eyes back on the road. Leaning back, I tilt my head and stare out the window at the flat expanse of nothing that is Nebraska. The monotony of the landscape lulls me into a light sleep. I dream of Sterling on a concert stage in the middle of a cow pasture as a backup dancer to BTS and don't wake until we roll to a stop at a gas station.

I rub my eyes, surprised to see the sun hanging so low in the sky. When I check the clock on the dash, it's already three thirty. The sun sets quickly this time of year. I'd guess we only have another hour or so of daylight.

There's a knock on the glass. On the other side of the window Ash holds up a bag of sour cream and cheddar Lays and a Monster energy drink.

"You want?" she asks when I open the door and step into

the crisp winter air. Small flurries tornado, circling the pavement around us. Even though I'm not as sensitive to the cold as a human, I rub my arms, wondering if I should dig my coat out of our luggage in the back of the van.

"Naw, I'm good." I scan the gas station, taking in the other cars and where the owners are. We need to switch White Whale's license plate, but we can't be conspicuous about it. I spot a gray SUV parked on the side of the station. Ash catches me eyeing the car.

"That a good candidate?" They all know we need to do this, but I'm the only one fixated on a clean escape. And why wouldn't I be? No one else is conditioned to stay under the radar. All four of the other angel-borns have always relied on the detailed planning of other Nephilim to keep them safe, whether in the academy or the communities they were born into. Only I have real world experience on how to be invisible—except for Tinkle, but he doesn't really count. It's unnerving how easy it is to slip back into my old mode.

A surprising rush of resentment clogs my throat, and I have to cough it down before answering Ash. I hate the way it leaves a bitter aftertaste on my tongue.

"Yes, that's the one. Let's get everyone back in the car."

I do a quick sweep of the area, looking for cameras, but I'm confident the SUV is parked in a blind spot. Once everyone is in the car, I direct Greyson to leave the station and swing around the back entrance, pulling up behind the other car. Sterling and I jump out, switching the plates as quickly as possible. Then we're back on the road with another nine hours and twenty-six minutes to go.

I tap my fingers nervously on the armrest, unable to contain the bubble of unease blooming in my chest the closer we get to our destination. I barely talk to anyone for the next several hours, content to let the others think I'm either dozing or deep in thought, when really I'm just trying not to freak out at the thought of seeing Steel again after all these weeks. I didn't anticipate being this nervous, but with every mile we inch closer to him, the knot in my gut tightens a bit more. By the time we roll into Pontiac, it's early morning, and I'm seriously concerned I'm going to yak.

"We're here," Greyson announces unnecessarily. Despite the late hour, or rather early hour, we're all awake and alert. Except for Tinkle of course, who's taking his fiftieth nap of the drive.

The first of the sun's morning rays barely tease the horizon as we roll past the city limits. The streets are empty, and the offices and store fronts we pass are dark. Not surprising. Who would be up at this time of day? Even the Forsaken will be hiding in their dens right now.

We have the address of the location Steel was at when he called me, but if he's not there anymore, we don't have any leads. If he's moved on there's no easy way to find him until, or unless, he calls again. Sterling brought two of his laptops just in case, but we have to find a place to set them up and connect them to the internet if we plan to use his hacker skills.

"What's the next turn?" Greyson asks his brother. He can't check the maps on his phone since they ditched them all back in Colorado before we crossed into Nebraska. We kept mine in case we need it to find Steel. It's currently stowed in a homemade Faraday cage—an enclosure used to block electromagnetic fields that prevents the phone from being tracked. We picked up basic pay-as-you-go phones at a pit stop in Iowa so we can still stay in touch, but they don't have any features or apps. Making and receiving calls is the extent of their bells and whistles.

"You're going to hang a right at University Drive. The address I pulled is a motel. If he's there we should see his bike parked in the lot."

"Are you sure he wouldn't have rolled it into his room?" Nova calls from the back of the van. "He has a special relationship with his Ducati. I'm not entirely sure he'd leave her out in the open." Her lips are curved into a smile, but I don't think she's joking. Both twins seem to be mulling it over.

"It's possible," Greyson concedes as we pull into the parking lot of the motel. The pavement is caked with ice and riddled with potholes. Mounds of snow are piled along the perimeter. We make a slow trek around the lot, but don't spot Steel's bike anywhere. "Well, none of us really expected it to be that easy, did we?"

Sterling raises his hand. "Yes. I absolutely expected it to be that easy."

"Where's the fun in that?" Greyson twists to grin at his brother.

"What now?" Ash asks.

"Now," Greyson announces, "we get to work."

I wish I'd known "get to work" was code for drive and walk around every street in Pontiac looking for Steel or his fancy motorcycle. That gets us a lot of nowhere fast and is boring as all get-out. Every minute that ticks by winds me tighter. By midday I'm sure I'm going to snap.

Eventually, we park White Whale next to a hotel, and Sterling "borrows" their Wi-Fi to hook into city-owned cameras. Ash, Nova, Greyson, and Tinkle take off on foot to search the surrounding area. I get stuck in the van with Sterling in case my phone rings.

It's tedious work, but after he makes it past the city's flimsy firewall—his words, not mine—Sterling starts searching the traffic cameras. Hours pass.

In the early afternoon he spots a recording of Steel zooming through an intersection several days ago, but that won't help us pinpoint his current location. At least we have visual proof he's been here, which means we traced the phone call to the right area. That'll be little comfort if we can't find him.

Ash and Nova—with Tinkle in tow—circle back with food around four PM. I'm ravenous and inhale the greasy burger and fries I'm presented with. It isn't long before Greyson returns as well.

At dusk I no longer have the nervous tingle in my gut over seeing Steel again; I simply feel defeated. We move the van to another area of town and send Tinkle into the spectrum world to see what he can find. I insist on hitting the pavement this time if for no other reason than to stretch my legs. I've been camped in that van for over a day.

We walk the streets and alleyways as a group. I'm not the only one with energy to burn. Sterling begged off computer duty as well. A smattering of snowflakes sprinkle from the sky, but the fall isn't dense enough to accumulate on the ground. Every flake is a pinprick of cold when it lands on my face.

"Why does it feel so much colder here? The temperature isn't even as low as it gets in Colorado, but I feel the chill down to my bones." Ash hunches farther into her puffer jacket. She's from Arizona and doesn't know what wet cold feels like.

"It's the humidity," I explain. "The dampness in the air

makes it feel colder than it actually is. Your clothes are less insulating here as well."

"How do you know that?"

"I've spent a lot of time outdoors." I had a vested interest in learning about weather conditions and the elements since I spent extended periods of time without proper shelter.

"Oh."

It falls quiet after that. The only sound is the shuffling of our feet as we walk down the sidewalk. Which is weird, because it's not that late in the evening. It's as if everyone ran out of this part of town when the sun went down. I can understand why. The buildings around us are creepy. At least half of them have For Rent or For Sale signs taped in the front windows. The ones that don't are dark inside. A few even have the windows knocked out of them.

I think I hear an engine rev and stop walking. The other four angel-born continue trekking down the street, but I stare down the road on my right. There's no one there, but a muttered curse echoes off the buildings. The hair on the nape of my neck starts to tingle.

The group is a solid block ahead of me when I turn and start down the street. Another muffled curse has my feet moving faster, and it's no time before I'm rounding the corner and skidding to a halt.

He's there.

7

*S*teel's hunched over his motorcycle, riffling through the saddlebag. All he has to do is glance up and he'll see me, but his attention is elsewhere. It's so much like the last time I laid eyes on him.

But also . . . not.

I take quiet steps forward until a jolt works its way through Steel's frame. His hands stop moving. His whole body freezes, and I follow suit. The only movement I detect is a muscle twitch along his jawline.

My heart thumps in my chest twice, and then his head hinges up. Slowly.

His face is a stone mask. But his eyes. His eyes contain emotion enough for his entire body.

Steel is furious.

We stand a car length away from each other, but it might as well be mere inches. His anger hits me in the face like the heat from a raging fire. I suspected he wouldn't be over-joyed to see me, but this reaction is a bit extreme.

In a very Terminator move, Steel stretches to his full height and stomps toward me.

His usual swagger is gone. His moves are stiff, like his muscles won't contract enough to allow his joints to bend fluidly.

And me. I'm just standing. And staring. Completely mute.

"She's this way," Sterling's voice calls out. The sound of feet beating against the pavement follows his announcement.

I know the instant they round the corner because Steel's eyes finally leave my face and track over my shoulder. Frustration replaces a measure of fury in his gaze.

"You told them," he sighs in resignation.

A pang of guilt strikes my heart, but I won't be sorry for what I did.

Tipping his head to the stars, Steel exposes the full column of his neck. He doesn't look back down until the rest of the group surrounds me.

"You just had to come, didn't you?"

"Did you expect any less?" Greyson asks his brother.

"What I expected was for you all to stay out of this."

"If you really wanted that you wouldn't have kept making stalker phone calls to your girl, bro." Sterling lifts both eyebrows. "Seriously, you know how easy it was for me to track you?"

Steel flicks a glare laden with accusation at me. I cross my arms over my chest. This is not the reunion I've been hoping for.

Taking a small step back, I blend into the group. Nova and Ash stand slightly in front of me. Steel's gaze roams in my direction more than once as he bickers with his siblings about whether or not we'll be staying to help or returning to the academy.

"Listen, Steel," Greyson finally says. "We either stay here and help you take care of our family issue, or we head back and Emberly goes on a little trip to the Council's compound."

"What are you talking about?"

"We were able to get away under the guise of escorting Emberly to her big Council meet n' greet. If you force us to return without you, we're going to have to actually take her to the Elders at their compound in Egypt. Do you really want that on your conscience?"

Clearing my throat, I purse my lips at Greyson. That's not exactly the truth. He's using my situation to manipulate Steel, and I'm not sure I'm on board with that.

A prickle of awareness skitters across my skin. I'm being scrutinized.

Sure enough, Steel's teal eyes are locked on me with an intensity that borders on obsession.

Nova steps forward, breaking our staring contest.

"Don't be a blockhead about this, Steel. Your chance of success only increases with our help." Tilting her head, she gives him a solid once-over. "From the looks of it you're not in a position to refuse us right now. You look awful. Unless you're going for heroin-chic, in which case you nailed it."

"Thanks, Nova. That was delicately said," Steel deadpans.

"Anytime. I enjoy throwing truth bombs. I like the sound they make when they explode."

Ash takes a half-step away from Nova, a concerned frown pulling down the corners of her mouth. I squish my lips together and hold a straight face. Nova's scary some-times, but her bark is worse than her bite. I hope.

After scrubbing a hand over his face and muttering for a solid thirty seconds—I catch words like "nuisance" and "family" and "annoying"—Steel finally relents.

"Come on, let's get you guys settled in the same dump I'm at. I'll update you on the situation when we get there."

When we arrive back at Steel's motel, Nova and Sterling firmly refuse to even entertain the idea of renting rooms there.

I keep my mouth shut, not seeing the problem. The rooms have a bed and a bathroom. Check and check. What more do we need?

But Nova insists she'll catch bed bugs, and Sterling goes on about how he's worried his hair dryer will short-circuit the whole place.

A fiery round of arguing ensues until Steel agrees to move to a different location. We settle on a low-budget hotel in a seedy part of town that still looks cleanish.

We grab adjoining rooms with two queen beds in each. Keeping the door between rooms open, we convene in one. Ash and I sit cross-legged on one of the beds. Nova props herself up against the headboard of the other. Sterling and Greyson settle on the floor.

Brave. It looks sticky down there.

We turn expectant gazes on Steel, waiting for an update on Silver.

Grabbing a chair from the desk, he flips it around before lowering his tall frame into it, and then his words flow. I don't ask many questions because he lays out the facts very simply, with an almost military precision.

He's tracked Silver for weeks. He finally caught up to her in this town and has been running a one-man surveillance team ever since. She's been here for a week and a day, which is the longest she's been in one place since our battle in Colorado. Three other Forsaken, all male, have been her travel buddies.

"And she knows I've been following her," he finishes.

"What makes you say that?" Ash asks.

Without standing, he rotates his chair and grabs his computer off the desk behind him. He punches some keys and then turns the screen toward us.

I lean forward and watch as Silver exits a hotel and waits near a valet stand. At first, I'm not sure why Steel is showing us this footage. But then, right before she lowers herself into the driver's seat, she looks right at the screen, smiles, and blows a kiss.

Sterling releases a low whistle as Steel puts his computer away.

"Sweet ride," Nova says. "Although I would have gone for black. The chrome is a little showy."

Greyson cranes his head to shoot her a flat look. "Too showy for *you*?"

"That's what I said." She almost pulls off answering with a straight face, but then the corner of her lips curl.

"I'd say that's a pretty good indication she's on to you." Ash tugs us back on topic.

Steel nods. "Right. Silver's left the hotel right before dawn five days this week. I tracked her to a night club in an old church on the outskirts of the city, not far from where you guys found me tonight. She holes up there all day, then returns to the hotel after dark. I was going to case the place this evening, but then the circus pulled into town."

"You were going to go to a club looking like that?" The horror in Nova's voice is so strong I can't hold back a sharp bark of laughter. I slap a hand over my mouth and duck my head.

Steel scans himself from his feet on up and shrugs. "So?"

He's wearing black boots, dark jeans that look like they're about due for a washing, and a long-sleeved thermal that gently hugs his muscles despite his slightly leaner physique.

I do a little internal shrug as well. Looks good to me.

"It's like I don't even know you anymore." Shoving off the bed, Nova catches Greyson's sleeve as she brushes by him.

"Let's go," she commands.

"What? Where?" But even as he's complaining, Greyson pushes to his feet.

"To get your brother something decent to wear to the club tomorrow night."

"Why do I have to come?"

"Because I'm assuming between you and your matching DNA strand, you're the one toting the cash."

"That's not a bad assumption."

"What?" Sterling looks to his brother. "How much cash you got, Grey?"

Ignoring him, Greyson shrugs his coat on and grabs the car keys.

"Let's make this quick," he says as he follows Nova out of the room.

The heavy hotel door slams shut after the pair.

"Well," Sterling claps his hands together and stands. Stretching his arms into the air, he does a few standing yoga moves. Weirdo. "Now that our plan of action is settled, let's order some pizza."

Tinkle pops into the mortal realm.

"Did I just hear pizza?" Tinkle—standing on the night-stand as a flying squirrel—rubs his white-fur belly. "Because I'm sure I could eat a whole pie myself. Let's have an eating contest."

Steel shoves out of the rolling chair. In the time it takes me to blink, he has a knife pulled and ready to throw at the Celestial.

"Dude, that would not be fair," Sterling says without missing a beat. Does he not realize his brother just pulled a weapon? "You'll just transform into some crazy large beast and eat all our food. I'm not falling for that . . . again."

"Steel, why don't you lower the knife?" I suggest. "There's no need for anyone to get stabby. We're all friends here."

"What is that?" He gestures to Tinkle with the pointy end of his weapon.

"This is Tinkle. A Celestial."

His jaw falls open, and the tip of the knife descends.

"Take a seat, we have a bit of catching up to do."

8

"Huh," Steel reclines in his seat. "So that's Tinker Bell?"

"Yep."

"And you're saying he can transform into any animal?"

"As far as I can tell." I lean forward, my arms resting against the table. A sly smile creeps across my lips. "You jealous?"

"Honestly? A little."

We glance over at Tinkle, who's snoring in Nova's lap. The pizzas arrived around the same time Nova and Greyson returned. Nova and Ash are watching a re-run of *Project Runway*. Every once in a while, Nova chucks a piece of food at the TV and boos.

After eating only a quarter slice of pizza—Sterling had a fit when Tinkle said he wanted to shift forms to fit more in —Tinkle crawled into Nova's lap, curled into a ball, and promptly fell asleep.

The little guy is becoming predictable.

"Taken a shine to Nova, has he?"

"You don't know the half of it. He practically worships at her feet."

Nova uses a finger to absently pet Tinkle's head. She's the only one he lets touch him that way. If I ever tried, I'm pretty sure I'd be left with only nine digits.

"I think it's good for her."

Steel cocks his head. Nova has been in a bit of a funk since before he left Seraph Academy. She may not have been in love with Steel like I once thought, but his actions still had a profound effect on her. I open my mouth to give a very high-level explanation of what I mean when Sterling shouts, "Skinny dipping!"

"In your dreams, dude," Ash yells back.

"You mean you don't want to take advantage of the pool here?"

"There's an Olympic-sized pool back at the academy. Why would we want to go into the dingy one here?"

"Yeah, it probably has bed bugs," Nova adds.

"That's not how bed bugs work," Sterling says.

She shrugs.

Steel shakes his head at his brother's antics and shifts his attention back to me. The smile slips off his mouth when he sees my face, which is most likely a lovely shade of ghostly white.

I can't help it. Whenever I consider getting into any body of water larger than a bathtub, my body goes into panic mode. I start to sweat in really uncomfortable places and my fingers and toes go tingly. If I didn't have a better hand on my phases, I'd probably be in the spectrum world right now.

I tell myself to chill the heck out.

"Are you all right?" Steel asks. His hand reaches forward

like he's going to touch me, but he pulls back before making contact.

I yank my hair up into a twisted knot to get it off my neck. Did someone turn up the heat in here?

"Yeah, fine. Just not really a pool kinda person."

I look everywhere except at Steel until it becomes obvious that I'm avoiding eye contact. It's not until my gaze returns to his that he speaks.

"You don't know how to swim?"

That wasn't hard to guess.

"Nope. No one ever took the time to teach me." I try to play it off like I don't care, even throwing in a toothy smile for good measure.

"Well, look at this," Greyson interrupts, plopping down in the seat next to me. "I never would have thought."

His gaze teeters back and forth between Steel and me. In turn, Steel and I shift our attention from each other to Greyson, confused at his comment. We have this weird triangle stare-down going on that's starting to get awkward.

"What do you mean, bro?"

"Just look at you two, getting along."

"Yeah," Sterling adds as he takes the remaining seat at the small bistro table. "We were expecting a lot of sucking face and yelling. Who knew you two could actually converse like mature young adults? I didn't think that was part of your mating ritual."

My blush comes on fast and intense. My cheeks must be cherry red. I reach up and brush my fingertips over my skin. I'm hot to the touch.

There's a sputtering sound behind me, and I assume Ash is choking on her drink.

This is so embarrassing.

Steel leans forward and punches Sterling on the arm . . . hard.

"Dude. That hurt." Sterling scooches his chair back and rubs his bicep. "Uncalled for."

"You need to develop a better filter."

"A better filter? *Any* filter." Greyson laughs, and I give him the stink eye. He's the one who started this.

Sterling scoffs. "Yes, because tiptoeing around a situation is so productive. You all would be lost without me."

"Keep telling yourself that, Sterling."

"All I'm saying is that these two—" Sterling uses his fingers to indicate Steel and me. Like that's necessary. "Have been—"

"Do not complete that thought." Pushing out of his chair, Steel stands. The levity between us is utterly shattered, and a fist forms in my chest.

For all of his bumbling, Sterling isn't wrong. There haven't been many moments of peace between me and Steel. We seem to operate on hot or cold. Having the opportunity to be with him, without tension hanging in the air between us, is . . . nice.

"I'm grabbing a shower. It's late, we should turn in soon." Turning on his heel, Steel stalks to the bathroom, slamming the door behind him.

I shoot Sterling a dirty look before stomping off to my room, intending to do the same.

My airway is blocked off. I can't breathe and instantly go into freak-out mode, swinging an arm out before my eyes even open. My flailing limb is caught mid-air, but I'm already geared up to kick a leg—never mind that I'm still horizontal—when a body lands on top of mine.

"Shh, it's just me."

Steel?

The fight leaks out of me as my eyes adjust to the darkened room. I blink to see that Steel is, in fact, flattening me with his body.

When he sees recognition flare in my eyes, he pulls his hand away.

"What the heck, Steel?" I whisper-hiss at him. "Get off."

Tilting his head, he looks down the length of both our bodies. We're meshed together from chest to toes.

"Shit. Sorry," he says and rolls off me.

Sitting up, I check the room to find Ash still fast asleep on the bed next to me, ear plugs and face mask in place. If a zombie apocalypse happens in the middle of the night, she'll be the first to get eaten.

On the other bed, Nova is turned on her side facing the other way. Her steady breathing says she's dead to the world as well.

"What's wrong?"

Steel bends over Ash's bag, riffling through the contents. He straightens, a piece of material balled in his fist.

"Let's go," he says and gestures for me to follow. Moving with the stealth of a ninja, he pauses at the door, checking over his shoulder to make sure I'm following.

I'm not.

I'm seated in bed, wondering if this is a dream.

Admittedly, if I were dreaming, Steel would most likely be shirtless. I'm not embarrassed to admit—at least to myself—that he's fit.

His facial features are hardly discernable in the almost

pitch darkness, but thanks to my angel-born eyesight, I see the thick slashes on his brow pinch as he waves me over.

Am I really doing this? I ask myself as I slide out of bed in only a tank and sleep shorts.

The answer is yes. Whatever this is, I'm definitely doing it.

I follow Steel as he noiselessly slips out into the hallway. Taking my hand, he pulls me along the corridor without so much as a word.

I'd be lying if I said I wasn't intrigued, but after a couple of turns, I lose my patience.

"Where are we going?"

He glances over his shoulder. "You'll see."

I grind my molars at the typical Steel response. Why did I even bother asking?

My feet pad soundlessly on the packed carpet as we tread down hallways and around corners. It's tacky and spongy. Yuck. I wish I'd thrown on some shoes before leaving the room.

Steel stops in front of an unmarked door and fiddles with the handle.

Is he picking a lock? His body blocks my view, but it sure sounds like it.

When the door pops open, he reaches for me again. The callouses on his palms brush against the sensitive nerves in my hand, and I suppress a shiver. I still find the touch of another person's hand to be incredibly intimate. It probably doesn't even register with Steel that he's holding on to me, but I couldn't be more aware.

Walking over the threshold, I'm hit with a muggy smell that hangs heavy in the air. I taste the chemical tang of it on my tongue.

A rectangular indoor pool, lit only by two underwater lights, stretches out in front of us. The water on the surface is smooth and still as glass.

"Here." Steel holds out a piece of pink fabric. I instinctively accept what he's offering before realizing it's a bikini. "Ash won't mind."

My heartbeat pulses in my throat, making it hard to swallow.

I shove the swimwear at Steel, already shaking my head, but he won't accept it. "I'm not getting in there."

"Yes, you are. Not knowing how to swim is a liability you can't afford. They should have taught you at Seraph." He gestures toward a door on the opposite side of the room. "Go change."

My stomach flips and butterflies flap a crazy cadence in my lower gut.

"This is happening, even if I have to throw you in there fully clothed."

I scoff as if he told a bad joke, but I know he's serious. Proving me right, he makes a move toward me, and I jump away.

"Okay, okay. Hold on." Taking a deep breath, I eye the pool with a heavy measure of disdain. I really don't want to do this, yet . . . he's not wrong. It is dangerous that I don't have this skill.

He crosses his arms over his chest. "Do I need to count to three?"

"Do I look like a toddler to you?"

Tilting his head he lifts his eyebrows, telling me he thinks I'm acting like one at the moment. I glare back at him, and he holds a finger in the air. "One."

Shoot.

"Stop."

Another finger ticks up. "Two."

"This isn't funny."

The curled corner of his mouth says that it is to him. "Thr—"

"Ahh!" I bolt toward the girls' locker room before Steel can pounce. The sound of my feet slapping on the porcelain tile almost drowns out his deep chuckle.

It takes me a good five minutes to work up the courage to leave the safety of the bathroom. Ash's swimsuit isn't scandalous by any means—all my important bits are covered— but I feel close to naked in the two-piece. A likely bi-product of not having spent any amount of time in a swimsuit.

I shove open the door to find Steel lounging on a chair, eyes closed, chest bare, with his arms behind his head as if he's sunning himself. His posture so relaxed, jealousy bubbles inside me. If only I could be as comfortable in my own skin.

"I was beginning to wonder if you were going to need help putting on your suit."

"Ha ha. In your dreams."

Tipping his head back he gives me a once over. "You absolutely will be wearing that pink number in my dreams."

I cross my arms over my chest and shoot him a look. "Cut it out. You sound like a sleazeball when you say stuff like that . . . or Sterling."

A single eyebrow arches as he shoves to his feet. "Good point."

I'm absolutely not staring at his ripped chest and abs. Nope. Not me.

Taking three large steps, he launches into the air,

drawing his knees toward his chest and wrapping his hands around his shins. His body crashes into the water with a slap, shooting liquid into the air and causing a small tidal wave to crest over the pool's lip.

The puddle on the ground reaches my toes. I curl them when wetness kisses the tips. The water feels warm, but a chill works its way up my body.

Maybe this wasn't such a great idea.

Steel surfaces with a grin. His hair flops over his forehead, and rather than reaching up to brush it away, he jerks his head and the wet strands fling to the side.

"No second thoughts," he says, as if reading my mind. "You're already committed."

"Under duress," I say, giving myself a mental pep-talk. *Okay, Emberly. You've got this. Lots of people swim without drowning. It's just water. You drink it and bathe in it every day. This is totally not a big deal.*

Tiptoeing to the edge of the pool, I lower myself, sitting primly on the perimeter. My arms tremble, but I cover the movement quickly. Dipping one foot into the water, I let it sink. Coolness slides up my leg as it submerges. The water is just a touch colder than my body temperature. I tentatively dunk my other limb and try to relax—a physical impossibility.

Steel treads water in front of me, but with a few powerful strokes he's at my side, folding his long arms on the ledge to my left. His bicep brushes my thigh as he settles, and I pretend not to notice.

"So what's your issue with water?"

The bluntness of the question throws me. Steel and I are good at dancing around topics, experts at building emotional walls. I'm not sure I'm ready to reveal this part of my history to him.

Vulnerability makes me twitchy.

"I like water just fine," I hedge. "From a distance."

Steel studies me, taking in my rigid body and inability to meet his eyes. "It's more than just not knowing how to swim, isn't it?"

Give this guy a gold star.

"Something happened to make you afraid."

A brittle laugh rattles my chest. "Do you mean the time I almost drowned when I got swept downriver during flood season, or when I slipped into the community pool and the lifeguard pretended not to see me?"

Steel's bicep bumps against my leg again as he suddenly tenses up, but I don't pay it any mind. My mouth is on verbal vomit mode.

"Or maybe you'd like to hear about the times I explained to my foster parents why I ran fully clothed into a lake or pool or river to escape the shadow beasts? That never went over well. People don't want to take care of a little girl they think is either a liar or insane."

I run a shaky hand through the tangled strands of my hair.

"Honestly, there were some days I wondered if I *was* going crazy."

When I stop talking, the only sound in the room is the gentle lapping of water sloshing off the sides of the pool. I concentrate on the ripples journeying along the surface rather than the person beside me as my cheeks heat from oversharing. Why did I say all that?

It feels like an eternity before Steel's low timbre echoes off the glass enclosure. "What happened to you wasn't fair."

I snort. "I don't want your pity. Life is rarely fair."

I sneak a peek at him when the silence descends on us again. Steel's gaze sears me.

"I don't pity you." The lines of his face are harsh, but he's not angry at me. He's angry for me. "But you should have grown up with loving parents who helped you understand our world. No one should have to live the way you did," he says, reading between the lines of everything I did and didn't say.

A burning sensation prickles the back of my eyes. Warmth settles in my chest, but with it something inside tightens. Staring back at Steel, I can't exactly identify what I'm feeling, but it's overwhelming. Breaking our contact, I search for an escape route.

Who says you can't run from your problems?

My gaze latches onto the red Exit sign at the top of the door at the other end of the pool. I'm a half-second away from bolting when something tickles my upper arm.

Steel trails the tips of his fingers down my arm. My skin tingles wherever he touches. When he reaches my hand, his own wraps around it.

"Come on. Time to learn how to swim."

Wading a few feet out into the pool, he tugs and I slide off the ledge, allowing him to pull me forward. Standing with my head and shoulders above the water, I start to shake. Some of my extremities go numb. I know my fear isn't rational, but it doesn't make it any less real.

This was a bad idea.

My pulse elevates and breaths quicken as my flight instinct takes over. Logical thinking becomes a distant memory.

The water is warm, but goose bumps break out on my skin at the same time moisture beads at my hairline.

The smell of chemicals fills my nostrils, making it feel like I can't get enough oxygen.

Blue and pink bursts of colors explode in my vision, but worries about phasing into the spectrum world are hardly at the top of my mind.

I take a baby step back, hoping to feel the pool's lip rough against my shoulders, but it's not there.

"Hey, look at me," Steel's voice booms in the relative silence. "I'm not going to let anything happen to you."

I want to believe him, but fear is a funny thing. I can face down a Forsaken with single-minded determination, yet a small pool leaves me paralyzed.

Go figure.

Steel squeezes my hand and uses his other one to tip my chin up, forcing my gaze from the blue-tinted water around us to the teal pool of his eyes as he draws closer.

"Deep breath in. Deep breath out. You've got this."

He's trying to calm me—I know he is—but the diminished distance between us only kicks my heartbeat up a notch.

I try taking deep breaths like Steel suggested, but the starbursts of color deepen and take over my vision as adrenaline pumps throughout my system. There's no stopping it now, so I give in and phase.

9

It happens just like any other time. From one blink to the next, I've traveled out of the mortal world and into the spectrum one. The sharp sting of chlorine is replaced by floral notes in the air. The water sparkles like a lit crystal chandelier, hiding my glowing white aura from any foes.

I'm grateful for that, but only that.

A flutter of my pulse is all it takes for me to panic. I'm further out in the water than I realized, and although the pool's edge is only a few lengths away, it feels like miles. I turn, and the water pulls at me like sludge.

My weakened knees bend and I submerge, inhaling water. I come up coughing. My body reflexively bends at the waist with each hack, and I end up dunking myself again.

Tentacles slip around my middle and behind my knees, and I'm tilted backward. I push against whatever is holding me, flailing and sputtering in the water.

It's hard to see anything clearly because the water sparkles like liquid crystals, blinding me.

The manacles wrap tighter, restricting my movements.

It isn't until his mouth is next to my ear calling my name and I'm sucking in a lungful of Steel-scented air that I realize it's him that has me, not some mystery monster from the deep.

I stop fighting, my ragged breathing filling the space around us. It's loud enough to disturb even the spectrum air, which shivers with each exhale. Steel keeps me pressed to his chest.

My arms warp around his neck in a near chokehold, and I've drawn my knees up so I'm almost in a ball. With my face buried into the side of his neck, the ends of his hair tickle my forehead.

Panic slowly dissolves, but I can't seem to force my arms to loosen.

Goose bumps are a thing of the past as my skin is now on fire.

"You ready for me to let go of you yet?"

I squeak a non-answer and plaster myself to him, eliminating whatever minuscule bit of space might have been between us the moment before.

Steel's chest vibrates with his near-silent laugh. "I guess we'll just chill like this for a bit longer."

This is so embarrassing. I'm only glad no one else is here to bear witness.

Correction, I'm glad Sterling isn't here. I'd legit never hear the end of it.

A few minutes pass and the tension leaks from my limbs. I hold them so rigidly, they shake with weakness. Clearing my throat, I loosen my hold on Steel. My cheek brushes his as I lean away, un-suctioning my chest from his.

His arms are anchored around my lower back and under my legs.

"Would you mind . . . um . . . letting me down."

I stare at the glittery water rather than his face as his arms melt away. Panic spikes again and I slam my body back against his and try to climb him like a flippin' tree. "No, no. Don't let go. Maybe just don't hold me like a baby anymore?"

"All right. I've got you."

I force my limbs to relax. I can only take a few inches of space between us—any more, and fear starts to churn in my gut.

My logical brain finally wakes up, but it only makes me feel worse about myself. I wish I wasn't like this—that a few incidents hadn't defined this part of myself. I'm probably the only Nephilim on the planet with a water phobia. I'm a freak by Nephilim and human standards.

"Read any more of those shirtless shifter books?"

"What?" My mind wipes clean of previous thoughts as I blink at Steel, trying to make sense of his question.

"I'm just wondering about those books you said you read. The ones with the guys who end up naked when they shift."

"I never said I read anything like that." I wrack my brain to think if I've even read a novel since coming to Seraph.

Steel's head cants to the side. A chunk of wet hair flops across his forehead, his smile nothing short of wolfish.

"Sure you did. When we were in the cave that first day, hiding from the Forsaken. You wanted to know what happened to my clothes when I shifted because of all the shifter romances you'd read."

I remembered that day and that conversation. That's not exactly how it went down.

"You're muddling the details a bit."

"Am I?"

"You know you are."

"Why don't you remind me then?"

"I'd rather not."

"Why is that?"

"This conversation is dumb."

"Are you saying you want to talk about something else?"

"Anything else."

"How about the fact that you're standing in the water without my help?"

What?

I check my surroundings and let out a small gasp. The sound echoes off the walls, causing ripples of sound to turn pink as they swim through the air.

He's right. I'm at least two hand lengths away from Steel. My arms are crossed over my chest rather than wrapped around him. He pushes the water back and forth with his hands, making gentle waves in the crystal brilliance.

He just used our conversation as a distraction. And it worked.

"I think we should start with floating."

"Floating?" He's not going to berate me for the major freak-out I just had? That's not very on-brand for him.

"Yeah. I think if you learn how to float, your anxiety about the water will lessen."

His reasoning has logic, but floating is terrifying. I'll have to lie back in the water and hope I don't go under.

"This is happening. Embrace it."

He reaches his hand out. The crystal brightness of the water caresses Steel's skin, illuminating its deep bronze shade, so much darker than my own ivory skin. My eyes trace a line from his palm up his forearm, over his bicep and the tight cords of his neck, to settle on his face. He holds his features still, but there's a challenge in his eyes.

I wrap my arms more tightly around myself and rub the goose bumps pebbling my skin, not sure I'm ready to accept his silent dare, but knowing that eventually I will.

Pulling in a deep breath of sweet-scented spectrum air, I force my arms to uncoil and take Steel's hand. A half-smile quirks the side of his mouth as he raises our clasped hands, leading me in a slow turn until my back is pressed up against his chest.

I clear my throat, slightly uncomfortable with our closeness. "Is this position really necessary?"

"Yes."

"You sure it's not just an excuse to cop a feel?"

Like, for real.

His chuckles cause his breath to puff against my neck. It feels too much like a caress, and I can't help the shiver that runs through my body. I'm only human after all. Or at least, part human.

"Can we just get on with—" A yelp slips past my lips as I'm pitched backward. He totally did that on purpose. Steel places an arm around my back and another under my knees to keep me afloat. I slam my lids shut and try to concentrate on not dying. My limbs shake so badly, water sloshes against the sides of the pool.

"Do I need to start asking about romance novels again?"

"Shut up."

"Did you know Sterling didn't learn how to swim until he was eleven?"

"Seriously?" The shaking turns into a moderate tremble.

"Oh, yeah. After he learned to swim in the mortal world, it was at least another year before he'd get in the water in the spirit realm. He was scared since the water sparkled, and he couldn't see the bottom. Fully convinced there were bloodthirsty mermaids waiting to pull him under and eat him."

An unwilling laugh bursts from my chest. "What gave him that idea?" It's quiet for a few seconds too long. "You didn't?"

"I haven't always been the perfect older brother. Besides, it's basically a rule that you need to razz your younger siblings. How was I to know Sterling would believe me?"

There is a familiar pang in my chest. Family. I thought I'd squashed these feelings—longings—years ago, but I guess the wound only scabbed over. I wonder what kind of sister I would have been?

"Of course, when I told Sterling and Greyson that the Fallen could enter their dreams at night and eat their brains, they didn't sleep for three nights straight, so I should have known the mermaid thing would mess with them. At least Greyson had wised up by then."

"Geez, Steel. That's savage . . . and really dark. How did you even come up with that stuff?"

"Neph kids grow up in a dark world."

"They're not the only ones."

For a while there's only the sound of the water gently lapping. The liquid passing over my limbs starts to soothe me rather than fuel my panic.

"Want to learn to tread water?" Steel's voice comes from my right, which I expect, but not at head level.

I blink open my eyes. His face isn't looming over me, because he's floating on the water's surface next to me—which means he's not holding me up anymore. Which means no one is holding me up anymore.

I jack-knife and immediately sink, sucking in a mouthful of chemically saturated water. I pop up sputtering and coughing.

"Whoa."

Steel snaps to attention and rights me, keeping his hands anchored on my biceps as he leads me to the pool's edge.

"We'll have to tackle treading water during the next lesson."

I nod rather than speak because I'm still clearing my lungs.

Dipping down, he plants his hands on my waist and hoists me into the air, seating me on the ledge. There's a long moment where we just stare at each other. And it should be awkward, I know it should, but it's not.

"Time to go back to the real world now, I guess."

The words were meant to be light-hearted, but they do something to Steel. The contours of his face harden and his mouth levels into a straight line. His eyes go from open and friendly to guarded. He's shutting himself off from me. Only now that it's gone do I realize we'd recaptured some of the levity from earlier in the evening.

With a nod, he pulls himself out of the water. Droplets fall on me as he strides away, phasing back into the mortal realm after only a step. I stare at the spot where he disappeared for a few long seconds before closing my eyes and concentrating on phasing. When I blink them open again, the sparkling light from the water has faded and chlorine burns my nostrils.

Steel dries himself with a towel. I pad over and grab a folded towel before sitting on the chair next to him.

As I dry off, I peer at him through my lashes, wondering what caused his mood to flip so suddenly. Whether it's the trauma of having just confronted one of my worst fears, or the fact that I was roused from a perfectly good night of sleep to do so, I don't hold my tongue.

"What just happened?"

Steel looks at me out of the corner of his eye, refusing to even turn his head in my direction. I wrap the towel around me, securing it under my armpits, suddenly self-conscious.

"Nothing. It's like you said. We had our break from reality, and now it's time to get back to the real world. We've got a lot coming up in the next day. I shouldn't have kept you up."

He grabs his clothes and starts for the door without waiting to see if I'm following. His hand is on the knob when I call out.

"Wait."

The muscles in his back tense, and for a moment, I don't think he's going to listen, but then they relax, and he turns his head in my direction.

"Yeah?"

"I just . . . um, thanks. You know, for the swim lesson. Or rather, float lesson. It was . . . nice."

What I really want to tell him is that no one has ever taken the time to help me overcome my fear of the water before. No one has ever cared enough to try, and the fact that he did, well, that means something to me. But the words are lodged so deeply in my throat, they'll never see the light of day.

I must broadcast my vulnerability because his demeanor softens fractionally. He opens his mouth and then closes it again. His desire to speak brushes up against me like a living thing, but he only nods his head in acknowledgement before yanking the door open and walking through it.

Releasing a sigh, I collect my things and follow. Both of us brim with unspoken words. Maybe one day we'll get so full they'll explode from us, but for now they go unsaid.

e spend the better part of the day learning everything Steel knows about Silver and her plans—which sadly isn't a lot—and coming up with ideas on how to trap her. Steel's adamant about capturing Silver rather than outright killing her. He believes she has information we need, and I agree.

Silver is a wellspring of knowledge. She orchestrated Blaze and Aurora's kidnapping to get to me, and we still have no idea why. And then there's the orb that was shipped to the Elders' compound to be studied. Where did it come from? Was it found or made? What else can it do? We have a mountain of unanswered questions, and Silver may be the key to answering them.

We all agree that capturing her isn't going to be easy. There are three other Forsaken with her—and those are just the enemies we know of. We may have the numbers, but when it comes to Forsaken, I don't like those odds. Silver is a proven formidable foe. She also knows we're coming for her—or at least she knows Steel is. We're hoping she isn't aware the rest of us are in town just yet.

Tonight's objective is reconnaissance. We spend hours poring over the blueprints of the club. Since the building used to be a church, it's undergone major renovations. By comparing both original and updated schematics, we identified several rooms that were unaccounted for during the upgrades—the perfect place to carry out nefarious deeds. Something is going down in that club, and we have to find out what.

We also use our time to plot exit and entry points, planning for as many contingency options as possible.

It's decided—after a decent bit of arguing—that the boys will scout the interior of the club this evening. We're even sending Tinkle in to conceal their aura from any enemies hiding in the spectrum world. The little guy argued against it, saying it's his job to shade me, but I secretly think he was more upset about being parted from Nova.

The girls' job is to keep surveillance on the hotel where Silver is staying, which admittedly is kinda lame, but I'm not complaining. The idea of going to a nightclub is preposterous to me. I've never set foot inside one before. I'm about as far from a party girl as a person can get, so I was happy to pick up a different task.

"What do you think about this top? This would be good for a club, right?" Ash holds a gold sequined number up in front of her for my inspection.

I scrunch my eyebrows as my gaze tracks from the shiny fabric to her face. "Why in the world did you pack that? And who cares? Only the guys are going to the club tonight."

"That's not *exactly* correct." Ash's tentative reply automatically puts me on edge. That tone means she's about to admit something I'm not going to like.

"What do you mean?"

Ash's gaze shifts to Nova, who ignores us as she pulls a bag of food out of her purse for Tinkle. Tinkle jumps up and down on the table, clapping his tiny squirrel hands, waiting for the processed goodness to fall on his head.

"Well . . . the boys may have miscalculated their need for backup tonight," she says.

I narrow my eyes, not buying that explanation for a moment. "Why don't you tell me what this is really all about?"

Ash bites her lower lip and scrunches her nose. "I have no idea what you're talking about."

I pin her with a stare, not buying her fake innocence for a single moment. "You need to take some lessons from Sterling. You're not half as convincing as he is."

Ash releases her lip and twists her mouth into a guilty grimace.

"The guys don't need backup, Ash. They're only scouting the club, and Tinkle will be shading their auras in the spirit realm the whole time."

"Which Tinkle is still upset about," the Celestial cuts in. His cheeks are puffed out and his mouth is ringed with orange. He spits cheese puff crumbs onto the table when he talks, and then immediately goes back to shoveling the Styrofoam-ish snack into his compact squirrel mouth.

"All to say," I continue, "that it's a relatively safe mission. So I repeat, what's really going on here?"

"We want to see what a club is really like." The words come out in a rush and then Ash covers her face.

I throw my hands into the air, berating myself that I

didn't see this coming. Ash and Nova argued with the guys about our task earlier in the day, but gave up relatively quickly. "Argh. You girls are killing me. I don't *want* to go to the club."

"Em," Ash whines. "We may never have an opportunity like this again."

I tell myself not to feel guilty, hardening my resolve even as I feel it crumble. "Even if I did want to go, I don't have anything to wear. I'll stick out like a sore thumb."

"This is killer." Nova pulls a blue garment from Ash's bag and holds it up in front of her. She twists back and forth in front of the mirror to get a better look at herself. "I definitely want to borrow this sometime. Blue looks great with my complexion."

"Oh, Ash. You didn't." I drop back onto the bed and squeeze my eyes shut. Nova is holding the bandage dress I tried on back in Glenwood Springs. I had completely forgotten Ash bought it the night I was attacked.

The bed dips and sways. I open one eye. Ash's face hovers above me.

"Being a bit dramatic, aren't you? It's just a dress. It's not going to kill you to wear it for one night."

"First," I tick a finger in the air, "it's not a dress, it's a glorified top. Second," another finger goes up, "it may just kill me, we don't really know. Hypothermia is a definite possibility in that thing."

Ash tilts her head and shoots me a droll look. "You're a Neph who can create and throw magic fireballs, Emberly. I don't think freezing to death is a valid concern here."

"And third," I continue, undeterred, "I'm not putting something on just so a roomful of dudes can drool over my cleavage and try to look up my skirt."

"Wait just a minute." Nova sounds pissed. I prop myself up on an elbow to see her. One fist rests on her hip and the stretchy blue dress is clutched in the other. A scowl mars her perfect face. "The point of wearing an amazing dress like this is not for guys, it's for you."

"How do you figure?" I'm genuinely curious.

"Do you think I dress the way I do to get male attention?"

Umm... Does she really expect me to answer that?

Her head tilts. "Well, I don't, okay? I dress the way I do *despite* the attention I receive. I wear what I think is cute. Maybe I'm feeling the color or the style. My clothes make me feel powerful and pretty. Like I need, or want, catcalls from dudes to make me feel good. I already know I'm fabulous." She uses a perfectly manicured hand to flip a chunk of dark auburn hair over a shoulder. "All I'm saying is that you shouldn't let the fear of what people think of you stop you from doing things."

"I don't—"

"Oh, yes you do. I remember what you wore when you first arrived at the academy. Men's clothes several sizes too large. You were trying to hide yourself in those rags. And since you were living on the streets when we found you, I can understand where you were coming from. But that's not your reality anymore, Emberly. With us, you can be free to be who you are. Or at least try to figure that out. We're not here to judge you. And who gives a flying flip what a few horny dudes at a seedy club are going to think, or not think, when they see you?"

I blink back at her. That was a surprisingly insightful speech. Not that I think Nova isn't smart—I know she is— but she brought up a point I'd never considered before.

"So here." Nova tosses the dress. It lands in a puddle on the covers beside me. "Try it for a night. If you hate the way wearing it makes you feel, at least you'll know. Heck, you can go back to wearing those disgusting men's shirts if you want. Just make sure you're doing it for the right reasons. Not to hide yourself from the world, but because you truly enjoy that style."

I glance at Ash, and she offers me a one-shoulder shrug that seems to say, *Worth a try, right?*

"Besides," Nova turns her back on us to face the mirror. She finger-combs her hair, then picks up a few strands and checks for split ends. "I'd love to see you stop dressing like an Ash clone. It's a little too Stepford Wife for me."

"Hey." Ash pops up. Her back goes ram-rod straight.

Nova cocks a brow and pins us with a look through the mirror. "Sorry to break up your slumber party, Ash. But you know it's true. Emberly isn't a dress-up Barbie for your amusement. The girl's got to find her own sense of style."

"Wear something sparkly. Everyone likes sparkles." Tinkle imparts his fashion advice with so much seriousness I have to cover my laugh with a cough.

Crossing her arms over her chest, Ash hunches and blows out a breath. The curls hanging over her forehead dance and then settle. Turning toward me, she eyes the crumpled dress in my lap and then fixes her gaze on my face. A smile spreads. "Well, that doesn't mean I can't still do your makeup."

I'm totally exposed.

Okay, so technically I'm not exposed, but it sure feels

that way. Even with the cropped leather jacket Nova let me borrow, I have more leg showing in public than I ever have before. I keep pulling down the hem. Nova slaps my hands away every time. I'm giving this dress a chance, but I'm pretty sure this isn't me.

What I am digging though are the black fringed ankle boots Ash let me use. The studded heels push my height well over six feet. I only teeter-totter a bit when I walk, and they make me feel like a rocker chick, which I'm surprised to find I like.

I pull the jacket tighter around my middle as a gust of frigid mid-western wind blows my hair behind me in a blonde and red tornado.

The ends of this stupid jacket barely touch together at my chest. Why would Nova buy something this impractical? Thank goodness for heated angel blood or I'd be a popsicle right now.

"Like we discussed, the guys are already inside." Ash adjusts a curl at her temple as we round the building. Parking was in the back, and it's a trek to the club entrance. We're lucky the night isn't as cold as the one before.

"I still think we should have told the guys we were coming. It's not like they could physically bar us from following them." I eye the long line of people waiting to be let into the club. Oh joy. I try hard not to notice the stares we're attracting. "Maybe we should try one of the other entrances. We don't want to draw too much attention."

Nova snorts beside me. "Like where we enter is going to make a difference. We're going to draw eyes either way. We look a-maz-ing."

We reach the end of the half-block-long line. Nova keeps walking when Ash and I stop. Without breaking stride, she glances over her shoulder and shouts back to us, "I don't wait in lines."

Oh, geez.

A group of girls in front of us shoot death glares as Ash and I scurry after Nova. We don't catch up to her until she reaches the front entrance. A muscled bald bouncer who bears a striking resemblance to Mr. Clean takes one long look at Nova—starting at her feet and moving up—before unclipping the cherry red velvet rope in front of us and letting her pass through.

"They're with me," she purrs at the gatekeeper. He frowns but moves aside, jerking his chin to indicate we can pass as well.

I feel the eyes of the angry partiers waiting in line and do my best not to glance up as I shuffle along behind my friends. The bass from the music inside the club thumps inside my chest, and we haven't even pushed through the doors yet.

A sliver of trepidation slides up my spine. I don't have to have been to a club before to already know this so isn't my scene. Nova, on the other hand, sways her shoulders and hips to the music. Ash appears a bit more reserved, her eyes wide and observant, but her head bobs along with the beat as well.

The best I could do is clap along, but even I know that would be awkward.

Ash and I follow Nova when she pushes through the front doors. Bright light strobes in my eyes, and I blink rapidly. It's a moment before I'm able to regain my bearings. When I do, it's as if I've stepped through a portal into another world.

We are in a tunnel. The ground below us as well as the

ceiling and walls to our right and left are black, but all twinkle with built-in lights. The effect is disorienting. As soon as I catch view of a light it blinks off and another grabs my attention.

Beyond the opening, laser beams of lights swirl and pulse to the rhythm of the music. Every few moments the lights in the tunnel strobe, making me blink rapidly.

How can people stand this? My stomach roils, a touch nauseated from the pounding noise and flickering lights. And some people find this entertaining?

Not just some people, but Nova in particular. Once we break free of the tunnel, Nova throws her hands in the air and heads right into the crowd. The mass of bodies in the small warehouse-like space swallows her immediately.

"Should we follow her?" I ask Ash. I have to yell to be heard.

Ash's face is tipped back. I follow her gaze until it settles on a woman hanging from the ceiling. Clad in what looks to be a sequined bikini, she is performing some sort of acrobatics while hanging on to red silk curtains. The ends of the draperies float only a few feet above the dancing crowd.

Shaking her head, Ash refocuses on me. "Naw, I think she's pretty comfortable out there. Let's move around the perimeter."

Grabbing my hand, she leads me around the sea of people congregated on the dance floor.

How are we going to find anything useful in this mess? A u-shaped bar rings three sides of the dance floor. Bodies press up against the counter three people deep, leaving only a very narrow path to navigate between them and the gyrating dancers. I'm thankful for my height or I wouldn't be able to see anything beyond the people crushing me on either side.

I struggle to stay alert. The longer we snake through the drunken horde, the more discombobulated I become. My angel-born senses go haywire.

The music is so loud it rattles my insides and attacks my eardrums. A headache pulses along with the beat. My eyelids flutter against the strobe lights and lasers flashing and flickering around the room, making it impossible for me to focus on the faces of the people around us.

I'm hit with a surge of body odor poorly masked by Axe body spray, and my stomach flips. The stench is so strong I can taste it on my tongue. The contents of my stomach start to mutiny, and I have to cup my free hand over my mouth and nose to keep from blowing chunks.

It's all too much.

Someone falls into me, and I lose my hold on Ash and stumble to the side, clumsily walking my way onto the dance floor. I'm jostled back and forth, not able to get my bearings.

I search for Ash's curly head of hair only to register flashes of people in between strobes. An elbow, a chin, a logo on the front of some dude's t-shirt.

I want to crouch into a ball with my hands on my ears, but fear I'll be trampled.

Some amazing angel-born warrior I am, conquered by a bit of loud music and a drunken crowd.

I'm bumped from behind and fall against a stranger. My hands land on his shoulder and left peck. The material beneath my palms is moist with sweat.

Yuck.

I snatch my hands away and rear back a step, but I

haven't gone unnoticed. The guy I just accidentally felt up turns fully toward me. After giving me a once-over, which leaves me wanting to tug my skirt down to my ankles, a lecherous smile grows on his face. His eyes light with interest even though it looks like he can't lift his lids past half-mast.

He's definitely drunk or high . . . or both. Humans' natural aversion to Nephilim is dulled along with their other senses when they are inebriated. I learned that the hard way with one of my foster dads. I was shipped off to a new foster home after embedding a fork in his leg when he tried to corner me in the kitchen one night.

I shake my head as beefy hands reach for my biceps. Taking another step backward, a barrier of bodies thwarts my retreat. I turn to push through the crowd, but a pair of sweaty arms wrap around my middle, jerking me back against a wall of clammy flesh. Before I even fully register what is happening, a face presses to my neck and over-heated breath wets the side of my face.

I really am going to be sick.

Moving quickly, I jab an elbow back and into the soft middle of the fool behind me. What I really want to do is introduce his face to the sticky floor, but that sounds like a lot of hassle.

The move has the desired effect, and his arms slide off me. I don't wait to see how he fared before shoving my way through dancers. I'm past caring if I'm rude. I just need to get out of this mess. But somehow, I find myself deeper in the sea of writhing bodies.

The EDM music pumping through the speakers mellows and the lights dim to match the mood. The softer beat would normally be welcome, but with only the spinning spotlights from above to illuminate the room, I have an even harder time seeing. When I strain to engage my enhanced sight, the flickering beams saturate my vision and then dump me in total darkness once again.

The throbbing pain in my head is like a spike hammering into my temple. Squeezing my eyes shut, I slap my hands over my ears and concentrate on sucking air in and out through my mouth.

The low thumping of the music still vibrates my body, and my skin heats uncomfortably. Lances of fiery pain shoot down either side of my spine, and I hiss at the sensation.

Shrugging my jacket off, I let it fall to the ground. Only a whisper of concern for Nova's garment brushes my mind before it's swept away by a deluge of sensory overload.

The sizzling pain on my back intensifies, and it's only then I start to process what is happening.

My wings are about to emerge. In front of humans. In the middle of a crowded club dance floor.

This is so bad.

Panic sets in.

Lights burst in my vision, but I have no idea if they are real or spectrum lights. I slam my eyes closed, but a pinwheel of colors still spin behind my lids.

I can't get enough air. What I do take in burns my lungs. I start gasping.

It's only a matter of time before my wings appear, most likely slicing and dicing anyone within a ten-foot radius, or I phase into the spectrum world. Either one of those actions is going to be a dead giveaway to any Forsaken in this club.

I tell myself to calm down, but it's not working. A bead of sweat rides a trail down my hairline.

A hand presses against my upper back right between my shoulder blades, and rather than freaking me out, a wash of coolness spreads from the contact. I exhale a relieved breath and crack my lids, hoping my lashes will block some of the beams of light.

A body glides in front of me and the pressure of the hand on my back skims forward to cup my shoulder. All I can see is a wide chest covered in a black t-shirt, so I force my gaze up.

Steel's eyes sweep my stricken face, and then he tugs me forward.

11

I go willingly into Steel's arms, burying my face in his chest as his hands caress my exposed back. My flesh cools under his touch, which makes zero sense, but I'm not about to complain. Somehow, he is the ice to my fire, able to temper the uncontrollable blaze inside. I don't understand it, but at times like this, I'm thankful for whatever magic is at work.

I drag in a lungful of Steel-laced air, and my heartbeat's frantic cadence reduces to only a slightly elevated rhythm.

Scooping up my hair, he places it over one shoulder and bends forward. With our faces pressed cheek to cheek, his lips brush over the shell of my ear when he speaks.

"I should have known you three wouldn't stay put. Let's get some fresh air." Talking directly into my ear is the only way I can hear him, and even then, he's practically yelling. Still, my body doesn't always respond to logical thought, and I can't help the shiver of awareness that zings from head to toes.

I nod, and my lips accidentally brush against his jaw.

We're still for a moment before he shifts, slipping his hand in mine and twining our fingers together. His grip is blessedly more secure than the one I had on Ash earlier.

The crowd parts for Steel like the Red Sea as he leads me off the dance floor. As if they sense his aura on a subconscious level, people simply know not to mess with him. If only I'd had that same effect growing up. Sure, my angel blood caused most humans to distrust and dislike me, but that didn't mean they always kept their distance.

I stabilize my focus on the back of Steel's head as we slide through the crowd of dancers. I should be scanning for Forsaken, but my stomach still isn't happy with me. Concentrating on one point seems to help it settle.

The colored club lights bounce off strands of Steel's black hair, reminding me of an oil slick, beautiful and hypnotizing. I don't notice we've left the crush of the throng until Steel tugs me down a shadowed hallway.

I engage my Neph sight because the flashing lights don't penetrate the narrow space. We're embraced by the darkness, and I let out a sigh of relief. It has a calming effect on me that, doubled with Steel's cool touch, allows me to feel in control of my body once again.

There's a metal door at the end of the hallway that Steel doesn't hesitate to push through, dragging me with him. I step over the threshold and out into the night air.

The door slams shut behind us.

"I hope it doesn't automatically lock."

Steel's face is expressionless except for a minutely arched eyebrow. "If it does, I'll just break the lock."

Right. Good point. Like something as trivial as a locked door would keep Steel out.

"You feeling better?" He doesn't look at me when he asks. Rather, he scans the alleyway behind me.

"Yeah. That wasn't my jam." Understatement.

The door let us out into a dead end. Glancing over my shoulder, I survey the rest of the alley while the cold night air chills my overheated skin. There's a streetlight near the entrance and I watch a group of three girls decked out in clubbing clothes stomp under its glow before disappearing behind the corner of the building. The rest of the alleyway is lit only by moonlight.

"Ash is with Sterling and Grey," Steel says. Oh, I'm *such* a crap friend. I completely forgot about Ash. "She was pretty freaked that she lost you."

I rub my forehead. My headache thumps, but I can tell it's dying down.

"I told her I wouldn't have a problem finding you. She's inside searching with them now."

"How were you certain you'd find me? I could have been anywhere in that mess." The closed door behind me is no match for the song blasting behind it. The jarring beats ricochet inside my head.

"You're not hard to find." Steel's gaze finally settles on me. "At least for me."

I straighten. What's that supposed to mean?

The question in my eyes goes unanswered as Steel steers our conversation in another direction.

"This is bold." He gestures to my dress and heat rises to my cheeks. I can get on board with Nova's idea of finding my own style, but stretchy bandage dresses aren't it. I itch to peel off the dress and throw on some sweats. I'll keep Ash's boots though and Nova's jacket—

"Oh, shoot!" I pat my arms, confirming what I already know. "I lost Nova's jacket."

Steel chuckles. "There's going to be hell to pay for that one."

"Don't I know it." I tip my head skyward, not seeing any stars. I once saw Nova go nuclear on a guy in our class for spilling soda on her, and that only ruined a cotton tee, not an expensive leather jacket. I absently wrap my arms around my middle while I contemplate what to tell her. Would she believe me if I told her a Forsaken stole it?

Steel's calloused palms brush over my biceps, startling me. I drop my gaze to find him standing in front of me. He slides his large hands slowly up and down my arms, warming the chilled skin.

"You cold?"

I'm covered in goose bumps, but I'm not cold. I shake my head, but Steel doesn't release me nor does he stop stroking my arms. An involuntary shiver works its way through my body.

"You sure?" He angles his head and moves a breath closer. He knows exactly what's going on, but I can't seem to drum up the energy to be annoyed. His once-cooling touch now has the opposite effect, causing warmth to fizzle in my veins, a delicious contrast to the cold kiss of winter air against my exposed skin.

Steel and I have been through a lot together. And the attraction that's been brewing between us, well . . . I may finally be ready to see where it leads. Our timing isn't perfect, but perhaps to an angel-born, there's no such thing as perfect timing. Maybe I need to grab hold of the moments I have whenever they come. The life of a

Nephilim can be long, but there's no guarantee of tomorrow.

Reaching between us, I lay a hand on Steel's chest while the other crawls up his neck. His pupils grow until there is just a sliver of aquamarine ringing the black. I step into him, playing with the longer hairs at the nape of his neck.

"I think I should be worried," he starts. "The last time something like this happened between the two of us, I got a fist in my throat."

"Are you saying you didn't deserve it?"

Bending his head and stepping fully into my space, he rubs his nose against my cheek before whispering in my ear. "It was well deserved."

He pulls back slightly, and my gaze dances over the angles on his face made sharper by the moonlight and shadows. He looks like some otherworldly creature sent to tempt me.

Maybe he is. Maybe it's working.

"Emberly, this thing between us." He brushes his fingers from my shoulder to wrist, and I close my eyes against the sensation. "I don't know . . ." I open my lids when he doesn't continue. "I'm not sure that it's real."

He voices the fears I dare not utter. Things are so intense between us at times. Is it genuine attraction or only out-of-control hormones? Or is something else at play here, something that strips our choices away from us?

Indecision causes me to tip away. Steel loosens his hold, but moves with me. My back skims the chilled door behind me, but I don't rest my full weight against it. The juxtaposition of the icy metal behind me and the heat coming off of Steel is doing things to my head.

The whispered word "mine" echoes in the corners of my mind.

His face tightens, unmasking his indecision. I watch doubt and worry seep into his mind. The light in his eyes begins to dim and his hold on me melts away.

I don't want that to happen. So as I watch Steel pull away from me, I do what comes naturally. I push.

"It's real for this moment, and right now, that's all I care about."

Steel's hands have dropped to his sides, but mine remain pressed against his chest and around his neck. Before he can sever our connection and ruin this moment for the both of us, my fingers tug on the soft material of his shirt, fisting it and stretching out the neck.

There's something I like about him looking slightly disheveled. A little less than perfect.

Perfection is overrated.

My hand on his neck no longer simply toys with his hair, but applies pressure, urging him closer.

In this brief moment in time, Steel is utterly enthralled with me, one hundred percent susceptible to my whims and desires. And my immediate desire is to be reminded what it feels like to have his lips slide over my own.

He angles his head to align perfectly with my own, and we only remain apart for a single heartbeat more. Our lips press together in a kiss so innocent, it probably should have been our first. I don't mind so much going out of order as long as each kiss moves me to my core.

Steel presses into me, holding me in place as he increases the pressure on my lips. The spots on my back where my wings fold out tingle, but instinct tells me they aren't going to emerge.

Our lips meet once, twice, three times.

Steel draws away just far enough for his gaze to sweep my face. His hand moves up to my neck, and his thumb strokes my pulse point.

"Emberly." He utters my name on a whispered breath. His eyes have taken on a feverish glow. I want to know what he has to say, but not as badly as I want another taste. My gaze dips to his lips as his hand slips into my hair. "So sweet."

I shift, leaning more deeply into his embrace, but it doesn't exactly work out the way I intend. The door behind me shoves open, and I clunk foreheads with Steel before flopping onto his chest.

He absorbs my impact with an "oomph" as we both get pushed several feet. My heel catches on some loose stones, and my ankle rolls. If it wasn't for Steel's reflexes, I'd be crumpled on the ground with a wet butt and probably a skinned knee.

"I'll check out here." Sterling's voice is unmistakable. "Oh, hey. Looks like I found ya."

I can hear and feel Steel's exasperated sigh. "Great timing, man." He keeps a firm hold on me until I regain my footing.

Once I'm stable, I bring a hand up to my face. Sure enough, my skin throws off heat like a furnace. My cheeks must be cherry red.

Ducking my head, I step away from Steel and turn to Sterling, lifting my eyes but not my face. The younger Durand twin is propped up against the brick wall to the right of the club door. His arms are crossed over his chest and one knee is bent as his foot rests on the wall behind him. He doesn't even try to contain the grin spreading across his face or the amusement dancing in his eyes. The word *smug* clangs through my mind.

"Sooo, tell me. What have you two been up to while we all were searching for you instead of Forsaken?"

"Nothing."

"Mind your own business, Sterling."

Could we sound more guilty?

Sterling releases a low chuckle, not fooled in the least. "Nice shade of lipstick . . . Steel."

I snap my gaze to Steel, who's wiping his mouth with the back of his hand. When he drops his hand, it's stained with a raspberry-tinted smear.

So. Busted.

Sterling's smile grows. "In all seriousness though, boys and girls, we need to get back in there. Our plan is going up in flames. You know what it's like when drunk humans get around us." Pushing off the alley wall, he lifts a hand to itch his forehead. "Even I'm getting annoyed by all the handsy females in there, so you know it's bad. And the girls straight up need bodyguards. Well, at least Ash does. Nova seems to be enjoying herself."

Steel shoves a hand in his hair. "We should have seen this coming."

"Yeah," Sterling agrees. "They're all over us like flies on poop."

"Ew. Real classy, Sterling," I say.

He grins showing off as many teeth as possible. "That's me. Classy to the core."

"I can think of a few other words to describe you."

"Handsome? Charismatic? Irresistible?"

I smash my lips together. Do. Not. Laugh. Encouraging

Sterling's bad behavior is never a good idea. He's like a toddler sometimes.

"Something like that," I answer as soon as I'm confident I won't crack a smile.

"Just as I expected." He slides up next to me, casually wrapping an arm around my shoulder and herding me toward the door. "Now, let's get going. I won't even tell you where Greyson was pinched. I'm sure he's going to want to relive that experience with you."

"Leaving so soon?"

Sterling and I freeze. A low growl rumbles behind me.

I shift my gaze toward the alleyway. I know we came here to find her, but a shockwave still boomerangs around my gut when my eyes land on Silver.

"It's actually her." I don't think Sterling is even aware that the words leave his mouth. Up until now he's only been *told* his sister is alive. Witnessing her on a video doesn't compare to seeing her with his own eyes.

"Hey, is that my little bro? Long time no see, kiddo." The click of Silver's heels creates an eerie echo as she saunters forward, cutting the distance that yawns between us.

Bold move.

"Silver?" Sterling brushes past me, looking like he's in a trance.

Silver throws her arms wide as if waiting for an embrace. "In the flesh."

Sterling doesn't make it another two zombie-like steps before Steel rushes past him in a blur, colliding with Silver even as her arms are still raised. He smashes her back into the building opposite the club with such force I swear the ground vibrates. Brick dust sprinkles down on the both of them.

The hit shocks Sterling out of his daze. His eyes harden as he stomps over to his brother's side. I follow in his wake.

Steel traps Silver against the alley wall with his forearm shoved against her neck, and a wicked, gold-handled dagger pushed against her side. He bares his teeth in an inhuman expression of anger. His beast side is extremely close to the surface and I can't be sure he isn't going to take a vicious bite out of her.

Silver is suspiciously calm. A secretive smile lingers on her lips, despite her compromising position. Her hands lift in the universal sign for "I mean no harm." When Steel presses his forearm harder against her throat, she only tips her head back farther.

I cast a glance around. Something isn't right. Steel and Sterling are too distracted by Silver's arrival to think clearly, but I don't suffer from that same affliction. I case our surroundings while Steel and Sterling interrogate their sister.

"Who are you working with?" Steel's words are barely intelligible above the growl in his voice. "We know you didn't stage the kidnapping on your own."

There's a garbled noise. I glance behind me to see Silver pointing to her throat. Steel lets up enough so she can wheeze out a few words.

"Is this really necessary, big brother? I'm obviously not fighting back."

"Don't call me that. You're not my sister. You're just the thing that killed her."

Silver's exaggerated eye-roll may have been funny under different circumstances, but her blasé attitude only makes the fine hairs on my body rise.

"We've already been over this. I *am* your sister, but I can understand your need to stay steeped in denial. Accepting that you've been lied to all your life by people you were supposed to trust has gotta burn."

"Cut the crap and just tell us what you know or Steel's blade is going to get real friendly with several of your organs." Steel twists the dagger after Sterling speaks. A spot of blood blooms on the white fabric over Silver's ribs.

"Ow. Uncalled for. As a matter of fact, I'd love for you to meet the boss. All you had to do was ask." Her gaze slides past the pair to me, and our eyes connect. The grin ratchets up on her face, and she winks.

In the blink of an eye, she snatches the arm shoved against her neck. Drawing both feet up, she kicks them out into Steel's stomach.

He's been trained to take punches, but Steel lets up just enough for her to slip out of his grasp. Steel and Sterling lunge for her, but she disappears.

"She phased. I'm going after her." Sterling vanishes before the word "wait" can form on my lips. Steel is still with me.

"It's got to be a trap," I say.

Steel stares at the place Silver just stood. His knuckles bleach of color, especially the hand clutching the dagger. He's going to leave an indent on the handle.

Lifting his head, he looks at me and simply says "I know," then phases into the spectrum world after them.

12

The air huffing out of my mouth fogs in front of my face. Snowflakes drift from the sky, getting stuck in my eyelashes. Indecision rides me. Hard.

Phase into the spectrum world, or search for help?

The choice gets taken from me a moment later when Sterling pops back into the mortal world, his shoulder a mess of mangled flesh. I spot muscle peeling back from bone.

He falls to his knees just as I reach his side. Blood streams from his lips and pools on the damp pavement.

"What happened?" He couldn't have been gone more than a minute.

He coughs and a glob of blood lands at my feet, splashing over Ash's boots. That's not good. Internal damage?

Throwing his non-injured arm over my shoulders, I force him to his feet. We stumble-walk to the club door.

I have to find someone. Sterling needs immediate help. I

don't have anything to press to his wound to stanch the flow.

Grasping the cold metal handle, I throw open the door and drag Sterling through, not even sure if he's conscious anymore.

The bass is as loud as before, but the long hallway muffles the sound a bit.

I have to find one of the others.

Setting Sterling down and propping him against the wall, I seriously consider yanking off my dress to tie around his shoulder. I probably won't get very far in my search for the other angel-borns if I'm running around in my underwear though.

I'm about to set off when Sterling's head rolls back. Pain glazes his half-closed eyes as blood continues to dribble from his mouth. His lips move, but I can't make out the words over the pump of the music and rasp in his voice. I lean in, placing my ear only inches from his face.

"They'll kill him," Sterling croaks.

Steel.

His words stab my heart. I cast a panicked glance at the closed door.

"Go." The urgency in Sterling's voice is real, but I can't go after Steel right now. If I don't find help, there's a real chance Sterling could bleed out.

Using his uninjured arm, Sterling tries to push me back toward the alley. His movements are sloppy and lacking in strength.

Standing, I turn to the dance floor and see Ash and Greyson shove through the crowd, a trail of pixie dust behind them. Seeing us, Ash's eyes saucer and Greyson's mouth opens. It's half a beat before they're running down the hall to us.

"Help him!" I shout over the music before pivoting on my heel and busting through the back door again. Grabbing hold of my panic, I let it wash over me and sweep me into the spectrum world.

Two steps out of the door and I've phased into a war zone.

Forsaken. Are. Everywhere.

There have to be at least three dozen. The bulk of them congregate down the alley in what looks like a mosh pit.

There's a roar, and a pale body is thrown. I duck to keep from getting hit by a flailing limb. It incites the mob of Forsaken and several more jump into what is obviously a fight.

A lion's bellow mixes with Forsaken screams.

Steel.

The mass of Forsaken blocks my view of what's happening, but the spurts of black and red blood splatter-painting the walls is indication enough.

That hidden part of me rumbles: *mine.*

I don't stop the possessiveness from taking over. Heat zings down my body as my wings burst free, cutting into a few Forsaken that have noticed me and tried to ambush me from behind.

Looking down at myself, I'm covered in golden armor. Weapons are strapped to my arms and legs, my torso protected by a shell of metal.

I'm finally wearing pants—thank goodness.

Crouching low, I spring into the air, giving my wings a few test flaps before dropping onto the horde of Forsaken attacking Steel.

I slash at the Forsaken with my wings and a dagger I yanked from the holster at my thigh. I manage to put a bit of distance between Steel and me, and the group of bloody monsters.

I spare Steel a quick glance. He doesn't look good. Besides the red and black blood soaking his fur, he's panting, and his frame is slimmer than I remember. The wear from the last few months shows.

I consider trying to convince Steel to phase back into the mortal realm, but the Forsaken would simply follow, most likely leaving human casualties in their wake.

We were wholly unprepared for an attack of this magnitude, and this time there won't be a small Nephilim army to rescue us.

The Forsaken circle us, hissing and spitting insults as they take turns lashing out with their claws and teeth.

"Filthy half-breeds."

"I'll spill your guts and shred your skin with my fangs."

"Those wings would make a pretty trophy."

"Let's skin the lion and leave his bloody corpse for the Nephilim to find."

"Now, now." A voice rings out above the noise.

Heads swivel in her direction as Silver makes her way through the throng. I don't know how she managed to gain authority over these creatures, but it's obvious she has. They quiet considerably, seeming to wait for her command.

"Let's not be hasty. You know we have use for the golden one." Her head tips in Steel's direction. Matted, greasy hair swings back and forth, a contrast to her silken mane in the mortal world. "This one, though, is a different story."

Silver steps toward Steel, and he swipes at her with his

paw. She deftly avoids his attacks. Fatigue and blood loss make Steel's movements sloppy and feeble.

"You've played your part to perfection, dear brother. You are wonderful bait, but I'm sorry to say I have no use for you anymore." Silver's gaze finds mine before she issues orders. A grotesque smile stretches her blood-leached lips. "Subdue her. Kill him."

There isn't time for dread to twist in my belly before the pack of Forsaken swallow Steel and me. I flare my wings and twist, trying desperately to dislodge the bodies weighing me down.

Steel's pain-filled roar breaks through the chaos and renews my strength. I'm able to shake a couple monsters free and flap my wings once, but just as I get a few inches off the ground, I'm hauled back to the earth.

Something punctures my shoulder, cutting through muscle and hitting bone. The pain is excruciating, but I don't have the luxury of reacting.

I thrash and buck, but can't break free. I can't see the spectrum sky through the mass of bodies pinning me to the frozen ground, and that frightens me.

Heat rolls through my body, building even as my energy drains. I can't feel my injuries anymore, only fire. It burns and scorches, cauterizing my wounds.

The Forsaken trying to rip into me hiss and back away. A white flame coats my body, seemingly burning any Forsaken who come near.

Finally free, I search for Steel, yet only see another horde of Forsaken. It looks like a football pileup.

Letting loose a cry of fear, I rush the pack, grabbing and flinging Forsaken almost without thought. Scorch marks appear under my hands wherever I touch.

Good. Let them burn.

Eventually they catch on that my touch burns and scurry a safe distance away, leaving Steel sprawled at my feet. His pelt is so saturated in blood—his own and Forsaken—I don't know where his injuries start or end.

Lumbering to his feet, he growls. We're backed against a wall, which limits our ability to escape, but at least there's one less side we have to guard.

Digging deep, I concentrate on letting my power pool in my hands. A golden ball of fire starts to form between my palms. I'm anxious to chuck it at our enemies.

Seeing the weapon grow in my hands, the Forsaken back away farther. Unease is heavy in the air. Tentacles of fear leak from the suddenly tentative monsters.

For the first time since entering the spectrum world tonight, confidence straightens my spine.

I'm seconds away from releasing my wrath in the form of a super-charged, fiery ball of energy, when Silver appears front and center. She narrows her bloodshot eyes and plants her hands on her hips like a petulant child, not knowing— or caring—she's seconds away from being fried.

Is she tapping her foot?

The ball in my hand sparks and shrinks in size.

Steel's growl refocuses my attention, and I force energy into my hands, re-growing the ball of golden fire. It turns an angry red color. The light it casts seems to bother the Forsaken. Some of them hiss and cower away from the rays.

"Very pretty, Emberly. But that's enough. Time to end the light show." Silver's voice echoes off the alley walls.

Is she for real?

My anger increases my power and blue sparks join the

fiery mix between my hands. A slow smile breaks over my face.

I'm so going to barbecue this group of monsters.

I draw my arms back in preparation when Silver snaps her fingers at a group of Forsaken. Holding my gaze, she tips her head to the left, indicating something in the crowd. When I see what she's gesturing toward, the breath freezes in my chest.

No.

Ash fights like a hellcat between three Forsaken. One is attached to each of her arms, and another has its beefy limbs banded around her middle. Her feet flail in the air as she struggles to break free. There are scratches on her neck, and blood runs down her right arm, but her captors also look worse for wear. Black blood oozes out of multiple wounds, and the creature behind her is missing an eye.

"Burn them all, Em!" Ash's shouted command rings clear, agitating the group.

A Forsaken jolts forward and hits her with an open palm, running its claws over her cheek on the downswing. Blood leaks from the slashes now marring Ash's beautiful face.

She's going to be all right, I chant to myself as I fight to keep it together.

"Sterling?"

"Tinkle's been holding out on us," she answers with a smile. I don't have the bandwidth to mull that over. It's enough to know he's okay . . . at least for the moment.

The ball in my hands grows in size, matching my fury.

"You throw that angel-fire and she's dead." Silver flicks her fingers in Ash's direction, and the Forsaken that holds her from behind opens its maw and places its mouth on Ash's thin neck.

I have too good a view of its elongated teeth pressing into her flesh. The white fangs are super visible against the contrast of her dark skin. They must have picked that Forsaken for its mouth size, because somehow it's able to engulf almost half of Ash's throat. Has it dislocated its jaw?

The beast moves only a quarter of an inch, but it's enough to break her skin and cause blood to run in rivulets down the column of her neck.

Ash stops fighting, and her eyes go wide. Her chest lifts up and down rapidly and her body straightens as her muscles lock.

My heart's going to explode. I've gone from cocky and confident to terrified in only a matter of beats.

Beside me, Steel lets out an angry roar, and then in a blast of light, transforms back into himself.

I thought he looked bad as a lion, but in human form, he looks worse.

Gashes mar every limb, some so deep I wonder how he's still standing. One of his ears is ripped, and blood covers his face like he's just had a bucket of the stuff dumped over his head, *Carrie*-style.

He holds an arm across his abdomen and I'm worried he's holding in his own guts. Nephilim are built to last and undeniably hard to kill, but at some point our bodies will give out on us. Steel needs medical attention, fast.

"Silver!" Even his voice sounds wretched, and it stabs my soul. "Call all your minions off and release Ash and Emberly. This is between the two of us. Time to take your revenge."

Revenge?

With widened eyes, Silver regards her twin for a count of three and then bursts into laughter. Her body bends forward as she doubles over. The sound and sight coming from her skeletal frame is eerie and so completely out of context with the gravity of the situation. Fire ants dance up and down my spine, and I shake out my wings to rid myself of the sensation.

Since Ash appeared, I've lowered my arms, but the ball of heated angel-fire still dances between my palms. Smaller than before, but not extinguished.

Silver gets herself under control and straightens. "Oh darling, this has nothing to do with you. In fact, this has very little to do with me, either. But it has everything to do with the golden beauty you've been panting over like a dog. If anyone has bargaining power here, it's her, not you."

Steel's gaze shifts to mine, his eyes filled with concern.

We're back to this. Someone, or something, wants me and I still don't know why.

"Now, Em—may I call you that?"

"No."

"So, Em," she continues. "If you want your friend to walk away from here with her head still attached to her shoulders, I'm going to need you to put that out." She points in the direction of my hands. "I won't ask again. This has gone on long enough."

My fingers ache from the tension running through them. With a glance at Ash, who attempts to shake her head but can't without risking exacerbating the tear at her neck, I drop my arms. The fireball dissipates.

"That's better. Now we get to the good stuff. Negotiation. I tire of these games. Bottom line is that I've been ordered to bring you in—and I will, one way or another—

but my timeframe has been pushed up. I'm not leaving this dank armpit of a city without you. So, here are your choices." She holds a finger in the air, ticking away what she believes to be my only options.

"You allow us to subdue you—and by that I mean knock you clean out without a fight—and I won't let Silas nom-nom your friend . . . at least any more than he already has. And as an extra bonus, I'll throw in a free pass for my big brother. We'll take you, and leave your friends to fight another day." Cocking her head, her eyes narrow on Steel before returning to me. "I'd say, considering our predicament, that's a very generous offer, wouldn't you?"

Ticking up another finger, Silver continues. "Now for option number two. You can do your best to try to blow some of us up with your underdeveloped angel-fire. By the time you manage to summon your power, Silas will have made a snack of your friend's neck, and in the process, separate her head from her body."

Putting a hand up next to her mouth she whisper-yells the next part, acting as if no one else can hear. "And in case you're wondering, that would for sure end a young Nephilim's life. Re-growing a head on top of your shoulders isn't part of the Neph skill set." She tips a shoulder. "Shame." The smile on her face says she finds this option enticing.

"While that's happening, a group of my associates here will be working on separating Steel's limbs from his torso. In case you haven't noticed, the theme of the night is dismemberment."

Taking a breath, she plants a hand on her hip. I've only let her continue to talk because I'm truly at a loss for words.

Silver is psychotic. She's a Forsaken, so this should not be surprising to me in the least, but it is. I must be in shock.

"I will admit, with your shiny wings and blossoming abilities, there's a slim chance you may escape. Make no mistake, your friends won't." She claps her hands together and the sound jolts me. My wings flare before settling at my back. "So, what'll it be?"

There's no real choice. I've somehow gone from the girl who'd do anything to save herself, to the girl willing to sacrifice anything to save her friends.

I don't know exactly when it happened, but it has. Over the past months, this group of almost-humans has become more important to me than my own well-being.

Too bad I've only had a taste of what living truly is. There's little hope that if I go with Silver, I'll make it back to Seraph Academy in one piece. I'm not giving up—that isn't who I am. But I'm a realist, and instinct tells me whatever lies ahead isn't looking good for me.

I start to move forward, ready to agree to Silver's terms, when Steel stops me with a hand on my shoulder. His fingers are wet with his own blood. His eyes tell me exactly what he's thinking, but he says it anyway.

"Don't do this. We can fight our way out." His words are soft and for my ears only, but firm with conviction. "This isn't the answer."

Maybe he's right. Maybe there is another way. Glancing at Ash, her neck still in the vice grip of the Forsaken's jaw, I know it doesn't matter. I'm not willing to gamble with her life. Ash is the first true friend I've ever had, and she means the world to me.

I find Silver in the crowd. A cat-like smile plays along the corners of her bloodless lips. She knows she has me. I'll bet Silver is the type of creature that likes to play with her food before eating it.

I hate her.

"Release Ash and Steel first." Steel's hold on my shoulder tightens with my words, and he tries to tug me back into him. I want so badly to find comfort in his embrace but I can't, so instead I break free and stride forward, putting several feet of distance between us. It only helps a little. I can feel Steel at my back like a soothing summer's breeze. "I'll agree to your terms, but only when you pull your beasts back so I know Ash and Steel will go free. And you promise to hurt no one else tonight." Throughout this battle, my mind hasn't been far from my other friends as well.

Silver brings a hand up to her chest and feigns a look of insult. "Are you saying you don't trust my word?"

Rather than verbally respond, I narrow my eyes and bare my teeth. Now that I've made a decision, I'm ready to be done with this.

She nods her head in Ash's direction. Silas growls, but shrinks his teeth enough to disengage them from Ash's throat without doing further damage. Even after he releases her, the rips in her neck weep blood. More than one Forsaken has its eyes fixated on the wounds, a glazed look in their eyes.

"Your turn to offer a boon."

Time to turn myself in. I take a step forward, but am jerked back two.

"No." Steel hisses the word in my ear. Silver's eyes narrow and her hands flex. The claws on the tips of her fingers shine in the iridescent spectrum moonlight. She may act flippant, but she's one wrong move away from losing it.

Closing my eyes briefly, I settle against Steel. *I'll only steal this single moment of time*, I tell myself.

One inhale. Two. Time's up.

Flaring my wings throws Steel off balance, and his hold on me dissolves. I spare him a glance over my shoulder before marching to my doom.

I consider grabbing him for a goodbye kiss. It seems like the appropriately romantic thing to do, especially when you aren't sure if you'll ever see someone again, but honestly, Steel is nasty right now and the thought of licking blood off his lips . . . hard pass.

It's funny how something can seem so ideal, but the reality of the situation is much grittier than the fantasy. Instead of a kiss, I can only offer Steel a lingering glance filled with longing.

If he's interested in more than that, he's going to have to do something about it.

"You said it was easy for you to find me. So prove it."

13

I come awake with a start, my face smooshed into a silk-covered pillow. I'm never going to get used to waking up in a strange location. The last thing I remember is Silver's sly smile before I was beaned in the back of the head and knocked unconscious.

Squeezing my eyes shut, I reach back and probe the throbbing spot with my fingers, wincing when they come in contact with a goose egg buried under a layer of hair.

Oh, that smarts.

Sucking up the pain, I force myself to assess the situation. With a groan, I flip and stare at sheer white fabric draped over the corners of petrified wood posts that make up the bed I'm lying in. The tips of each branch reach for the others, creating a center point above my head.

Throwing off the covers, I crawl to the edge of the ginormous bed and slide off the mattress. I notice I'm back in my bandage dress as my bare feet sink into an animal-skin rug—bear head still attached. *Sorry, big guy.* It's cold. The air puffing from my lips mists in front of my face before disappearing. I rub my hands over my chilled arms.

I cast a glance around the room and then freeze, my blood turning to sludge in my veins.

The only window in the room is covered with dark stained glass, but there's a tell-tale shimmer in the air. I release a strong whistle, and the sound drifts on visible currents. Breathing in through my nose, I smell honeysuckle.

I'm still in the spectrum world even though I should have phased back to the mortal world when I lost consciousness.

Unease coils in my gut. The spectrum world means monsters and pain along with the beauty and wonder.

I'm a captive either way, but if I had a choice, I'd pick the mortal world. At least the Fallen don't exist there. One less enemy to worry about.

I try to phase several times, but something blocks me, reminding me of the orb Silver used to keep the Nephilim out of the spectrum world. After the fourth try, I give up and start checking for a means of escape.

The room I'm in is over-the-top. It looks like it's outfitted for an ice princess with a nasty vendetta against color. Its furnishings are white with a splash of silver here and there. Bleached white stone lines the walls and floor. There's a fireplace with an ice-encased log. An oversized high-backed accent chair is placed to the left of the useless hearth. A small table supported by one long spindle leg connected to a round base sits next to it. The only other piece of furniture in the room is a white lacquered armoire pressed up against the wall to my left. Just beyond that is the door.

Bingo.

I tiptoe across the room as if the task requires silence. Grasping the knob, I'm not at all surprised when it doesn't turn, but I still yank on it several times for good measure.

I press my ear to the flat surface. Nothing.

Next, I eye the armoire. Flinging open its doors, I find gowns hanging on the left and rows of drawers stacked on the right. Neatly placed shoes fill a cubby that runs along the bottom. As I look through the drawers, I notice every piece of clothing is white, silver, or gold, down to the undergarments.

What the heck?

Glancing down at myself, I take in the grimy piece of stretchy fabric covering me. I can almost hear Ash's lecture about ruining the dress, one hand on her hip and the other wagging in the air.

My eyes prickle and well. What I wouldn't give to be stuck listening to one of her lectures right now.

No time to wallow.

Bypassing the hanging gowns completely, I rummage around the drawers, searching for practical clothes to wear.

Ugh. Everything looks like it was made for a formal affair. Nova would be in heaven, but I need pants.

I toss clothes out of the way until I find something usable—white skinny jeans, a gold tank top, and a baggy off-the-shoulder sweater. I'm going to look like a real housewife of Orange County, but whatever, it's better than a dress and will offer me some warmth against this glacial air.

Quickly shedding the blue dress, I shimmy into the new clothes. Finding a single pair of sneakers in the back—also white with gold glitter soles—I tug those on as well. The clothes and shoes are a perfect fit, including extra length on the legs for a tall angel-born. I chalk it up to coincidence, not wanting to consider the alternative. Tossing the worn dress in the corner, I twist my hair up and into a knot.

The door was a bust, so it's time to try the window. I crack my neck and put on my game face.

Forty-five minutes later I'm still stuck in the strange white bedroom. I've done everything I can think of to open or bust through the only two possible exits, including, but not limited to, kicking and punching, throwing furniture—the white sofa chair now lies in scattered pieces—and pretending I know how to pick a lock with a splinter. The room is in shambles, but there isn't a scratch or dent on either the windowpane or door.

I swat a sticky lock of red-tipped hair out of my face. My knuckles burn and ache from abuse. The skin is torn, cut up by the rough wood surface of the door. A few drops of blood have stuck to my clothes, marring the pristine surface, and that makes me glad.

If I can't get out of here, I'm going to weapon-up.

Snatching the skinny accent table, I use my foot to crack off the base and top, leaving me with a two-foot length of wood thin enough to wrap my hand around—longer than a traditional dagger, but shorter than a sword. It's an awkward size, but it will have to do. Both ends are splintered and jagged, just how I want it.

I spend the next few hours assembling makeshift weapons by stripping whatever materials I can tear or break apart in the room. Using ribbons of the silk sheets, I wrap glass shards from the accent table's broken top to the tip of some of the spikes. I bloody the tips of my fingers pulling nails from the furniture to embed in the ends of the wooden rods I fashioned from breaking apart the bed, chair, table, and armoire drawers. Whenever I stop working, my mind floods with worries over my friends.

Did Silver hold true to her word and release Ash and Steel? Was Sterling okay? Did any or all my friends escape?

Sleeping is out of the question. Closing my eyes is a dangerous game. Images of sharp Forsaken fangs cutting into Ash's neck or the blood coating Steel's body play unbidden behind my lids. My mind concocts a never-ending stream of horrific possibilities for what may have happened after I was knocked unconscious.

As time drags on, my armory grows.

I stash some of my creations around the room, but keep my favorites—one with nails sticking out from the end like a porcupine and a particularly sharp stake—within arm's reach. I'm practicing jabbing when I hear movement on the other side of the door.

Soundlessly, I grab my arsenal and slide into position to the left of the entrance.

When Silver's matted head appears, I don't hesitate to attack. Her bloodshot eyes widen, and she slams the door closed. My body smashes into the wood.

I beat at it in frustration, doing more damage to me than whatever strange tree created the impenetrable planks.

"Drop the weapons, Emberly, and move to the other side of the room."

I slide back a few steps and crouch into a defensive stance, waiting for Silver to open the door again.

"Have you moved away from the door?" Silver calls out, her voice muffled.

"Yep."

"You ready to disarm yourself?"

As if.

"Sure."

"Why do I feel like you're lying to me?"

Maybe because you're only half as dumb as you look? I choose not to voice my opinion.

"Drop whatever weapon you're holding. I want to hear it hit the ground."

I glance between my hands. Pointy stake or makeshift mace?

Letting go of the sharpened stake, I wrap both hands around the nail-riddled piece of wood. The stake clatters on the ground before settling.

"I dropped it. Time for you to uphold your—"

The door swings open. I should have been ready, but wasn't, and so I fumble for half a second before arching my weapon at Silver. Silver's arm points in my direction, and something slams into my ribs. From one blink to the next I go from ready-to-land-the-mother-of-all-death-blows, to twitching defenselessly on the ground.

My body is a mess of muscle spasms and pain. My vision sputters before clearing. When it does, Silver stands over me with a self-satisfied grin, my weapon in one hand and a Taser in the other.

"You . . . cheated," I force out between convulsions.

Just as the electricity seems to finally filter from my body, she pushes the trigger, and the pain cycle starts all over again.

"Whoops. Slip of the finger."

"Hate . . . you."

"Don't care," she sing-songs. "Now, this is how this is going to work. You're going to get up and walk out of this room without trying anything sketch. If you look down you'll see the probes still in your side. If you take one step that I don't tell you to, I'll lay you out again. If you try to rip them out, I'll lay you out again. If you breathe funny in my direction . . . well, I think you get the point. Nod so I know we understand each other."

Through gritted teeth I nod while flipping her the bird.

"Perf. Now stand up."

Everything hurts.

I struggle to my feet. The soreness permeates my body on a cellular level. Even my teeth ache. I didn't know that was possible. The electrocution caused my hands to contort into claw-like shapes. I imagine them wrapped around Silver's thin neck. It wouldn't take too much to break it, and I'll bet it would make the loveliest snap.

Silver chuckles, her eyes casting over the ruins that were once a bedroom. "Nicely done."

I bare my teeth. My hand goes to the tender area on my side where the Taser's probes are embedded in my flesh. I'm zapped by a short bolt of electricity. The current is only a whisper of the intensity of the first few shocks, but it doesn't tickle.

"Ah-ah." Silver wags her finger. "I told you that's against the rules."

I'm too busy riding out the residual muscle spasms to bother with a witty response.

"All right, enough playtime. Let's go for a walk." Silver jerks her chin toward the doorway.

I have an urge to argue simply to be contrary, but rotting away in this room won't help me escape, so I exit silently in front of Silver. My hands itch for one of the handmade weapons I'm forced to leave behind, but with this Taser still stuck in me, there's no way I'd be able to grab one before I'm laid out again.

The hallway is made of the same colorless stone blocks as the room I was just locked in, and lit by torches of green and blue flames that jut out of the wall every ten feet or so.

"Where are we?"

"Canada. Quebec to be exact."

My toe catches on nothing, and I have to steady myself before I pitch forward. "Oh." What else was there to say? In no version of this conversation did I expect she would tell me that information so easily.

"Why are we still in the spirit realm?"

"Did you really think we'd lair-it-up in the mortal world?" Her tone makes clear how stupid she thinks that assumption was.

"Maybe," I say under my breath. "Why can't I phase back?"

"You'll find that out soon as well."

I roll my eyes. Cryptic non-answers are lame. If she's trying to psych me out, it's not working.

A couple dozen more paces and the hall ends at a door, which opens to a stairway. Silver jabs me in the shoulder to keep me moving. I tilt my head back as far as it goes to check out the spiral stairway we start to ascend.

The lighting isn't much better here than in the tunnel we traversed, creating the illusion that the climb goes on forever. Staring up makes me dizzy, so I refocus on a point a few stairs ahead of me.

A distant roaring noise increases in intensity as we climb the corkscrew stairway. Occasionally, I make out elevated shouts, though the words are unfamiliar.

"So, you and my brother, huh?"

She can't be serious. I press my lips together, not wanting to encourage this conversation. As we continue up, weak rays of light start to filter down from above.

"I'm slightly surprised. I always thought it would be Nova. But then again, with you out of the picture, maybe it still will be. They were so tight as children, our parents were practically planning their union."

I'm aware she's trying to bait me, so her words bounce off easily. What does stick with me is Silver's familiarity with life before she became a Forsaken. When she talks like this, it's harder to believe she's really gone.

How would a Fallen know so much about its vessel's life? The Nephilim is completely erased when the possession occurs. Is a Fallen able to access its victim's memories? Or is it as Silver claims, and there are Forsaken out there that have retained some of their Nephilim souls?

"I get it," Silver continues, despite my silence. "Steel always had the ability to catch the attention of the opposite sex. Even when we were little, he used to charm everyone. He could get away with murder, that one. I should know."

"We're just friends," I grit out behind clenched teeth, ready to be done with this conversation.

She chuckles low in her throat, the sultry sound bouncing off the walls. Spectrum daylight makes it bright enough to see the steps between the torches.

"Friends? Do you know how all your friends taste? If so, you just became marginally more interesting to me."

I stumble over a step.

"What is this?" I snap. "Girl talk?"

"I'm getting bored with zapping you."

I'm about to roll my eyes when I'm hit with an electric current strong enough to cause a spasm. My body shudders and muscles lock as I pitch forward. My kneecaps crack on the stone, but I manage to catch myself with Jell-O arms before face-planting into the edge of a whitewashed step.

"I was wrong, it's still fun."

I bite my lip hard enough to draw blood and call Silver every filthy word I know in my head.

"Come on, we still have a ways to go."

Silver can't seem to keep quiet as we continue to trudge up the spiral stairway. Funny, her twin doesn't seem to suffer from the same affliction.

"You should be thanking me."

I snort.

"I did you a favor. Steel can't be trusted. When things get hard, he's always only going to look out for himself."

I struggle with trusting people and even I know Steel's not like that. If anything, he puts himself in unnecessary danger for the people he cares about. "You were nine the last time you spent any significant time with him," I scoff. "As if you truly know what type of man he is."

"I'm the only one who really knows what he's like," Silver growls. It sounds like she's juggling a throat full of pebbles when she talks. "If you truly knew the selfish heart that beats beneath that layer of flesh, your little infatuation with him would be crushed."

We both fall silent after that last comment. My mind whirls with reasons for Silver's laser-focused loathing of her brother. It has to have something to do with what happened to them on that mountaintop all those years ago. But how can someone blame a child for their fate? What could Steel have done that was so bad? And as a Forsaken, why would Silver even care how Steel treated her vessel?

We have one more spiral to go. The noise from the

crowd is now loud enough to be seen moving on iridescent waves around us. It makes the last curve of stairs undulate, and I have to close my eyes a few times and use my hand on the wall for navigation to keep from getting disoriented.

Bits of stone dust rain down on my head as we round the final curve, making me cough, but I don't slow my steps. The knowledge that I'm going to finally get an idea of the structure of my prison keeps my pace steady despite the exhaustion of just having climbed a million steps.

We crest the stairs and march through a high arch. I'm greeted by the bright spectrum sun and its gilded rays. I blink against the light as lavender snowflakes collect on my lashes.

If I thought the roar of the crowd was loud before, it's deafening now. The intensity slams into my chest like a physical blow, forcing me back. Silver shoves me forward, and I catch myself on a carved, waist-high railing. When I lift my gaze, terror shoots through me in a hot flash. I'm on a balcony in a coliseum, surrounded by hundreds, maybe thousands of enemies. They litter the multiple tiers that ring an oval-shaped pit in the middle.

The shred of hope I've clung to dissolves into nothing.

Silver slides next to me, unbothered by the sun's rays. A small smile lifts the corners of her blood-leeched lips. She turns her head slowly to me, and her fangs elongate as her smile turns into a chilling, Joker-like grin.

"Welcome to Whitehold," she says evenly. "Let the games begin."

*T*he arena below is empty, but the black blood staining the white sand floor suggests it hasn't been that way for long. My mind whirls with possible scenarios of what goes on down there—none of them anything less than horrifying.

"What is this?"

"Are you daft? I just told you—games. We've made it just in time for the best part."

I can only hear her because the crowd has simmered down.

The sly look in Silver's eyes does nothing to calm me. She's anticipating my reaction to whatever is yet to come, which makes me more than a little leery.

I jump when horns blare, creating angry waves in the air that sweep across the coliseum in broad strokes. The creatures renew their shrieks and roars. I cringe, which I'm sure makes Silver happy.

The atmosphere is a blur too messy to see through until there's a clang of metal striking metal. A detonation in the middle of the arena below throws a gust of wind outward in all directions, blowing my hair back and clearing the static from the spectrum air, despite the ruckus.

A lone figure appears in the center of the arena, clad from head to toe in silver armor that gleams in the midday light. He stands tall while the mass of creatures in the tiered seats goes wild.

A slight glow of an aura surrounds him. It's weak, so I squint my eyes, straining to make sense of the hazy image below. I've never seen an aura like it. It carries the white glow of an angel-born, but is mixed with veins of darkness. Light and dark pulsate at different intervals, battling each other. Forsaken don't have auras and humans can't phase into the spectrum world, so I can't wrap my brain around what I'm seeing.

A sliver of trepidation takes root and anchors in my gut as the minutes tick by and the Forsaken whip into a frenzy. They pound on their seats while jumping up and down, letting loose awful, ear-bleeding screams.

My fingers tighten on the cold stone beneath my hands. Snow has collected on my hair and shoulders, and my breath fogs in front of my face after every exhale. Terrified I'm about to watch an execution, gladiator-style, my gaze stays glued to the unmoving figure and his warring aura.

A soft drum-beat starts up, thumping rhythmically, and it isn't long before all the Forsaken are stomping along. Their blows shake the whole structure. The vibrations travel up my legs and rush down my arms. The rhythm pounds in my chest as the drumming becomes so furious there aren't any pauses between beats. And then as if a switch is flipped, everything stops. It's utterly silent.

The Forsaken have frozen and seem to be holding their

collective breath. The crowd is motionless. I search for movement to make sure I haven't stepped into a time-stalled reality. The purple snowflakes lazily dropping from the sky are the only indication that the world is still moving forward. Even Silver has gone eerily immobile next to me.

Chains rub against each other as gates around the periphery of the arena floor rise. I can see six from where I'm standing, though I'd guess there are eight in total. The clank of each link booms around the coliseum.

The tunnels yawn open, black holes that devour the light.

Dark gray mist slithers out, making short work of gobbling up the white sand floor.

Too busy watching the fog creep across the arena to notice movement from the tunnel, I'm caught unaware when the crowd roars back to life. Releasing a yip of surprise, I stumble away from the balcony railing.

Silver's gaze flicks in my direction before she looks skyward, shaking her head. I scurry back to the overlook.

Eight gray-skinned beings—both male and female—stride toward the man in the middle of the arena. They're easily a foot taller than the warrior they march toward, and even from this distance, I can tell the fighter in the silver armor is no shorty.

The dark fog churning below drips off these creatures like water off melting icicles.

Their only armor is hardened leather shells that cover their chests, leaving their arms bare save the weapons and shields some of them carry. Thick capes drag behind them at odd angles.

Wait—those aren't capes.

My breath catches as my eyes widen.

Wings flow from each of the creature's backs, skimming the ground behind them as they advance. The feathers range in hue from muddy brown to pitch black.

Snapping my gaze up, I scan the coliseum, noticing other winged creatures dotted in the crowd among the Forsaken.

I refocus on the gray-skinned monsters below. They are terrifying to behold, but the reason my heart stutters in my chest as these new beasts stride forward isn't because of their horrifying appearance.

It's because I know these beings. The Fallen.

Before being taken in by the Nephilim, I was only ever able to half-phase, which left me physically present in both realms but blinded to some objects in the spectrum world. The monsters that stalked my nightmares were never more than formless dark smudges, dreamlike and shrouded. But the scars I carry on my body are real enough.

The silver-clad warrior holds his weapon at the ready as the Fallen draw near.

How can this be considered an amusing sport? He's ridiculously outnumbered and will be ripped to shreds before the crowd can work up a decent bloodlust.

The Fallen stop their forward progress a couple body lengths from their prey. They take a measure of caution with their next moves. Their gazes tick from one to another as they gauge who will make the first move. None of them appears particularly eager to be the first to engage the warrior.

My hands ache from gripping the railing. An urge rises in me to aid the lone combatant, but a lifetime of survival instincts beats it back.

I don't want to watch the man be torn in pieces, but I can't seem to look away.

It's a Forsaken, it has to be.

Watching any living being fight to the death for sport is deplorable, but my conscience doesn't prickle at the thought of Fallen and Forsaken ripping each other to shreds. As much as I fear the worst, I reassure myself it must be a Forsaken and ignore the voice inside reminding me that Forsaken don't armor-up for their battles, or fight with shields and swords . . . or have auras.

The combat commences when a Fallen charges. He doesn't slow his momentum as he swings a war hammer through the air, aiming the blunt end at the smaller fighter, who ducks and rolls at the last second to avoid decapitation.

The Fallen quickly changes his trajectory and arcs his weapon down with the force of both arms.

A flash of light reflects off the armored warrior's sword as he snaps it up, catching the handle of the hammer before the spiked end can make contact with his chest.

The breath I've trapped in my lungs begins to burn. I release it in a rush, my gaze glued to the combatants bearing down on each other in the pit below.

The rest of the Fallen stand like statues around the two warriors. The hits the combatants rain down on each other look to be bone crushing, but they keep hammering away. Black blood oozes from a handful of wounds on the battling Fallen's arms and legs, yet the smaller fighter remains unscathed.

Several minutes tick by and the Fallen appears to flag, his movements growing sloppy and slow.

Fatigue hasn't yet set in for his opponent, who jumps, ducks, and rolls out of the way of the Fallen's strikes with ease. He slashes his sword with vicious accuracy, nicking the Fallen in areas that cause the blood flow to increase, and for the first time I wonder if the armored fighter is playing with him.

Despite the blood leaking from multiple wounds, the Fallen rallies and presses the silver warrior back with a series of blows so quick, his opponent is only able to block.

They battle to the edge of the circle of Fallen, and the silver-armored warrior is pushed past the ring of monsters. The second his foot makes contact with the white sand beyond the closest Fallen, she becomes animated and joins her comrade in battle.

Seeing what happened, the silver fighter crouches down and then jumps into the air, launching himself over his two foes and back into the middle of the circle.

The female Fallen is just as tall as her male counterpart and fights with a broadsword easily the length of my body. The reach on her weapon is long enough to make it difficult for her smaller opponent to return her blows.

The silver warrior battles with a Fallen on either side of him, pushing back one only to have to turn and deal with the other.

Bloodlust drips from the spectators' gazes surrounding me—Forsaken and Fallen alike. Several fights have even broken out around the stands.

To my left, a group of Forsaken heave one of their own over the railing and onto the arena floor. A beast on all fours darts out from one of the darkened tunnels and pounces on the Forsaken before she can get her footing. Its jaws—as long as an alligator's with rows of teeth visible from my perch—clamp down on the Forsaken's shoulder. The animal-like body is shaped like a giant dog but rather than fur, iridescent scales cover it from head to toe.

It gives its head a vicious shake, and a shriek of pain

rises from the Forsaken. The crowd cheers as the beast drags its prey into the darkened tunnels.

What was that?

"Didn't I tell you the Nephilim don't know everything?"

The bloodthirstiness isn't lost on Silver. Her eyes shine with savagery and her fangs have grown long enough to pierce her bottom lip. She swipes her tongue over the black liquid that oozes from the puncture wounds, and then shoots me a wicked smile.

The roar of the crowd spikes, and I look down just in time to see the head of a Fallen drop to the ground. The decapitated body sways on its feet for a few seconds before succumbing to gravity and thudding against the blood-splattered sand.

Another Fallen breaks from the ring to replace the one that was felled. Rather than surround their foe, both Fallen advance on the silver warrior, forcing him to fall back.

For the second time, he crosses the invisible barrier around the combat circle, and a third Fallen joins the fray.

The warrior has proven his skill, but there's no way he can hold his own against three Fallen.

The battle becomes a flurry of motion and sound. Weapons strike together in a continuous clang. The silver warrior's movements blur with speed as he defends himself against his opponents.

My feet itch to move but remain rooted in place.

Despite his best efforts, the Fallen have managed to corral the fighter to the boundary another time, and yet another Fallen joins the fight.

It's four-on-one with only three Fallen remaining on the sidelines.

The silver warrior cuts his way out of the smaller circle

of Fallen that have closed in on him, hacking off the arm of one of his foes as he breaks free.

The victory doesn't last long because the armless Fallen continues to advance, swinging at the warrior with his remaining arm.

Without realizing it, the warrior steps over the boundary again and a fifth Fallen rushes him from behind.

My shouted warning is swallowed by the crowd's roar.

The warrior will be cleaved in two.

The Fallen raises her sword and brings it down in a brutal arc. I force myself to keep watching, when what I really want to do is squeeze my lids shut.

I'm sure I'm about to see another flow of black blood spray through the air when wings erupt from the warrior's back.

Silver-tipped feathers deflect the blow. A shower of sparks falls where wing and blade meet.

Twisting, the warrior flares his wings and they cut cleanly through the Fallen, severing her body in half at the waist.

I can no longer deny what I'm seeing—what this warrior is.

That's not a Forsaken fighting for his life, it's an angel-born. And even though he's doing an admirable job leveling the playing field, I can't let him battle alone anymore.

15

I grip the railing and vault over it, feeling the Taser probes rip from my side as Silver's angry shouts ring in my ears. Instinct kicks in and I morph before my feet hit the sand. When I stand from my crouch, I flare my wings and grab the dagger at my thigh, wishing I had a weapon with a longer reach.

A beast the color of night darts out of the tunnel closest to me and charges. I'm stunned for a moment. The creature is even more terrifying up close, with its red eyes and drool dripping from its jowls.

It's almost upon me when I snap out of it, launching my dagger when it's only a few body lengths away. The blade makes contact with its shoulder, but slides off iridescent scales that act like armor.

I palm two more knives as the beast jumps at me with its jaw wide. Its elongated mouth could bite me in half.

With the monster in the air, I dive under its body, but point my sharp wings up in a move inspired by the silver Nephilim. Wetness pours on my back, and I hold in a gag.

I only spare the disemboweled being a half look to make sure it's down for the count. It twitches in the sand with its guts several feet away from its body.

Good enough for me.

Taking a half-second to locate my discarded dagger and store the knives back in their sheaths, I snap my attention to the battle between the Nephilim and Fallen, ready to join the fight.

I've drawn the unwanted attention of the two unoccupied Fallen, who now sprint toward me. Their blood-red gazes are nothing short of hungry. Shadows continue to drip off of them as they draw closer.

What have I gotten myself into?

Easily eight feet in height, the former angels are the picture of violence. The ones headed my direction have a battle axe and spear clutched in their clawed hands. I don't know why they bother carrying weapons—those hands of theirs are lethal enough. Their skin is stretched over bulging cords of muscles, yet their gray pallor makes them look like reanimated corpses.

Very fast and agile corpses, like super-sized zombies on steroids.

If the Fallen were terrifying when I could only half-phase and see them as shadow beasts, this is next-level terror. I'm glad I wasn't subjected to their real form all those years. If I had, I probably would have found a hole to curl up in and never emerged.

I don't have time to mess with these two. In the distance is the battle I have my eyes set on. I don't think these two are allowed to enter the fight until the silver fighter steps over the borderline again.

With a mighty downward thrust of my wings, I lift into the air. I wobble on the second flap, but am high enough to sail over the heads of the advancing Fallen.

Not ready to give up their prey so easily, one of the Fallen cocks his arm back and chucks his spear at me. The shaft slices through the air at the perfect trajectory to impale me. I bank to the left just in time for the sharpened tip to spark against my metal breastplate and wings.

Close. Too close.

The sloppy flying has me careening toward the ground and second-guessing my rash rescue attempt.

I smash into one of the battling Fallen and end up in a lump several feet away. He lumbers to his feet, looking shell-shocked. Drawing a knife, I stretch forward on my belly and slash at his ankles, cutting through both Achilles tendons and sending the giant crashing back to the ground with a howl.

Clamoring on my hands and knees, I scurry to his head and plunge another knife into his eye socket, sinking the blade through his squishy eye and into his brain.

The huge form of the Fallen remains still, and so I think I'm in the clear to move on to the next obstacle.

Three Fallen still battle the silver angel-born. The armless one has been dispatched and is lying face-down on the other side of the brawl. The two Fallen who chased me are standing a ways away, snarling and shifting from foot to foot in obvious agitation.

Good, I was right about them not being able to join the fight.

Popping up, I sprint to the Nephilim's aid. I only have to wait a split second to see an opening, and I jump into the fight, positioning myself at the angel-born's back as I've been taught to do.

The Nephilim spares a quick look over his shoulder. His helmet covers most of his face except for a "T" that exposes his eyes and runs down the center of his face. I only catch a flash of blue before he's turned back to the two Fallen bearing down on him.

The third Fallen attacks me.

I'm focused solely on staying alive as the minutes tick by. The angel-born slays another Fallen, but sometime during the fray, he must have stepped out of bounds again because a new Fallen replaces the deceased one.

I must have become an honorary combatant, because the moment I step out of bounds, the last Fallen joins. The odds are four-on-two again in no time.

I steal the sword from a slain Fallen to defend myself. My muscles shake from fatigue, burning as if poisoned by venom.

I'm terrified but also strangely exhilarated. Exhausted, but focused. My world narrows to the smell of blood, the cold kiss of shadow fog on my legs, and the heavy clang of metal meeting metal.

Anticipating an opening, I swing the cumbersome sword with a battle cry, separating a Fallen's head from his shoulders. The feeling I get from the victory is euphoric, but I don't stop to rejoice as another enemy advances.

This monster dispenses with his weapons and comes at me with his claws flashing. I bring the sword up to deflect his blows, but his aggressive movements are faster without the added weight of a weapon.

His arms rain down on me. Black blood streams from

deep cuts over his forearms where my blade blocked his attacks, but it doesn't slow him.

Catching me on the thigh, he rips a jagged path past my protective armor and through the muscle.

I have a few minor nicks and cuts, but this is the first major wound I've sustained. Red blood flows freely from the injury.

The Fallen stops and inhales a deep whiff of blood-scented air. He tips his head back and howls.

The terror that has been waiting on the sidelines decides to rush into the game and zips throughout my body. I limp away in a feeble attempt to escape.

Behind the Fallen, the angel-born notices my predicament when the two Fallen he's battling give up their fight with him and sprint toward me.

Are they like sharks that frenzy at the smell of angel-born blood? Didn't Tinkle say something about me being tastier than a regular Nephilim?

I really don't want to be eaten. That sounds like an awful way to go.

Crouching, the Nephilim shoots into the air and lands in front of me before the first Fallen can tear into me.

The Fallen is so distracted by my blood, it makes it easy for the angel-born fighter to sink his sword through her hardened breastplate and into her chest.

He leaves the sword in place as he scoops me up, anchoring his arms under my knees and along my lower back.

"Playtime's over." The words are dismissive, but the tone of his deep voice is hard as stone.

With a flap of his wings, he launches us into the air.

Caught unaware, my breath catches in my throat. His movements are more assured than mine. I've never flown this high on my wings.

I drip onto the crowd as we sail over the tiered seating. The Forsaken are whipped into a frenzy as they fight over the droplets. My stomach churns to think they're ravenous for the taste of me.

My nails scrape against the warrior's rounded shoulder spaulders. My body tenses as I wait for Fallen to give chase, but it doesn't happen. Instead we clear the top ridge of the coliseum without issue.

I expect us to fly clear of the archaic compound, but instead the angel-born heads straight for a spire on the far end. A pulsating light glows at the tip of the tower, reminiscent of the orb that was sent to the Council's compound. Except this one emanates a bright silvery glow like a star, rather than a warm blue or gold color.

I crane my neck from side to side, battling the wind blowing my hair in every direction to scout as much of the surrounding area as possible. As far as the eye can see is an endless range of snow buried mountains.

The frozen air claws at my exposed skin as we slice through the icy drifts. The fluffy lavender snow has become razors slicing my face and arms.

I try not to focus on my hamburger meat thigh or that I'm plastered against a stranger's chest. My mind hazes from blood loss. I tuck my wings as close as possible to protect myself.

This is bad.

Our descent slows, and within moments, we glide through a large arched opening high up on the tallest tower and touch down. The angel-born sets me down on an ornate white chair that allows my wings to comfortably hang over the low back, and I proceed to bleed all over it.

Straightening, he throws a hand up and a ball of fire shoots from his palm into the stack of wood in the fireplace next to us.

I start, not only because of the blaze, but also the ability. I've never seen anyone else control fire like I can. My heart thumps, and I can't say if it's in excitement or trepidation.

Things are happening super-fast, and I have to stay focused. I'm a captive, and even though this angel-born may be like me in some ways, that doesn't automatically mean he's my ally.

Grasping the front of his helmet, he jerks it off and drops it to the stone floor. He tugs his gloves off next and shucks off his breastplate and spaulders in record time, his eyes locked on my bleeding mess of a leg the entire time. But since the instant he yanked off his helmet, my gaze hasn't left his face.

Holy. Angel. Babies.

This guy is beautiful.

His skin is like polished marble, so pale it has a silvery glow to it. His eyebrows—in contrast to his silver blond hair—are dark slashes above sapphire eyes only a shade lighter than black.

But his physical appeal isn't the only reason my mouth hinges open and my eyes remain glued to his face. He doesn't fit the typical angel-born formula. I've only ever seen one other Nephilim like him.

Me.

Questions bounce around my head as I watch the

warrior bend and riffle through a drawer. He pulls out gauze, disinfectant, and a bottle of clear liquid. Squatting in front of me with the materials neatly laid around him, he finally meets my gaze.

"May I?" he asks, indicating my mangled leg. His voice is deep and smooth and reminds me of honey. I haven't found my voice yet, so I simply swallow and nod.

When he peels back the buckled gold cuisse from my thigh, the skin around his eyes tightens. The rest of his features remain stony.

Uncorking the bottle of clear liquid, he mutters "water" before using it to clean the bits of sand, dirt, and congealed blood out of my wound. It feels like my thigh is being stung by bullet ants, but I bite my lower lip and don't allow the whimper choking my throat to escape.

He finishes the task and the entirety of the injury is revealed. I make the mistake of glancing down. A wave of nausea and light-headedness rolls over me. The Fallen's claws ripped through skin and muscle, exposing parts of my body I could have happily lived a lifetime without seeing. If I were human, this injury would be life-threatening, or at the very least lay me out for weeks, and take months of physical therapy to recover from. As an angel-born, the worst of it will be healed in a day, but that doesn't make the sight any less gruesome.

My upper body sways as the blond stranger prepares to disinfect the wound. My vision goes wonky until a hand grips my arm, shaking me back into the here and now. I blink back at him. When he seems satisfied I'm not going to pitch forward, he goes back to tending to my thigh.

I hiss when he sanitizes the wound.

"I'm sorry this happened. The sport got a bit out of control."

A bit? And also, *the sport?*

"What were you doing in the pit?" he asks without lifting his gaze, still busy bandaging my wound. He jerks his chin to indicate I should lift my leg so he can wrap the gauze around it.

"Helping you?" The way he's talking about what just happened makes me think he never needed my help in the first place.

His head snaps up at the honest confession. "Helping me?" His brow pulls tight as he tilts his head. Sitting back on his heels he asks, "Whatever for?"

"So you didn't get torn apart by those Fallen." I mean . . . duh.

"You thought . . ."

With a shake of his head, he stands and moves across the room, grabbing items off a shelf. I let my eyes peruse the space for the first time. It's obviously a bedroom. A really large one. The size is closer to a great room than a traditional bed chamber. Through the window, I can only see the tops of buildings and the white-capped mountains beyond.

I'm startled to find him standing in front of me when I twist back around. He's stealthy for a large dude. He holds a damp towel out to me. "To clean up some of the mess."

I accept the cloth and murmur my thanks. Looking down at myself, I'm not sure where to start. Black blood is splashed across my armor and wings. Gritty sand from the arena sticks to me everywhere and has managed to find its way into some super uncomfortable places beneath my armor.

Grabbing a chair from a wooden desk behind me, the

blond stranger hauls it over and drops it in front of me, lowering himself into it with a labored sigh. His wings fan out on either side of the seat, metal-tipped feathers scrape against the stone floor as he settles. Closing his eyes, he rubs both hands down his face before leaning forward on his knees and pinning me with a stare.

"What's going on?" I ask, finally finding my voice and hopefully my backbone as well. "What am I doing here? What are *you* doing here?"

"This is where I live." He gestures with his arm, indicating the giant room we're in.

My eyes widen as I lean away from him. He lives among the Forsaken and Fallen? I don't even attempt to hide my shock.

"I take it Silver didn't explain the forum to you?"

"Silver didn't explain *anything* to me."

His face hardens and something flashes in his eyes. His lips press together into a line before he opens them again to speak. "She'll be reprimanded for that."

My eyebrows lift. Reprimanded? Like a child or subordinate?

He talks as if he has some sort of authority over her. Maybe he does, but if so, what world did we slip into where Forsaken and Fallen obey the orders of a Nephilim?

"Who are you?" I ask.

He tilts his head ever so slightly. The hair lying against his forehead shifts, and I notice a scar that runs at an angle through his left brow and disappears into his hairline. He brushes a calculating gaze over me, like he's trying to uncover hidden secrets.

"You may call me Thorne."

The way the statement is phrased makes me wonder if that's truly his name.

"How is it that you live here with these . . . creatures?"

He sits back and crosses his arms over his chest. An eyebrow cocks. "I don't just live among the Forsaken. I rule them all."

CHAPTER SIXTEEN
STEEL

The porcelain lamp shatters against the wall. Remarkably, I don't feel any calmer in the sudden silence that follows the impact, so I pick up a crystal vase and give that a try. Shards scatter in every direction as it explodes, leaving yet another dent in the drywall. The rage inside is a living thing, and it demands destruction. Grabbing a wooden chair, I lift it above my head, and with a downward swing it smashes against the hardwood floor.

"Steel!"

I ignore the shout as I search for something else to destroy. It's not right for the space around me to remain intact while my world crumbles to pieces.

My eye catches on a painting: a black and white image of a man with wings sprouting out of his back, dropping red hearts onto the sidewalk. The vibrant hue of the hearts reminds me of Emberly's red-tipped hair.

It has to go.

I march across the room, intent on shredding the artwork into a thousand bits when a pair of slim hands slams into my chest. Nova curls her fingers just enough that the sharpened nail ends dig into my chest without breaking skin.

I drive forward, a growl rumbling in the back of my throat. The animal parts of me prowl beneath the surface, even in the mortal realm, clawing to be released.

Nova slams her eyebrows down over fiery green eyes. Her mouth is set into a hard line. I've known her long enough to recognize her "I mean business" look, but it's going to take more than her glower to bend my will.

"Yo, Hulk Smash, I'm talking to you. You need to chill out."

"Yeah, Mom's already going to scalp you for trashing another room, but if you touch her Banksy, she'll disown you." I crane my neck to see Greyson surveying the room from the doorway.

Sterling brushes past him and lets out a low whistle. "Nice work," he tells me. His gaze travels to the painting I almost destroyed. "Mom won't be too upset, though. Banksy's one of us, so she'll just ask him to paint another."

They need to shut up about the stupid painting.

"Two. Days," I grit out. The room falls silent except for my labored breathing. My jaw aches from clenching it so tightly. "It's been almost two days since they took her, and we're sitting here twiddling our thumbs rather than getting her back from those creatures."

"Um, ouch." Sterling holds up his hands. "Dude, my fingers are starting to chafe from being online for so long. I only got up from my workspace to get some more snacks when I heard you raging in here."

It's true. Sterling's the only reason why we know what's going on with the investigation. The Council isn't filling us in, and when Sable found out what the others had done—misleading her and my parents so they could find and help me—she was furious enough to ice us out. Words like, "immature," "irresponsible," and "reckless" were thrown around during that initial call.

I tunnel my hands into my hair and fist the strands. Tipping my head back, I close my eyes and concentrate on my breathing, forcing myself to calm down.

I feel my blood pressure start to drop when a ball of sparks floats into the room and lands on Nova's shoulder. The sparks flicker and then disappear as Tinkle transforms into his flying squirrel form again. Useless Celestial.

"We're all doing our best here." Tinkle's high voice grates on me.

"You're one to talk," I spit out. He shrinks back against Nova's neck. She lifts her hand and rubs a finger against his tiny head.

"You're not being fair," Nova says.

"Fair?" I bark a bitter laugh. "His whole reason for existing is to protect his charge, and he lost her."

Tinkle jumps into the air and disappears. Nova shoots me a stern look. "You know why that happened."

"Yeah, he took his eye off the ball."

"In order to save your brother. Do you wish Tinkle would have let Sterling bleed out in that club hallway? Because that's exactly what would have happened if he hadn't stayed to help Greyson and Ash. Sterling would be dead right now."

I can't look her in the eye because, of course, she's right. Tinkle saved my brother's life, and for that, I should be grateful.

The hard truth is that it's my fault Emberly's gone. I was

in the alley with her. I let her slip through my fingers. I'm to blame. I had a chance to bury a blade in Silver's heart and I hesitated, pressing her for information instead of going in for the kill. We lost our advantage.

Turning my back on everyone, I stalk to the window and stare down on New York City, not really seeing anything. Raging isn't doing anyone any good, least of all Emberly. I need to get my head on straight.

Sucking in a lungful of air through my nose, I hold it for a five-count before releasing it and turning. Greyson, Sterling, and Nova are all still in the room. They know me. We've ridden highs and lows together throughout the years. They'd go to Hell and back with me if I asked, no questions.

Well, on second thought there'd be a lot of questions, but regardless, they'd have my back.

"You're all right." The words are easier to get out than I thought they'd be. "I've been an ass, and it's not helping anyone."

With a nod, Nova crosses her arms over her chest. "So, what are you going to do about it?"

"For starters, pull my head out of the sand and get to work. I have a contact in the Keepers who's cursing the day we ever met, but I may still have some sway with her. We need to find out exactly what they know."

"Now you're talking my language." Sterling gestures with his head for us to follow him.

As I follow my brother through the penthouse, Emberly's last words before she was ripped away from me echo in my mind. *You said it was easy for you to find me. So prove it.*

That's exactly what I plan to do.

17

I don't just live among the Forsaken ... I rule them all.

Impossible. There's no way the Forsaken would stand to be ruled by an angel-born. Unless I'm wrong to assume he's a Nephilim.

"What are you?" I demand.

"A Nephilim, just like you, of course. You can see with your own eyes." He splays his hands to show he's not holding back. I glance at the white aura around him, darkness shooting through it like mini thunderbolts, and I know that's not the whole truth.

I straighten in my seat. My leg screams at me. I have to tread carefully.

"How old are you?" It's impossible to guess a Nephilim's age. Someone who appears to be in their thirties might actually be centuries old. From what I know, angel-born are much more likely to die a brutal death in battle than of old age. I've yet to see anyone who could pass for more than mid-thirties.

Thorne, in comparison, seems oddly ageless. The thin

white scars on his face contrast the perfection of his marble-like skin, adding interest to his striking features rather than dulling their effect. His eyes carry the weariness of a lifetime of hard living, yet the curves and slopes of his face give him supermodel good looks.

"I've seen twenty years."

So young.

"If you're their ruler, why were you fighting? You could have been killed."

"Not likely."

The smile that twists his lips is nothing short of smug. Steel's self-assured grin flashes through my mind. My chest constricts, and I take a deep breath through the pressure. I still don't know what's become of him beyond Silver's weak assurance that he lives.

"Once a season for the last seven years," Thorne continues, "I offer the Fallen the opportunity to challenge me. If they choose to enter the forum and overtake me, they can claim my kingdom and my body."

This is madness. "You mean . . . ?"

"If I yield or am injured instead of killed, the Fallen responsible will be given my body as their vessel."

Thorne's dark gaze remains unblinking as he waits for my response. Seven years. That means he's been fighting gladiator-style against Fallen since he was twelve? And here I thought I had a rough childhood.

I take two shallow breaths before responding. When I do, the words feel sticky in my throat and come out only a touch above a whisper. "Why would you do that?"

"To prove my worth as a ruler. As you can see," he indicates himself with a wave of his hand, "I've never failed."

"And the battle lasts until you've killed all the Fallen or are defeated yourself?"

"Yes. I've bested countless combatants in the pit."

"If you always win, then why do they keep challenging you?"

"I am one of the most powerful beings in existence. To have control over my vessel is to have access not only to the mortal realm but all my power as well." He's not boasting. His tone is too matter-of-fact for that. He's simply relaying the truth.

"There are many powerful Nephilim, but the Forsaken don't bow down to any of them." Not to mention other angel-borns don't have darkened auras or metal-tipped wings. I want to know what makes Thorne—and me—so different.

Something flashes in Thorne's eyes—a spark of interest I'm not wholly comfortable with. A satisfied look settles on his face, softening his stone-like features.

He's pleased that I'm suspicious, but why?

"You're right, the Forsaken do not bend the knee to Nephilim. I'm sure you know by now that you and I are something more than our angel-born brethren."

He lets his statement hang in the air. My body strains forward with anticipation, mentally urging him to go on. The weight of the unanswered questions that are a constant pressure on my shoulders might finally start to lessen. I can't help but gobble up the bait he's dangled in front of me.

"What do you mean?" I prompt when the silence lengthens.

"What do you know of your sire?"

I grit my teeth. I don't want to be questioned; I want

answers. I want to know why I'm different from even my own kind. I want to know everything.

"I'm not asking to be evasive." Frustration must be written over every part of my face. "To properly explain, I have to know how much you already understand."

"Little. I understand very little," I grind out behind clenched teeth. "Especially after what I witnessed today."

Something flashes in his gaze.

"You've most likely been told there were no seraph angels cast out of heaven during the uprising."

I nod. That was an early lesson at the academy.

"Do you know that isn't written in the Book of Seraph? The belief that no seraph angel was cast out of glory was verbally carried down from one generation of Nephilim to the next."

I don't consider myself an expert on the Book of Seraph, only having scratched the surface of the text myself—studying giant tomes in a language I only half-comprehend is not my idea of a good time—but I assumed the bit about seraph angels was written in the text somewhere.

"No, I didn't know that. But it's not as if it's verifiable."

"I'll provide you with a copy of the Book of Seraph if you'd like," he offers.

"No thanks." I know what he's hinting at—that there are seraph Fallen—but I'm curious to know how he plans to prove his claim.

It's a beat before he responds. A calculated gleam lurks in the depths of his gaze when he does.

"You know you're different. Even if your physical appearance wasn't dissimilar from the others, you feel it inside." He presses a hand to his chest. "The desire to belong yet not quite being able to fit in any particular place. The longing you most likely struggled to ignore while being raised by humans."

Leaning back, I cross my arms and pin him with a stare. "That's not a hard thing to guess about me. I'm assuming you looked into my background and know how I lived the majority of my life. No one could grow up like I did and not feel that way."

He nods in acknowledgement. "That's true. Those are the typical responses to being abandoned by your parents and race and forced to grow up relying on the charity of strangers ignorant to what you really are."

I flinch at his blunt words. His description of my childhood is accurate, but I don't like feeling as if it's being thrown in my face.

"But it's not only that, is it? Don't you wonder why you still feel that way even though your eyes have been opened to the real world? The pressure of living with a group of Nephilim who will never quite understand what it's like to be you? Feeling like, yet again, you are on the outside looking in. You want to be one of them, but you can't rid yourself of the nagging voice inside that tells you you're not."

His words feel manipulative, but I can't deny he's right. How many times have I questioned why I still don't feel complete?

"It's because you don't truly belong with them. You belong with someone of your kind. Another child of the mighty seraph. You belong with me."

Ignoring the protest from my shredded thigh, I stand, shoving my chair back, and it tumbles to the ground. I teeter a bit, putting weight on my uninjured leg.

"Are we siblings?" My gut is a knot of emotions as I wait

for his response. I can't decide if I want his answer to be yes or no.

Surging to his feet as well, he shakes his head. "No. We are not brother and sister."

"Cousins? Aunt and uncle? Half-siblings twice removed?"

"Twice removed?" He stares at me like I've lost it, and perhaps I have. "No. We're not related at all, at least not in that sense."

My brain doesn't quite know what to make of that. The sharpened tips of our feathers, our blond hair and dark eyes. We have too many shared physical characteristics to not have some sort of familial connection. "So you're saying we're both descendants of the seraph line, but have different parents?"

"I'm saying we both have seraph sires, not watered-down lineage like the rest of the Nephilim. I'm saying we are the only two beings in existence with seraph blood running through our veins *and* the ability to phase into and out of the mortal realm at will. I'm saying we are superior to our Nephilim kin and weren't born to serve the human race or any other, but rather created to rule." His aura flares. The dark lightning zaps through the white.

A shiver skates down my spine at his words, and my wings bob twice before settling. Nothing good ever came from someone claiming to be a superior race.

Electricity dances along my arms. Sparks shoot off my fingertips as I retreat another step. He moves forward, gobbling up the space I just created.

"No, no. Don't take another step." I hold my hands out in front of me like I know what to do with them. This is defi-nitely one of those times I ache to have control of my powers. Random sparks and adrenaline-fueled fireballs aren't going to protect me unless I have mastery of them. Frustration flares in my chest like a flash fire.

"I've seen this movie, read this book. There's no way I'm becoming your queen of darkness and bearing the heir of the apocalypse or whatever sort of weirdness you have planned. I want no part of your creepy evil scheme."

There's a stretched beat of silence after my outburst, and then Thorne explodes in laughter. It isn't one of those hair-raising villainous cackles, it's a full-body laugh. It sounds rusty, as if it's something he doesn't do often, but it's undeniably filled with humor.

That throws me.

His face transforms, mirth radiating from every curve. Laugh lines appear next to his eyes as a smile stretches his mouth. He's breathtaking in a whole new way now.

As his amusement wanes, he rubs a hand across his face as if he can wipe his moment of temporary insanity away. He scrubs at his mouth until his lips straighten, and I notice the tips of two fingers on his left hand are missing. Another flaw I find intriguing.

"I'm sorry. I shouldn't have laughed. It's just . . . heir of the apocalypse . . . really?"

I lift a shoulder in a half-shrug. My cheeks flame. "When anyone starts crazy-talking about being born to rule, it's only a matter of time before they reveal their plan to destroy the earth."

"I don't want to destroy anything. What would be the point in that?" Some tension begins to drain from my muscles, but they lock back up as he continues. "I simply refuse to kneel before inferior beings, and don't think my subjects should either."

Subjects. He means the Forsaken and Fallen.

I must be in the upside-down. Is it Opposite Day?

"That sounds ominous. If you consider the destruction of the mortal world to be counterproductive, what's your endgame? Simple world domination? Enslavement of the human race? Annihilation of any and all Nephilim who don't share seraph blood or bow to your rule? Those all seem like sufficiently evil villain lifegoals."

Thorne's eyes narrow slightly. He allows the silence to stretch to an uncomfortable length as he stares at me. His gaze doesn't stray from my face, but it feels like he takes in my full measure.

After a slow blink, he settles back into his wooden chair, dominating the space as if he were seated on a throne.

"I'd like for you to spend the next few days getting to know me and my subjects. Perhaps you could attempt to withhold your judgments about us until I've had a chance to properly educate you."

"That almost sounds like a request."

"We both know it isn't." His smile is wide enough for me to see a mouthful of teeth, making the gesture more threatening than comforting. Are his incisors extra sharp, or is my mind playing tricks on me? "The Nephilim have had you for months. It's only fair that we take a few days of your time to combat their prejudices."

I can handle a few days, but I don't believe he'll just send me on my way after that. I don't think the Nephilim are aware this place even exists. There's no way he'd let me scamper off and tell them. And the more he shows me, the more he has to lose if I leave.

No, he's not going to release me, but I'm curious to see how easily he lies.

"And after a few days, you'll let me go?"

One corner of his mouth turns up. He leans back and folds his arms across his chest, which is still splattered with blood and gore from the arena. "Let's cross one bridge at a time, shall we?"

"You're good at making it sound like I have a choice."

He tips his head in what might be agreement.

A high-pitched shriek snaps our collective attention toward the room's balcony. The noise is followed by a roar from the coliseum crowd that up until now has been an easily ignored low-level rumble.

When I swing my gaze back to Thorne, all levity drops from his face. He stands and strides for the opening.

"Wait!" I hobble forward a few steps, wincing at the pain. "You can't leave. I don't understand what's going on. I don't understand anything."

He twists toward me, locking his gaze on mine. His eyes are cold and distant, the blue only a half-shade above black. "It's because you've been kept in the dark. But don't worry," he assures me, "I intend to bring you into the light."

18

With that creepy, cultish statement, Thorne slides his armor back on and then leaves me in his enormous room. Large shutters slam shut behind him after he flies away, presumably to restore order in the coliseum. After a failed attempt to break through them, I scarf down a plate of fruit and cheese I find sitting on his desk and then lie on his oversized bed when I get bored. Resting doesn't suit me though.

I'm hobble-pacing back and forth in front of the sealed balcony shutters when they slam open right before he comes gliding back through.

"Sorry for the interruption. That couldn't be helped," he says when he lands. He's covered in even more gore than before. Black blood drips off his once-shiny armor. The ends of his wings are also covered in blood. It puddles where he stands.

"Um . . . yeah."

His eyes flick over the dirty bedding behind me before settling back on my face.

"What? You told me to rest."

"And I'm glad you did," he answers as he yanks off his helmet. A clump of white-blond hair flops over one eye. His disheveled appearance almost makes him normal from the neck up. If I squint and tilt my head the right way, he could be a college student who just played a pick-up game of soccer or returned from the gym. But then he lifts a gloved hand to push the hair off his forehead and ends up smearing blood over his cheek, instantly transforming into an other-worldly warrior.

He stares at his hand with a grimace, realizing the mess he just made. "Let me take a moment to clean up."

Striding past me, he pushes his hand against the wall. There's a grating noise and a section depresses, then hinges open like a door. He shoulders past it and disappears into another room.

Water splashes, and I can't help but inch forward to look through the opening. Thorne has shucked his heavy armor and is pulling his shirt over his head. I rear back with a squeak.

If the dude is changing, why the heck didn't he shut the door?

My cheeks heat. Turning my back on him, I shuffle over to the yawning opening. The view from this tower is breathtaking—snow-capped mountains as far as the eye can see—but that's not what holds my attention.

My stomach hollows when I get an unfettered view of the compound. There are half a dozen large buildings, each flanked on either side by smaller structures that connect them all together in a rectangle. Thorne's tower is located in one of the corners. I spot the coliseum, sitting in the belly of the compound. I have a partial view of the arena floor.

The seats of the coliseum are cleared, but down in the arena, Forsaken drag what's left of the Fallens' bodies—and various body parts—away. An unwelcomed shudder works its way through me as I remember fighting in that pit. And to think, it was all for naught.

Dragging my gaze away from the arena, I cast a critical eye on the wall that rings and connects the entirety of the fortress. I consider making a run for it right then and there, but the sentries along the wall—both Fallen and Forsaken—stop that escape plan in its tracks. Between the lookouts and my poor flying skills, I won't make it a hundred yards.

I may not be ready to flee at the moment, but when the time is right, I'll take the chance. If I'm getting out of here, it is going to have to be a stealth mission. Outrunning my captors outright is not an option.

"The armory is the squat building to the left. The one that's a slightly different shade of white."

I whirl to find Thorne prowling toward me. He's changed into leather pants and a long-sleeved shirt. His wings are nowhere to be seen. A damp tendril of hair hangs over one eye, and he bats it back impatiently as he joins me. He's morphed from medieval knight to modern-day rocker. The change is jarring.

"It burned three years ago, almost taking out the barracks on either side with it, so we had to rebuild."

"Huh?" I'm so eloquent.

Casting me a side-eyed look, the corner of his mouth tilts up. I notice another scar running down his jaw. The white line is barely visible, but it's there.

"I figured I'd help you case the fortress. If you're planning an escape, you'll need some decent weapons."

I slant my gaze toward the dagger at my thigh and lift a brow.

"That's not going to get you very far. It's a close-range weapon. You'll need something you can use from a distance to fight your way to freedom."

"Why are you telling me this?"

He crosses his arms and looks over his domain. "I don't intend to hold you captive here. I believe given some time, you'll see this is the best place for you. You'll need to know your way around your new home."

I frown, my gaze pulling outward to the space beyond the walls of this fortress. What a joke. There's no way he would offer information so easily if he ever intended to let me leave.

"What is this place?"

"This is The White Kingdom."

I snort. "Rather pretentious."

The side of his mouth upturns again. "Built by Forsaken from the white rocks in this mountain, my people have been using this place as a refuge and training center for over a millennium now. Although I agree, the name is a tad pretentious. I prefer Whitehold."

"So this fortress isn't inhabited by humans in the mortal realm?"

"It's not inhabited in the mortal realm at all. We only send forces beyond the orb's reach as lookouts. The residents here dwell in the spirit realm."

My gaze sharpens. "So that's what's keeping me from phasing?"

"Precisely. It's perched above us." I cast a glance up, as if I can see through the ceiling . . . which I can't. "Would you care for a closer look?"

"Maybe when I'm feeling better and can fly myself."

The corners of his mouth lift in a knowing smirk, and I train my gaze out the oversized window. The sun hangs low, bleeding pastels across the western sky and dyeing the stark interior walls of the compound.

Sucking in a breath of sweet-scented spectrum air, I marvel at the normalcy of this conversation. "How long have you lived here?"

Is there a chance he was once a captive like I am now? How else would a Nephilim have found a place among these beasts?

"For as long as I can remember."

"You grew up in the spectrum . . . er . . . I mean spirit realm?"

"Yes. I can move between realms, just as you can, but have spent the majority of my time in this one."

What must that have been like? To have been raised apart from other Nephilim is one thing, but to have grown up in a completely different realm . . . My brain simply can't comprehend that existence.

"But, who raised you? The Forsaken?" I pull a face as soon as the words leave my mouth.

Thorne studies me out of the corner of his eye, easily reading the revulsion splashed across my face.

"In a way," he hedges.

Horror washes over me. What hope would someone raised by such evil creatures have? Would a kernel of humanity be able to grow in their soul, or would their heart blacken and shrivel to match the beings that raised them?

Thorne doesn't appear to be bent toward evil like the creatures roaming this compound, but what have I really learned about him in the past few hours? Nothing. He could simply be a good liar. Even psychopaths know how to fake empathy.

"How's the leg feeling?" he asks, changing the course of our conversation.

I add a touch more weight on my injured leg, testing its strength. It holds, but there's a bone-deep soreness under the bandages. My muscles protest even that small movement, but I'm not going to admit that to Thorne. Sometimes predators like to see their prey weakened before they strike. I've already shown enough weakness for one day.

"I'm fine." Only a half-lie.

Thorne's eyes sweep my body, weighing its language as well as my words.

"Hmm," is all he says. And then a moment later, "Would you like to get cleaned up?"

"Oh gosh, yes." The words fly out of my mouth without thought. I've been trying to ignore the sand chafing my skin under my clothes and armor, but it's become increasingly difficult.

"You're welcome to use my en suite. Your new room is being prepared. I was told you weren't pleased with your first accommodations." He gives me a look that says he knows how I tore apart the last room. I shrug, not the least bit repentant.

"Your body needs rest," he goes on. "You can get familiarized with the fortress tomorrow." Turning, he strides toward the still-open door at the back of the room, expecting me to follow. I bite my lip, trying to keep my limp from showing even though he'd have to have eyes at the back of his head to see me.

His bathroom is spacious, clean, and stark—just like his

room. The ceiling vaults at least two stories up, and a giant chandelier dips down from its center.

Thorne makes quick work of showing me where everything is located and how to work the bath and shower before leaving me to it. Looking down at myself, I'm not sure where to start. I've never had to take off the armor before—it's always disappeared when I phased back into the mortal world.

I start with the breastplate wrapped around my torso. I flare my wings and contort my arms awkwardly to find latches or straps, but come up empty. While turning circles, my metal-tipped feathers bash into the vanity. I jerk my wings away only to get them tangled in a towel rack. The ruckus brings Thorne back. He rushes into the room to find me tugging a white towel snagged on my feathers off my head.

He skids to a stop and stares.

With a groan, I give up and let the fabric go, but it swings like a flag of surrender where it's still attached to my left wing.

"I don't know how to work around all this," I admit with a swipe of my hand to indicate my clothes and metal appendages.

Thorne's mouth pinches as he crosses his arms over his chest. "Then shed your battle gear."

"Shed?" I get an image of my wings and armor flaking off my body and thumping to the ground. "You mean . . . transform?"

He gives a slow nod.

I bite my cheek and grind out, "I don't know how." It stings to admit as much, especially to a seasoned warrior.

Thorne arches a single dark eyebrow.

"Really?" is all he says after a prolonged pause.

"Just get out," I snap. "I'll figure something out."

"I don't mind you redecorating." He points to several gashes I unknowingly made in the walls. "But I'd like to keep my en suite functioning for a while longer. Getting building materials to this location can be a real pain. How long have you been able to transform?"

I shrug. "Not long. The first time was a few months ago."

"Well, that's understandable then." There's a soothing note to his voice that helps me drop my guard. "This is new, and with no one around to teach you, I'm sure this has all been . . . a bit much."

Understatement.

"I can help."

His steps are sure as he approaches, and my hackles rise. I slap away his hands when he gets within reaching distance. "Yo, hands off, dude. I'm not letting you undress me."

"I didn't mean it like that."

I narrow my eyes. Maybe, maybe not.

Bringing a hand to his face, he rubs his lips, considering. He nods to himself as if deciding on a course of action. "You have a spark inside you, Emberly," he starts. "When it ignites into a flame, your body pushes past the restrictions of a normal angel-born body because you aren't a typical angel-born. Not even close. As a daughter of a seraph, your capacities surpass those of our brethren."

I watch Thorne closely when he talks about our abilities as seraph Nephilim. There isn't pride in his voice, like I would have expected. Rather . . . resignation? He sounds almost weary. Odd.

"In order to return to your normal state, you need to

learn to extinguish that flame. To focus on where that fire is coming from and find a way to put it out."

"How do you find that place inside?" I ask, not knowing how exactly to put my questions into words. Introspection isn't really my thing. And sharing all of this with a stranger makes me extra skittish.

"Close your eyes and search inside yourself." He waits for me to follow his instruction, but I don't trust him enough to close my eyes in his presence. When it's clear I'm not going to obey, he gestures over his shoulder with his chin. "How about I go out there and talk to you through the door?"

"That'd be best. Can I lock it?"

He shakes his head. "No locks. No one would dare enter my private rooms." A bit of hardness returns to his features, as if he's imagining what he would do to someone who stepped uninvited into his domain. I imagine it wouldn't be pretty.

I nod my agreement, and he slips from the room, firmly shutting the door behind him. His slightly muffled voice comes only a moment later.

"Close your eyes."

I comply this time, squeezing my lids shut.

"Take a few deep breaths," Thorne orders. "Through your nose and out your mouth."

What is this, a yoga class?

"Listen to the breath going in and out of your lungs." Thorne is silent for a few minutes while he waits for me to find a rhythm. "Feel the strength in your muscles and the hardness of your bones. Count the heartbeats as your blood travels through your veins."

The world slowly starts to fall away as I focus on my

body. The only outside influence that has any bit of my attention is the deep timbre of Thorne's voice.

"Roll your shoulders and feel the weight of your wings."

Three more breaths. In and out.

"Now I want you to take stock of your body. Everything from the tips of your fingers to the ends of your wings. Feel each part and search for the source of warmth inside."

Still skeptical, I do as he says, starting with my toes and working upward. Thorne's voice is smooth as it washes over me. "Imagine you can see inside yourself. That the energy you feel powering your body flows through bright pathways of light you can travel along. Pick one and follow it."

In my mind's eye I see burning trails of golden lava, ebbing and flowing. I mentally travel one up my leg, and the path grows brighter and hotter as it nears my center. Moving past my gut, the pathway reaches my chest and burrows deep before it dead-ends. Light flares behind my closed lids, and I suck in a sharp breath of air, breaking my calm flow as sweat beads on my skin and drips down my back.

The light grows so bright, my eyes begin to water. Searing heat roots behind my spine, and I grit my teeth to keep from releasing a pain-filled shout.

Thorne may still be talking, but I'm not listening anymore. The brightness condenses into a burning ball. Yellow flames lick the perimeter. Shocks of white lightning pulse with the beat of my heart.

I press a hand to my chest, and my fingers are seared by the heat. It's more than I can bear.

Now that I've found it, I just want it to go away. The last

time something like this happened, Steel's cool touch coaxed the flames to abate.

"It's burning me from the inside," I choke out.

"You're stoking the flame rather than putting it out." Thorne's voice brushes against my eardrums.

I snap open my eyes to find him standing in front of me rather than safely tucked away on the other side of the door. He lifts his arm, perhaps to reach out for me, then balls his hand into a fist, stopping himself. I don't have time to be annoyed that he invaded my privacy because I'm on fire.

My skin glows with a warm, buttery light and flames lick the ends of my wings. I'm a hair's breadth away from full freak-out mode.

I make small flapping motions, which only spread the blaze farther up the feathers. "Ahh!"

"Emberly!" My name leaves Thorne's mouth with a snap of authority.

I freeze as the fire continues to burn from within and without. I cast Thorne a gaze filled with panic.

"Put it out. Demand that it obey you," he orders.

"How?" I squeak, my voice embarrassingly high.

"How do you make your toes wiggle, or flap your wings? How do you take air into your lungs or sing a song? You are the master of your own body and this power is a part of you. Control it!" he roars.

Slamming my lids closed, I drive back my panic through sheer force of will, locking it in a buried place. I imagine ribbons of ice reaching inside my chest, burrowing through flesh and bone to grab hold of the seemingly uncontrollable ball of pure power that pulses behind my spine.

It sputters when the chill connects with it, encasing it in

a sheet of frost. The sphere shrinks the longer it's exposed to the cold, until only a spark remains inside a bubble of ice.

I release the air I've held inside my lungs and it cools my lips as it breezes past. I taste fresh winter snow on my tongue before it evaporates.

My lashes flutter as they open. Thorne leans against the carved vanity across from me, arms folded and a smirk threatening his mouth. His eyes hold the glaze of appreciation, as if I'm a fine piece of art rather than a person.

Rather than truly seeing me, he appraises my value. I can feel him weighing my worth as an acquisition.

I don't like it.

My reflection blinks back at me from the mirror behind him. I'm still caked in grime, but I'm back in white skinny jeans and a sparkly off-the-shoulder sweater. My skin has returned to its normal porcelain hue under the splashes of sand and blood, my aura a soft white glow rather than a golden blaze. There's not a lick of fire anywhere on me. Even so, I pat my arms and legs just to be sure.

I'm as good as new. The same can't be said for Thorne's bathroom.

Oops.

"Singed" would be the best description. The towel that was caught on my wing is a pile of ash on the ground behind me. The other towels lie in a heap of half-burned cloth still smoldering in the tub. A layer of soot covers the glass panes and dirties the previously white stone walls. The room needs a washing as badly as I do.

Thorne glances around the bathroom. "I'm not sure this space is going to be much use to you anymore."

"Sorry." I'm not sure I actually am though.

He waves a hand through the air, dismissing my weak

apology. Shoving off the vanity, he gestures for me to follow as he strides back into his bedroom. "Your room should be ready by now," he throws over his shoulder. "You can get cleaned up in there."

"Does it lock from the inside, or out?" I ask.

He turns to me with a dark look. "You can hardly expect me to give you free rein of the compound."

"You said I wasn't a prisoner."

"I prefer to think of you as a reluctant guest. Besides, confining you when you don't have an escort is as much for your safety as the safety of the Fallen and Forsaken who live here. You have a . . ." His mouth twists as he searches for the right words. "An allure that is particularly enticing to the Fallen. If left to roam, you'd find yourself in more trouble than you can imagine. Speaking of—"

He picks a bracelet up off his desk. I don't remember it being there before. "I had intended to give you this after you'd bathed, but considering that," he tips his head in the direction of the wrecked room, "it's best not to wait."

He reaches for my wrist, but I jerk my arm out of the way. "You have an issue with personal space, don't you?"

"Here." He extends an outstretched hand, palm up, offering me the clunky piece of molded gold. There's a single milky stone embedded in the tarnished metal.

"Um. No thanks. I don't think we're at the jewelry phase in our relationship yet." I'm joking, but also serious. I don't want anything from him unless it's my freedom.

"I'm not trying to impress you with a trinket. It will keep your power muted from the Fallen so they'll be able to control themselves around you. Without it, I'll be forced to slaughter my subjects day and night to keep you safe."

I grin, showing all my teeth. "I don't mind the sound of that."

He smashes his lips together. I get the distinct impression he wants to scold me. Then something wicked flashes in his eyes, and his mouth slowly twists into a grin. "If you don't put it on, I'll be forced to confine you to this room. How do you feel about moving in together?"

I choke on nothing, but shoot back the moment my throat clears, "How do you feel about castration?"

His grin freezes and then disappears.

"Just wear it. Please." He forces out the last word behind gritted teeth.

I stare back at him, unimpressed with his coercion skills.

"I won't be able to allow you to leave *your new* room without it."

I run a tongue along my teeth, frustrated I'm going to bow to his demands. The hours Silver left me to rot in the last room felt like an eternity. I can't go through that again, at least not if I can help it.

Snatching the bracelet from Thorne, I give a grunt of annoyance before slipping it over my hand. My fingers spasm when it settles around my wrist, an electric charge zapping me.

"What the—?" My gaze snaps to Thorne, seeking answers and throwing an accusation at the same time.

"The gem was simply activating." Is that supposed to clear everything up for me? "I would caution you against taking it off." The words are spoken lightly, but the hard glint in his eyes says the warning is anything but.

"What is this?" I tap the stone with the tip of my finger.

"Something else the Nephilim don't know about. They're

called spirit gems. Small ones like these," he nods down at my bracelet, "are scattered throughout the spirit realm. They have various uses and properties. The one on your wrist helps conceal your powers. Other gems can amplify abilities, create shields, control objects or people—the list goes on and on. And there are likely more out there that haven't been discovered."

"Why don't the Nephilim know about them?" Some angel-borns must be aware of these magic rocks—the Council of Elders at the very least.

"As a rule, Nephilim don't spend time in this realm. They pop in and out during skirmishes, but they never spend a moment longer here than they have to. Is it any surprise they don't know the wonders of this realm?"

I tuck the information away to think on later.

The metal sits hot against my skin. A low-level vibration hums through it, as if it's filled with an electric current. I twist my wrist to inspect the jewelry and realize the scratches are in fact deliberate etchings.

"What are these?" I ask.

"Enochian runes. It's an enchantment that works with the gem to lessen the effects of your aura. Makes you less of a temptation to Fallen."

"You gave me something with Fallen language on it?" I move to tear the protective jewelry off, but Thorne's hand stays me.

"They're just words," he says.

"Sometimes words are more powerful than the sharpest weapons."

He tilts his head in agreement. "Even so, you need to wear this."

I want to argue, but I also want to remain safe. Safety

wins out over the minute possibility of contracting Fallen cooties.

I shake out of his grasp but leave the bracelet in place. Thorne nods his approval. "Now that's settled, let's get you comfortable in your new accommodations."

19

*T*horne takes me to an equally lavish and white-washed room a floor beneath his. It's equipped with a huge bed, crystal chandelier, working fireplace, en suite bath, and iron-barred windows. I clean myself—glad to have found more pants and a sturdy pair of boots in this room, even if all the clothes are still white or silver—and go about re-building my armory of weapons, this time with more discretion. Nothing says "I'm hiding sharp objects" like a conspicuously trashed room.

I tell myself I won't fall asleep, but it's been an eternity since I've had proper rest. Sitting on the soft mattress, I prop myself up against the headboard. I stare at the door, convinced I'm only giving my muscles a rest.

Each time my lids close, it's that much harder to get them back open. The slow blink and fluttering of lashes is my last clear memory before I'm swept away.

I don't immediately recognize that I'm in a dream. At first I'm simply disoriented.

Turning in a slow circle, there's only fog, fog, and more

fog in each direction. Opening my mouth, I try to yell a greeting into the void only to find my voice not working. Sound is as elusive as sight in this strange place.

As I debate what level of freak-out I should be ascending to, the world around me begins to take shape. A desk appears—Sable's desk. The Book of Seraph is flipped open to the eighth chapter. I scan the text, unable to read any of the words at first, until my gaze snags on verse twenty-eight. The wavy letters start to take shape until I'm able to read.

"The powers of the halflings varied greatly in both strength and ability. Some gained wings and the gift of flight, able to soar above their enemies. Yet others developed an aptitude in controlling one or more of the elements, causing flowers to bloom or a storm to descend with a single command. And a chosen few carried the fire of angels in their souls. And to them was given the power not only to burn through the materials of this world, but to the innermost parts of a living creature."

The innermost parts of a living creature? Is that just a nice way to say fire can char through flesh? Because if so . . . duh.

Peals of laughter echo from somewhere outside Sable's office. Forgetting the ancient tome resting on her desk, I rush to the door, throwing it open. I sprint down the hall, pulled in the direction of merriment, and skid to a halt in front of my history classroom.

The door is ajar, and through the crack I see students seated in the back corner of the room, their desks pushed together in a circle. Limbs hang over the backs of chairs and arms rest on desktops. The door is silent when I nudge it open and slip into the room.

No one notices me standing motionless in the entrance.

With the exception of Tinkle, they're all there: Nova and Ash have their heads tilted together as Ash whispers something in Nova's ear. Nova's laughter bursts through the din, deep and throaty. Sterling chucks a wadded up piece of paper at the pair, which Nova swats out of the air before it connects with her face. Greyson nudges his brother, either to say, "cut it out" or "good job," I can't tell.

And with his back to me—legs stretched out in front of him, one arm slung over the back of his chair, head slightly tilted—is Steel.

This can't be real. I know it can't, but the emotion that clogs my throat is authentic. My eyes start to tear, and I blink rapidly to clear my vision. A small sound of distress hiccups out of my throat.

Dream Steel drums his fingers on the tabletop next to him, but when the noise leaves me, his fingers freeze. His whole body tenses as he slowly swivels his head to check behind him.

When our eyes connect, it's clear he can see me. He's out of his chair and striding toward me in a flash. I open my mouth to speak, but before any words can emerge his arms wrap around my back and he's crushing me to his chest.

"You're here." He whispers the simple words against the side of my head, his breath skimming over the shell of my ear. I shiver.

Pulling back only far enough to check my face, he raises a hand and cups my cheek before rubbing a thumb against my jaw. My gaze drops lazily to his mouth, remembering that last kiss that was stolen from us. I may not have all my feelings toward this boy sorted, but there's no denying the attraction is there.

"So soft. I can almost believe this is real." He stares at me like he's trying to memorize every angle of my face.

I tip forward a fraction, hyper-focused on his lips.

Almost. There.

"Where are you?" he whispers, his lips feathering over mine.

"Who cares?" I answer. We're in a dream after all. Does anything in the real world really matter right now?

"I can't find you. You're trusting me to, and I'm failing."

Maybe an answer will shut Dream Steel up. My arms wind around his neck while I say, "I'm in a Forsaken compound somewhere in Canada."

Dream Steel rears back. "What?"

A bubble of frustration wells up at my inability to control this dream. Seems like I'm stuck playing along.

"Silver took me to some sort of fortress in the mountains. I don't know where it is, but there aren't any easy ways in or out. It's crawling with Fallen and Forsaken." The words stumble out of me.

Dream Steel blinks a few times and then unwinds my arms from around his neck and takes a step back. I huff, feeling rebuffed.

"That's oddly detailed for a dream," he says as he knits his brow.

"Well, since this is my dream, I think I get to say what's appropriate and not. Maybe we should stop talking about this and just kiss. If I'm going to have a dream with you in it, that's what I want to be doing."

Dream Steel isn't shocked by my forwardness. Instead his mouth pulls into a frown. "Your dream?"

Now I'm not even sure I *want* to kiss him anymore. He's being extremely difficult—very authentic Steel. My subconscious re-created him a little too faithfully. Boo.

"But . . . are you really here?" he asks.

Why do I feel like this is turning into a "who's on first" conversation?

"Yes. Of course."

"So this isn't a dream."

"Of course it's a dream . . . isn't it?"

"But yours or mine?"

I sigh. We're talking in circles when we could be doing something so much more interesting. Typical.

Dream Steel glances over his shoulder. Our friends are still conversing, oblivious to our presence at the front of the room. He marches over to Greyson and waves a hand in front of his face. Greyson doesn't make any indication that he sees Steel.

"What are you doing?" I ask as I make my way to the back of the room.

"Trying to get their attention. We need to find out if this is actually a dream or not."

"How is waking up Dream Greyson going to help you figure that out?"

He stops clapping his hands in front of Ash's nose to tilt his head in my direction. "Dream Greyson?"

I point at my friends one at a time. "Dream Greyson. Dream Sterling. Dream Ash and Dream Nova."

He makes a sound deep in his throat that might be a chuckle but then refocuses on jarring one of them.

Heaving another sigh, I join him in front of Ash. Her facial expressions are happy as she laughs and jokes along with Nova and the twins, but underneath the merriment she looks tired, worn. There are dark rings beneath her eyes and even her curls seem to hang limply.

I do a quick check of the rest of the group and find similar hints of stress and exhaustion on all their faces.

"Why do they all look so worn?"

I'm speaking to myself, but Steel answers, straightening to look me in the eye. "None of us have gotten much rest since you were taken. We're doing everything we can think of to locate you. It's taken a toll."

"My mind must be showing me what I'm hoping," I mumble. "But I wish it showed everyone healthy."

Reaching out, I pull one of Ash's curls straight before letting it loose. A high-pitched squeal shoots out of her as she jumps from her seat.

"Something touched me!" she yells, head on a swivel until her gaze snags on me. "Emberly? Is that really you?"

"Yeah?" My dream friends are acting really weird. Is it possible . . . ?

In three steps she has me in a hug that's part choke hold. "Are you all right? We're all so worried."

"Am *I* all right? Are *you* all right? The last time I saw you a Forsaken was ready to bite into your throat like it was a juicy steak. And you . . ." I swivel my head in Steel's direction, really seeing him now that I'm coming to realize this might not be a dream—or at least not an ordinary one. Just like the rest of my friends, he looks tired, but he's alive and uninjured. Either this dream-state doesn't allow me to see his injuries, or he's already healed from them.

I feel Steel's gaze like a cool brush of air as it passes over me from head to toe and back up again. My heart starts to thump faster.

"Yes, we're fine." Ash's voice snaps me out of my Steel-trance. "Silver held to her word and pulled back her Forsaken thugs after they knocked you out. We tried to give chase, but they left their injured behind so they could move quickly." Regret shines in her eyes, and I squeeze her hands.

"It's okay. I'm just glad you're all okay."

With a wobbly smile, she yanks me around so she's facing the group. "You guys, can you believe . . ." Her words trail off mid-sentence when she eyes Nova, Greyson, and Sterling, all still in their own bubbles of unawareness. "What's going on?"

"That's what I was trying to figure out," Steel says. "You were like them until Emberly touched you. I think she pulled us all here."

Ash's surprised gaze turns back to me. "Really?"

"I have no idea," I answer. "I'm just as confused as you two are. Is dream communication a Nephilim power?"

Ash shakes her head. "Not that I know of. But one of the primary functions of angels has always been to act as messengers. Perhaps one of your ancestors had the ability to dreamscape or dreamwalk or dream telecommunicate— whatever you want to call it. If you're in control of this, Emberly, that's probably why your touch made me aware of your presence. Try it with one of them."

"Here goes nothing." Standing in front of Greyson with Ash and Steel at my back, I pinch his arm.

"Ow," he says, and then rubs his arm. His eyes grow wide as his gaze tracks up my body.

"I didn't pinch you that hard."

"Oh my gosh, you're okay!"

I'm tackled in another hug. The moment Greyson releases me, Steel tugs me back, widening the gap between us. Craning my neck, I shoot him a what-the-heck look. His eyes are fixed on his brother though, so he misses it.

Greyson cocks an eyebrow in response. "I told you you

needed to phase and let that pent up aggression out." Making a big show of it, Greyson shoves his hands in his jean pockets. "I assume this isn't really a dream."

"We don't think so," Ash says as I move on to wake up Nova.

Nova keeps her cool when I brush my fingers over her shoulder and give her a gentle shake. "Wicked cool," are the first words out of her mouth. "Glad to see you're still alive."

We all turn to Sterling after catching Nova up.

"Do we really have to wake him?" Ash asks with a chuckle. "I'm enjoying this too much."

Sterling seems to be having a debate with . . . himself? His hands fly through the air, punctuating whatever point he's making. I'm not entirely sure whether he's winning or losing the conversation, but he's definitely all-in.

I position my hands on either side of Sterling's face and bend over so we are eye to eye. When my palms meet his cheeks I say, "Boo!" right as Sterling's eyes begin to focus on me. With a yelp, he tips back in his seat and tumbles to the floor with a crash.

"Sorry. Couldn't help it." The grin on my face probably isn't convincing.

He looks over each of us from his angled position on the floor. "What's happening?"

"We're all dead," Greyson answers with a straight face. "This," he swings his arm in an arc to indicate the classroom, "is our afterlife. We're not allowed to move on to a better place until you actually pass a class. Which means we're all doomed."

"Grey," Steel groans.

"Couldn't help it. Check out his face."

"You suck," Sterling shoots at his twin as he lumbers to

his feet.

Ash takes a moment to explain what's happening and our only working theory that I might have somehow pulled everyone into a dream together. Sterling takes another look at our surroundings.

"A classroom at the academy?" he says. "Couldn't you have dreamed us somewhere tropical instead? Preferably with a beach and a bunch of bikini-clad women."

"And that's why we woke you up last," I reply.

Sterling shoots me a wink, and there's a low growl behind me.

"Steel's getting a little territorial," Greyson says by way of an explanation.

"Ohhhhh. You should have phased earlier today like we said and released some of that tension, dude."

"Shut it. This is serious, and we're wasting time. Ember-ly." Steel gently pulls me to his side and away from his brothers. "We need to know as much as you can tell us about where you are. You mentioned Canada. Do you know which province you're in? What is the terrain like? Even the temperature will help us."

"Right." Bringing my hands to my face, I rub circles on my temples with my fingertips. How can a headache possibly be brewing? Whether I've brought my friends here or not, this is still technically a dream. I shouldn't be suffering through a migraine in my subconscious.

I do my best to recount as many details as possible. Quebec, the mountains, the spectrum world—anything I can think of that might be of interest. When I pause to take a full breath, the only thing I haven't told them about is Thorne. I open my mouth to speak, but then close it again, steeped in indecision I don't entirely understand.

"There's something else," Ash says as her eyes study my face.

I force the words out. "There's somebody here. Another angel-born like me."

I remember Aurora's words from several months ago about there being someone out there "like me." Could she have meant Thorne? And if so, how would she have known about him? That little girl is chock-full of secrets.

"What do you mean?" Ash tips her head ever so slightly, the way she always does when she's trying to work something out. "Like you how?"

I rub at a spot on my neck at the base of my skull. The tension headache has worsened. "Thorne. He claims to also be a seraph angel-born. But he . . ." Are they even going to believe what I'm going to say next? I'm still having trouble believing it myself, and I saw it happen with my own eyes. "He seems to be in control of the Fallen and Forsaken—at least the ones at the fortress. Like he's their leader or ruler."

Greyson and Sterling share a look, their faces mirrors of skepticism. Ash lets out a little yip of surprise. Nova's expression doesn't change, but I think she's stopped breathing. I don't look at Steel, but I can feel tension rolling off him in waves.

"Is that even . . . possible?" Ash directs her question at the group.

"It's not anything we've ever heard of before, but neither was Emberly's existence, yet here she is. It's improbable considering all we know about the Nephilim's history with Fallen and Forsaken, but I suppose it's not impossible." Steel's response is more balanced than I expect. "But if this leader is like Emberly, he's going to be more difficult to kill than maybe even a Fallen or Forsaken."

A boulder presses against my chest at Steel's words, making it hard to breathe.

"No." The breathy word is past my lips before I even decide to speak.

Darkness starts to churn in Steel's eyes. His pupils expand, shrinking the ring of teal around them.

"If he leads the Fallen and Forsaken, he's already marked for death," he growls, some of his inner beast floating to the surface. "Besides ordering your kidnapping, how many people do you think have died on his orders? Countless, most likely."

"We don't know that. I just . . ." I peter off.

Steel's not wrong, but I have an uncomfortable instinct to protect Thorne. "What if he's the only other one of my kind?"

"We're your kind."

Are they? Are they really?

I glance over the five of them—all their dark hair and light eyes. They were raised in loving families and supportive Neph communities, secure in the knowledge of who—or at least *what*—they were from birth.

None of them gets it. None of them understands.

"He said he could teach me about my powers. That's something no one has truly been able to do since I arrived at Seraph Academy. Not really. But it's more than that. What if he knows something about where I'm from? I'd be a fool to pass up this opportunity."

Steel's body is tense. His shoulders hunch to practically his ears as he leans forward. "So what are you really asking of us? You want us to leave you there? Or maybe we should rescue you, kill all the Fallen and Forsaken but leave him alive so he can tutor you in the secret art of seraph powers?"

Steel's words drip with sarcasm and my hackles rise.

"I'm just saying that I'm not comfortable putting him on the To Be Assassinated list quite yet," I say with cold determination.

It's quiet for several heartbeats as Steel and I face off. Ash's quiet voice finally breaks the silence. "But at what cost, Em? Is that knowledge really worth your life? Is it worth the life of another angel-born or human down the line? Because sometimes that's the trade-off when you hesitate to take down an enemy."

I stuff my conflicted feelings about Thorne into a hidden spot inside. I haven't worked through anything myself, so arguing about this is pointless.

Covering my indecision with a stoic mask, I jerk a quick nod acknowledging I've heard her.

"You guys. Something is happening." I look over at Sterling, and his silhouette is blurred. He's turning a hand back and forth in front of his face while he wiggles his now fuzzy-looking fingers.

"Are you waking up?" Greyson asks.

"Maybe? Honestly, I don't know how I even fell asleep in the first place. The amount of energy drinks and sour candies running through my blood stream should have kept me awake for several weeks, at least." His body starts to go semi-translucent. "Last thing I remember is searching the network for news."

"Maybe she's powerful enough to suck you into a dream while you're still awake?"

"I wouldn't be surprised." Sterling winks at me. I can hardly make out any of him now. "Rad power by the way, Em," are his last words before he disappears completely.

"Shoot. Looks like I'm next," says Nova.

My heart sinks. They're all going to disappear, and I'm going to wake up alone.

"Give Tinkle my love."

A sad smile crests Nova's face. "I will. Poor little dude is pretty broken up about all this." The static around the edges of her body gets worse, and I can see through her to the chair she's sitting on. "You've got this. Give 'em hell."

Pressing my lips together, I nod.

"I think that means it's my turn," Greyson says before Nova has even fully faded. "Looks like we're waking in the order you linked our awareness."

I turn to Greyson the moment Nova's gone. Rising from my seat, I throw myself in his arms, not caring if Steel gets prickly about it.

Greyson wraps me in a bear hug. "We don't have an organized plan yet, but the information you gave will help us find you. I'm sure of it. Keep your eyes out for a signal."

Leaning back, I search his face. "What signal?"

"You'll know it—" He doesn't finish his sentence before he blinks away.

"Em, I'm just—" Ash sniffles behind me. I turn to see tears dripping down her cheeks. "About what happened at the club. I'm so sorry. If it weren't for me—"

"No. Do not even finish that sentence. Silver and those Forsaken were never going to stop coming for me. Even if we'd been able to take them all, another wave of Forsaken would have just replaced them. Now that I see this place—understand it even a little—I know this was always going to happen."

Her chin wobbles but she nods bravely. "I love you," she whispers as she fades away.

My breath catches in my throat. Has anyone ever said

that to me before? That they love me? I don't think so. But I don't have time to dive deeper into how that makes me feel because . . .

It's just Steel and me now.

"I'll see you soon," he assures. "But in the meantime, keep yourself safe."

Of course he couldn't help but issue a command.

"Even with what I told you, you might not be able to find me." It's the nagging thought I can't seem to stomp out.

"I will find you." There's a deadly growl to Steel's words that warns me against contradicting him. His outline starts to go a little blurry. "I will *always* find you."

He takes three determined steps in my direction. His eyes broadcast his intent, and butterflies take flight in my stomach.

My mind's first command is to flee, but I'm so glad I don't when his mouth descends on mine, crushing our lips together. He wraps his arms around me, anchoring one hand at the back of my head and the other on my lower back.

He holds me like he doesn't intend to ever let go. I'm glad. I want this kiss to go on forever. It's fierce and emotional and wild and so *so* hot.

When he pulls back, his form is transparent. I start to lose the sensation of his hands buried in my hair and pressed against my back.

"Just wanted to make sure the dream lives up to all those expectations."

The dark smirk curving his mouth is the last thing I see before he blinks out of existence.

20

I wake up with the taste of Steel still on my tongue.

Yum.

I know I should pop out of bed and assess my surroundings, but I steal a moment to wiggle into the bedding and smoosh my smiling face into the pillow, savoring the tendrils of warmth still lingering in my belly. It's a delicious feeling too rare not to enjoy.

That boy knows how to kiss.

There are only two explanations for what happened last night: Either I truly dragged Steel and my friends into a dream, or I have the most creative subconscious on the planet. I've never considered myself to be particularly imaginative.

As consciousness creeps further in, ruining my dream-buzz, I stretch and flip over. Fully clothed from the night before and lying atop the bedding, it's easy to slide my feet to the floor.

In the full-length mirror across the room I see that I'm

rocking some serious bed head. Odd, since I usually don't move in my sleep. Ash likes to say I sleep as still as the dead. So motionless, in fact, that I once awoke to her face hovering inches from my own. She was trying to determine if I was breathing or not. That had been a rough morning for both of us. I had a mini heart-attack and Ash got a bloody nose when my forehead connected with her face. Lesson learned.

My fingers race as I plait my hair into a braid. I hadn't intended to fall asleep last night, but I'm not sorry. Besides potentially having reached my friends and discovered a new, completely kick-butt power, my body feels rested and aware. Only a slight twinge of pain remains in my thigh, and I have full use of the muscles again. All that's left of yesterday's wound is probably only a thin scar that will disappear before the day's end.

Going to the barred window, I watch the gilded rays of first light chase away the bruised night. Dark blues and purples in the spectrum sky lighten to a greenish hue. Eventually the sky will be awash in pink pastels. It's a beautiful sight, but I miss the blue skies of the mortal world.

From my perch, I spot movement on the ground. One of the figures below is Thorne—his light hair is a dead give-away. The other could be Silver, but I'm not positive.

I squint, but I'm simply too high to be able to tell for sure since so many Forsaken share similar features. The air around them is also somewhat blurred, indicating raised voices.

Thorne slashes his arms through the air, getting loud enough for me to hear his parting words to the female Forsaken: "That's final!" He turns away from my tower and heads in the opposite direction.

His companion watches Thorne leave before turning and disappearing into the tower at least a hundred feet below.

Reaching down, I check to make sure the shiv I made last night is securely in place. It's tucked in a spare sock to keep from slicing me while wedged in my boot. It makes for a tight fit against my right leg, but I'll put up with the physical discomfort for the mental peace its presence gives me.

Swiveling to the door, I lean back against the window and wait. Only a few minutes pass before the bedroom door is shoved open. Silver narrows her bloodshot eyes at me.

"You're up to something."

I shrug noncommittally.

"Whatever it is, you shouldn't bother. The only thing you'll manage to do is piss off Thorne. And trust me, you don't want to see him in a bad mood." She licks her blood-leeched lips, and her eyes shift to the side before returning to me.

Interesting. She's scared of him.

"Noted."

"Come on," she says and then heads down the hallway, leaving the door open behind her for me to exit on my own. I pause only a moment before following.

"What, you aren't going to tase me this time?"

She mirrors my earlier shrug, only glancing over her shoulder to make sure I'm following. "Ran out of batteries."

At the end of the hall is an old-fashioned elevator, the type with a gate that needs to be pulled back manually in order to enter the car. Even though it looks ancient, it still seems out of place in this gothic structure. I thought there'd be another winding staircase rather than an electric lift.

Silver pulls a lever to call the car. I can hear it clank from several floors below as metal grinds against metal.

When it stops at our floor, Silver hauls the grate out of the way and saunters into the car.

"Maybe we should take the stairs," I suggest, eyeing the decrepit interior of the box. Made completely of iron, spots on the walls and floor have rusted away. Step wrong, and half my leg will reach the ground floor before the rest of me does.

"Get in or I'll bring something stronger than my Taser next time to motivate you." She's checking her dark, claw-like nails as she threatens me. The words are right, but the usual venom is missing from her tone. She sounds bored.

"Getting tired of playing babysitter?" I ask as I gingerly step into the death box.

"Don't worry about me. I'm headed out for some big game hunting after I drop you off at daycare." The wicked grin that slowly stretches over her face when she makes eye contact is nothing short of chilling. It's a smile someone gives you when they know something you don't . . . but should.

I'm immediately uncomfortable, but do my best to cover it with a fake smile of my own. "Oh, nice. You're being let off your leash for a bit."

My barb doesn't seem to hit the mark. Silver's black eyes gleam with unconcealed excitement, and the smile doesn't slip from her lips.

We reach the ground floor and the elevator jolts and bobs a few times before settling. Silver studies me for long seconds before shoving off the wall and pulling the grated accordion door out of the way for us.

It's a short walk to a thick wooden door—also ancient

looking—and then we're striding through the spectrum morning sun. The warmth from the gilded rays doesn't do much to ward off the frosty chill in the air, but I'm glad for the light anyway.

"I'm surprised you're not begging for more information about your friends."

Normally, I would be, but if last night's dream was real, I already know how they're doing. "I don't feel like wasting my breath. You either honored your word or you didn't."

She looks at me out of the corner of her eye. "And do you think I'm good for my word?"

"No. Not particularly." A flash of anxiety runs through my body. If that dream was only a nighttime fantasy, there's every reason to believe my friends could be hurt or worse.

She chuckles darkly, but doesn't confirm whether or not she's trustworthy.

"Where are we going?" Something I should have already asked.

"I'm taking you to Thorne."

"Ahhhh, so you fetch as well. You know lots of tricks, don't you?" A muscle spasms under her eye.

We're walking along the eastern wall of the stronghold. There's a wall connecting each of the buildings along the perimeter of this fortress. It soars several stories into the air, but it's not unscalable for someone with wings.

"Aren't you worried I might try to fly over these walls and escape?"

Silver snorts. "No. Not at all. You're a sloppy flyer, and that's putting it generously." Throwing me a side-eye, she gives me a judgmental once-over. "Not to mention you can't even manifest your powers on command. Sentries are posted on our walls twenty-four hours a day, and if by some miracle you were able to get by them, our thermal imaging cameras would catch you. Honestly, I think it would be amusing if you tried, so be my guest." She misses my smirk as she gestures to the wall.

Thanks for the free intel, Silver.

Dragging my steps, I drop behind her a few feet—if for no other reason than to further irritate her. Juvenile, I know, but it gives me a measure of satisfaction.

"Keep up. Thorne's waiting for you," she snaps over her shoulder a minute later.

My strides remain slow and steady, so Silver stops to wait—hands fisted on hips and booted foot tapping against the crushed rock beneath our soles.

"So impatient," I chuckle when I catch up.

"Like I said, I have places to be."

I keep my gait unhurried so she's forced to match my leisurely pace if she doesn't want me falling behind. "I'll bite. What are you hunting?"

"You'll find out soon enough."

And I bothered asking because?

I mentally brush off her cryptic response. She's just trying to get under my skin. I can now see Thorne in the distance, striding toward us, a training field of sorts behind him. Already a few sparring matches are happening in several of the circular pits dotting the field.

"Good morning," he says with a smile when he reaches us. He's dressed casually in ripped jeans and a fitted long-sleeve thermal—not a speck of armor or leather pants. He exchanged last night's rocker look for indie-boy-band today. His hair is even tousled in *just* the right way to tip me off that it's been purposefully arranged.

"Morning." I lift my arm and wave lamely, feeling the need to do something with my hands.

"Am I cleared to leave the hold now that I've delivered her to you safe and sound?" Silver asks. Thorne's eyes narrow as he frowns at the sass in her voice. Seeing his reaction, her face blanks and head dips in respect.

Well, well.

"Yes," Thorne finally says. "Make sure to check in with your progress."

"Of course." She goes to leave, but stops and turns her head in my direction. "I'm sure I'll see you soon, Emberly." With her face pointed away from Thorne, one side of her mouth tips up and she winks before swinging back around and leaving.

My stomach sours as I watch her go. Releasing Silver into the wild is never going to be a good thing for humans or angel-born.

"You okay?" Thorne's voice startles me, and my attention snaps back to him. He moves his arm as if he's about to place it on my back, but then drops it. I take a covert step away to discourage the gesture.

"Yeah, I'm fine. Silver's just not my favorite Forsaken."

His mouth pulls down into a frown as he watches her saunter away. "Silver is . . . rather unusual. Even among her kind."

My interest peaks.

"Is that so? What makes her different?"

Thorne's face remains neutral, but I know he's trying to decide how much to tell me.

"Do all Forsaken have memories from their vessel's life? Silver seems to be particularly. . . in touch with those memories. And she kept her host's name as well."

Using words like "vessel" and "host" leave a bitter taste on my tongue, but since that's how Fallen and Forsaken seem to think of Nephilim and the humans they've possessed, playing nice might help loosen Thorne's tongue.

I try encouraging the conversation when he still doesn't respond. "She mentioned something before about how Silver, the original one, wasn't really gone."

Thorne looks away sharply, eyeing the closest sparring match about twenty feet away. The combatants tear into each other. Even from this distance I can clearly see bits of gore and blood splatter over the sand at their feet. A Fallen oversees the match, yelling commands at the pair as well as instructions on how to disembowel an opponent. It makes my stomach turn, but I don't even think Thorne sees the carnage.

"Walk with me," he finally says, and I'm instantly deflated that he's not going to entertain a conversation about Silver. If there's more to the Forsaken than the angel-born know, I want to find out what it is.

Thorne carries himself as if we're strolling through an English garden rather than weaving through a blood-stained training field. Fallen and Forsaken battle in clusters to our right and left. This training could not be more dissimilar to the high tech-facility in the bowels of Seraph Academy. Angel-born are educated in multiple weapons and fighting techniques under the watchful eyes of instructors. We run through a regimented set of drills each day and take precautions so we don't seriously injure ourselves or each other.

Thorne throws out an arm to stop me from getting beaned in the head with a severed hand, gesturing me forward after the appendage thumps to the ground several feet away.

I grimace. How gallant.

The Fallen and Forsaken obviously don't share the same concerns as Nephilim fighters. It's like watching gladiator matches that only end when one of the opponents loses a limb.

Oh wait, no. I'm wrong. That doesn't end the fight. The Fallen and Forsaken tearing into each other battle on, even though the Fallen only has a bloody stump where a functioning hand should be.

"Don't worry. Shayna can regrow a hand." Thorne misinterprets the look on my face as concern.

"Relieved to hear it," I mumble back.

We reach the opposite end of the training fields and stop to watch the closest match. The Fallen has the height and weight advantage, but the Forsaken is speedy and scrappy—two traits I always rely on in a fight.

Unsheathing a sword holstered at his hip, the Fallen goes after the female Forsaken. The weapon is extra-long because of the Fallen's height, so the reach of the blade is ridiculous. The Forsaken, in contrast, is only using her claws and teeth, her movements animalistic. Every blow she lands elicits a grunt from her larger, winged opponent. I can't decide if the Fallen's wings are a help or hindrance.

"Keep fighting like this," the Forsaken taunts, "and it will only be another few centuries before you earn yourself a vessel."

The Fallen spits something in Enochian back at the Forsaken. I don't need to understand the language to know it was a curse.

The winged fighter picks up his pace, but it isn't long before his armor is slick with blood, and his movements become sloppy. He swings at the female and misses; she jumps to the side and ends up behind him. Before the Fallen can spin to face his opponent, the Forsaken wrenches both of his wings back.

The Fallen roars when both appendages snap at uneven angles. I flinch at the sound and pinch my face into a wince.

Hindrance. The wings are definitely a hinderance.

Dropping the useless limbs, the Forsaken snatches the discarded weapon and knocks the Fallen out with the handle.

"Why do you allow the matches to get so . . ."

"Vicious?" Thorne finishes for me.

"Yeah."

Thorne faces me, and I mirror him, glad for an excuse to block out the sights and sounds from the training pits around us.

"How else do you expect them to get strong? If they fight with blunted weapons and padding, they'll never be able to survive in either realm. Angels will pick them off in this world and the Nephilim in the other. Learning to fight through pain is an advantage in battle."

"But they're tearing each other apart. Surely using half your army as training fodder isn't a wise strategy."

"The Fallen and Forsaken heal quickly."

"What about the Forsaken who've taken human vessels? They can't regenerate as fast."

A shadow crosses his face as he twists his mouth into a frown. "I don't allow Fallen to use humans as vessels, so that's a non-issue among my subjects."

I consider Thorne. Not allowing Fallen to use humans for vessels is interesting. Just the idea of it appears to anger him. Could there be some hidden humanity lurking beneath that poker face?

"Human vessels are weak," he continues. "Fallen trapped in a human shell have only done themselves a disservice. I have no use for them in my army."

Well, there goes that theory.

"Why did you want me to see this?" I ask, tipping my head toward the field we just slogged through.

"I want you to get used to the way they fight. Learn these techniques as well as the ones the angel-borns no doubt drilled into you over the last several months. We'll start training here in the mornings, both in powers and fighting skills."

"But . . . why? For all intents and purposes, I'm your enemy. Why would you want to teach me anything?"

I should keep my mouth shut. Getting stronger and learning more about my powers and abilities is a better way to spend my days in captivity than being trapped in a cell—no matter how lavish that cell may be. But Thorne's interest in me is baffling.

Reaching forward, he takes my hand. The gesture feels more friendly than suggestive, but I still have to force myself not to yank from his grasp. I don't like being touched.

"You and I are the same, Emberly. We could never be enemies," he says by way of explanation. He tips his head away from the training fields. "Come. I have more to show you."

he creatures lash against the bars of their cages, rattling the metal and shaking their prisons. I'd almost forgotten about the mysterious beasts that had been unleashed in the arena. Was that only yesterday? It feels like weeks have passed.

"What are they?"

We're in the depths of the coliseum, having entered through an exterior door and then twisted through dank tunnels and down stairs for a solid ten minutes before coming upon this chamber. Rows of cages large enough to fit a man line both sides of the low-ceilinged room. There are twenty cages in all, each holding a single beast.

"They're called barghest."

The serpentine, dog-like creatures emit keening howls, making short ripples in the air of the spectrum world. It's almost too much for my sensitive hearing, but I don't allow myself to wince.

"Bar-guest?" I parrot, having to raise my voice to be heard. "Never heard of them."

"I'm not surprised. I told you the Nephilim couldn't teach you about our world the way I can. There are many things you'll never learn if you remain in their clutches." His face hardens. It's clear he wants to continue disparaging the angel-born, but he moves on instead. "Barghest are common in some human mythology, even though they've never set foot in the mortal realm. You're probably familiar with a more common term—hellhounds."

Oil-spill scales cover the howling creatures from the ends of their elongated muzzles, down their bodies to the bottom of their claw-tipped feet. Spikes streak along their spines in parallel rows that extend at least a hand's length. Tufts of needle-like hair shoot up from the tops of their heads as well.

The creature in front of me gnaws on a metal bar of its cage, trying to saw through the solid material to reach me. I have a perfect view of its shark-like teeth—several rows of triangular, jagged blades, dripping with sticky saliva. I scrunch my nose. The sweet smell of the spectrum world is swallowed by the stench of sulfur.

"Hellhound" is a fitting name.

"And to think I used to like dogs," I mumble.

"They have their uses," Thorne responds.

Taking a step back from the cage and the rabid creature inside it, I turn to Thorne. "Yeah, like for entertainment value. It's always fun to watch one living creature rip into another."

Gesturing forward, he walks me around the room. He stops now and then to inspect one of the barghest, getting far closer to the cages—and their snapping jaws and sharply clawed feet—than I feel comfortable with.

"Angels aren't the downy-winged lute-playing messengers of peace humans portray them as," he says conversationally when we reach the other end of the room. "Fallen or full angel, they are warriors first and foremost. Made to keep creation in line and defend a higher power. Violence is part of our nature. It's pointless to pretend otherwise."

"We're also part human," I argue.

He chuckles, as if I've said something amusing. "There's plenty of evidence to suggest their race is capable of even greater malevolence than angels."

Fair point. I've seen glimpses of the darkness that lurks in the human soul. I haven't even been exposed to the worst of it, but it makes my skin crawl to think of. I brush my hands up and down my arms to rid the goose bumps.

"We're all responsible for our own actions. We can choose to be better than our natures if we really want."

"We have a choice?" His eyebrows make perfect arches as he cants his head. "Is that what you think?"

I'm about to answer that yes, I do believe we have the capability to overcome our baser instincts, when Thorne lifts a hand to his mouth and releases a long, shrill whistle. The room falls silent as the barghest drop to their bellies. Pointed ears flatten in submission, and they don't release so much as a yip or whimper.

I turn wide eyes on Thorne. "You have them whistle-trained?"

He chuckles. "They're no use to me if they can't be controlled."

His words bounce around the walls of my brain as he moves back down the row of cages. Does that philosophy extend to everything in his life?

Coming to a stop, Thorne issues a sharp command in a language I don't understand—most likely Enochian. The barghest get off their bellies and stand rigid at the front of their cages. All twenty heads turn in his direction like a pack of robot dogs, waiting to receive their next command. The pack is completely different from the uncontrollable beasts they were moments before. The transformation is chilling.

Thorne strides to the closest cage and utters another Enochian command. The barghest inside curls its upper lip to show a row of razor teeth, then drops to its butt.

Going down the line, Thorne issues different commands to each beast. One lies on its side, another releases a single bark, and so on until he's lapped the room. I do my best to commit the strange words to memory.

"Are you trying to show off?"

"Maybe a bit," he concedes with a smirk. "They have dedicated handlers, but I like to come down here at least once a week to work with them myself. They're magnificent creatures. Hungry?"

"I could eat."

"Perfect. I know just what to show you next."

Thorne extends an arm, inviting me to walk in front of him. The moment he steps over the threshold behind me, the barghest go ballistic again.

"Control is a precarious thing," he says as we walk back the way we came. I try to pay attention to the twists and turns we make to get back to the surface, but I'm not sure I've memorized the route correctly.

I still think I can hear the phantom howls of the hell-hounds when we step back into the light of day.

I worry my bottom lip as I stare at the dress laid out on my bed. I don't know what I was expecting when I agreed to have dinner with Thorne, but it wasn't formal attire. After having lunch in the mess hall, ignoring the hostile stares from both Fallen and Forsaken, Thorne took me on a tour of the walls connecting each structure in the compound. I was disappointed but not surprised to learn that sentries are posted along the entire perimeter of the stronghold, just like Silver said. And if Silver is also correct about the infrared cameras, escaping—or breaking into—Whitehold will be nearly impossible.

My mind was filled with strategy, memorizing the exact layout of the compound and the distance between watches when Thorne casually brought up dinner. I agreed before even processing his words.

On the other hand, could I have refused? For as hard as Thorne tries to treat me like a guest, I'm acutely aware of my prisoner status.

My gaze drifts over the offending garment. The gold and white dress is floor length, but the slit up one side and the V on the front and back won't cover much. I'll probably feel about as exposed as I did in the blue bandage dress Ash and Nova had talked me into wearing to the club. Considering how well that worked out for me, it's no wonder I feel squeamish about wearing another one so soon.

Thorne's words from the kennel echo in my head.

"They're no use to me if they can't be controlled."

Staring at the lovely piece of finery in front of me, I can't help but feel as if I'm another one of the creatures he wants to control.

"Screw this."

Droplets of water from my wet hair leave a constellation

of drips on the dress and bedding as I spin to the wardrobe. If I have a choice, I'm not letting someone dictate what I wear. In this situation, clothes are like armor, and I intend to dress for battle, not a ball.

I pass my fingers over the hanging garments, shuffling through them like a deck of cards. I fly over a few pieces and then pause, backtracking until I find what caught my eye.

"Now this I like," I whisper. It only takes a few more moments to find the rest of the ensemble.

My still-damp hair hangs in clumps around my shoulders and down my back when Thorne knocks on my door. I don't bother answering, since we both know the knock was a simple courtesy rather than a true request to enter.

I'm leaned up against the window, the thick bars pressing into my back, when he pushes open the door. His gaze flicks to where the dress still lies on the bed and then to me, taking a quick sweep of my body from head to toe. A half-smile quirks his lips upward. "Didn't like the suggested attire?"

"Don't particularly like being dressed up like a doll."

"Glad to hear it."

I frown at the unexpected reaction.

Shoving off the windowsill, I take a few measured steps forward. "Why pick something out for me if you didn't want me to wear it?"

"To see what your reaction would be, of course." He's playing a game, I'm just not sure what it is. But I can't afford to not win.

The outfit I settled on is a pair of white ripped skinny jeans, a simple silver tank, and chunky white army boots with gold laces. The whole outfit is anchored by an amazing cropped white leather jacket that looks like it was splatter-painted gold. It's officially my favorite thing I've ever worn —I think I might be in love. Nova would be proud.

"Also, do you have something against color?" I ask, not knowing how to respond to Thorne's comment about my reaction. "I look like a sheet of paper. And with the walls and décor," I float a hand around the room to indicate the sea of whites and creams. "What's the deal?"

Thorne brushes some of his light hair off his forehead. "What's wrong with the color white?"

"I don't even think white *is* an actual color."

"Point taken. I can have some other things sent to you. Any particular requests?"

"Maybe something that doesn't show blood so well?" I ask, fiddling with the red tips of my hair.

He nods in concession and then gestures toward the door. "Ready?"

We take the ancient elevator down a few floors. The gears grind to a halt, and Thorne pulls the grated accordion doors open. I'm surprised we're not on the ground floor. Instead we exit the death box, and Thorne leads me through an exterior door that opens to the wall connecting this tower to the next of the compound's structures—the Fallen's barracks.

Blistering winds toss the ends of my hair, drying the still-moist strands. Our auras give both of us a slight glow in the darkened spectrum night. Thorne's is just as bright as mine despite the lines of black lightning streaking through it.

Thorne nods at a sentry as we pass. The Forsaken's eyes track my movements, his lip curling to reveal a pearly white fang. His gaze is like a slimy touch. I keep my pace steady despite the sudden urge to scamper ahead. It's physically hard to turn my back on the hostile creature.

As we near the barracks, I notice something on the ground, tucked into the corner where the wall meets the side of the building. A pit of unease forms in my stomach as the full spread comes into view.

Thick furs are laid out on the stone ground. A single lantern throws a soft glow over a dinner of shaved meats, fruits, nuts, and loaves of bread.

Thorne plops down, positioning one of the many pillows scattered about behind his back so he can lean against the wall more comfortably.

He waves me over. "Come, sit."

"What," I have to clear my throat because it's suddenly dry. "Is all this?" I finish.

"Dinner, of course." Taking in my words and the rigidity of my body, Thorne's face falls. "What's wrong?"

I shift my weight from one foot to the next. My gaze bounces anywhere but to Thorne, first looking at the pile of pillows next to him where I'm supposed to sit, then the food, then off into the distance above his head.

"All of this makes me a little uncomfortable. It's a bit more . . . intimate than I was expecting." My cheeks heat as the words leave my mouth. I half-turn so I don't have to watch Thorne's expression at my admission.

"Oh."

The wind tunnels in and out of the silence hanging between us.

I hear movement and watch Thorne come to stand from the corner of my eye. Staying where he is, he rests his elbows on the ledge behind him.

"My intention is simply get to know each other better.

I'd like to believe if my focus was seduction, I'd be able to come up with something more original than a moonlit picnic."

I force myself to turn my head so I can measure Thorne's sincerity. He looks properly contrite, but he could just be a good actor.

"How can I put you at ease and convince you of my sincerity?"

I have an opening here I can take advantage of. "Answer any questions I have, honestly and without evasion."

He crosses his arms over his chest. The skin on his exposed forearms isn't even pebbled, despite the subzero temperatures of late December in the Canadian mountains.

"Only if you agree to the same terms."

He won't know if I'm lying. But by the same logic, I won't know if he is either. Sorting through half-truths and white lies will be better than nothing. Knowledge is a currency I need to horde if I'm to survive this ordeal.

"Agreed."

"Then please, sit. I promise to keep several feet of distance between us at all times." He's joking, but also not.

Feeling only marginally more comfortable, I walk to the opposite side of the furs and sink to my knees, delighted to find that this spot is protected from the wind. I start to re-heat immediately. The lantern between us also seems to be giving off some warmth.

Only when I've settled does Thorne finally return to his spot on the far side of me. We munch on the food in silence as we both stare up at the stars above—tiny pinpricks of light in a black-washed sky. In the spectrum world, the stars twinkle with a reddish glow.

I'm strategizing which information is most important to

push for and how to go about it when Thorne breaks the silence.

"When I was young, I used to think the stars were angels, high in the sky, burning radiance for the world to see. I was crushed to find out they were burning balls of gas rather than beings watching over me through the night." He chuckles softly, but I pick up the note of sadness in his voice.

"Why am I here?"

It's a simple question, but I'd wager the answer isn't. Thorne has gone to an awful lot of trouble for me. I want to know why.

He finishes chewing the grape he popped into his mouth and swallows. Heaving a sigh, he rubs his forehead before tipping his face in my direction.

"You had to start with a hard one, didn't you? You couldn't have just asked my favorite color?"

"I already know what that is . . . white."

"Touché. But for the record, it's viridian. It's a dark shade of spring green. Between true green and teal."

"Pfft. I know what viridian is." Liar liar pants on fire. I'd never heard that word before in my life.

As if sensing my fib and finding it amusing, he grins.

I clear my throat. "So, back to my question."

His grin falls. "Right." He searches my face, but I don't know what he's looking for. "My people have known about you almost from birth. They searched for you for many years and when their efforts provided no useful information, they eventually waned. When I learned of your existence—that there was another seraph angel-born child—I renewed the search for you. It was just bad luck that I only got a pin-point on you at the same time you were taken by the Nephilim and brought to Seraph Academy."

"But . . . how did you possibly know about me when none of the Nephilim did?"

Thorne picks up his cup and drains the purple liquid inside. These dramatic pauses of his are killing me, but when he finally speaks I can understand why it took him a bit to get the words out. "A Forsaken tried to kill you as an infant."

Boom. There it is.

"B-but, why?"

I bury my hands in the folds of fur beneath me to cover the shaking. I'm suddenly no longer hungry. The little food I have eaten sits heavy in my gut. I always knew I was in danger, even before I learned about the world and creatures that existed beneath the layer of the mortal realm. But hearing about a murder attempt on the defenseless, infant version of yourself is jarring.

"Isn't being a Nephilim baby reason enough?"

"To Fallen or Forsaken, I suppose so. But is that all?"

His features twist. I bet he wishes he never agreed to honesty at the beginning of dinner. He releases a breath in a rush forceful enough to stir the short hair lying against his forehead.

"I don't exactly know, and I'm not willing to burden you with my guesses." His posture tells me I'm not likely to get any more information on this topic, even if I keep pushing, so I go back to my original question.

"You never answered my question. Just because you knew I existed, and we are from a similar line, doesn't mean you had to abduct me. You could have, I don't know, tried to talk to me first."

He laughs. "As if the angel-borns would have allowed us even a simple conversation. Your place is here, with me. The Fallen and Forsaken are more your kind than the Nephilim ever will be."

Six months ago there didn't seem to be a single person on the planet who wanted me, but now two opposing ends of the supernatural spectrum both claim me for their own.

"I don't know why you think that, but whatever the reason, I should be given a choice."

"You are. I knew you'd never agree to make this place your home without a chance to get to know what we're like —without getting to know me. So to answer your question, that's what this is all about. You've had months with the Nephilim, it's only fair I steal a few days of your time as well."

"And what happens if at the end of all this, after you've shown me everything you want me to see, I decide I don't want to stay?"

Thorne's body is angled toward me. He moved closer as we spoke, but with a blink he lets his body fall back against the cold stone wall. Disappointment shutters his features, but he wipes it away a moment later. "If after everything you didn't want to stay . . . you'll be freed. I've already told you this."

He has, but just as before, I know it can't be true. And if that's the case, what other lies or half-truths has he fed me?

"My turn now."

It was too much to think he'd forget about that part of our bargain. I shift, adjusting my jacket like the armor I wish it could be.

Thorne places a finger on his lips as he regards me. "Tell me about . . ."

Oh boy, here it comes.

"... your favorite food."

What?

He chuckles at my WTH look.

"You're serious? That's really what you want to know?"

He shrugs. "Why not? We need to get to know each other. It's a place to start."

"Okay. Umm . . ." What *is* my favorite food? Consistent meals are a luxury to me. I don't like to dwell on what I can't have.

Thorne laughs again. The sound is rounded and full-bodied. "That's not supposed to be a trick question."

I chew on my bottom lip, tipping my eyes toward him. "It's just . . . I don't think anyone has ever asked me that before."

The smile drops off Thorne's face, but it isn't pity that settles over his features, it's understanding. The deep kind. Like when you look at someone and realize they reflect parts of yourself back at you.

That doesn't happen to me often, and I'm not thrilled that it's happening right now.

"Pizza," I say, thinking that's a convincing answer. "My turn again."

We spend the rest of dinner exchanging questions while I pick at food. My inquiries are geared toward uncovering whatever secrets I can about Thorne, Whitehold, the Fallen, and Forsaken, or his general intentions for me. He's a master at answering without giving away anything substantial, and after several back-and-forths, I've learned little about anything of import. Thorne never met his father; Whitehold houses twelve hundred Fallen and Forsaken; the angel-borns don't know everything about the spectrum world. Blah, blah, blah.

My only comfort is that he hasn't learned much from me either. His questions are all surface-level, and I answer with whatever comes to mind first rather than with what might actually be true.

After an hour, we're both frustrated, but Thorne is a tad better at hiding it than I am.

"I think I'm done." Done with dinner. Done with this fruitless game.

Releasing a sigh, Thorne pushes to his feet and extends a hand down to help me up. I accept the help and for the moment it takes me to stretch to my full height, the warmth of his hand heats my numb fingers. I slip my hand free, and we head back the way we came. Neither of us speaks until I'm back in my gilded cage and Thorne's hand is on the door, about to shut it and lock me in.

He offers me a sad smile. "I'll make sure you have some more variety in your wardrobe, starting tomorrow."

"Thanks." The word is lifeless, but he accepts it with a nod.

"Make sure to get rest tonight," he says, "for tomorrow, we battle."

CHAPTER TWENTY-TWO
STEEL

"I'm really not sure this is the best idea." Greyson voices his opinion for the seventh time as he hovers over my shoulder.

I heard him and responded the first six times, so I ignore him now, studying the topography on the map in front of me. I trace the southeast edge of Quebec with my finger, skimming over seven hundred miles of land in mere moments, trying to commit it to memory. It's going to take a considerable amount of time to scan the area from the air, but what else can I do? Sterling is the computer genius. Greyson is the family diplomat—if anyone will be able to lobby for more help, it's going to be him. I can't just sit around and do nothing.

I woke up this morning with Emberly's strawberries-and-cream scent lingering in the air. I would have preferred a few seconds to savor the dream, but my brothers were standing over me sporting matching looks of anxiety. They'd had time to convene with the girls before waiting vigil at my bedside. It took no time at all to verify they'd all experienced the same thing.

"Mom and Dad are working on getting a battalion together to search the area. Striking out on your own could be suicide."

"I won't be on my own. Tinkle is coming with me."

Greyson crosses his arms over his chest. "That hardly makes me feel better."

I don't disagree, but I'm not going to voice my agreement. Instead I grunt noncommittally.

We did the responsible thing and told my parents about the dream, then relayed the details to Sable and Deacon. They picked up the baton and ran with it, alerting the proper channels all the way up to the Council of Elders.

I'm glad to hear they're rallying the troops, but it isn't enough. Not for me. A full twelve hours has passed since we dreamscaped with Emberly. A lot can happen in that amount of time. I can't help but think this other angel-born is filling her head with lies. I don't like seeing sympathy in her eyes for someone who condones and orchestrates kidnappings and murders Nephilim.

I re-focus on the map in front of me, paying special attention to the Laurentian Mountains, the primary mountain range in Quebec. The range runs along the south-eastern coast and dips into New York, hundreds of square miles of snow and ice to hide an evil mountain fortress of nightmares.

That's where I'm focusing my search. It's a large area, but I can cover it as an eagle.

Tinkle said he can sense Fallen or Forsaken, especially in

large groups. I'm skeptical since he missed the horde of Forsaken at the club. I'm hoping it was an off day and that he's back on his game. If all goes well, when we get close enough, he'll be able to sniff the fortress out like a hound. At least that's the idea.

It isn't a great plan, but it's all I have with the limited information we possess, so I'm going with it.

"We won't be able to get a hold of you if you're flying around in the spirit realm."

"I'll phase back every few hours and check my messages," I reply, only half paying attention to Greyson. My mind is running over supplies I'll be able to carry on my person and forecasts for the next several days. The weather this time of year couldn't be worse. I'm going to have a few frozen days ahead of me.

"Steel!" Greyson slams his hands down on the map in front of me, slapping a palm over Montreal.

I fix him with an icy stare and lean back in my chair, crossing my arms over my chest to let him know he has my attention, and my anger.

"What's this really about, Grey?"

"It's just—" He shoves a hand into his hair. Rake marks track through the mop, evidence he's been plowing his hand through it all day. "We never should have left Seraph Academy."

I lift my eyebrows. Not insulted, but surprised at the admission. "Agreed."

"You shouldn't have left either."

A dark mood instantly rolls over me. Shoving out of the chair, I stride to my closet, set on gathering my things so I can get on my way. "That was my decision."

"It was a bad one."

I throw an icy look over my shoulder, warning him against continuing this conversation. As usual, he ignores me.

"It's just—" His hand scrapes through his hair another time. He's going to bald himself if he keeps that up. "I thought we could do this, I really did. But I was wrong. We're no match for this amount of Fallen and Forsaken. They're organized like we've never seen them before."

"I don't plan on fighting the lot of them."

"See, that's the problem. You don't plan. It's been this way for as long as I can remember, but especially these last few months. When the twins went missing, you struck out on your own looking for Silver and almost got yourself killed. Now you're about to do it again. You're going to get yourself in some serious trouble. You're going to get others hurt. When are you going to learn you don't have anything to prove?"

I squeeze my hands into fists, and even though we're still in the mortal world, I feel a beastly growl crawling up my throat.

I stomp up to Greyson, crowding him and pushing him back a step with a chest bump. I'm only an inch taller than my brother, but I use it to my advantage, going nose to nose with him.

"This isn't about proving anything. It's about protecting the people I lo—" I choke on the next word, having almost said something I can't take back. "It's not about that, and you know it."

"You're so damn arrogant to think you can always do it on your own."

"I have to," I roar in his face.

"No you don't!" Taking a step forward, he shoves into

my chest, but I refuse to concede. There's a fire in Grey's eyes I don't often see. "We're not lone wolves. The angel-born rely on each other—it's been that way for millennia, since the days of The Great Revolt. If we didn't band together back then, we'd all still be enslaved by the Fallen. We're more powerful as a group than individuals. When will you see that?"

Grey and I stand tall. Anger has elevated our breathing, and we huff air in and out of our lungs. Our jaws grind and hands clench as we restrain ourselves from using fists instead of words.

This isn't an argument he can win, but he's never going to understand why—at least, I hope he never learns the truth.

"I'm not explaining myself to you."

The noise that comes from Grey's chest might be a self-deprecating laugh. "Why do I even try? You're Steel Durand. What could anyone ever teach you that you don't already know?" He shakes his head.

It's not like that. At least not completely. But there's no way to explain my motives to my brother without carving into my chest and laying my innards out for him to see.

I curl my lip in a snarl, trying to force his retreat.

The door behind Grey slams open, and Sterling walks in, another energy drink in one hand and a half-eaten sand-wich in the other. He starts talking around a red piece of licorice hanging from his lips.

"Hey guys, I found some good possible—" He freezes when he catches us posturing in the middle of the room. "What's going on?"

Grey's gaze narrows, but he finally breaks eye contact and turns his back to me. His stride is stiff as he walks away.

"Nothing but the usual," he says to Sterling before he leaves the room, slamming the door in his wake.

"What did you do this time?" Sterling's tone is mocking, but I see real concern etched across his brow.

"Sterling," I warn, wiping a weary hand down my face.

"Think he's gonna go tell Mom?"

Dang, I must be tired because I don't care if he does. "Just tell me what you got, man. And make it fast. I need to get on the road."

My eagle form slices through the air, cutting along icy currents. The spirit realm night sky is bruised purple, reddish stars winking through the dark. My vision is superior to the average angel-born in this form, so I don't mind the lack of light as I search for signs of life below.

I'm making good time. It's deep into the night, several hours since I took off, but I'm already northwest of Montreal. Tinkle transformed into a hawk and keeps pace with me easily. Unlike me, he can speak in his animal form, but he's only given a few updates since we left, all of them to let me know he hasn't picked up anything. If I were to put money on it, I don't think the Fallen fortress is this far south, but I keep my gaze sharp, just in case.

The Laurentian Mountains aren't any more like the Swiss Alps than the Rockies, but my mind can't help drifting back in time as I soar over peaks and valleys.

"Steel! It's getting dark. Should we go home?"

I turn toward my sister, throwing her a smile as she trudges along beside me. She frowns and wraps her arms around her bubbled torso. Her puffer coat is silver, of course. She wants every-thing to match her name these days. Girls are weird.

"I just want to see what's over that ridge. I'll bet there are some epic ice caves."

"Why can't we just come back tomorrow with Mom and Dad?"

"Because we're already almost there."

She stops walking, forcing me to halt as well or leave her behind. When her eyes narrow, a seed of unease plants in my gut. That look is never good. I don't want to know what wicked thoughts are going through her brain. A slow smile spreads on her face and the unease blooms into full worry.

"I'll keep going with you, but you have to let me have Thun-dersinger for a full week."

"Silver," I whine.

The spirit realm's light purple snowflakes collect in her hair, graying the dark, tangled strands. She shakes her head, dislodging some of them. "Take it or leave it. I don't know why you're so attached to that sword anyway. You know once you morph, you'll fight in animal form."

Not if I end up pulling the short straw and only morphing into a bull. I don't voice that concern. It's a touchy subject for me. "I have to be prepared to defend myself before that. We won't morph for years."

"Pfft. In a few weeks we'll be spending most of our time wrapped in a bubble back at Seraph Academy. Nothing can hurt us there. We only get a few short breaks a year to spend with Mom and Dad. It's not like we're ever away from their watchful eyes."

I spread my arms wide. "Yet here we are on a snowy mountain all alone."

She sticks out her tongue. "So are you gonna give me Thun-dersinger for the week, or should I turn around now?"

I tip my head back. Sisters are so annoying. I should have

brought Sterling or Greyson with me instead. "Fine. Just hurry up."

She throws me a smirk and does a little shimmy victory dance before hopping to it.

We walk in silence for several more minutes but the crest we're trying to reach doesn't seem any closer. Ten more minutes and the sun has sunk beneath the horizon and the spirit world sky dims. The snowfall has worsened as well, and the last gust of wind almost pushed me off my feet.

I sneak a peek at Silver, wondering if we should give up and head back. She's hunkered down in her coat, her lips flattened into a thin, purple line. She's freezing. Maybe this wasn't such a great idea after all.

"Yo, lover boy." Tinkle's voice snaps me back into the present. "There's something down there."

My eyes work like a telephoto lens in this form, allowing me to enhance and magnify objects in the center of my field of vision. I scan the gorge beneath us but see nothing.

"Not there, you doofus."

I caw at the Celestial. How did Emberly put up with this creature for so many weeks?

"It was back there." Tinkle tilts and loops around. I follow in his wake, letting him lead me to where his Spidey senses say we should go.

We circle the air, slowly descending while we search. I still don't see anything. Tinkle lands on a relatively flat area, and I set down next to him, changing back into my natural form immediately. Tinkle's hawk explodes in a cloud of sparks that reveal his flying squirrel form when they clear. His little body can stand on top of the snow without sinking.

"Burr. It's cold."

"Then why didn't you transform into a polar bear?"

His round Yoda eyes blink up at me. "Why would I do that? That wouldn't change the temperature."

It's not worth it. "Which way?"

His nose twitches as if he's sniffing the air. He points in a direction, and I set off on foot.

"Hey, wait up. I want a ride."

The tiny creature scampers after me, and then climbs up my pant leg and the back of my coat until he's perched on my shoulder.

"It feels like there's something in front of us."

There's nothing in front of us except a jutting wall of rock, covered in ice several hundred feet away. There aren't any footprints in the snow either.

"You sure about that?"

"No. It feels . . . weird."

"Weird?"

"Yeah."

"Care to expound on that?"

"No."

Great.

I trudge forward in the direction he indicates, the sword at my back thudding against me with each step. I haven't used it since I was a child, but instinct urged me to bring Thundersinger on this quest.

Snow swirls in the air around us, funneling upward. The details of the rocky wall we're traversing toward start to take shape, but it's the cave chiseled into the side of the mountain that has my attention. My mind drags me back in time.

Full dark has settled over the night, and the cold seeped through my clothes and into my bones an hour ago. Silver shivers beside me. The wind flings her hair in different directions, making it extra hard for her to see through the tornado of snow. I'm more than a little worried, but I try not to let it show.

"I'm sure the chalet will be over that ridge." I'm not sure of that at all. I thought that about the last three ridges we climbed and was wrong every time. We are good and lost. We both know it, but refuse to voice it. Mom and Dad are going to kill us when we get home. Strike that, they're going to kill me, since this was my idea.

Silver's face is pinched as she nods, keeping up the charade that either of us knows what we're doing.

We slog forward, picking up the pace when we near the next crest. My stomach bottoms out when we reach the top to discover nothing but another snow-covered descent.

"Steel. I'm scared." Silver's eyes dull as she turns toward me. She stumbles when a gust of wind slams into her body. I reach out to steady her and get blown sideways a step myself.

"We just have to find somewhere to ride out this storm. I'm sure Mom and Dad are already looking for us."

"They're going to lock us in the attic for this."

"Don't worry. There aren't any attics in our penthouse." I smile to lift her spirits, but the expression is all wobbly.

"Like that will stop them," she huffs, but the corner of her mouth quirks up. "Hey, look over there!" She points to something in the distance, halfway down the slope in front of us. I tilt my head to get a better look, eyes straining in the darkness.

"Is that a cave?"

"I think so! Let's go check it out."

We whoop and holler with renewed energy and hope as we slide and stumble down the decline. The cave opens halfway to the bottom. We slip past it and have to claw our way back up through the snow. Collapsing in the opening, we fall to our knees to catch our breath.

The enclosure is still cold, but bearable because it's protected from the howling wind. Icicles like thin teeth drip from the top of the entrance. We knocked a few to the ground when we dove into the cave—they're as thick around at the base as my leg. Snow and ice layer the ground of the cave for the first few feet after the opening, and then there's only the craggy green rocks of the spirit realm. They're slightly luminescent, casting a sickly green glow over both of us.

"Wow," Silver mutters.

"See. I told you it would be worth it. This place is wicked cool."

"Maybe even worth the frostbite," she agrees as she traces a gloved finger down one of the icicles.

My eyes are on the glowing rocks, wondering if I can pry one loose to take back with me when we're rescued, as I step a few feet further into the cave. There's a shuffling sound and a pebble comes rolling out from the darkness beyond, only stopping when it bumps into my boot.

Silver and I freeze.

Something emerges from the shadows, striding with the gait of a seasoned predator.

I've never seen a Forsaken in real life. They are the monsters in our nightmares, the boogeymen of our parents' warnings, but even having been told about them practically from birth, I'm not prepared for the sight in front of me.

"What do we have here?" His words hiss around the giant fangs his lips can't conceal. "A few lost Halflings. How fortuitous. I was in the mood for a midnight snack."

Tinkle is chattering in my ear, but I don't hear what he's saying. We haven't quite reached the cave, but there's a familiar green radiance that chills my blood and sends my heart racing.

It's not the same cave, I know that. We're not even on the

right continent. But it doesn't stop my body from reacting, my brain from remembering the second Forsaken that appeared from the shadows that night. Silver and I fled the cave, slipping and falling down the mountain, only making it as far as the bottom of the ravine before the creatures snagged us with sharp claws. Silver's blood dripped to the snow when the Forsaken shredded her coat and sank its maw into her shoulder. And worst of all, the horrible game they forced on us for their amusement.

Wind freezes the tears to my cheeks. Snowflakes like small razors cut into my skin.

"What's it going to be, little Halfling? Are you going to fight me for the chance to save her, or trade her life for your own?"

Silver's eyes shine with wetness, but it hasn't spilled over yet. She isn't fighting against her captor anymore, and her body shudders from more than just the cold, but she hasn't given up hope yet. She thinks I can beat him, when I know I can't.

We're standing at the entrance to the cave. Tinkle is going on about something being in there, but not being able to pick up exactly what. He paces a few inches back and forth on my shoulder, but I'm as rooted as a tree. My mind is trapped in a fog of memory until the object of my musing steps from the darkened abyss, materializing in front of me as if summoned by my thoughts.

"Hello, Brother."

23

My head slams into the ground, and I get another mouthful of grit. Arms shaking, I push to my feet, spitting out sand and blood.

After four straight days of training with Thorne—aka, Emberly gets the stuffing beat out of her first thing in the morning—I know when I start to get the upper hand, he's just going to turn up the heat. Which means I'm going to bleed harder, ache more, and suffer longer than I was a few minutes before. Thorne's version of "training" makes me want to curl up in a corner and raise a white flag, except the stupid pit we're in is round.

Sparring with Steel and Deacon wasn't a cake walk, but this is next level.

It doesn't help that the training pit is ringed with Fallen and Forsaken. Like Pavlov's dogs, more than one of them starts drooling every time Thorne opens a new wound. Saliva drips from their chins, and their fangs grow to monstrous lengths.

The Fallen, however, are interested in me for a wholly

different reason. Their eyes fill with desire as they size up a new vessel—especially the female Fallen. Whether it was Thorne's intention or not, he's put me on display for my enemies. Their hungry eyes search for weaknesses to exploit, and they're finding plenty.

We've been battling for more than an hour, and all Thorne has to show for it is a healthy glow and a single scratch on his cheek.

I, on the other hand, look like I've been thrown into a wood chipper. Even in my full battle armor I drip blood from multiple shallow wounds and scratches along my arms and legs.

Thorne doesn't bother with armor when we battle. He's shown up at my door each morning in athletic gear and zero protective outer wear—not that he needs it.

The wounds littered across my body are either from the twelve-inch dagger he fists or the ends of his wings. He's trying to teach me to use my wings in combat as well, but he never issues verbal instructions or commands. He teaches by example.

Who knew there'd come a time when I missed being yelled at by Deacon?

Thorne side-swipes me with his wing and my shoulder takes the brunt of the hit, but I remain standing. Frustration shines in Thorne's eyes at my weak attempt at a block. I saw his move coming, but I just couldn't make my body respond fast enough.

I'm done, I know I am, but they don't believe in conceding fights here. Sparring only stops when one opponent is dead, or almost there.

A fist slams into my jaw, whipping my head back.

I didn't see that one coming.

Like a slow falling tree, I topple to the sand.

Timber!

From the ground the sky looks fuzzy. Two sets of identical orange clouds float above me. I blink and one disappears.

Is it over yet?

Thorne's foot collides with my side, sending me flying through the air, and I know it's not. I smash into the two-foot high barrier that surrounds our designated fighting zone.

I can't breathe. Can't move my legs.

My head flops to the side, and I look down my torso. There's a dent in the side of my armor about the size of the toe of Thorne's shoe.

I try to push myself upright, but I still can't move my legs and my arms are wet noodles.

The metal ends of Thorne's feathers catch the spectrum sun and a ray of light flashes across my vision, reminding me he's still advancing.

I tell myself that he won't kill me, but from the damage he's already inflicted and the murderous set of his jaw, my brain doesn't believe me.

Pure unadulterated terror rises up from the hollow of my soul and chokes me.

I'm going to die. The phrase repeats in my mind over and over.

Thorne rolls his shoulders, his silver wings arching at the same time, as he prepares to make his move. I stop thinking all together.

Throwing my hands out in a fit of rage, I release the full power of my wrath. It comes shooting out of me in the form of blazing globes of fire directed right at Thorne's chest.

Without time to fully dodge the attack, he manages to curve his wing enough to intercept the brunt of the assault.

The balls of angel-fire explode in a shower of sparks. Some ricochet off Thorne's wings and into the throng of spectators. Pain-filled shrieks follow after, and the swarm around us retreats several feet.

I'm not sorry if someone else got injured.

I slump back to the ground, completely and utterly spent, forced to watch Thorne's retaliation from a cockeyed angle.

My breath wheezes in and out of my lungs and some wetness trickles from the corner of my mouth.

Thorne inspects the part of his wing that took the hit. He plucks a few silver feathers and inspects them, singed black and deformed. Melted in parts.

He lifts his gaze and surveys the crowd, which has grown suspiciously quiet. The barest hint of a smile plays on his lips.

"We're done here," he calls out. "Disperse."

"She's still conscious!" a voice booms from behind me. I don't bother to try to see who it is because Thorne sends a lethal glare in that direction. No way would anyone argue with that look. I should know. I've received several of them over the last few days.

As expected, there aren't any more complaints as the crowd thins. Thorne waits until there are no more loiterers before crouching down beside me.

"Not bad."

"Screw. You." It hurts to get the words out.

"No seriously, I was only holding back about twenty-five percent this time. And nice job with the angel-fire. Do you feel like you're getting an understanding of where it comes from inside?"

I only have the energy to shoot him a glare.

"All right, let's get you up." With surprising gentleness, Thorne tries to right me to a standing position, but my legs aren't working. I crumple like a rag doll, moaning when I hit the ground again and then cough up a clump of partially congealed blood. It lands on Thorne's white sneaker. I'm glad.

When his face comes back into view, concern is written all over it. Rather than trying to help me to my feet this time, he scoops me up. An arm wraps under my knees and another behind my back. The world tilts then rights itself as he hauls me up and into his embrace. The weight of my wings drags my torso back, so Thorne readjusts so I don't topple out of his grip.

"You broke my back, you jerk."

"Among other things, apparently." His face is a stormy mask as his eyes scan the training field. He always insists on using one of the pits in the very center, so there's no way for a quick escape. It isn't until Thorne swears under his breath, however, that I start to notice the attention we've re-captured.

Thorne takes long strides as he navigates through the training pits toward the tower that houses his apartment and the jail cell he likes to refer to as my room.

Fallen and Forsaken creep their way forward. Their gazes devour my broken state and come alive with interest. They're like a pack of sharks circling their prey.

The bracelet around my wrist can only do so much to dissuade the monsters. A female Fallen as tall as any of the males goes as far as to lunge at us. Thorne quickly spins out of the way. Crouching, he flares his wings wide and then jumps, at the same time performing a powerful downstroke. We shoot into the air.

This ride is not as smooth as the last. My legs dangle uselessly in Thorne's hold and my wings keep catching the wind awkwardly, throwing off his trajectory. The snap of cold air feels good on my overheated skin, and I'm enjoying watching Thorne struggle. We eventually touch down on his balcony—landing a bit rough as well—and he takes three steps forward before steadying himself.

Moving to his bed, he gingerly places me on top of the covers. I'm leaking blood everywhere, but once again it makes me happy to see something of his ruined.

Thorne throws a frustrated glance over his shoulder toward the rising shouts of Fallen and Forsaken from the training grounds. Sounds like a brawl has broken out.

"I have to deal with that, but I'll be back quickly. Don't move."

"Is that a joke?" I snap.

"No," he growls, his agitation growing with every second. There's a shriek from somewhere outside. "I have to assert order or things will go sideways quickly."

"They haven't already?" Another wet cough wracks my frame, and a colorful curse word leaves Thorne's mouth.

"I'll send up a healer. You're a mess."

None of the cuts on my body are as deep as the gashes the Fallen carved into my thigh in the arena, but there are so many open wounds, not to mention internal damage. Thank goodness angel-borns are tough to kill.

"Yeah, thanks for that."

He winces before spinning on a heel and dashing for the giant opening in his room, not bothering to seal the shutters. We both know I'm not going anywhere in this state.

Everything from the waist up hurts. From the waist down I only feel an occasional tingle, which tells me my spine is trying to heal itself. Once it knits back together, the true agony will begin. From the angle of my leg, I can tell my knee is out of joint. I want to pass out before I regain feeling, but my agony rides the edge—keeping me awake and sharp, but not strong enough to tip me into oblivion.

This is going to be so bad.

Ghost pains race up and down the backs of my legs as the stones on the wall to the right of the bed groan and grind. A section of the wall depresses, revealing another secret door in Thorne's room.

Through the doorway steps a female Forsaken. Her dark red hair hangs in greasy clumps that fall around her face and down the back of her head and shoulders.

The thought that I should be worried about being so vulnerable in front of a Forsaken passes through my mind, but dissolves as I continue to watch her in silence.

Keeping her head bent, she shuffles into the room. Something is wrong with her gait, almost as if she's dragging her left foot along after each step.

She's carrying a silver tray with various jars and cloths on it. Stopping at the edge of the bed, she mumbles, "Master sent me to tend your wounds." She's so short that the mattress rises to the bottom of her chest. She has to be a whole foot shorter than me.

"Master? Thorne makes you call him 'Master'?" Revulsion sours my stomach. If Thorne is trying to put his best foot forward, he's bombing today.

The Forsaken hunches her shoulders, bringing her

height down another inch or two, and doesn't respond. She gestures to the items piled on the tray, most likely asking for permission to start. I nod that it's okay, but since she's staring at the ground, she doesn't see me.

"It's fine."

Reaching out with her skeletal hand, she dips a clean cloth in a bowl of water, then starts the task of mopping the blood off the exposed parts of my body. Her arms are like flesh-encased twigs, all bony angles and lean muscle striations. Black veins are visible through her paper-thin skin. Only bits and pieces of her face peek through her curtain of rusty tangles.

Considering her hair color and height, she must be in a human body.

"Thorne told me he doesn't allow Fallen to take human vessels."

Her hands stop for a moment before resuming their efficient work. She finishes cleaning off half my upper chest and one whole arm, then carefully picks up her supplies and shuffles to the other side of the bed, where she starts working again.

I want to keep questioning her, but the pain in my lower body ramps up and I have to grit my teeth to stop myself from yelling out. Buried in a sea of agony, I don't notice when the Forsaken finishes her task and moves on to the next one. As she dabs a thick warm salve on each of the cuts, the pain lessens. By the time she's moved to my legs— finding more than enough exposed injuries through rips in my pants—enough of me is numbed that I come back into my right mind.

The pile of red-soaked cloths continues to grow the

longer she tends to me. I don't know how it's possible she isn't reacting to the smell of my blood.

"This needs to be put back in place," she rasps.

She isn't asking for permission, but I manage a weak "Do it" just before she grabs hold of my kneecap with one hand and the bottom of my leg with the other and jerks roughly.

There's no holding back the scream of agony that rolls up my raw throat. I feel the bone slide back into place and wish I hadn't.

Quickly lurching to the side, I lose what little food I ate that morning for breakfast. Vomit splashes against the stone floor with a disgusting sound that makes me heave again. My throat burns against the acidic assault.

When I roll onto my back again, the Forsaken hands me a small towel that I use to wipe the throw up from my lips. Already the throbbing in my knee lessens as my super-charged body works overtime to heal my wounds.

"This is the best I can do unless you can get rid of all that." She waves a limp hand up and down my body, indicating my armor.

The hair in front of her face parts a few inches as she lifts her chin a notch and waits for my response. It's just enough of a gap for me to make out one brown eye, her small nose covered by a smattering of freckles that contrast with her paper-white skin, and half her peeling and chapped lips. But one thing stands out to me more than anything else: Pressing into her bottom lip is a filed fang, blunted at the end and only as useful for tearing through skin as a back molar would be.

What happened to this creature?

"Chances are I'd set the bed on fire if I tried morphing back," I finally push out, unable to stop staring at that fang.

She dips her head in acknowledgement and gathers her materials, placing everything back on the tray. Moving to the side of the bed, she starts cleaning the sick off the floor.

Something squeezes in my chest, and I can hardly believe what it is. Pity. I'm having a twinge of sympathy for this creature, and I don't know what to do with that.

Thorne comes gliding back through the window while she finishes mopping up my vomit with her last clean cloth. Hearing his return, she finishes quickly and tries to jump to her feet. Her movements are sloppy, and she knocks some of the jars off her tray and onto the floor. I wince when I hear glass shatter.

"I'm sorry. I'm so sorry," she repeats over and over while she frantically picks up the broken shards with her bare hands. I can tell she's cutting herself as she's doing it, because bits of the glass she deposits back on the tray are covered in a thick black substance—Forsaken blood.

Thorne seems completely unaware of her presence as he strides forward, his eyes evaluating her handiwork.

Dumping the last bit of glass back onto her tray, the Forsaken makes a hasty retreat—or as much of one as she can while bowing and hobbling backward toward the still-open doorway.

"Not a word of this," Thorne barks.

I think he may be addressing me until I hear her quiet "Yes, master" before she leaves. The stones grind as they return to their place in the wall.

"What the heck was that?"

"I've told you weakness is seen as an opportunity among my people. I had to take a moment to remind them who was still in charge."

"No." I point a finger toward the wall where the Forsaken healer just exited. "What is going on there? You told me you didn't let Fallen take human vessels. No *way* was that the body of a former angel-born. And she looks like she's being . . ." The word sticks in my throat, and I have to swallow to loosen them. "Abused. Did you file her teeth down? Is she even being fed?"

There's a single crease running vertically between Thorne's eyes, bisecting his brow. The rest of his face is emotionless.

"What do you care about a Forsaken? Aren't you of the belief that the only good one is a dead one?"

"Well . . . yeah. Especially if you're going to abuse them. It's like abusing an animal. I don't have to like a creature to not want to watch it suffer."

"Would you like me to call her back? I can easily end her life if that's what you wish." His eyes spark with interest as he measures my response.

I rear back as far as my half-prone position will allow.

"Oh my gosh, no. You're serious. You'd actually call her back just to kill her if I asked."

"I'd do a great many things for you if you only asked." Thorne's voice has gone quiet, but the intensity of his gaze doesn't diminish. I've gotten so used to seeing his aura that it's only the flash of dark lightning that draws my eye to it now. He's gone deathly still, but the pulse of his black-streaked aura betrays deeper emotions. "Her life would be as easily ended as a snap of my fingers."

Am I being tested again? Does he want to know how heartless I can be, or does he truly not care one way or another if the poor creature dies? I honestly don't know which scenario is worse.

Bile starts to boil in my stomach, threatening to make another appearance.

"You're a monster," I whisper.

"I don't pretend not to be, but my point in all this is for you to evaluate your own prejudices. Do you feel sadness for the creature? Pity? If her existence shouldn't be snuffed out without thought or reason, why should any Fallen or Forsaken suffer the same fate?"

"You can't make that comparison. Forsaken prey on humans. Killing them, drinking their blood, planning their destruction for sport. And the Fallen want to see Nephilim bred as meat suits for them, effectively enslaving and then killing every angel-born on the planet. What you're talking about with that half-starved Forsaken is not the same."

"Not every angel-born's existence is snuffed out when they're turned into a Forsaken."

"What? What are you talking about?" My mind is spinning. I can't grasp what he's trying to say.

"Silver is a prime example. Becoming a Forsaken changed her, there's no denying that. When she was an angel-born she was little more than a naïve young child. But not all Nephilim lose themselves when they merge with a Fallen. If their spirit is strong enough, dominant enough, they retain their essence, and it's the Fallen who fades away."

And there it is. The truth about Silver that he's been reluctant to tell me, and the very same thing the Nephilim refuse to believe.

"If what you're saying is true, and Silver retained enough about herself during the merge to still be herself, then what is she doing here with you, fighting a war against her own family who searched for her for years? A family who mourned and loved her. Why would she choose to fight on your side?"

Thorne leans back, running two fingers back and forth across his bottom lip.

"She has her reasons, but they're hers to tell. If you're brave enough, you can ask her yourself. She's back."

That was fast. I wonder if she's been gone the full four days, or just avoiding me?

My body hates me for it, but I lean forward until I'm sitting upright. Gritting my teeth, I start the painful process of standing. Thorne makes a movement toward me, but I hold up a hand. I don't want to be touched right now. I don't want to be touched by *him*.

"I'd like to return to my cell now."

"It's not a cell, it's your room."

"It's not my room until I'm free to come and go as I please."

Thorne regards me for a minute, a look of contemplation on his face. "You're being difficult on purpose," he states. "I don't think I like it."

I have the instant urge to stick my tongue out like a petulant teenager, but rein myself in. "I really don't care what you like right now."

Thorne's gaze follows me as I hobble to the other side of the bed. The wings weigh heavily on my back. The ends scrape along the ground with each labored step, grinding against the stone floor. I don't even care about setting anything in Thorne's room on fire, I just don't have the energy to force the change back.

When I reach the wall on the other side of the bed, I start pushing random spots, trying to get the doorway to appear once again.

"Stupid thing," I mumble under my breath. "Where are you?"

I scan the cracks and crevices along the wall but can't find an outline for a door anywhere.

Thorne's hand reaches out from behind me and presses against a non-descript stone. A panel of the wall groans, recesses, and then slides to the left. The slab rides along a track embedded in the floor, and when I duck my head through the opening, I find gears and pulleys rigged on the ceiling.

I limp forward and start down the narrow set of stairs.

"Let me just carry you down."

Oh, now he wants to be chivalrous?

I ignore Thorne and keep going. My lower back aches like it's broken, even though technically it's at least somewhat put back together now. My knee is swollen, and the cuts and gashes over my body sting like a thousand fire ant bites. But I wouldn't accept his help right now if my life depended on it.

He growls with frustration and shifts his wings, but doesn't try to touch me.

What feels like eighteen days later, I finally make it to the next floor. Of course there's no visible door, so I have to wait for Thorne to push the magic spot on the wall to get it open.

The room Thorne locks me in is just down the hall, and I speed-hobble toward it faster than anyone should want to get back to their jail cell. At the moment I don't even care that I'm going to be bolted inside, I just want to find the bed and sleep for a year. My body needs the rest in order to regenerate and heal.

Flinging open the door, I shuffle to the side of the bed, but wait for Thorne to leave before falling into it.

He doesn't say anything for a while, but I know he's still there. I can feel his stare heating the back of my neck. Pulling my wings up and together, I flare them slightly to shield me from his gaze.

"Are you angry . . . about the training this morning?"

Among other things, I want to say, but keep my mouth shut. I want to be left alone.

The sigh he releases sounds labored and drained. In my mind's eye, he swipes a tired hand down his face before rubbing the back of his neck.

"It's just our way. We don't stop to put Band-Aids on cuts and check to make sure our opponent is all right because we aren't afforded that luxury outside these walls. It is a kindness to push each other to be our best. To learn to use our strengths and beat our weaknesses out of each other so our enemies don't do it for us."

He ruffles his wings; the feathers brushing against one another sounds like blades rubbing. He waits for me to say something . . . anything.

They're no use to me if they can't be controlled.

That one phrase of his still haunts me, even days later. When will the time come that he thinks the same about me? Maybe it's already here.

I turn to face him, hoping to gauge his response. "What's your endgame? I've been here for the better part of a week and all you've done is show me your fortress and beat the ever-living crap out of me. You say you want me to see how you live, well fine, I've seen it. Congratulations, I'm impressed. You have a very big castle and a strong and brutal army. Yippee for you. So what? How am I supposed to decide on anything when you're keeping the real point of all this hidden?"

"It's not time yet."

"Time for what?" I press.

"You don't know enough about us yet. But in a couple of days I'm sure—"

"No." I slash an arm through the air, instantly agitated from his attempt to put me off once again. "I don't need a couple of days. I've put up with your song and dance long enough. What's really going on here? You must need me for something. I want to know what it is."

Thorne and I glare at each other, each of our stares intense enough to make a normal person squirm. But as he's repeatedly reminded me, we're not normal.

"You're not ready," he snaps.

"I'm not ready?" A brittle laugh rattles my chest. "You mean *you're* not ready because whatever it is, you know my answer is going to be *no*. I've seen all you have to offer and what I'm ready to do is call in your promise. Let. Me. Leave."

Thorne's nostrils flare as he inhales.

"You don't mean that. There's no one else on this planet or in either realm that will ever know you like I do."

"I do mean that. We may very well both share the blood of the seraph, but if I've learned anything over my lifetime, it's that blood doesn't dictate your family."

A muscle under Thorne's eye ticks. "Your mother would be disappointed to hear that."

My stomach bottoms out. "My mother? What are you talking about?"

"She's the Forsaken who tried to kill you."

I catch my breath and it feels like time freezes for a moment.

"You're lying," I whisper.

"You can choose to think that if it makes it easier for you."

I wrack my brain for tidbits of what Tinkle revealed about my mother, which admittedly wasn't a lot. I sit down on the bed behind me.

"I was told she was murdered."

"The Nephilim would likely consider her transformation to Forsaken as a murder."

And apparently so would a Celestial.

"Is she still alive?"

Thorne seems extra reluctant to offer information, most likely regretting his loose tongue. I squeeze my hands, nails biting into my palms as I wait for him to answer.

"Yes."

"Is she here?"

"No."

"Then where is she?"

"I honestly don't know anymore."

Pieces start to fall into place.

"That's how the Fallen and Forsaken found out about me at all. How you found out about me. Because my own mother told you."

Betrayal stings like a fresh slap, heating my cheeks. I suppose it's not fair of me to feel that way; once she became a Forsaken, she wasn't truly my mother anymore. But logic doesn't soothe my jagged emotions. Like an exposed nerve, they vibrate with agony.

I'm staring at my hands when Thorne's softly spoken words drift over me.

"You're going to help us one way or another. I'd just like it to be willingly."

It takes a moment for his words to register, but when they do, blood turns to sludge in my veins. Muscles tense, I snap my gaze up to his face.

"That sounded an awful lot like a threat."

The moment stretches between us.

"You'll be brought your meals," he finally says with a shake of his head, then leaves without meeting my eyes, closing the door soundlessly behind him. The bolt on the door slides into place, locking me inside.

24

*S*omeone is here.

My eyes pop open, and I jackknife up, my gaze landing on the platter of food at the bottom of the bed before anything else. No light filters through my window, telling me I've not only slept through someone entering the room to deliver food, but also the day.

Dang. I'm getting rusty.

"Your soup's cold."

Swiping my hand under the pillow, I palm my makeshift mirror blade and send it sailing through the air. Silver only just manages to move her pasty face out of the way. The weapon sinks into the chair's stuffing where her head just was—pity—but manages to slice off two oily tendrils of hair. She picks them up and shoots me a "what the heck" look.

I'm on my feet in an instant. "What are you doing in here?"

My wings and armor have disappeared during my nap and I'm left in what I had on before I morphed—yoga pants, sports bra, and loose fitting t-shirt. Not exactly the protective gear I want to be wearing if I'm about to have a faceoff with a vicious Forsaken, but it'll have to do.

"You could have seriously hurt me."

Is she expecting an apology?

"I'm only upset that I missed."

"And that's the gratitude I get for bringing you a gift."

"What are you talking about?"

A slow smile spreads across her face, stretching her cracked lips.

Gosh, Forsaken really are ugly.

She gestures to the foot of my bed. "Your dinner, of course."

My gaze flicks to the platter again. "There's not even soup on there."

She raises a shoulder in a half-shrug. "Details."

"Great, you fetched my food. Time for you to run along."

Silver stands and moves to the fireplace, pretending to warm her hands in front of it. "Oh, I don't know that I feel like leaving just yet."

"Why not?"

"Because I enjoy your sparkling personality."

I cross my arms over my chest and lean back against the footboard of the bed, feigning nonchalance, when what I'm really doing is taking a mental catalogue of the weapons I have stashed throughout the room as well as visually probing Silver to see what she might have on her that I could use. I have another two mirror blades hidden between the cushion and arm of the seat Silver just vacated and in the nightstand drawer behind me. Sharpened wooden stakes wait under the foot of the bed and the clawfoot tub in the bathroom. And in a pinch, any of the furniture, chair-sized or smaller, can be used against an enemy.

Silver places a hand on the fireplace mantel and turns fully to me. She cants her head, and a few clumps of hair fall in front of her face. She doesn't bother moving them. It's shocking how different Forsaken look in the spectrum world than in the mortal one. In the other realm, Silver is one of the loveliest girls I've ever seen. Piercing teal eyes framed by raven black hair that waterfalls to mid-back. Petite, fae-like features, like her mother. Yeah, she's a little pale—never being able to stand in the sun will do that to a person—but it plays into the Snow White look she rocks. But here, in the spectrum world, the only look she's rockin' is skeletal-vampire-zombie-chic.

Admittedly, her clothes are still nice, but they hang off her frame and everything clashes with her chalk-white, black-veined skin. Her hair looks like it's never been brushed and was cut by a chainsaw. Rosy-red and plump in the mortal realm, her mouth is now dehydrated, chapped, and cracking. Her lips hold a tint of pink so pale, it almost looks like she doesn't have any lips at all.

She's surprisingly confident despite her off-putting appearance. But I suppose with the exception of Thorne, she's in good company. In my opinion, all the Forsaken are equally hideous and the Fallen aren't much better.

The silence that hangs between us as she studies me is uncomfortable, but after several days at Whitehold, I'm somewhat used to it. Almost every minute I spend outside this room is scrutinized by hostile eyes. I plan to wait her out. Eventually she'll spill the reason why she's here and then leave me to keep planning my escape.

"What did Steel tell you about the day I was captured by Forsaken?"

My lashes flutter, but besides that, I keep the splash of surprise off my face. I debate whether to lie or refuse to answer, but I don't see the harm in admitting the truth. Maybe it will loosen Silver's lips.

"Nothing. He never talks about you. My roommate told me what happened."

A muscle twitches in Silver's jaw, but her poker face is firmly in place. Bending, she picks up a piece of firewood from the rack at her feet. The bark is white, and she turns it over in her hands. "That makes sense. If I were him, I wouldn't be keen to air my cowardice either."

I scoff and roll my eyes. She lifts her gaze at the sound. "You were children. Seems petty to hold a grudge against a nine-year-old because he couldn't save you."

The laugh that comes from Silver is as brittle as the kindling in her hands. "He tried to save me? Is that the story you were told?"

I keep my lips pressed together. Uncrossing my arms, I plop a hand on my hip.

"The truth is far more nefarious than that. I may look like a monster now, but make no mistake, he's the one who made me this way."

She chucks the piece of wood into the fireplace, and the small blaze erupts in sparks and embers, startling me. I lift my arms in defense as she strides past me toward the door. With her hand on the knob she glances over her shoulder, a hint of vulnerability in her red-rimmed gaze. "He doesn't deserve your loyalty, but he does deserve everything that's coming to him."

With that ominous statement she breezes out of the

room, slamming the door behind her hard enough that the mirror in the bathroom rattles.

Silver may have been able to overcome the monster who tried to claim her body, but it left a scar. There's no denying the darkness living inside her. Something . . . unhinged.

The rapid pounding of my heart belies the cool façade I put on for Silver. I don't move as her clicking heels recede down the hall, and she wrenches open the elevator grate. I hold my breath as I wait to hear the faint clanging of gears as it lowers, taking Silver with it.

I remain immobile for another two minutes. I count out exactly one hundred and twenty seconds, eyes glued to the door the entire time. Because when Silver stormed out, slamming the door behind her, there was no telltale *clink* of the lock sliding into place. In her emotional turmoil over an event I'm starting to believe I know next to nothing about, Silver made one very grave mistake. She forgot to throw the lock on my cage, and there's no way I'm letting the opportunity for escape pass me by.

Pressing my back into the stone wall, I will the shadows to darken around me even though I don't have the power to perform that miracle. After complaining to Thorne about my bland wardrobe, I was given an abundance of black clothes—a not-insignificant win as I will myself to disappear into the night. I would have been spotted the moment I snuck out of the tower in one of the white ensembles. Although I'm sad I had to leave my new favorite gold and white leather jacket behind, sacrifices have to be made if I'm going to make it out of Whitehold alive.

My breaths are shallow as I creep along the shadows, moving painfully slow as I scan the dark for movement. The sentries along the wall are conditioned to look for threats from outside, not from within, but I'm not taking chances. Besides the lookouts, a Fallen or Forsaken could emerge from one of the buildings at any time. It's not as if the compound has a curfew.

As always, the night is cold. Lavender snow has collected on the ground, making my footprints painfully obvious to anyone looking. Flurries twist and blow hard enough to create ripples in the spectrum air. With any luck they'll cover my prints quickly.

I mentally run over the aspects of my plan. I stockpiled every detail I could about Whitehold over the last six days, feigning interest in different aspects of Thorne's fortress. I now know the number of sentries along the wall and rooftops—always twenty-four—and the purpose of every building in the compound—all twelve of them. I memorized the layout and figured out where the cameras are mounted along the walls—I hope. I even determined what area of the mountain range offers the most coverage. All to give myself the best chance of survival for this exact moment. My escape strategy isn't foolproof, and hinges on several variables going my way, but it gives me a sliver of a chance.

A twinge of guilt tickles my gut as I creep along. Thorne hasn't been completely forthright with me—the bomb he dropped earlier today about my mother is proof of that—but I do believe his desire to see me join his cause—to join him—is sincere. It just comes with a warped sense of right and wrong. That the strong should rule the weak, and that power should be taken rather than granted.

I've been the weak one before, and how I was treated by

the people who should have protected me wasn't right. Thorne was raised with Forsaken and Fallen as his guides and mentors, and it shows.

I inch closer to my destination, the coliseum. It reaches into the sky at least five stories—shorter than the wall that protects the compound, but still high enough to be intimidating. It takes me only a few short minutes to locate the door Thorne took me through. It opens easily, free of any locks. I slip inside and out of the cold, shutting the door soundlessly behind me.

I brush snowflakes off my coat and shake them out of my hair, hoping like crazy that the thin layer of leather and my angel-born abilities are enough to keep me from freezing to death in the Canadian mountains when I escape.

Before moving into the maze beneath the coliseum, I take a moment to listen—stretching my sensitive hearing to the limit. When all I pick up is a faint dripping echoing somewhere in the tunnels, I take off, doing my best to follow the same path I traveled with Thorne.

As I glide deeper into the underground belly of the coliseum, I fist my hands to keep them from shaking. This part of my plan is more than a little dangerous. Even though I don't hear as much as a yip from the barghest housed somewhere in this labyrinth, my mind's eye works overtime to remind me about the jaggedness of their teeth, their foul breath, and sharp claws. I mentally recite the Enochian words I memorized to keep the beasts from tearing me to pieces when I free them. If they aren't released, I won't have a diversion to use to sneak beyond the wall.

I realized early on that with the sentries' hawk-eyes on the terrain, and the thermal imaging cameras scanning the mountains surrounding Whitehold, the only way I'm going to escape is by creating chaos. The name of the game is *controlled* chaos—or at least chaos I cause with a purpose. One of the sticky variables in my plan is how well I'm going to be able to control the hellhounds. I have a reasonable amount of confidence I can get them out of the coliseum without being torn to shreds. But I also need to lead some of them out of the hold to be released into the mountains with me.

Chaos from within and without. Extra thermal signatures to confuse the cameras, so my captor's don't realize I've slipped out as well. I'll flee on foot, then by air. Eventually the reach of the orb will run out and I'll be able to phase back into the mortal world. Then I'll only have Forsaken to worry about.

I make another turn and expect to come upon the door leading to the kennel, but the tunnel in front of me doesn't look right. There's no wooden door on the right, just another long passageway.

"Shoot." I must have made a wrong turn along the way.

Backtracking gets me horribly lost within a few short minutes. Stopping, I press my forehead against the chilled wall. Perspiration has collected along my hairline regardless of the cold temperature, so the rough stones provide some relief.

"You can do this," I whisper to myself. "Think. Think. Think."

How long do I have before someone, most likely Thorne, discovers I'm not locked in that room anymore? Maybe until morning when he comes to collect me for training, or it could be much sooner. I have no guarantees beyond the next few moments and here I am, wasting precious time.

I mentally retrace every twist and turn I took to get to

this exact spot. My eyes pop open when I realize my mistake. I head back in the direction I just came, making three left turns and a right, sure I'm now back to the spot where I made the wrong turn to begin with.

My steps are sure but silent against the hardened ground. I'm speeding along the tunnels when I hear a cough, followed by a whimper.

Halting, I tilt my head to the right, the direction the noise came from. A T-shaped intersection leads in the opposite direction I'm meant to travel. Only a few seconds pass before there's another cough, this time followed by what may be someone crying. My feet pad soundlessly over the stone floor in the direction of the noises before I realize I've made a decision.

Later, I'll wonder what might have happened if I hadn't heard the cry or had ignored it and continued on my way. But right now, my heart beats double time as I follow the sound.

I've completely lost my bearings after four turns and two sets of stairs, but I'm close. To what, I'm not sure, but I can hear soft moans and sniffles. There's an open doorway down the corridor.

Whatever I've been tracking is there. I'm sure of it.

Slowing my steps, I hold my breath as I near the entrance. A wet cough vibrates the air, followed by muffled words I can't make out. I know immediately they're not Enochian. The cadence is too smooth for the guttural language.

A few feet from the doorway, I press my front against the wall's cold stones. Forcing myself to take slow, even breaths, I inch my head to the side to peek into the doorless chamber.

I tell myself that once I've satiated my curiosity, I'll renew my quest to find the kennels and release the barghest. I tell myself I still have time to execute my plans and that this is just a short detour. I tell myself that whatever is past this doorway is none of my concern and that the ball of worry writhing low in my belly is for nothing.

And then I get my first glimpse of what lies inside the chamber, and I realize I've just told myself a bunch of lies.

25

I have to blink twice before my eyes adjust to the light. Water stretches out in front of me and to the sides. I'm not sure what this place is, but I don't think it's an underground sewage system. It would smell if it was. Maybe it's Whitehold's fresh water source?

Across from me, situated on a rough stone peninsula connected to the back of the cavern, a group of people huddle together. A group of humans.

Shock squeezes the breath from my lungs. Humans can't enter the spectrum world, yet here is a ragged group of about twenty-five or thirty men and women cloistered together in the belly of an enemy stronghold.

Their clothes are worn and dirty. Ripped sleeves, dark stains, frayed edges, missing shoes. Not a single one is wearing a coat. This space is protected from the elements, but is not heated. The chill is uncomfortable to me and I have angel-blood running through my veins, which means the temps here could cause hypothermia in a human.

The water's usually flattering luminescence only amplifies their pallid complexions, making them all appear sickly. Darkness sits beneath their eyes, standing out against the pale hue of their skin.

Butted up against the wall, with water on the other three sides, they sleep on thin pallets. There aren't enough blankets to go around, so bodies are huddled together for warmth.

A middle-aged man on the edge of the group lies on his side, coughing, phlegm rattling in his chest. With a round bald spot on top of his head, he's dressed in slacks and a button-down shirt that might have been white at one time, but certainly isn't anymore. He's one of the few people who still has two shoes on his feet—brown leather Dockers that have no business being worn in the Canadian wilderness. If he was cleaned up, he'd be dressed for a casual day at work.

There's a woman with shoulder-length black hair sitting vigil behind him, rubbing his back. A few streaks of gray frame her face. She's wearing a thin pink sweater torn at the seam, leaving one of her shoulders half exposed. The man turns his head to give her a weak smile. She tries to return the gesture, but isn't able to manage more than a slight upturn of the corners of her mouth before they sink again.

Pulling my head back, I lean against the wall.

What do I do?

I can't un-see this. I can't scrub the memory of these people from my mind, but with every moment that ticks by, my chances for escape grow smaller.

I wrack my brain for a plausible explanation for why Thorne would be holding a group of humans in Whitehold, but I can't come up with anything except the obvious: they're food. Barely living blood bags for the Forsaken to munch on.

I've been on the wrong end of a Forsaken bite before. The terror that rushed my body had been paralyzing, and I'd been educated about Forsaken and their particular eating habits. Who knows what these humans have been told. They probably think they're being held by a group of vampires. I can't decide what's more horrifying: the truth, or what their minds might have come up with to explain this strange reality.

A voice inside my mind screams at me to walk away. To turn around and do whatever I need to do to keep going. Free the hellhounds, escape Whitehold, find shelter.

What can I really do for these people now, anyway? Wouldn't it be more helpful for me to escape? Then the Nephilim will know this place exists and there might be a chance of a future rescue . . . at least for the ones that make it that long.

Can I really do that? Turn my back on people who are obviously suffering in order to save myself?

There's a tug-of-war in my soul. As my fight and flight instincts battle against one another, I'm crippled with indecision. My mind is so deeply steeped in shock, clear thinking becomes impossible.

A small whimper pierces the quiet and my mind is made up for me.

Emerging from the shadows, I enter the room, but only make it a step past the doorway before my muscles lock. There's at least a body-length of ground between me and the water's edge, but I'm hesitant to get any closer.

"Mama, I'm hungry," a child whines. Her cries are high-pitched but muffled as a woman rocks her back and forth.

"I know, sweetling." The woman speaks gently as her hand moves in smooth circles against the small child's back.

With a full head of honey-blonde hair, she can't be much older than seven or eight. Tears trek down her mother's face. "But it's time for rest now."

Hopelessness hangs over these people like a heavy cloud. My heart breaks in a way I'm not sure it will ever be put back together again.

"*Que etes vous?*" The male voice is loud enough to stir several of the exhausted men and woman around him.

Drowsy eyes blink back at me as people come awake. The man who spoke is on the younger side, probably early to mid-twenties. His hair is caked with dried blood, and his face is smudged and dirty, but even so, there's a sharpness in his gaze that many of the other are lacking.

"*Que fais-tu ici?*"

Nope. I do not know that language.

"Who are you? What are you doing here?" he demands in heavily accented English.

Most of the group has come awake by now, their gazes a mixture of fear and cautious curiosity. The woman who was comforting her child pulls her little girl fully into her lap, angling her away from me. The only part of her visible to me now are a few matted locks of blonde hair.

"I . . ." Emotion clogs my throat and I have to push past it to speak. "We need to figure out a way to get you out of here." I eye the deceptively beautiful water. "Can you swim over? I'm pretty sure I can navigate us through the tunnels."

Wait, did something just move under the surface? The brightness of the water makes it impossible to see clearly.

"Are you here to save us?" someone in the back asks. I can only just make out a pair of eyes and a mop of brown hair behind the mass of bodies.

I swallow hard. "I'm going to try."

I don't mention I have zero ideas on how to go about this. How in the world am I going to lead this group through a mountain range? And that's only *if* I can get them away from the Fallen and Forsaken first. My plan to use the hellhounds is completely shot now. Maybe I can figure out how to disable the cameras instead and then I only have to sneak—

"We can't get to you," the man with the French accent answers. "There's something living in the waters." As if on cue, a scaled eel-like creature crests the surface, flashing a row of sharp teeth before sinking beneath the ripples.

Oh. Heck. No.

I take a step back, shaking my head. "What is that?" My hand trembles as I point.

"We don't know, but we already lost someone who tried to swim across."

I swallow, wetting my suddenly dry throat. Taking a deep breath, I tell myself to chill the heck out. Casting my gaze around the space, I note the low ceiling. Flying is out of the question.

"Over there," someone shouts. "The lever drops a walking bridge."

Swiveling, I search until I find a wooden handle attached to the wall and pull it. Something groans behind the stones as a structure begins to descend from the ceiling. When it halts to a stop, a plank reaches from one side of the chasm to the other, connecting the peninsula to the shelf of rock where I stand.

Encouraged by the others, the young man takes a tentative step onto the bridge. It sways slightly from the chains suspending it from the ceiling.

"Be careful, Andre!" a woman warns.

The plank is at least two feet wide, but there are no safety rails. There are a few gasps from the ragged group as he traverses the bridge, but he makes it across.

One by one the group crosses the shaky plank until only the mother and her small child remain.

"Hurry," someone hisses behind me, keeping their voice low.

"We don't have time to wait," says a guy to my left. "Let's get out of here."

I give the dude the side-eye. I'm in no way the most compassionate person on the planet, but that was a bit harsh.

"We all leave together," Andre snaps back before turning his attention to the terrified pair across from us. "Angeline, your *maman* will be with you. You must come to us now though. We must go."

Little angel. The irony of her name is not lost on me.

I can see the child shiver from the expanse between us. It's obvious Angeline isn't going to move, so her mother bends over and picks her up, holding her against her chest. The child isn't large, but the woman is frail, and most likely starving and sleep deprived as well. She staggers under the additional weight, but makes it halfway across the plank bridge. I finally feel as if I can take a full breath when one of the water creatures crests the surface. Angeline squeals and wiggles in her mother's arms, throwing their balance off.

It's almost as if I watch both of them topple into the sparkling water in slow motion.

Cursing under his breath, Andre sprints forward. I follow without thinking, and the plank bridge swings wildly under our combined weight, throwing us both off balance.

Heat blasts my back and skin splits. My wings burst

free, but it's too late. I hit the water with a splash. My gilded wings do nothing to aid my non-existent swimming skills, and I'm dragged under the water by their weight.

I kick and flail, desperate to reach the surface. It's a mercy only my wings emerged. If I'd fully morphed, the added weight of my armor would have sealed my fate.

My booted feet do little to propel me to the surface and after a few heartbeats, I'm no longer even sure which direction is up.

It's bright under the water, distorting my vision. Dark objects snake back and forth throughout the crystal liquid bubbling around me.

Something darts at me, and I suck in a lungful of water on a gasp. It veers at the last second and circles me like a shark.

My body jerks reflexively, searching for air, my movements becoming less than useful to save myself.

I am going to die.

If only I could go back in time and take my swim lesson with Steel more seriously. I might have had a chance of surviving this.

Steel.

My heart doesn't pang with remorse for what could have been at the thought of him, but the image of him yelling at me to fight does.

The dark water-serpent decides to strike, and I have enough presence of mind to grab one of the makeshift daggers hidden in my boot, and lash out. My underwater movements are painfully slow, but I manage to embed the jagged mirror-blade into the creature's eye only after it latches on to my forearm.

Agony rips at me, but it takes a backseat to my need for air.

With a scream that vibrates through the water, that beast swims away, leaving streaks of black blood in its wake before disappearing from my fuzzy view.

I renew my desperate attempt to reach the surface, flapping my wings to move me, but with a lungful of water, energy quickly drains from my body. Only the angel blood running through my veins has kept me alive this long.

With a final jerk, I can no longer move my muscles, and my eyes begin to close.

I'm only half-aware when something latches onto my bicep and pulls me upward.

Breeching the surface, I gag when I try to breathe. Grabbing onto whatever I can, I barf out the water I inhaled before I take a staggering breath. The air burns as it fills me up, but it's a welcome pain.

Andre yanked me up far enough so my arms drape over the plank-bridge. His eyes are wild as he takes in the top part of my wings. There's no time for explanation. He jerks his chin behind me with the command to "get her" before dunking beneath the water.

Still hacking, I snap my gaze to the left, where I spot the child struggling to reach safety. Her slick blonde head bobs up and down in the water. She's close, but I'll have to leave the side to reach her.

I don't let myself think of how close I came to drowning as I shove away from the bridge. Reaching the girl, I wrap one arm around her and furiously doggy paddle with the other to reach the ledge. A few of the braver humans crouch on the side, reaching for us.

My fingers just make contact with a hand when something latches onto my ankle, and tugs.

Shoving the child forward, I gulp in air right before I sink below the surface for the second time. One of my weapons swam away in the eye socket of the last creature that attacked me, but I'm not defenseless. And so close to relative safety, I have a renewed sense of survival.

I have a blurred view of a jaw clamped onto my ankle. The end of the eel-thing lashes as it tries to pull me deeper.

I only just keep myself from sucking in another mouthful of water when a second water serpent sinks its teeth into my shoulder, my leather coat the only buffer between my flesh and its jaw.

Fear walks the razor's edge, threatening to trip back into panic at any moment, but if I let that happen, I'm dead. I'm not going down this way.

Not bothering to reach for another one of my stashed weapons, I grab the creature attached to my shoulder and rip it off me with my bare hands as I slice my wings down. The sharp tips of my feathers shred the eel attached to my foot. I use both hands to crack the lower jaw off the other water serpent before releasing it. Black blood blooms in the water as I kick to the surface. When I break through, I'm hauled out of the water. Crawling as far away from the edge as possible, I drop into a wet, bloody heap.

The child shivers against the wall only a few feet from me. She's soaked, but breathing and seemingly free of injury, so I'm going to call this a win.

A clap sounds, and I search for whoever is stupid enough to make more noise. My gaze snags on a figure standing tall behind me.

"You didn't think it was going to be that easy, did you?"

26

*T*he humans scatter as I stagger to my feet and face the female Fallen. She's at least a half-foot taller than me, and blocking the only exit in the room with a pair of onyx wings. Hair cascades to her waist in a sheet of liquid silver that shimmers when she cocks her head and runs a narrow-eyed assessment over me. She doesn't seem impressed, but I'm too thrown off by her presence and exhausted from the ordeal in the water to really care.

People sprint down the tunnel along the narrow ledge that runs in both directions, most likely figuring their chances of survival are better in the underground labyrinth than making a stand against a Fallen. They might be right.

A small group of humans remains huddled on the other side of her, including the young man who saved me. He stands as if protecting the small bunch. The little girl's mother is crouched behind him, her wide eyes trained on her daughter.

Water pulls at my clothes. A puddle forms at my feet as I use the wall to steady myself.

"Let us go," Andre demands. "You can't keep us here like this. We're not livestock, we're human beings." His hands are fisted at his side and shake from nerves or anger, I'm not sure which.

The Fallen angles her head in his direction, her red gaze detaching from me to land on him. He flinches but holds his ground.

The Fallen's skin is pale gray with a pearlescent sheen. Despite her fair complexion and light clothing, darkness drips from her, pooling as shadows on the ground.

This is not a normal Fallen.

My stomach bottoms out even as my limbs shake with fatigue.

"You're right," the female Fallen purrs as she takes a few measured steps toward him. Her boots click on the stones beneath her feet. The sharpened points of her silver-tipped nails scrape along the wall, creating sparks. I'd bet money they extend to claws. "You're not livestock. You're less valuable than that. At least livestock are mute."

Andre's face darkens to red, practically vibrating with righteous anger. When he opens his mouth, the Fallen lifts her arm, snapping her wrist in a whipping motion. A streak of fire shoots out from her closed fist and wraps around his neck. He doesn't even have the chance to utter a word before she yanks her arm back, pulling the leash of flame taut.

His head separates from his shoulders and hits the ground with a hollow thud. Screams fill the chamber as his body crumples. His head rolls and falls into the sparkling water. There's a flurry of dark movement underneath the surface as the creatures below devour it.

I press a hand to my belly.

Fallen can't manipulate the elements because they were stripped of their specific angelic powers when they rebelled. Nephilim use this disparity to their advantage. But this Fallen just demonstrated exactly the kind of power she's not supposed to have.

"You . . . killed him," I whisper, the horror of the act plainly written across my face. My insides clench, and I keep the vomit from coming up through iron will alone.

Thorne was right about one thing: angels were created for violence. The Nephilim bred into the world for similar purposes. Humans can be vicious and cruel and house a great many evils, but even so . . .

I glance behind me. Only four people remain, including the small child who is openly crying. Turning, I find the child's mother on the other side of the Fallen. Her terror-filled gaze bounces between her daughter and the place where the man's head disappeared.

Just because someone isn't as strong as you doesn't mean they are your prey.

"Not as smart as I was told, it seems. Pity. But that's not the only lie my son told me about you." The Fallen places a hand on her hip. Her silver off-the-shoulder sweater and white leggings seem out of place on such a vicious creature. There's not a drop of blood on her despite the savage death she just caused.

"Son?"

"Yes. He severely downplayed your compassion for these creatures."

By creatures, she means humans. Ironic, since I refer to Fallen and Forsaken the same way.

"Who is your son? One of the Fallen who watched me

spar in the training pit. Maybe one of the sentries along the wall? No wonder your intel is bad."

I barely know what I'm saying. I couldn't care less who her spawn is, but wasting time with conversation allows me to wrangle the heated energy coursing through my body. I will it into my hands, and with any luck, I'll be able to chuck a raging hot ball of angel-fire at her face.

Since she herself has fire powers, I doubt my attack will do much damage, but my objective is to distract so I can reach into my boot, grab the remaining mirror-blade tucked inside, and attack her. My best shot at taking her down will be to aim straight for her neck. It's going to take a fair amount of hacking and sawing with the seven-inch makeshift blade before she's truly defeated, but what other choice do I have?

"He didn't tell you." Her head snaps to the side, a half-cocked move that reminds me of a bird. In a strange way I find the fact that she's as creepy as the rest of the Fallen somewhat comforting. "Interesting. I wonder what else Thorne kept from you."

Tiny sparks dance across my fingertips. I fist my hands to hide the telltale signs of an impending attack.

"Thorne was actually very forthcoming with information."

"Hmm."

She snaps her fingers and electrified sparks of fire dance along the tips. "Forthcoming, you say? Yet he failed to mention that Mommy Dearest is a Fallen seraph."

No.

The power building in my hands wanes. The sparks on my fingertips putter out.

Female Fallen can't get pregnant. It's the reason male

Fallen bred with humans in the mortal world. She can't be Thorne's mother . . . can she?

"Did you know that angel pregnancies last over twice as long as human ones? Nephilim should be glad they inherited the human gestation period because *oy*, carrying a bun in your oven for two years is tedious. But I suppose by now I'm used to waiting. Hasty plans are often sloppy. I prefer to play the long game."

I swipe back through my memories, wracking my brain for every detail Thorne told me about his parents. The only real information he ever gave me was that he never met his dad. I hadn't thought to ask about his mother; I assumed she'd been human.

He'd done an excellent job distracting me whenever the topic popped up, luring me down a different rabbit hole with morsels about my family tree or a new detail about Whitehold. I now understand why he has darkness streaking through his aura.

The Fallen takes a step forward, and I retreat a pace, my wings skimming the ground behind me. I'm distracted. We both know it.

"I can see the rusty wheels turning. A cartoon light bulb might as well have just popped into existence above your head."

Her insults barely register. Instead of focusing on her words, I imagine her and Thorne side by side, the resemblance now obvious. It's only then I realize her wing-feathers are some sort of black metal from tip to quill. Not a bit of the vane looks soft or downy, but . . . metal, like the tips of Thorne's and my wings. There are other subtle similarities. The tilt of their eyes, the high cheekbones, thick lips. The lightness of her hair.

To believe Thorne had been abandoned by his parents like I had was a stupid assumption.

I give myself a mental shake. I can mull over and obsess about Thorne's lies another time. The most immediate issue is standing in front of me.

"I don't care who, or what, you are. I'm leaving and taking these humans with me. I don't mind cutting you to pieces if I have to."

"Escape might have been an option if you hadn't wasted so much time with this lot of garbage."

I flinch at her words. How many times had I been called the same over the years?

"You dislike my level of regard for these creatures?" Lifting her hand she flicks her wrist, gesturing toward where the remaining humans cluster like a flock of terrified sheep. Whimpers and cries burst from some of them when she waves a hand in their direction, and the group shuffles back even farther. I don't blame them. They just watched one of their fellow captives get decapitated by a power they never knew existed.

The Fallen chuckles at their fear. The smile is still on her face when I send a surge of fire-coated energy her way. Not wasting time to see how she reacts, I yank the shiv from my boot and fly at her.

My power strikes her shoulder, charring a patch of skin and marring her marble-like complexion. She regains composure a nanosecond before my blade punches through her carotid artery—the instant is just long enough for her to spin out of the way. The mirror-blade skids across one of her metal wings and shatters, leaving me weaponless, except . . .

Spinning, I flare my wings, blindly hoping for purchase,

but this Fallen is too smart for that. She has her own set of hardened wings and uses them to sweep me off my feet.

I land on my back. Hard. The tip of my wing hangs over the water, and an eel snaps at it.

I scramble to regain footing. I'm only able to peel the top part of my body off the ground before her wings cut forward and punch into both of mine, pinning them—and me—to the stone floor.

There's murder in her eyes. Yet another similarity between her and her son.

"Mother!" Thorne's familiar voice echoes up and down the tunnel. "That's enough."

I struggle against the pressure of her wings as she glances over her shoulder. Her eyes narrow when they connect with something out of my field of vision. Someone doesn't like being given orders. "I let you have a chance, but you failed."

"We don't know that yet," he argues.

Her laugh is filled with dark humor as she gestures with her chin. "I caught her trying to free these slaves. I think that's a pretty solid indication that she's not willingly joining our cause."

"I haven't had the opportunity to explain everything to her yet."

"I believe that. She seems disgustingly naive. But your time is up." Her burning red gaze fixes back on me, and her nails elongate several inches. The pointed ends curve to create crescent-shaped sickles on each of her fingers.

Thorne steps forward and places a hand on his mother's uninjured shoulder. His face is riddled with tension. "Mother . . . please."

Some of the fire dims in the Fallen's red eyes as she bird-tilts her head in his direction, then huffs out an annoyed lungful of air. "Fine," she bites off. "You know what has to be done if she doesn't agree."

His lips press into a hard line before he nods once.

The pressure of her wings against mine lifts, and I crab crawl away. Bumping against the wall, I clamber to my feet. A quick peek at my wings reveals several of the feathers bent and misshapen, but no further damage.

The humans have all fled at this point. All except Angeline and her mother. I hope the ones who ran make it out of this place—I truly do—but they'll most likely be rounded up and dumped back on that peninsula.

The child behind me doesn't make a peep. Her mother is on her knees behind Thorne, wailing for her little one. I spread my wings to protect the innocent, defenseless child behind me.

The Fallen—Thorne's mother—spins toward the open doorway. She casts her gaze toward the crying woman, and I think that's all she's going to do, except right before she steps over the threshold she flares her metal wings, disemboweling the woman.

On a gasp, I spread my wings even more, hoping to shield the child's view of her dying mother.

The woman's wails are cut off immediately. Agony paints her face as she tips forward and splats in her own guts.

"Mother!" Thorne snaps, but the Fallen's mirthless chuckles are the only sound as she strolls away.

If I thought the young man's beheading was awful, this is so much worse. I can't take my eyes off the woman's twitching form as a red puddle forms around her. Droplets of blood slip over the edge and into the water. A group of black eels whip into a frenzy.

I'm not sure if the woman is still alive. In fact, I hope she's dead. A fast death would be a mercy.

Forcing my gaze from the grizzly sight, I look to Thorne, words tangled in my throat.

He rubs a hand down his face then turns and slams a fist into the stone wall hard enough that bits break off under his knuckles and crumble to the ground.

My muscles seize, ready for an attack that doesn't come. I steal a glance over my shoulder. The child is still balled on her side, silent and most likely in shock. Blessedly faced away from the remains of her mother.

As my anger grows, the horror fades.

"Who was that?" I know what she said, and what my eyes and logic tell me, but I want to hear it from him. I want to hear him admit that murderous thing is his mother.

Thorne's shoulder and back muscles bunch beneath his long-sleeved shirt. He places a hand on the wall next to the divot he just created and leans heavily against it.

"Seraphim. Mother of all seraph angels." There's a heavy pause before he admits, "My mother." I'm about to lash out about his deception, but get stuck on the "mother of all" part.

"*All* seraph angels?"

His head—hanging low—bobs in affirmation. "In a way. She is the first."

Holy. Angel. Babies.

"Who is your father?"

"A human. No longer alive."

I release a brittle snort and see Thorne wince. Maybe he

didn't lie to me about that part after all. It hardly matters now.

I swallow, wetting my dry throat. Fury makes my words shake. "And why do you have human prisoners here?"

He turns his head to look at me. "For exactly the reason you believe."

The small flicker of hope that I'd misread the situation snuffs out, dying a fast and complete death.

Sorrow shines from his eyes when he watches that last bit of trust vanish from my gaze. My already rigid muscles tighten even more when I realize what's next.

Only one of the two of us is leaving this tunnel alive.

"Will you even give me the chance to explain?"

"What could you possibly say to make this okay?" My arm sweeps out to indicate the body of the woman lying dead in her own entrails, as well as the man's headless body.

Pushing off the wall, Thorne drops his head into a hand and mumbles, "Then she was right."

With a roll of his shoulders, his silver barbed wings punch out of his back, shredding the back of his shirt. When they fully extend, he straightens and turns to face me.

"I was hoping it wouldn't come to this." The words aren't cruel, but his voice is devoid of emotion. Like he flipped a switch, and a wall sprang up separating him from his humanity.

Goose bumps break out along my arms as I take a half-step away. There's only so far I can go with the child huddled behind me.

"You said I'd be free to go after I learned about your people."

His eyes narrow in irritation. "And you were. Who do you think allowed your door to remain unlocked?"

That throws me. He had Silver do that on purpose?

"But you didn't just try to leave," he continues. "You tried to take something of ours with you. Something that didn't belong to you."

"These are people," I argue. "Not possessions. They don't belong to you. They don't belong to anyone but themselves."

"They are inconsequential."

A bitter half-laugh of disbelief burns my chest.

"You think I hate them, but I don't," Thorne says, his tone chillingly stoic. "I have no more malice against them than I would any inferior being. They serve a purpose: to help grow our army and feed our troops. Beyond that, they are nothing. If you would only accept that, we could skip this next part."

His presence closes in on me, even though he hasn't moved an inch.

"No. These are people—deserving of life just as much as you or I. They have hopes and dreams. Families and friends. Why do you think you have the right to do whatever you want with them and to them? Simply because you're stronger?"

This time he does take a step toward me, and I have to force myself not to retreat farther. My only two options at this point are to stand and fight, or grab the girl and flee. I won't make it far with the child, but my conscience won't let me leave her.

"Yes. It's the way of both realms. It's our way."

"That's ridiculous. That's not the way of things." My voice comes out stronger than I feel.

"It isn't?" he challenges. "Look at animals—the strong survive and the weak perish. Human history has forged ahead since the beginning of time on the bloody backs of the oppressed. Look to the Creator himself. Does He not rule over all because of superior strength?"

There are complexities and layers to each of those examples that can be pulled apart and analyzed, but right here, right now, my mind is clogged, choking on equal parts fear and fury.

"Th-that's different," I stutter. "Just because that's the way things have been doesn't mean it's right. It doesn't mean that's the way it *should* be. You don't know any better because you were raised this way, brainwashed to believe these barbaric ways are the only ways. Relegated to the spirit realm so you wouldn't see the truth."

His voice drops to barely more than a whisper. Every word carries an icy chill. "Don't fool yourself, Emberly. It's your way as well. You can only fight your nature for so long. Someday you'll see, but I'm sorry to say today isn't that day."

He's done a good job distracting me, so when he strikes, I don't see it coming or have a moment to lament my end. One moment I'm there, and the next there's nothing but darkness.

27

"*Emberly! Emberly!*"

Someone yells my name. Darkness fills my vision, and my first thought is that I'm dreaming. But the pounding in my head is too painful for even a nightmare. Second thought is that I'm dead—but I dismiss that for the same reason.

My pulse thuds, whooshing through the tiny veins in my head and making me want to rip them out with my bare hands, but it's another confirmation that I'm still alive. I'm not sure I want to be at the moment, though.

There's a loud clang, and it feels like there's a spiky metal ball bouncing around empty chambers in my mind, smashing against the sides of my skull.

I release a low moan, but the sound doesn't stop. If anything, it gets worse.

My arms must be weighted because it takes a thousand years to drag them up and press my palms against my ears, muting the noise just enough to give me a measure of relief.

Releasing a sigh, I crack an eyelid. I already know I'm

lying face-up. The hard surface beneath me sucks the warmth from my backside, but it's the least of my current discomforts. I check my surroundings through a slitted gaze.

It's dark, but with enough ambient light that I can see minor details. I'm staring at a low hanging ceiling. It takes all of one second to realize I'm in a cell. Not a fancy room with a bolted door, but a real cell this time. Stacked stones make up the walls. I suck in air permeated with a dank musk so strong it isn't covered by the flowery spectrum air.

Very dungeon-esque. How unoriginal.

My name is shouted again, the sound adding to the clanging chorus of agony tormenting my poor head. I tilt my head back as far as I'm able, searching for the source of the noise. My upside-down view takes in metal rods stretched from floor to ceiling, but there isn't anyone on the other side of them.

Flopping over, I crawl toward the bars, ignoring my instinct to curl in a ball in the corner.

"Sss . . ." I want to yell for it to stop, but my throat is too dry and refuses to push out the word. My next "stop" sounds more like a toad croaking than an actual word, but it does the job. The harsh repetitive clanks cease as I lean my body against the solid iron bars that make up the fourth wall of my cage.

"Emberly." The word is barely louder than a whisper this time, and I'm finally with it enough to recognize the voice.

There's a thick wall separating my cell from his. It's impossible to see into the other area, but my eyes widen as an arm reaches out in my direction, patting the ground between our cells.

Blunted nails and raw knuckles. Dried blood covers

patches of rough skin. Have I ever seen anything so wonderful before?

Shoving my hand through the bars, I reach as far as I can, finally covering the hand with my own—the cool skin a comfort. A tear tracks down my cheek and splashes to the cold, harsh dungeon floor.

"Steel?" My voice is rough and clogged with emotion. What is he doing here?

"Thank the Creator." His hand squeezes mine almost to the point of pain, but I don't care. "I saw them bring you in, but you were unconscious and bleeding from a head wound."

"Head wound? What head wound?" I bring my free hand up and touch a tender spot on my forehead. My fingers come back sticky and coated in garnet blood. Oh, that head wound. "Never mind."

"I thought you said you weren't being hurt," he growls, the familiar animal undertones comforting.

"So it wasn't a dream?"

I don't have to explain what I mean. Steel knows. "No. It *was* a dream, but you pulled all of us into it. When we woke up, we confirmed we'd all had the same experience."

I want to take a moment to wonder at the marvel of my new ability, but there are more pressing matters. "Steel, what happened? You shouldn't be here. Are the others here as well?"

"You said you were being treated well." Another loud clang makes me wince. He must have hit one of the bars with his free hand. "You said that some Nephilim male, Thorne, wasn't hurting you." He practically spits the name, and the growl in his voice intensifies. Pushy male. I'm not getting any answers out of him until he calms down.

"Please stop hitting the bars. I think I have a concussion. Or maybe it's just a killer migraine."

"Answer the question, Emberly," he demands, but doesn't punctuate it with an aggressive outburst this time.

"I *was* being treated well." Probably not the time to mention the beat-downs I took in the training pits. "I couldn't figure out how to connect with you guys again, so I'd convinced myself it hadn't actually happened, that it was just a regular dream. I was locked in a room for the past week, but it was left unlocked today. I tried to escape, but . . ." My stomach dips and loops when I remember the humans. The poor young man and the mother Seraphim brutally murdered. The child who was going to be, at best, scarred for life.

"Emberly, what is it? What happened?"

Steel's hand tightens around mine, grinding bone against bone, but I don't let go. He needs the assurance I'm here, alive, and in the flesh. And I need the same.

"They're keeping humans here. I'm not sure exactly how they got them into the spirit realm, but I have a guess. I found a group of them. When I was trying to free them so we could flee together, I was caught. I'm not," I have to swallow through the dryness before going on. "I'm not sure what's happened to them, but they're not being cared for properly. They're being fed on. There's even a little girl."

I cover a sob with my free hand. Steel doesn't speak for several beats. Without being able to see his face, I can only guess that he's trying to tame his own emotions.

"We'll figure something out." The conviction in his words is firm, but it's not as easy as that.

"How long have you been here?"

His short chuckle is devoid of any type of humor. "That

depends. How many days has it been since you dream-scaped with us?"

Dreamscaped . . . is that what it's called?

"Four. Actually, probably five now."

"Then it's been about three days. I set out to find you the night after that dream and . . . ran into some trouble."

Silver. Her hunting mission. It had to be that.

"And it's only you? None of the others are here?"

". . . Yes. It's just me." I don't miss the pause before Steel answered.

"There's something else."

"No. I'm the only one here. Everyone else was still in my parents' penthouse in Manhattan, where I left them. I was on a scouting mission. I can only hope that by now they've figured out the location of this place."

"Whitehold. That's what they call this compound. This fortress."

"Pfft. How original." I can imagine Steel's eyes running over the rough white stone walls encasing him in this dungeon.

Steel's hold on my hand loosens. Glancing down, I take note of the blood caked and flaking off his knuckles. "Are you all right?"

"Yeah." I detect a note of exhaustion in his voice. "I'm fine. Don't worry about me."

There's nothing I can do but take his word for it.

Silence blooms between us as we both get lost in our own thoughts. My back starts to ache from the awkward position I've contorted myself into in order to reach Steel's battered hand, but I stay put.

"I don't want to be rescued." The words are softly spoken when they fall off my lips. "This place . . . it's dangerous. I don't want anyone else to get hurt or die for me. I wish I hadn't reached out to you and the others. I wish . . . I wish you hadn't looked for me."

I pull out of Steel's grasp before he can do anything about it. Leaning back against the bars, I fold my knees against my chest and wrap my arms around my legs.

"Emberly." Steel's voice is more growl that anything else. "I promised I'd find you."

"And as a reward, you get to die with me. What a prize."

There's a shuffling noise as Steel stands. His footfalls echo as he paces back and forth within his confined space. "You would have preferred I left you here to fend for yourself?"

"Yes," I say on an exhale.

He roars and then hits the stone wall separating us hard enough that chunks of rock smack against the hard floor.

"You should morph into one of your beasts to release your aggression. Maybe as a bull you might be a match for these bars or one of the walls." I'm only half-joking.

"Can't. They slapped some sort of jewelry on my wrist and it's keeping me from phasing."

I glance down at the bracelet Thorne gave me. The milky stone winks up at me from its gold casing. He said it would lessen the effects of my seraph blood around the Fallen and Forsaken, but now that his nefarious side has been exposed, I can't help but wonder what else it might be for.

I tug at the ring around my wrist, planning to toss it away from me, but it feels fused to my flesh. Fantastic.

"I have one too. I'm not sure what it does because I can still morph, but I can't get it off either."

"It only does as I said. Shields you from Fallen."

The words bounce off the walls from down the corridor. I may not be able to see into the cell next to me, but I can see down the hall a bit. Thorne comes striding into view. He stops on the opposite side of the bars from me. I stand and put several feet of space between us.

"How's your head?"

A low rumble comes from Steel's cell. Thorne's gaze only flicks in that direction before returning to me.

"Where are the humans?"

"Back where they belong."

"You're a monster."

The darkened lightning in his aura flares—the only indication he's bothered by my words.

"I came to say goodbye."

"Why don't you save yourself some time and kill me already? All this," I indicate the cell. "Seems a little pointless."

Thorne's gaze softens as he places his hands on the bars. His voice is quiet when he speaks. "We're not going to kill you, Emberly." I don't have time to be surprised before he goes on. "At least not the way you're thinking." A ball of ice forms in my chest. I want to have misinterpreted his meaning, but I don't think I have.

"Seraphim then?"

His lips press into a straight line as he nods.

"That was the arrangement I worked out with her. If I couldn't make you one of us willingly, she was allowed to take you as her vessel. I once told you we could never be enemies. This way we won't be."

Something slams into Steel's cell bars so violently, stone dust rains down on my head and the walls tremble.

"No!" he roars. He must be ramming himself into the bars, because it happens again, and again, and again.

I want to soothe him, but I can't show any weakness in front of Thorne. I certainly don't want to show Steel any affection and make him more of a target than he already is. Steel swears and throws insults at Thorne. I'd smirk at some of the more creative ones if I wasn't so numb.

"What are you doing with him?" I have to raise my voice to be heard over Steel's raging.

"There's to be a tournament. The Fallen who is victorious can claim him as their vessel."

Both of our fates, sealed.

"You can't do this!" Steel yells.

Thorne turns his head, locking his gaze on Steel. Any softness on his face melts away, leaving an icy shell behind.

"So this is the infamous Steel, the angel-born who's plagued our Silver's nightmares all these years." Thorne strides toward Steel, but his profile remains visible through the bars of my cage. "You look a bit worse for wear."

Barbed wire tightens around my heart, squeezing painfully. What I wouldn't give to be able to set my eyes on Steel right now. I let a bit of the pain leak onto my face since Thorne's attention is elsewhere.

After his rampage, Steel's deadly calm is eerie. "I know you."

Say what now?

Thorne raises his eyebrows a half-inch. "Is that so?"

"You can't have her."

Thorne's chin notches a fraction in my direction. "Neither can you."

"We'll see."

Steel's arm darts between the bars as he makes a grab for Thorne, who jerks out of range.

"Did you really think—" Something strikes Thorne in the temple, cutting him off. He slaps a hand to his face. His cool façade slips as he bares his teeth at Steel in a feral snarl.

The wound is on the side of his face pointed away from me, so I can't see the damage. I do notice a hunk of rock lying on the ground behind Thorne. A piece of the stone wall that cracked off during Steel's tirade perhaps? He must have chucked it at Thorne.

When Thorne pulls his hand back, blood drips from his fingertips. Wordlessly, he extends the blood-coated hand at Steel, and a blast of fire shoots from the tips.

Crying out, I charge the bars, but still can't see into Steel's cell. I hear his body slam against a wall with an "oomph," and then he's silent.

"Steel!" I yell, not concerning myself with the desperation in my tone. "Steel, are you okay?"

He doesn't respond.

"What did you do?" I spit at Thorne.

He turns his controlled gaze back to me. "Nothing he won't heal from . . . eventually."

I beat my hands against the metal rods keeping me trapped. All semblance of my control has crumbled. "How can you do this, Thorne? I trusted you!"

"You never trusted me. If you had, it never would have come to this."

With that, he turns on his heel and stalks away.

28

I now know why Steel was pounding on the bars and yelling my name. Patiently waiting for him to regain consciousness is impossible. I pace in the ten-by-ten box I'm trapped in, one hand gripping my hair in frustration and the other fisted at my side. I periodically call out his name, begging him to answer.

"He's a peach," he finally croaks.

Lunging for the wall that separates us, I lay my palms on it and hunch my shoulders, placing my forehead against the rough material. "Are you okay?"

"Define 'okay.'" He coughs and then groans. It sounds like he's trying to get to his feet. After a moment I think he gives up and sinks back down.

"Steel . . . this is bad."

He heaves a sigh loud enough for me to hear. "I know."

One thought kept appearing in my mind the whole time he was out.

Silver.

If she could retain some of her autonomy after her possession, maybe we can, too.

"I have to tell you something. It's about Silver."

Something cracks, and I think Steel might have tossed a piece of stone at the wall.

"What is it?" I imagine him bracing himself against whatever it is I'm about to say. Fortifying his heart against the pain.

"I think it really is Silver—as in *your* Silver. I don't think the Fallen that possessed her took over her mind."

"Impossible." This time he does shove to his feet. He grunts once, and then moves to the bars, rattling them out of frustration or to search for a weakness. "Fallen possession doesn't work that way. They consume the soul inside the body."

"Maybe not every time though. I think Silver, and maybe a few other Forsaken, are different. Thorne said—"

"You can't believe anything that psychopath told you."

I press my lips together, unsure how to proceed. He's not only been conditioned to believe it's impossible for Forsaken to retain their angel-born autonomy, but he doesn't *want* to believe it either. It's probably easier for him to picture Silver as a beast that inhabits his dead sister's body, rather than a transformed version of the family member he once knew and loved.

"Steel, I've talked with her. I think . . . I think it really is your sister."

"Emberly. Don't." Despair leaks into his words, impossible to miss. I hate to labor the point, but he needs to know we have a chance. That when the time comes, maybe there's something we can do to fight back.

"I wouldn't press this—I know how hard this must be for

you to consider, but we need to be prepared. There may still be some hope."

There's only silence from Steel's side of the wall.

"Steel, the things she knows about you and your family. How can that be?"

"Maybe Forsaken can access some of their host's memories."

"I considered that as well—assumed that was the case. But the emotion behind those memories is so real. I don't think that's something a Forsaken can fake. It's just . . . If there's a chance, we need to be prepared to fight."

He sighs, and I hear his hands slide over the bars before he sinks to the floor again. His voice is weighed with exhaustion. "Even if it were true, I'd rather die than live as a Forsaken."

I squeeze my eyes shut. "Don't say that, Steel," I whisper. "Death isn't preferable."

"Trust me, it is. Look at Silver—if that's her in there, being a Forsaken has changed her, and not for the better. If the worst happens, I'd expect you to do whatever you could to end my life."

"I wouldn't do it." That's not something he can ask of me.

Turning, I sit against the stone wall. Tipping my head back, I stare at nothing on the ceiling.

I chew on my bottom lip, steeped in indecision. My interactions with Silver over the past week churn in my mind. "Steel, what happened with Silver all those years ago?"

There's only silence from Steel's side of the wall until he says, "Whatever Silver told you is probably true."

"She hasn't told me much," I confess.

"Everything that's happened to her is my fault." Steel's

voice is flat and devoid of emotion. I always assumed some of his issues were due to an extra-large dose of survivor's guilt, but maybe there's more to the story.

"But you were so young. Lost in a snowstorm on the side of a mountain. It was a miracle either of you made it back unscathed. No one could have predicted that a group of Forsaken would find Silver before the Nephilim did. Blaming yourself for what happened to her seems a bit extreme."

The silence stretches for so long, I'm sure he's not going to respond. When he does, his voice is low. I have to strain to hear him.

"The Forsaken found us when we were lost in the storm. I used Silver's life to barter for my own."

I crawl over to the cell's bars, disbelieving my own ears.

"You what?"

The story spills from Steel's lips. The sordid tale pulls at my heart and brings tears to my eyes. The heaviness Steel carries with him begins to make sense as he explains how they were attacked by Forsaken and the life of one twin was bartered for the other. The impossible situation he was put in and the decision no loved one should have to make. The horror of the consequences of his choice. I'm struck silent, the breath held inside me when his voice tapers off.

"I ended Silver's life that day the same as if I'd run a blade through her heart. Even if part of her is still alive within that hardened shell of a creature, she's warped and distorted, capable of killing without remorse." He drags in a labored lungful of air. "I'm not looking for her forgiveness. I'll never get it, nor do I deserve it, but it's my responsibility to end this."

I don't know what to say. I don't know if there's

anything to say. What went down all those years ago was undeniably sinister. The right and wrong of the situation isn't as clear as black and white. The shades of gray that exist in their tale are multifaceted.

Silver's anger toward Steel is both justified and not, but one thing is for sure, he's tortured himself for years over what happened. Besides mental anguish, his emotional walls are ironclad, and he's taken the role of protector to ridiculous lengths.

In a way, he's as much of a shell of the person he could have been as Silver is. More than one life was destroyed that fateful day.

"Steel, I—" The words catch, but I'm determined to get them out, so I steamroll the knot of emotion lodged in my throat. "I can't say what you did was right or wrong. You were placed in a no-win situation. You were untrained children going up against supernatural monsters. There was no way you or Silver could have both escaped unharmed." I curl my hands against the ground. Gravel and dirt collect under my nails. "You can't change the past, you can only move forward. Something you'll never be able to do if you don't forgive yourself."

Silence fills the breach between us once more. His voice is low, barely above a whisper when he does respond. I strain my ears to pick up each syllable.

"Some acts are beyond forgiveness."

A fissure rends my heart. I ache to comfort him. He truly believes that forgiveness is an impossibility. If I could give it to him myself, I would. Especially now, when we're both facing the end. But it's not something I can force until he's willing to accept it.

I open my mouth, ready to offer a weak drop of comfort,

when footsteps sound from down the darkened corridor. Both Steel and I shuffle to our feet, wanting to face whatever is coming for us standing.

A group of six Forsaken march into view wrapped in armor uncharacteristic for their race. They each hold a single gold-tipped spear and swords are sheathed at their waist. This is the first time I've seen Forsaken decked out in weapons.

When they come to a stop in front of my cell, one of them breaks rank. Stepping forward, the female Forsaken inserts a key into the lock on her side of my cage. When it catches and clicks, letting me know the lock is disengaged, the other five warriors point their spears at me.

The door swings open with a rusty screech.

"It will be easier on everyone if you come quietly," she says before a wicked smile splits her face. "But we would enjoy the fight. We're not supposed to injure the merchandise unless provoked."

"Hey, you. The extra ugly one in the front." Steel rattles the bars on his cell. "Take me instead."

She only spares him a side-glance and a sneer, but it's enough of a distraction to give me an opening. Bursting from the cell, I take her out first. She doesn't have time to block my blow, and I catch her across the jaw.

She recovers quickly, but not fast enough. Taking her head between my hands I twist, breaking her neck. She's not dead, but she's not getting up to fight anytime soon either.

The rest of the Forsaken come at me as a pack, using their spears to nick my skin here and there, but never a full thrust. Of course they've been ordered not to kill me, and that works to my advantage.

I manage to duck under the strike of one and come up

behind two of the warriors. I take them out one at a time. Part of me marvels at how easily it's done and wonder if Thorne's lessons the last few days have made the difference.

Swiveling to face my next opponent, I'm cracked on the back of the head by the butt of a spear. I fall to a knee, but shake off the blurred vision. I'm ready to enter the fight a moment later when an arm wraps around my throat from behind, pressing on my airway.

"We were ordered not to kill you, but we didn't get the same order for him."

My heart jumps to my throat. The battle has brought me several cells down the hall in the opposite direction of Steel. There are three remaining Forsaken warriors. One holds me captive; another pants in front of me, saliva dripping from his mouth because my blood is flowing. And the third is at the mouth of Steel's cell. Long spear pointed forward, ready to jab at a moment's notice.

Steel beats against the bars and shouts my name. I still can't see his face, only his hands as they rattle and pound the iron rods he's trapped behind.

Closing my eyes, I raise my hands in front of me. The pressure eases up on my throat, but not much. Instead of letting me walk freely, the Forsaken hauls me down the hall, away from Steel. I try to call back, but the arm clamps down again against my neck and my words are cut off. We walk forever before I can't hear the echoes of Steel's bellows as he calls my name.

29

I'm fairly certain it's the same day when I'm led through the pathways under the arena floor by four Forsaken I don't recognize. Two at my back, and two in front. I have a weird sense of déjà vu as we march through the darkened tunnels. The sounds from above shake the walls and the ground beneath my feet. Fine stone powder trickles down from above as the very foundation of the coliseum quakes.

The merchandise is going to get dirty, I think as dust settles on my bare shoulder.

The Forsaken they'd assigned to ready me had all been human at one time. It was evident in their hair and skin coloring, as well as their stature. I wondered where they'd been hiding during the days Thorne had paraded me around the compound. They were another reminder of the lies he spoon-fed me, and further sealed my motivation.

After the initial shock, I didn't fight the Forsaken stripping and washing my body. Conserving my energy was more important than modesty. They'd spent hours scrubbing and preparing me, and I endured it all without complaint.

My skin was pink and shiny when they finally finished. My hair was brushed until it glistened, the top part braided into a red and blonde crown. The rest falls in loose waves down my back. An overly generous amount of makeup was applied to my face.

When I caught a look at myself in a mirror when they were finished, an ethereal, unfamiliar creature blinked back. Onyx-lined cat eyes sat above silver tinted cheekbones and bee-stung, pale pink lips. My skin radiated a dewy sheen unnatural for either the spectrum or mortal worlds.

After I was scrubbed, brushed, and powdered to near perfection, they dressed me in an outfit worthy of a warrior queen.

Even with a cursory look at myself in the mirror, I can't help but feel as if I was unmade and put back together again as a different being altogether. But I suppose that was the point. Seraphim ordered her vessel to be prepared to her standards, after all. I'm not meant to feel like myself anymore.

The sheer fabric of the white cape attached to the low back of my corseted breastplate, and the red overlay skirt belted around my waist, billow behind me on unseen currents of wind as I move forward. The Forsaken surrounding me have set a brisk pace. I have to speed-walk to keep up. Under different circumstances, I wouldn't be as quick to rush to my own demise, but I'm anxious to find out what happened to Steel.

We ascend another spiral staircase, going up up up until I'm sure we'll emerge into the gold spectrum clouds.

My nerves are locked tightly away, buried so deeply

inside I'll have to dig to unearth them. My mental shields are up as high as they can go as I prepare for what's to come. I don't plan on giving Seraphim the satisfaction of seeing me come undone.

I haven't admitted defeat, but I also haven't figured out how to achieve victory. My mind stalls when my thoughts trail to Steel, my concern for him outweighing my need for self-preservation. His convictions on becoming a Forsaken are more than clear—he'd rather die. With that perspective, there's no way he'll overcome the Fallen who claims him as a vessel. For there to be any hope, I have to make something happen before the merging begins.

At last, we reach the top of our climb. Only a door separates us from the open arena. The shouts and stomping of the Fallen and Forsaken beyond are hardly muffled, sending wild ripples flying throughout the air. The lead Forsaken yanks the door open, and I'm slapped by a rush of light and sound strong enough to make me turn my face away. I'm prodded in the back by one of the guards, my eyes watering as I'm pushed out into the open. The end of the Forsaken's spear pokes me again between my shoulder blades and I whirl, grabbing the shaft and yanking it from their hands. I twist the wooden rod, slamming the blunted end into the guard's stomach before the other three restrain me.

The injured guard wheezes out a few breaths from his hunched position before snapping his face up. Murder churns in his eyes as he bares fanged teeth. I don't bother fighting against my captors as they muscle me away.

A horn sounds, and just like before, the ripples obscuring the spectrum air clear from the coliseum. Fifty feet to my left, Seraphim reclines on a cushioned lounge, looking like a Roman empress swathed in a flowing white gown. Her midnight wings brush the stones of the balcony behind the chaise, and opaque fabric hangs above, shielding her skin from the gilded rays of spectrum sun. All she needs to complete the image is a servant feeding her peeled grapes.

I look down at my mostly white ensemble. Now I know who made all my original wardrobe choices.

Four Fallen stand at attention on each corner of the balcony, but appear to be more for decoration than anything else; they're practically buried in armor too cumbersome for actual combat.

I frantically search for Steel. I can't quell the anxiety that roils in my gut and spreads up into my chest, but I don't let it show on my face.

The arena floor is clear except for a raised platform set up in the middle. It's round and draped in red like a giant tablecloth with two wood poles shooting out of the center. Manacles attached to thick chains are fastened to both—a His and Hers matching set. Cute.

When her minions quiet, Seraphim smoothly rises and takes several measured steps toward the front edge where she can see, and be seen by, the crowd.

She shouts something in guttural Enochian that sounds a bit like "Sh-gra-nite-gu frag-ka," before sliding over to English. "Today is a special occasion." Her melodious voice carries, echoing off the massive structure as she speaks. "After millennia of searching, I've finally found a worthy vessel."

The coliseum erupts again. A small smile curves on her profiled face. She allows the ruckus for a short time, then lifts a graceful arm and the crowd instantly quiets. With a barely visible tilt of her head, she signals to bring me forward.

My gaze levels on her face as I'm led toward her. Her eyes sweep over me, familiar desire shining within. It's the same look I've received from Fallen all week as they sized me up.

"Where's Thorne?" I demand. His betrayal sits sour on my tongue, but there's a small hope I might still be able to appeal to him. This isn't what he wanted.

She lets out a low chuckle. "Not here to help you, if that's what you are thinking. He left an hour ago."

I ignore the dip of disappointment in my gut. It was a long shot anyway, and Thorne made it clear he wasn't on my side. I curl my lips into something very close to a snarl.

I'm still unbound, so when I reach her I consider striking out. How far would I get in a fair fight? Something heated circles my wrist, startling me from my stare-down with Seraphim. Another cuff has been snapped in place. This stone is ruby red and glowing.

"In case you get any ideas about morphing."

My fingers wrap around the metal, tugging and pulling as I search for a way to remove the band, feeling like a complete and utter idiot for giving her an opportunity to trap me when I was doing something as stupid as trying to murder her with my eyes.

Turning away from me, she addresses her subjects once again. "As tradition dictates, the ceremony will begin at nightfall. But before that we will all have the pleasure of a tournament. The victor will claim a rare Nephilim as their vessel—a Cherubim with the power of three beasts rather than one."

Her gaze slides toward me as she assesses my response.

Gritting my teeth behind closed lips, I don't give her the satisfaction of anything beyond a cool glare. This isn't a surprise, but my heart still pounds behind my fitted breastplate.

"Bring in the vessel!" she shouts.

Chains clink and groan as a single grated door on the arena floor begins to open. I can't see anything but darkness beyond the flattened iron bars as the door rises. When it docks with a clank, figures emerge from the shadows.

As much as I mentally prepared, I can't stop myself from lurching forward when Steel steps into the light. I'm immediately hauled back by two sets of hands. I strain against their hold as I take Steel in.

Scruff shades his jaw and the hollows of his cheeks. He squints, lifting a chained arm to block the light and survey his surroundings. I'm too far away to pick up the slight nuances of his facial expressions, but he's most likely doing his best to not show emotion.

Prodded in the back by a spear, he throws an angry glare over his shoulder before moving. He strides forward, head held high as he scans for something.

I know he's found what he's looking for when his gaze lands on me.

Even from this distance I can see the physical effect I have on him. Muscles bunch under his torn, dirty shirt and jeans. His hands fist and strides lengthen. He advances toward me, ignoring the red platform in the middle of the arena floor completely.

As expected, Steel looks a bit worse for wear. They didn't bother fancying him up, like they did for me. His hair juts in all directions. Blood stains his clothing where he was wounded. There doesn't appear to be a single spot on him that's clean.

But he's never looked better. Dirty or not, I still want to run and throw my arms around him.

As he nears, the intensity of his gaze sharpens. I jerk against the hands holding me in place, but they don't slacken. His eyes flare when he notices the Forsaken restraining me. His arm muscles constrict and I know he's dying to transform and rip through a couple of Fallen or Forsaken. The spirit gem on his wrist catches the spectrum sun and winks red.

It isn't until he's traversed to our side of the arena that any of his Forsaken guards attempt to restrain him. Shock squeezes the breath from my lungs when a rope lassos Steel's neck and pulls tight. The arena erupts in cheers.

Three Forsaken yank on one end of the cord. Steel jerks back, losing his balance and almost dropping to the ground. Lifting his hands to his throat, he pulls at the rope cutting off his airway as he works to free himself.

With a scream, I rip away from my guards and charge toward the edge of the balcony. The familiar pit opens inside of me and something deep within roars *mine*. The new cuff wrapped around my wrist heats, and the gemstone flares bright red. An instant later, a wave of cold air washes not only over me, but through me as well, dousing the burning fire that heralds my transformation.

Wings or not, I'm prepared to plunge over that edge to reach Steel.

I make it a half step away from the drop before I'm tackled to the ground, my face squished against the dusty stones and my body crushed underneath the weight of Forsaken bodies. I squirm to catch a glimpse of Steel. Out of the corner of my eye, I see him fighting wildly in the pit below. He's abandoned trying to free himself from the noose and is instead attacking Forsaken with his fists and feet. New wounds weep blood, but after only a few short moments, he's defeated all four of his guards.

A gust of frosty wind picks up the red ends of my hair and tosses it everywhere as I'm yanked to my feet. I'm now restrained by four sets of hands instead of two. Seraphim steps in front of me, blocking my view of what is going on below.

She grasps a tendril of my wind-blown hair between her thumb and forefinger. Her eyes track down my body and back up again, noting every smudge and tear. Annoyance flares in her eyes, and I'm glad her pristine little vessel is dirtied.

With a flick of her wrist, she directs the guards to haul me to the side.

Craning my neck, I catch a new group of Forsaken closing in on Steel. They stop several body lengths away from him. After discarding the noose, he rolls his shoulders, readying himself for another battle. The Forsaken in the arena have their heads turned in our direction, and the crowd has quieted.

"Unleash him," Seraphim orders.

Steel's gaze snaps to her when she issues the command. A single Forsaken inches forward, and Steel's attention is drawn back to the enemies circling him. The Forsaken moves steadily forward with her hands up in front in the universal sign for "I mean no harm." I don't trust her, and Steel's body language says he doesn't either. Her mouth moves around her elongated fangs, but there's no way to tell what she's saying.

I tense as she gets within two feet of Steel, but then he holds out his arm to her.

What is happening?

She removes something from her hip—it looks like a crystal shard—and then with a quick movement slams it into Steel's wrist, sending red sparks flying. I don't have time to be alarmed before Steel transforms in a burst of light. My mouth drops open when the brightness dims.

Steel was right; he doesn't just transform into a cow. Stomping the dusty ground of the pit below is something much more than your ordinary farm animal.

30

I will never make fun of him for this form again. The giant black-haired bull stomping in the arena and ringed by no less than ten Forsaken is terrifying. He's easily three times the size of a regular bull. His horns stretch a body length in each direction and one of his hooves is the size of a single Forsaken skull.

A cloud of dust rises from where he paws the ground. A few of the Forsaken circling him back up a half-step.

Throwing his head into the air and shaking it, he lets out a bellow that vibrates throughout the arena. The noise rises above the cheers and screams of the Forsaken and Fallen crowd. As the roar tapers off, fire blasts from his muzzle.

I can do nothing but marvel at the spectacle as an unfortunate Forsaken gets charred before my eyes.

Steel dips his head and charges the other Forsaken. Some scatter as others hold their ground. They swipe and claw at Steel as he attacks, bowling over any and everything in his way. He sustains a few injuries, but he's clearly coming out ahead. If I didn't know better, I'd say he was even enjoying himself.

The coliseum erupts in another round of ear-bleeding shrieks and screams when Steel stomps on one of their defeated comrades. The Forsaken's guts splatter the ground as Steel moves on to another victim.

A guard tries to sneak up on him, but Steel's reflexes—even in such a large form—are honed and lethal. With a jerk of his head he spears the Forsaken with a horn through his belly, lifting him off his feet. With a shake, the Forsaken is flung free of Steel's horn. He slams into the arena wall and slumps onto the ground. It's doubtful that killed the monster, but he's at least knocked clean out.

Why in the world has Steel never transformed into this tank of an animal before? The Forsaken are no match for his size and strength, and he picks them off one by one with hardly any injuries to himself.

When at last all of the Forsaken in the arena are either dead or knocked out, another burst of light overtakes his body and he transforms into an eagle. With a powerful downstroke he's airborne and torpedoing toward me.

For the first time in the last day, hope balloons in my chest. We may just make it out of this mess alive.

It's time to fully unleash the energy I've been conserving, and with a series of quick movements, I maneuver out of my captors' hold. It only takes a few seconds to deliver jabs and kicks to sensitive parts of their bodies and rip out of their loosened grips.

I'm primed for the short run off the edge—confident Steel will catch me and fly us away from this nightmare—when he crests the top of the balcony. He beats his wings and the flimsy canopy shakes with the force of the displaced air.

I don't have time to be impressed; I need to get moving, STAT. Muscles fire as I sprint and launch myself off the edge and into the air, swan diving toward the arena floor below.

Coming up behind me, Steel's talons curl around my biceps. He swoops down to cushion my fall—turning what could have been a jarring impact into a shallow swing. I hang awkwardly from his grasp, but if this is what it takes to escape, I'll endure it.

Steel flaps his mighty wings twice and veers away from the balcony. The Forsaken and Fallen filling the coliseum are a blur as we bank left and gain altitude.

We're going to make it.

A whip of fire wraps around the base of Steel's wing and a loud cry bursts from his beaked mouth.

We tilt and lose altitude. Our trajectory veers back toward the arena floor.

The ground rushes to meet us. Steel twists, taking the brunt of the impact. His grasp on my arms releases, and I bump and roll before coming to a stop.

Rough hands haul me to my feet, but I come up swinging. I've miscalculated the Fallen's height and end up throat-punching her, but it works to my favor when she drops to the ground clutching her indented windpipe.

Power surges in my veins, but can't be unleashed because of the stupid gem Seraphim slapped on my wrist. Fire pools along either side of my spine, straining painfully for release and reminding me of the first time I morphed. Even the cool sensation from the spirit gem can't quench the blaze inside.

I'm back down on a knee before I even realize what's happened. A headache stabs my skull, muting everything in the spectrum world except the pain.

Pushing through the agony, I force open my eyelids, searching for Steel. I spot him to my left, back in his natural form, using only his fists to fight off several Forsaken. His movements are sluggish, and his punches poorly aimed. One shoulder of his shirt is burned off and the skin underneath is scorched. It's only a few seconds before he falls under his enemies' attacks.

Shoving to my feet, I sprint for him while Forsaken bind his hands behind his back and then force him toward the red platform in the center of the arena.

Reaching his first captor, I rip the Forsaken away from Steel. I reach my hand forward to clamp down on the second one, but I'm jerked away and flung to the ground before I connect. The wind knocks out of me when I hit the ground.

Charred air fills my nostrils, and a scorch mark is slashed across my middle. Before I can think about regaining my footing, a hand clamps around my throat and lifts me into the air.

Seraphim's face hovers below my own as she snarls up at me. "That will be quite enough."

She walks over to the platform while I dangle in her hold. Stepping up, she crosses it and then lowers me to the ground. I don't have the opportunity to be relieved I can breathe again because she slams me back against one of the wooden poles with her deceptively strong arm. My back screams in protest, my wings fighting to be released, as my arms are bound behind me and around a pole.

"Let me go!" I scream.

Seraphim's backhand snaps my head to the side, and I watch as Steel is secured to another pole a single body length away.

"I may have to hose you down before we merge. You're filthy." Seraphim's words draw my attention; her face bunches in distain.

Blood has collected in my mouth and I spit it at her, spattering her face and the white fabric covering her chest with red. When she rears back, my laugh sounds crazed even to my own ears.

"Now we're both dirty."

Seraphim composes herself, throws me a glare, and turns her back. Walking to one edge of the platform, she raises her arms as the crowd I blocked out over the last several minutes quiets.

"Now that you've gotten a display of his powers, let the tournament commence!"

The familiar clang of rusty chains scraping against each other rings out, coming to an abrupt halt after a few seconds. Eight Fallen males march out from the darkened depths at various sides of the arena, ready for battle.

We never had a chance.

She simply wanted to give her people a demonstration of Steel's power. The only part that hadn't gone to plan was my participation, but it hardly mattered. Steel and I have both been rendered harmless, secured to these thick metal beams.

Seraphim rattles on as the Fallen champions move into position around the arena—spread out equally around the perimeter of the circular platform. Seraphim's voice carries around the coliseum's acoustics, but at least she's projecting in the opposite direction.

Ignoring her, my eyes lock on Steel. His head is bent forward, his body slumped as if only his bindings keep him standing.

"Steel, talk to me. Are you seriously injured?"

His head slowly cranes to the side. Hair flops in his face and I can only make out one half-lidded eye. "That form . . . drains me. I get a large burst of energy, but I can't sustain it for long." He takes a heavy breath. Even something as simple as that seems hard. "It's why I don't change into a bull very often."

I offer a watery smile. "And here I thought you were embarrassed."

The weak smile he shoots back doesn't reach his eyes. "Well, there's that too."

I have a vague notion that Seraphim has given the word for the Fallen to start battling, but I ignore the violence raging around us.

"Steel, please keep fighting. Don't give up on me now."

Sad eyes connect with my own. He knows what I'm asking. I want him to fight the merge. To fight for control when the Fallen tries to take over his body.

"Emberly." My name takes shape on his lips, but it's uttered too softly to hear. He lifts his head higher and then shakes the hair from his face so I have the full effect of his striking teal gaze. "Don't you know by now that I would do anything for you? I would search for a thousand years and tear down ten thousand doors to reach you. I'd rip the world apart and then find a way to stitch it back together if you willed it." His Adam's apple bobs when he swallows. "Please don't ask this of me."

His words rip me apart and put me back together. How

is it possible to be utterly devastated yet filled with incandescent lightness at the same time?

A hot tear streaks down my cheek.

Steel's eyes flare, his muscles straining as he pulls against his bindings to get a few inches closer to me. "Death isn't powerful enough to extinguish the fire between us. This isn't our end. If there's anything I believe in, it's that."

A million unspoken things pass between us in that moment.

"How can you say these things and ask me to let you go so easily?"

"Because now you know that whatever happens, in whatever reality that exists after this one—I'll wait for you."

31

A horn blares, and the intimate bubble I've imagined around us pops. The chaos of the spectrum world rushes at me on a growing roar from the crowd.

The battle among the Fallen has finished. A single blood-drenched combatant remains standing. From the look of the carnage scattered everywhere, it was a violent event. Various pieces of Fallen are littered over the arena floor. I can't see the entire scene from my point-of-view, but it appears like a couple of the Fallen are still alive. I watch as a Fallen drags himself toward one of the dark arena tunnels—he's missing a leg from the knee down and his wings hang akimbo.

The winner strides toward us, his hungry gaze locked on Steel—his victor's prize. His gray skin is a macabre canvas for the oily blood splattered everywhere.

Reaching the platform he jumps up, only breaking his stare with Steel when Seraphim directs him to face the other direction and address the crowd.

"Legion," Seraphim starts, "you have proven yourself the

most worthy. As your reward for faithful service in my court, and for demonstrating the superiority of your combat skills this day, you may claim the cherub vessel."

Seraphim throws her arm out with a flourish, arcing it up and then back toward Steel. Another sound wave erupts as the Fallen and Forsaken around the arena stomp their feet, roar, and screech their delight.

Steel has mustered the strength to stand tall with his head held high. Distain and disgust are the only emotions broadcasted on his face.

"Steel, what happens next?" I have to yell to him to be heard over the crowd.

He refocuses his attention from Seraphim and the Fallen —Legion—to me. "There isn't a Nephilim still on this Earth who has witnessed a merging and lived to talk about it."

In other words, he has no idea what comes next either.

"Tales of the process were considered too horrific to pass down through the generations." Steel's brow lowers, his eyes broadcasting the seriousness of his intent. "If presented with the opportunity, strike fast and true."

He means for me to end him if the merge happens . . . no matter what the outcome.

I'm going to throw up. It doesn't matter that my belly is empty, whatever digestive juices are currently burning a hole through my stomach lining are going to make an appearance any moment.

"The enchanter may come forward to start the ceremony!" Seraphim's voice booms, and the coliseum quiets.

A red robed figure makes their way toward us from the edge of the arena. A large hood is pulled up and over their head, making it impossible to see who it is. Considering their height, I'm guessing it's a Forsaken rather than Fallen.

Their steady steps are unhurried, as if they might be savoring each of these moments. It isn't until they're standing in front of the platform and pull back the hood that I see who is beneath the ceremonial garments.

Silver's eyes shine with satisfaction. A tiny cat smirk curves her lips upward.

Steel's cool finally breaks and he tugs and jerks against his bindings in a fruitless attempt to free himself.

A thin circlet of gilded leaves rings Silver's hair like a halo. She's swathed in a white linen dress. The hem brushes the tops of her sandal-clad feet. A completely ridiculous outfit for the weather, but she hardly seems to mind the cold. She's probably warmed by the fire of revenge burning in her soul.

Skirting the platform, she ascends on the side and saunters toward Steel. Lavender snowflakes collect over her matted black hair and settle on the ends of her eyelashes before melting.

Steel's chest is heaving by the time she reaches his side. His muscles bunch and strain. I know he's trying to morph and break free from his chains, but doesn't have the strength to do so. He's completely tapped out of whatever supernatural mojo he needs to make the transformation.

"The day has come, Brother. Justice will finally be served, and what a sweetness it is for it to be delivered by my hand."

Whatever fight is in Steel leaks out of him in that moment.

Legion steps forward, positioning himself in front of Steel. Silver stands to the side of them, facing my direction.

"Silver," I cry frantically. "Don't do this. He's your brother."

Her gaze flicks to mine and holds. "And yet I was his sister and he delivered a much harsher blow."

Without preamble, she locks a hand on both Steel's and Legion's shoulders. The deep, guttural language of the Fallen begins to fall from her lips.

"No!" I scream, knowing the ceremony has already begun. Steel's body tightens as his head flings back. The pain of whatever is happening is evident on every inch of his face.

"Silver, stop!"

She ignores my begging and speeds up, words pouring unfettered from her lips. A whirlwind appears at Legion's feet and cyclones up his body.

I yank against my bindings, bloodying my wrists. Heat grows in my body, excruciating without an outlet, but I don't stop my power from rising.

Twin tornadoes swirl at Steel's and Legion's feet. The Fallen is hazy behind the twirling wind that now engulfs him.

No. No. This can't be happening.

The whirlwind has reached Steel's chest when he forces his gaze to Silver and pushes words from his chest. "There's nothing I have ever regretted more than what I did to you."

Silver's guttural words falter for a moment before returning to their former cadence.

"I won't ask you for forgiveness, because I know I don't deserve it. Just know I've never forgiven myself either."

I'm a trapped animal, beyond frantic to escape my bonds as Steel's words continue.

"You deserved more than what you've become, and if I spent a lifetime trying to right that wrong, it still wouldn't be enough."

Silver's face twists into an expression I can't decipher, and it's only when the semi-transparent Fallen grunts a harsh word at her that I realize she's stopped chanting.

With a shake of her head she continues, and the wind swallows the rest of Steel's form along with whatever other words might have been his last.

Legion's form hazes completely out, leaving a formless mass of darkness in his place. With one final yelled word, the darkness ignites into a flame that rushes Steel, absorbing into his body through his skin and pouring into his open mouth.

My scream of rage and despair scrapes my throat raw. I choke up a wad of blood and it coats my tongue before dribbling out my open mouth.

Something snaps and I fall to my knees, my eyes still locked on the darkened inferno that is Steel's body. Silver takes a measured step backward, her face a stony mask, as smoke billows from his pores before clearing.

When it does, Steel has been transformed. His skin is leeched of its healthy bronzed tone, replaced with a chalky pallor. His hair was a mess before, but now any hint of shine has been dulled. Strands hang loosely over his forehead and ears. I notice red veins running through the whites of his eyes when he's released from his shackles and starts rubbing at the raw skin on his wrists. His lips peel back in disgust, and pointed incisors grow an inch, dimpling into his bottom lip.

I still have a sliver of hope stored deep inside that he's made it through the merge, but Steel slowly cants his head in my direction and stares down at me with the soulless eyes of a killer. I know he's lost to me now.

I thought I knew what pain was, but up until this

moment, I've only ever experienced a small echo of true suffering. If a Fallen stepped forward and split me open from nose to navel, it couldn't hurt any worse. And at the moment, I almost wish one would.

Even knowing it's not him, I can't stop his name from leaving my mouth. "Steel?"

Smelling my spilt blood, his fangs grow even larger. Blood lust blooms in his gaze. "Steel is no more, little lamb. My name is Legion."

32

If presented with the opportunity, strike fast and true.

I'm free of my bindings. Small puddles of molten metal are sprinkled around me. Did I somehow melt my manacles?

I'm not sure how I did it, and only have a vague recollection of when, but I'm not going to take my liberated state for granted.

Right now I have two objectives. End Legion. Free myself.

Whipping an arm out, I latch onto one of Legion's booted feet and yank hard enough to send him crashing. If I were armed with any sort of sharp weapon, I could have ended him then and there, but I have nothing.

With a grunt, I launch myself off the back of the platform and sprint for the nearest body. Between the Forsaken Steel took out in his bull form and the Fallen who were defeated in the tournament, there are several to choose from.

The nearest is a Fallen. There's a broken double-sided

axe lying on the ground beside him. The axe head is easily three feet from blade to blade. Not a weapon I would usually be able to wield, but I don't hesitate to snatch it, swinging at a Forsaken that jumps at me from the left.

The axe's sharp edge sinks into the Forsaken's skull, and the creature keels over without uttering a sound.

Shoot. Now I have to find another weapon.

A Forsaken lies facedown ten feet away, and I make a run for it. It's one of the oddly armored ones. Thankfully it still clutches a spear in its hand.

Perfect.

I'm not sure if it's a male or female because the head is missing and the body is covered in armor, but even in death this Forsaken doesn't want to relinquish its weapon. I give the shaft another yank and it finally comes free.

Standing, I face the next Forsaken closing in on me. There are twelve in total, including the ones trying to creep up on me from behind. A quick glance at the coliseum stands shows hundreds of enemies that would happily join them.

I can't fight them all alone. I have to figure something out.

Another flash of heat burns through my veins, and I gasp at the intensity but refuse to drop to the ground or release the spear. I grit my teeth and hold my ground.

The Forsaken stop advancing, leaving me in the center of a twenty-foot ring.

Are they waiting for me to attack?

I'm about to do just that when two of them step to the side and Legion, wearing Steel's body, stomps forward. He rolls his shoulders and flexes his fingers, probably getting used to his new shell. He looks to his right and left, taking note of the Forsaken on either side of him.

"This height will take some getting used to," he rumbles.

Steel's Forsaken form is changed enough that I can tell myself it's not him anymore, but that voice . . . it sounds just like my Steel. A clawed hand latches onto my heart and squeezes.

I lift the spear higher, directing it at Legion's head, telling myself to push through the pain. It's what Steel would want, after all.

Legion lasers his attention on me. Steel's once striking teal eyes are now pools of hatred ringed by bloodshot veins. He crosses his arms over his chest and tilts his head, assessing me.

"What do you hope to accomplish by this show of rebellion? You're surrounded. There's nowhere to run. No hope of escape."

My eyes narrow. The tip of the spear I'm holding starts to shake from my fatigued arms failing to keep it steady. It would be easier to be swinging and plunging it into Forsaken skulls than holding it still in the air.

"There's always hope."

Legion just defeated several of the fiercest Fallen and is also wearing Steel's face. He's strong and powerful. If I'm going to beat him, I can't go at him head-on.

Spinning, I strike out at the enemies creeping up behind me. I catch the Forsaken by surprise, felling one with the blunt end of the spear and impaling the other in the shoulder. The one on the sharp end of my weapon falls and I use the momentum to catapult over his head.

Not bothering to pull the spear free, I sprint for the nearest exit in my periphery. The gates are still open, and I'd rather take my chance in one of the dark tunnels than against a stadium full of enemies.

I'm tackled from the side and go down hard, absorbing the full weight of whatever nailed me. There's a grinding pop and a shooting pain. I'm half convinced I've dislocated my shoulder, but I don't have time to baby myself.

Flipping over, I try to squirm out from under the weight bearing down on me, but am sucker punched in the jaw before I can break free.

Through a hazy gaze, Steel's distorted face grins down at me.

I shake my head.

Not Steel. Legion.

"I like fighters," he says. His fangs grow to impossible lengths. A bit of drool drips down his chin and lands on my neck.

Barf.

"Too bad you aren't sticking around. You would have been fun to play with for a while."

Bile burns the back of my throat as I'm engulfed in another wave of rage.

I attack with the heel of my hand, jabbing it into his nose, forcing bone and cartilage into his brain. Snarling, he jerks back. Black blood immediately faucets from his face.

That'll keep him down for a few minutes.

It's enough of an advantage to shove him off me and scramble back to my feet. I glance around wildly, scanning the arena until I spot the opening nearest to me, and then sprint toward it.

The Forsaken and Fallen in the crowd roar with delight. Nothing entertains them like a good bit of murder and mayhem.

My eyes catch on a spark of light that doesn't fully register until I've zoomed past it. When my brain catches up with my feet, I skid to a stop—kicking up dust and sand and leaving a deep divot in the arena floor.

Lying on the ground behind me is the female Forsaken that approached Steel before he morphed into a bull. Hanging on her belt is the crystal she used to shatter the spirit gem.

I need it. I'm fully juiced and ready to explode. If I can just free myself of the spirit gem's binding, I can blast several of these Forsaken away and take off.

I'll never make it out of here with my powers bound.

In a fraction of a second, I assess the distance between me and the crystal and Legion, who is now steam rolling toward me at full speed.

I jolt forward, convinced I can make it there in time.

I don't slow when I near the crystal. Instead I pick up speed, hunching over at the last moment to snag the fist-sized gemstone and then using momentum to jump as high as possible.

Legion isn't expecting that move, and I sail over his head. The moment my feet have purchase on the ground, I slam the crystal against the red stone embedded in the bracelet.

A wave of fiery air blasts me, scorching the earth beneath my feet in a ten-foot radius.

Legion's cries of pain are loud enough to make me flinch.

Wings punch through my back and relief flows over me. I don't have to look down to know that I'm gilded in gold and ready for battle.

Without a second thought, I create an energized fireball. It glows and crackles in my open palm. Deadly.

Turning, I take aim at Legion. He's bent over. His back is burnt and charred, but he's still very much alive.

If presented with the opportunity, strike fast and true.

My mind chokes on Steel's last wish, but it's what he wanted. If there's even a bit of him in there, this isn't an existence he wants to endure.

I hesitate a mere moment, knowing I can't afford to, but not quite able to make myself end him.

He turns his head to look over his shoulder at me, and what I see in his eyes almost brings me to my knees.

Legion isn't looking at me from half a seared face—Steel is. He gives me a slow nod, encouraging me.

It's him. He's right there, and all I want is to run and throw my arms around him. But what he's asking me to do instead is kill him.

His gaze hardens as his lips form a sneer, letting me know that Legion has taken control once again.

Pushing past the pieces of my shredded heart, I cock my arm, readying myself for what comes next, when a ribbon of flame wraps around my forearm, staying my hand.

The fire licks at my skin but doesn't burn. I can't decide if I'm disappointed or not that I was stopped.

"Enough!" Seraphim's voice jars my attention. The end of her fire whip dissolves, and I spin around.

My stomach bottoms out.

Wrapped in Seraphim's arms is the human child I pulled from the water, the same one whose mother Seraphim brutally killed. Seraphim presses the girl's face into her stomach and holds a dagger to her back, positioned just right to plunge into the girl's heart.

I stride toward the pair, my gaze locked on the little girl. The child trembles. Her muffled cries reach my ears.

"Seraphim, what are you doing?"

"Forcing your submission. I tire of these games. And besides," her upper lip peels back from her teeth, "you've made a disgusting mess of my vessel. I don't want to end up having to re-grow a limb because of this little insurgence of yours."

A gust of wind blows lavender-tinted flakes through the air. I'm only a few arm-lengths from Seraphim now. The Fallen and Forsaken on the arena floor have backed away.

The wind buffers against my wings, and I think about how easy it would be to take a few mighty flaps and flee. I have enough stored energy in my body that I'm confident I could blast anything in my way, including the ebony-winged Fallen in front of me.

Humans have never done me any favors. I was only ever tormented and neglected by their kind. Why should I relinquish my body, my freedom, to save one of them?

The child makes another sound of distress. She's so tiny, only skin and bones.

"Where are the others?"

Nothing on Seraphim's face changes except the faintest upturn of the corners of her mouth. It changes her look from menacing to psychotic, and despite the heat coursing through my veins, I shiver.

"You killed them all?"

I know she did. I've witnessed the ease with which she ends human life.

"I'd say they died well, but that would be a lie."

"What do you care about falsehoods?" The horror of the situation—that she slaughtered dozens of people, either by her own hand or at her command—turns to rage, further fueling my power. An inferno licks over my exposed flesh. I welcome the heat.

Her head quirks in her signature bird-like movement. "Lying is not part of our nature."

The sound that erupts from my chest could be construed as a laugh, but is actually a bitter ball of disgust unlodging in my chest. "Thorne promised me I'd be released if I didn't want to stay and fight for your cause, yet here I am." I throw my arms wide. "Still a prisoner."

"Silly girl, I'm trying to release you, but you keep running."

"Death isn't a release."

"Of course it is. I'll inhabit your body and your soul will be released. Thorne never lied to you about how this would end."

"Deception is a form of lying."

"Now you want to argue semantics?" She looks heavenward as if irritated with an annoying child. "I grow weary of this exchange. I could force your capitulation easily. A few more minutes of this and I will."

Lifting a palm, I urge my powers to condense, creating a ball of angel-fire in my hand once again. The flames are so hot, they burn white and blue. "Are you sure about that?"

Her eyes flare ever so slightly. She isn't.

"I'm sure I can end this youngling's existence with a simple flick of my wrist, and you could do nothing about it."

She's not wrong. She could easily kill Angeline and I've stalled long enough. I knew what was going to happen the instant my eyes landed on the human child shivering in Seraphim's hold. What kind of monster would I be otherwise?

"I want assurances that the girl will be returned to the humans . . . unharmed and unchanged."

Seraphim dips her chin in agreement, the chilling psycho-smile back in place. "She'll be released and deposited wherever she wants to go."

As my resolve starts to harden, a strange sort of peace folds me in a tight embrace.

I don't want to die. I really don't. Every living creature is built with the innate desire to survive and I'm no different. But I never thought my life would count for much. Giving it to save an innocent is a more noble way to go than most.

"Legion, are you well enough to perform the ceremony?"

Legion lumbers forward, tearing the pieces of what's left of his shirt off as he passes me. His facial burns are deep red, but the skin has knit itself together. His back is not pretty. The damage there is much more severe. Skin is bubbled and blackened, split open and oozing black blood.

"It would be my pleasure," he snarls in my direction.

Seraphim's fingers twist in the child's hair, getting a firmer grip. "After you."

33

*I*t takes only moments to reach the red draped platform. Silver no longer stands on top, but instead watches from the side. I follow Legion to the middle, his mangled back leading the way until he stops and turns to face me.

We wait as Seraphim drags the girl over and secures her to the side of the platform. As a shackle is snapped around her petite wrist over her threadbare shirt, I half-wonder if the child could simply slip her hand through the manacle. But even if she could, where would she go?

Finally released from Seraphim's grasp, the girl sinks to the ground and rolls into a ball. The only parts of her visible to me are her rounded back and blonde head. My gaze remains on the poor child until Seraphim joins us.

"This isn't exactly how I planned this," she says on a huff. "But let's move forward anyway."

Legion stands to my right and Seraphim's left. Mimicking Silver's actions from earlier, he lays a hand on both our shoulders. His grip on me is biting, but I don't show it bothers me.

When several moments pass without anything happening, I chance a look around. Full night has fallen, the spectrum sky having darkened to a puzzle of dark indigo and deep purple splotches poked with crimson starlight.

The moon is large and bright, but torches are being lit throughout the arena. Silver and a few other Forsaken place them around the platform. The blue flames light the platform for the spectators.

The crowd is in an unusually somber mood as they wait for the ceremony to continue. Once the last torch is placed into the sand, Legion starts talking.

I squeeze my eyes closed, not wanting to see the look of satisfaction on Seraphim's face, but Legion's voice—even uttering the alien words—sounds too much like Steel's. *It's not him. It's not him. It's not him,* I chant over and over to myself. Even so, I have to take a look at his altered visage to remind my heart he's truly gone, or else I may beg for him to stop.

The unknown words he utters are filled with spite and hate. I don't need to know the meaning to understand the intention behind them. His fangs have shrunk in size, but still poke into his bottom lip on certain words.

Looking into the dark abyss of his gaze, I think, *whatever happens next, I'll find you, Steel.*

"This is my favorite part," Seraphim whispers to me conspiratorially as the cyclone starts at her feet and steadily moves up her body.

A tugging sensation begins low in my belly, and despite my former belief that I'm resolved to my fate, my body jerks, rejecting what's about to happen.

My breathing increases tenfold and sweat begins to bead at the back of my neck.

Legion's words spill from his lips—Steel's lips—every syllable slamming into my chest with the force of a physical blow.

Seeing my distress, Seraphim laughs. The sound is husky and soon swallowed by the funnel of air that wraps around her head. She's still visible through the wind, but her features are distorted.

The feeling of being pulled from my body intensifies even as the Enochian language Legion speaks pounds into me.

The pain is like nothing I've ever experienced before. I'm being struck by a hundred fists while invisible hands reach inside, wrenching my soul from its bodily shell.

I want to fall and curl into a ball, but my legs are frozen, captured in the cyclone making its way up my legs.

I don't want to do this. I can't do this. I change my mind. But it's too late.

My power builds as the ceremony continues. Molten lava runs through my veins, adding the agony of fire to the other sensations.

Whatever magic facilitates the merge reaches my chest. Across from me, Seraphim's form begins to blur.

I can no longer hold back my tormented scream of anguish. For what's happening to me. For what's happened to Steel. For what's happened to all the humans and angel-born sacrificed to greedy Fallen in the past.

It starts subtly but as the magic consumes me, rising over my head and making the outside world a fuzzy unreality, I feel her—Seraphim. Her essence burrows past skin and bone, seeping into the deepest crevices of my being, trying to harness the power coursing through me.

I'm complacent for only half a heartbeat. That's all I can stomach handing over to her.

I still have enough control of my functions to stoke the fire inside. Ignoring the pain, I let my power burn hotter than it ever has. Every lungful I breathe is like sucking in liquid fire, but I don't stop. Can't stop.

More of Seraphim's essence absorbs into my body. It feels like black sludge snaking trails through my mind.

I think of Silver, and I know I still have a chance. Seraphim is undoubtedly powerful, but I've spent a lifetime suppressing and hiding my true self—no more.

With an unheard cry, I reach into the deepest parts of myself, the well I haven't yet dared breach, and put everything I have behind it.

I detonate. And for a shining moment, the world is no more.

34

I'm a flame. A burning ember that can never be extinguished. A power like the world has never seen.

Fire skates over my body, undulating in waves and crackling at the ends of my fingertips. With a mere thought, I can direct it wherever I want.

Something strikes my arm, but it feels like the brush of a feather. Power surges, lashing out at whatever dared to attack. My gaze shifts in time to see Legion land on his back and then topple off the platform.

Silver stands wide-eyed behind him, mouth ajar as she takes me in. I'm so intoxicated by the power, I don't concern myself with Seraphim, simply content that she's no longer there.

I stretch my wings. Currents of energy flow to the tips of my feathers. It's glorious.

A horrible shriek breaks through my new utopia, scratching my eardrums. I create a flaming ball of energy as large as a soccer ball between my hands and launch it in the direction of the ear-splitting annoyance. It goes streaking toward the coliseum seats, exploding in a shower of gold and red when it makes contact, sending Fallen and Forsaken diving for cover.

When the brightness of the explosion fades, two charred bodies lie prone in the stands. Deep satisfaction that they were so easily ended permeates my mind, and a smile grows on my lips.

A small blossom of worry at my own blood-thirstiness starts to form, but I stomp it out. They deserve even worse, every one of them.

Fallen and Forsaken within the radius of the blast beat at small fires that have started on their clothes. Within moments three of them are set ablaze; they rush for help, but their fellow warriors flee rather than lend aid. Their anguished cries are once again grating to my ears, and I send several consecutive rounds of fireballs at them to end the noise. Just like the others, only their scorched remains are left behind.

"You killed her!" Legion roars from the side, his voice heavy with accusation I'm not going to deny.

"And if I could resurrect her to do the same over and over, I would."

Silver stands behind Legion and tries to catch his arm before he rushes me, but he moves so quickly she's left grasping at air.

Legion barrels toward me with single-minded focus and a war cry on his lips.

Without retreating a step, I lash out with my wings, swatting him like a fly. He goes sailing backward over Silver's head and lands in a heap on the sanded arena floor.

I march toward him, Steel's impassioned words a broken record in my mind: *strike fast and true.*

Between Seraphim's absence and my rain of fireballs, the coliseum has broken into a circus of chaos. Some Fallen and Forsaken flee, while others shove through the crowds and drop onto the arena floor, fighting each other on their way to challenge me. It's the perfect moment to escape, but there's a steady drumbeat in my chest that I can't ignore. It's pounding to the beat of *kill, kill, kill.*

I no longer want to simply escape this place. Instead, I want this White Kingdom to go up in a blazing inferno, and I want to watch until the last writhing beast is nothing but ash in the wind.

The flames dancing on my fingertips creep up my hands, over my wrists, and continue to climb up my arms. The fire spreads with every fury-filled heartbeat, and I'm glad.

Something skids through my mind and gives pause to my assured steps. The child.

The desire to preserve Angeline's life wars against my newfound bloodlust, and for a few stretched seconds, it's a toss-up on which one is going to win.

With a grunt, I spin, searching for her. My blood runs cold when I spot her, standing at the edge of the platform, free and unshackled. It's my first look at her face since Seraphim dragged her into the arena.

Her bloodless lips are peeled back from her teeth, the snarl revealing two sharp fangs. Claws extend from her fingertips and her skin carries a familiar pasty hue. Her blonde hair hangs in dirty clumps down her shoulders and over one eye.

She's a Forsaken. They turned an innocent into a monster.

With a child-like scream, the Forsaken rushes me. My mind trips over itself to reconcile what I see with what I know—that it's truly possible for Seraphim to be monstrous enough to have allowed a Fallen to invade the body of a child. That Thorne would have allowed it.

Fallen can't possess humans without permission. What had been done to the girl to make her give them permission?

With a flap, I launch into the air. The Forsaken barrels past me. She spins unnaturally fast and charges me again the moment I land.

Without forethought my arms whip out, grabbing the creature by the throat to keep its claws from raking across my face.

It doesn't take any more than that to end it. The flames on my skin lick over the distorted child-like features immediately. The Forsaken screams in my hold as its body becomes engulfed in flames.

Its throat disintegrates under my hands until I'm left with only char and ash dirtying my palms.

Oh my gosh. I killed . . . a child.

Not a child, I remind myself. A beast that took possession of her body and killed her.

It's not until that moment, in my state of semi-shock, that I stop to consider how I look. Am I the same person I've always been, just with super-sized powers, or am I now a Forsaken?

I do a quick assessment of what I can see. My arms are pale under the blue and orange flames, but that's not unusual. They don't appear to have the chalky pallor of a Forsaken.

Inspecting a chunk of my hair is useless. It's covered in a mix of red and black blood and coated in sand.

I don't release a sigh of relief until my tongue slides over my blunted teeth, my incisors only coming to a normal, dull point at the end.

I don't know how it's possible, but I'm still me, and Seraphim is gone.

I push the recent horrors out of my mind, scrubbing Angeline's remains off my palms.

My senses buzz as I twirl. Legion swings at me wildly with a broadsword. I duck and roll, narrowly missing the sting of the blade.

Popping up, I send every ounce of my power at him in a super-charged stream of fire, fueled by fury.

It ignites immediately on contact, and the impact sends him flying. He skids, flopping lifelessly over the sanded ground for twenty feet, bouncing like a stone skipped across water. He's encased in a ball of fire, burning whatever—or whomever—comes within ten feet of the blaze.

I drop to my knees. My hand goes to my mouth with the realization of what I've just done.

Steel was still inside that creature, I know he was.

If presented with the opportunity, strike fast and true.

The blaze coating Steel's body continues to burn. The flames go from red to orange to green as they work to devour every bit of him.

I know it's what he wanted, a definitive end rather than eternity as a prisoner, but regret still rips me apart.

What have I done?

This act can't be taken back and there's nothing I can do but watch his corpse disintegrate to nothing.

But . . .

His body isn't turning to ash like it should under the fire's intensity. His clothes aren't even burning.

My eyes widen as the wounds I caused on his back knit themselves together. Golden skin forms over the ugly ridges before it smooths completely.

His body shudders before it twists and bows. His spine arching into a U-shape, arms flung out on either side, head thrown back and mouth open in a scream swallowed by the inferno raging around him.

I move forward and into the blaze. The heat buffers against my skin like soft kisses, the flames wrap around me like an embrace, and it isn't long before I'm standing only feet from Steel's tormented body.

I have no idea what is going on. Nor do I have any idea what to do.

Kneeling in the sand next to him, I run a finger over his palm, whispering his name. His eyes pop open on a gasp. Teal oceans churn within his irises, and I grasp his hand, my breath caught in my lungs.

Something seeps from his pores and starts to rise, creating a black and gray cloud above his body, but still holding his shape. It twitches and arches along with Steel's movements until at once, Steel's body relaxes. The shadowy form above him releases an unholy scream that tears at my eardrums before bursting and raining ash down on Steel's body.

"Emberly?" he croaks, blinking up at me. His skin carries a healthy golden hue. The fangs indenting his bottom lip are gone and his hair . . . is still a matted nasty mess, but the rest of him is completely restored.

The inferno I created has dissipated. The ground below us is now a giant plate of cooling glass.

This time, I don't care that he's dirty and bloody and covered in gore.

I rain kisses over his face. Across his high cheekbones. His scruffy chin. His eyelids and even his eyebrows before he becomes frustrated, grabbing the sides of my face and directing me exactly where he wants me.

When our lips connect, a whole new fire is lit. It swirls between us, building in intensity. I swear I see fireworks behind my closed lids, but still it's not enough. My mind craves more confirmation that he's come back to me alive and well and for good.

At some point Steel wraps an arm around me and pulls me down so I'm resting on his chest. His hand tangles in my hair, catching on the knots and snarls, but the feeling of his soft lips against mine forces away the pinpricks of pain.

This moment, this one right here, is the one I never want to end. But it has to.

With a herculean effort, I pull back from Steel. His eyes blaze with irritation, and I bite my lip to keep from smiling. All it does is direct Steel's gaze back to my mouth, which is . . . distracting.

Also distracting? The ear-shredding screams and shrieks from the arena.

Our eyes widen as we come back to ourselves and reluctantly force ourselves to stand.

Some trained warriors we are. Making out in the middle of a battle is a sure-fire way to get yourself dead fast.

Worth it.

"Where's the seraph?"

I shake my head, not knowing how to explain. Now's not the time for the long version anyway. "Gone."

"Thorne?"

"Not here." I'm distracted when I answer because none of the Forsaken or Fallen are attacking us. In fact, they're all fleeing. The Fallen with wings fly clear of Whitehold altogether. The others stampede over themselves for the exits. "What's going on?"

"They're scared of you."

"Me? Why? Up until now, they all wanted to nom-nom my flesh or wear it like a prom dress."

Steel waits until he can hold my gaze. "I didn't fight my way free. I tried. I really did. But it wasn't going to happen. You blasted Legion—me—with pure, raw angel-fire. You literally burned the Fallen out of me." His eyes sweep over me as if for the first time. "If there was any question about your parentage, it's gone now. Only seraphs have the ability to wield pure angel-fire. And there's never been a being alive who could restore a Forsaken. They're scared of your power. Scared you're going to burn through them like you did me."

"Well, that's food for thought, but later."

"Agreed."

I turn a slow circle, making sure enemies aren't sneaking up on us, but the coliseum is almost completely cleared now.

"We need to free the humans and figure out how to bring them with us," Steel says.

"No we don't," I say, using my eyes to convey the sorrow of their fate.

He presses his lips together so tightly they almost disappear. His hands fist, but he gives a curt nod to let me know he understands.

"Can you shift into an eagle? Flying is the only way we're going to make it out of here. And we need to do it fast, before they realize I can't duplicate whatever mojo I used on you. At least not without getting super-charged again. Eventually one of them is going to get up the nerve to challenge me."

Steel seems distracted. He scans the arena floor, but manages a quick "Yeah, I'm good," before taking off. A few yards away, he drops to one knee, turning a body over in the sand.

The once-white shift Silver wore is now stained with black blood and sand. The gold-leafed crown has slipped to the side and is tangled in her matted hair. One side of her skirt is burned away, and the skin on that leg is scorched and blistered, as is half of her face.

I don't even remember doing that.

"Is she . . ."

"No. She's too stubborn to die."

I saw my teeth back and forth over my bottom lip as I consider the situation. "Should we take her with us?"

Steel's chest expands as he sucks in a breath. "We can't. We need to move fast, and I can't do that if I'm carrying her. If she wakes up, she'll be doubly difficult to manage." It's clear he's already thought this through. "I have to leave her." But even as he says it, it's clear that isn't what he wants to do.

"Are you going to . . . end her then?" Since Silver appeared several months ago, that's been the single focus of Steel's existence—to kill her.

Using his thumb and index finger, Steel picks up a clump of her hair and moves it off her face. Passed out, Silver doesn't seem quite as frightening. Her skin is still pale enough to see the snaking black veins beneath the surface. But with her eyes closed and pointed fangs not peeking through her lips, she looks a bit like a sleeping princess with her delicate features.

"No, I'm not going to kill her." With one more sweep of his gaze, Steel stands.

I nod, but lift my eyebrows in question.

His hand rubs his forehead. "If you can bring me back, there might be some hope for her someday."

That's a lot of pressure. "I'm just as likely to burn her to ash as restore her."

"Worth a try, though. That is, if she ever appears again." Steel cracks his neck and turns his back on his sister. When he wraps his hand around my own, a small flock of butterflies flutters in my stomach. "Let's go. We'll fly south. It may be a while, but we're bound to reach something eventually."

The urge to flee is growing exponentially, killing the butterflies mid-flight. But we can't go just yet.

"We have to take the orb with us." I use my chin to point upward at the star-like orb sitting on the tallest point of Thorne's tower.

"It's what keeps us from phasing. They're using it to bring humans into the spirit realm."

Steel's face hardens, reading between the lines of what I'm saying. This orb should not be in their hands.

"I'll get it. Stay behind me and we'll leave from there. Try to weave a bit when you fly in case they decide to shoot at us from below. It'll make you harder to hit." In a bright flash, he transforms into an eagle.

I take a deep breath and launch into the air, staying close behind him.

It takes hardly any time to reach Thorne's tower. The orb glows brightly. This close, the silver waves of its energy are visible as ripples in the air.

Steel swoops low. His sharp talons wrap around the stone, and my breath catches. With hardly any effort it comes loose and we're on our way.

As we soar unchallenged over Whitehold's wall and into the dark night, I think we might just make it.

CHAPTER THIRTY-FIVE
STEEL

We fly through the darkest part of the night. I keep Emberly in my periphery. She's struggling. Having never attempted a flight like this, she has to be exhausted. It shreds me. There's nothing I can do about it. I'm not even able to talk to her in this form. We don't have any choice but to press on.

The urge to look over my shoulder or scan the ground for shadows of Fallen or Forsaken never dissipates. My body is a knot of strained muscles. The sun is just peeking over the horizon by the time we stumble upon a ski village. The lights from chair lifts are the first thing we spot. It's not until we crest the mountain that we see the red, green, and white roofs nestled into the valley below.

I caw to get her attention and bank left, circling back the way we just came. I imagine she's cursing me in her head right now, but I won't be able to explain until we land.

I descend onto a rocky plateau, a short distance from a cave I scouted. Setting the orb down in the snow, I shift back into my form in a blast of light. For a single heartbeat

I'm nothing before I reform again. Unlike my shift to a bull, my powers reenergize when I'm an eagle.

Emberly lands with the grace of a newborn fowl, her legs shaking then buckling when they take the full brunt of her weight. I react on impulse, my arms shooting out to steady her. Her skin beneath my palms is freezing.

"Are you okay?" I rub my hands up and down her biceps, heating the skin with the friction. "You're freezing."

"I'm okay, just really sore."

I press my lips together, stopping myself from arguing with her. She's not okay, but there's nothing either of us can do about it at the moment. My first priority is to get her to safety. Then she'll be able to rest and recuperate. With the amount of power she expelled today, it's a wonder she's even functioning at all.

I force my hands from her arms, worried that if I keep touching her I won't be able to stop.

Emberly rolls her shoulders and winces. She's quiet for a moment, introspective, before frustration tightens her eyes. Blowing out a breath, she swats at a few strands of red-blonde hair that lie over her forehead before asking, "Why are we here?"

Right.

"We have to phase back to the mortal world to call for help. That's not going to happen carrying that orb." I tip my chin toward where the glowing orb is cushioned on the snow a few feet from us. "It's got to be stashed for safekeeping. A team from the academy can retrieve it later."

Truth was, I couldn't be more glad to ditch the thing. These orbs have only ever brought trouble down on our heads. The implications of its discovery and the stones Emberly refers to as "spirit gems" are going to be far-reaching for the angel-born, but that's the Council's problem, not mine.

"I spotted a cave. Give me a minute. I'll go hide it."

"Where's the cave? I'll go with you." Emberly moves toward the orb, her hands already reaching for it, but I slide in front of her, blocking her way. I'm not about to let her touch it.

"I got it." When she plants her hands on her hips I add, "we don't know if it's going to react to you in an unusual way like the last one."

Her hands drop to her sides. "Fair point."

For once she doesn't fight me.

I can't help giving her another once-over before grabbing the orb and jogging to the cave. I hurry to stash it, not completely convinced she won't keel over while I'm gone. After finding a hidden alcove, I dig a shallow hole in the hard ground and cover the round object, hiding its glow. When I rejoin Emberly only minutes later, her teeth are visibly chattering and her eyes have glazed over.

I release a curse under my breath. "Your lips are turning blue."

She slowly blinks, her gaze making contact with mine. "I'm pretty tired."

"No sleeping in the snow for you." I'm not going through that again. My heart almost gave out on me the time I found her sleeping half-frozen in the snow. She'll never know how traumatic that experience was for me.

"Funny." A shiver punctuates the word.

Moving forward, I lift my hand, taken over by the urge to brush my fingers over her full lips. I gain control of myself before I make contact, squeezing my hand into a fist and forcing it to drop to my side. "Can you make it a few more miles? We can fly most of the way."

She nods, but it's not convincing.

"I can fly us both."

"No, really. It's okay. It's just a little farther."

I transform back into an eagle, and we glide toward the town we spotted. Two mountain peaks stand between us and the means to contact the angel-born. Two peaks, and then I can take a full breath.

We're over the first summit when Emberly starts to wobble in the air. I fly closer, spotting the ground for a place to land. She's not going to make it. But I can't find a patch of flat surface. Everything up here is steep angles. If she can just hold it together a little longer . . .

We've just crested the last peak—snow covered gables are visible in the valley below—when she starts to go down. Panic seizes my muscles. I've pushed her too far.

"Steel," she shouts.

I let out a high-pitched caw. There's a patch of flat snow to the left, but she's not paying attention.

Thin evergreens have sprouted up from the white ground below. Her feet slap against the pine needles, and after a moment so do her arms. I make a grab for her with my talons, but once her wings clip the treetops, she starts to spin, and wraps her wings around her body.

She's bounced back and forth like a pinball from one spiny tree trunk to another within the shell of her wings.

She slams into the snow covered ground in an explosion of white powder.

I shift back before my feet even touch down, the foot and a half of surface snow absorbing my weight. Stumble-running to where she landed, all I see are gold feathers.

Stupid, I berate myself. *I should have forced her to let me fly us both.*

"Emberly!"

She doesn't answer as I drop down in the snow above her head and pry her wings apart. Her eyes are sealed shut. I don't see rivers of blood, but I'm still not breathing easy.

"I think I'm done with flying for the day," she croaks.

"Where are you hurt?" My hands are already smoothing over her limbs, checking for broken bones. Nothing seems to be protruding and she hasn't winced away from my touch.

Good. That's good.

"Everywhere?"

I huff out a half-laugh. She's going to be the death of me, but I can't say I'm sorry about that. "Only you. How about you consider giving me a day or two off from worrying about you."

"Where would be the fun in that?" She ducks her head as I help her sit up, but I don't miss the blush coloring her cheeks.

Gosh. This girl.

"Where indeed," I mumble with a shake of my head. "Doesn't look like anything is broken. Can you stand?"

Rather than answer, Emberly pushes to her feet, trembling like a leaf. No way am I letting her walk the rest of the way. And I'm not planning on asking this time. I tilt my head, eyeing her wings. Those could be an issue.

"Let's see if we can phase back. We might be out of the orb's range by now."

I wait until she's able to phase back to the mortal world before following after her. There's zero chance I'd leave her unprotected in the spirit realm, even without any obvious threats.

After being in the spirit realm for so long, the mortal world seems even more muted when we return. White on white and a blue-tinted gray sky. Emberly has her eyes shut, her face tilted toward the sun. She's dressed in the blood splattered white and red garb she wore when I first spotted her on the arena balcony. As she greedily gulps the pine-scented air, my chest tightens with the realization of how close I came to losing her. To losing myself.

But I did lose myself. I forfeited control of my being to the monster, Legion. And she brought me back. That hour as a Forsaken is filled with darkness and shadows. There's very little I actually remember, and I can't decide if that's a mercy or not.

"Okay, let's go." She shakes out her limbs and turns in the direction of the town. I come in behind her, scooping her up before she finishes her first step. She yelps when her feet lift off the ground.

"I've got you." My voice is gruff and it feels like I'm juggling pebbles in my throat. I start marching through the knee-high snow.

"Put me down. I can walk." There's no bite in her words. She doesn't mean it.

"Want to."

Her arms are already twined around my neck, and I catch her eyeing a spot on my shoulder to rest her head. I keep a secure hold on her with an arm under her knees and another wrapped around her lower back and rib cage. I have to force myself not to crush her to my chest.

She feels good in my arms. Maybe even too good.

It's barely a minute before her head drops to my

shoulder and her eyes slip shut. I release a silent chuckle when her breathing evens out. I don't deserve her, I know that, but it doesn't matter anymore.

This girl is mine—she just doesn't realize it yet.

"Emberly." I waited too long to wake her, but I'm not sorry. I could have walked around the world—twice—with her in my arms, her warm breath puffing against my neck. If she doesn't wake soon, I'm going to have to dump her in the snow or risk giving in to the urge to find somewhere safe and lock her away from the world.

She snuggles her face into the curve between my neck and shoulder, and I swallow a groan. Next, the tip of her nose drags along the column of my throat, and a full-body shudder works its way down to my toes.

Was that intentional?

Pulling back, I search her face. Her eyes are half-lidded, and her gaze sleepy, but she ducks her chin to hide a smile.

Absolutely intentional.

The amount of strength it takes to set her on her feet and move away from her is astronomical. I have to pretend I'm scouting the empty area to the right of her while I get control of my body.

We're in a forested spot on the outskirts of Mont-Tremblant, a small ski village in Quebec. I need her awake and on her feet so we don't attract too much attention when we march down the street.

I answer Emberly's questions about where we are and what I have planned without meeting her gaze. I hand her a coat I nicked from a chalet we passed when she was sleeping.

Thank goodness for trusting people who leave their coats outside with their snow gear.

It's not until I'm sure she's wrapped up in an insulated puffer jacket that I allow my gaze to track back to her face.

Putting her in an oversized coat did not tone down her appeal. She doesn't need me all over her right now. She needs food and rest, and perhaps a shower—I know how much she loves those.

"Where did you get this?" she asks, oblivious to my wayward thoughts.

Tilting my head down I lift a single brow, a smile curving the corners of my lips. Cute question. "Borrowed them."

"Sure ya did." She zips up the coat and wraps her arms around herself. "Mad props for grabbing something without waking me. Skills."

"Not really. You were dead to the world. I was only worried your snoring would wake the homeowners."

"Funny." She shoots me a droll look, but the color reddening her cheeks is unmistakable. I could spend a life-time making her blush.

Hmmm. Interesting thought. Maybe I will.

"This way?" Emberly points a thumb over her shoulder, and I pull myself together.

Mumbling confirmation, I stalk past her. She falls into step next to me as we navigate the European-style streets of Mont-Tremblant. The street signs and storefronts are in French, which is typical of this part of Canada. We hear French, English, and a smattering of other languages before we push through the revolving doors of a sprawling hotel lobby.

Guests clomp past us in heavy plastic ski boots and skis slung over their shoulders on the way to catch the morning's first powder. I keep my gaze sharp, looking for threats as we step up to the front desk. After a brisk conversation in French with the concierge, I manage to snag us a suite and ask for clothes from the gift shop to be sent up to our room. Emberly blinks back at me when I steer her toward the elevator.

"You speak French?"

"My whole family does." I shrug. It's not a big deal. Generations of our family have come from France, so it's only natural.

Her eyes are wide as we enter an elevator with a built-in couch and a bellman. It strikes me that this is probably the nicest place Emberly has ever been to before. It's easy to forget she's not used to the luxury most angel-born are. Accumulating wealth isn't difficult when you're around for several hundred years.

Anger rises in my gut at the parents who clearly abandoned her. If I ever find her father, angel or not, it won't be pretty.

The elevator stops on the sixth floor and we get out. I lead the way as we twist through long-carpeted hallways. We reach our room and I unlock the door, holding it open for Emberly to enter.

Passing me, she makes a beeline for the mini fridge, grabbing a bottle of orange juice and then a couple of bags of nuts. I head for the phone and dial the one number I have memorized. It's only seconds before I'm connected. I quickly explain the situation to the Keeper and am told a bird will be dispatched immediately to retrieve us. After ending the call, I drop down in the seat across from Emberly. In the short time I was on the phone, she went through four bottles of sugary drinks and three bags of snack foods.

"I was hungrier than I realized," she explains when she sees me eyeing the carnage she left behind.

"I can see that." Her body demanded calories. I'm glad she listened to it. Guilt twists in my gut that I couldn't get her fed sooner. "Help's on the way, but it's going to take them about an hour to get a bird up here."

"That's good."

There's a knock on the door, and I go gather the items I asked for. Emberly's eyes light up when I return with a stack of fresh clothes. "I asked them to send these up if you want to change."

Picking out the larger sized items for me, I hold the rest out to her. She snatches them up and hugs them to her chest. "Clean clothes! How I missed you."

"There's a bathroom in there." I nod to the door behind her.

Jumping up she calls over her shoulder, "I'll be out in five minutes." There's a pause when she enters the bathroom. "Make that ten," she yells as the door clicks shut.

36

I'm a new person when I emerge from the bathroom. A cloud of citrus steam billows out from behind me. It doesn't matter that I'm wearing sweats at least two sizes too big without underwear or a bra, or that my hair is leaving a damp spot on my back. I've never been more comfortable.

There's a smirk on Steel's face as I float in his direction. "Feeling better?"

His hair is wet as well, and he's wearing a thermal shirt and pair of sweats with the hotel logo on it. I should be annoyed that the casual wear looks so much better on him than me, but I'm not. I give him a prolonged once-over that he doesn't miss.

"You have no idea."

Lifting a hand, he scratches the back of his head. "I think I do. I was in that cell for days and it's not as if I had access to indoor plumbing."

Scrunching my nose, I gingerly lower myself onto the cushion next to him. "I really didn't need to know that."

The hand at the back of his head slides to his cheek, and he rubs the five-day scruff on his face. "You're probably right. But I'm going to need more than a quick shower to rid myself of the stain of that cell." He's staring at nothing, eyes haunted.

"Steel?" When I lay a hand on his shoulder, his gaze clears. "Are you okay?"

"Yeah, I'm going to be fine. The important thing is you're free."

"But," I bite my lower lip, wondering how far to push it. Steel is such a private person. I want to ask him about what happened when he merged with Legion. Was he truly all right? Can a person really ever be okay after having another sentient being invade your body and mind?

Surprising me, Steel frees my lip with his thumb. "Haven't I already told you your lip's too pretty to abuse?"

I stop breathing because rather than lowering his hand, he gently outlines the bottom curve of my mouth. It sends a sensation to the bottom of my belly that warms me in a completely different way than my powers do.

The feeling only intensifies when Steel slowly lifts his gaze, giving me the glazed look of someone who's mind is singularly focused on me.

"I . . ." Was there something I was saying? I honestly don't know.

When I inhale, I get an intoxicating lungful of Steel. All sugary male spice and citrus shampoo.

Oh, my. We are close. When did that happen?

The hand that isn't leisurely tracing the contours of my face is draped around the back of the couch behind me. He crowds me in the most amazing way as he outlines the shell of my ear with the tip of his finger. His light touch is nothing short of delicious.

Leaning forward, his nose grazes my cheek as he takes in a long draw.

My lids lower to half-mast.

"Mmm." The sound rumbles in his chest, which is now grazing my shoulder and arm.

My hands itch to touch him. To run up his chest and wrap around his neck. To bury themselves in his hair and pull him closer.

We're not in a life or death situation right now. I'm not overcome by the shock that he's alive. But I'm slowly becoming overcome by something else.

The bright light of the day shines on us and whatever happens next can't be explained away by a life or death scenario, blamed on the heat of the moment, or classified as a mistake.

Whatever happens next can't be taken back.

His face is next to mine, and if I tilt my head just right, our mouths will align.

He waits for me to make that move. To let him know this is what I want and to step out and take it.

Some of his scruff brushes against my cheek and there's no helping the goose bumps that break out over my body. There's no denying that I'm dizzy with desire, but my only confusion is why I haven't moved yet.

Sliding my lids closed, I release a quiet breath as I allow instinct to take over.

Soft pillowed lips whisper over my mouth. I can't wait a moment longer.

Bang. Bang.

I break apart from Steel on a gasp, eyes popping open. Adrenaline spikes and then—

Lights burst and I'm in the spectrum world. Sagging back, I punch the couch with my fist and groan loudly.

Closing my eyes, I phase back into the mortal world. Steel's rubbing his lower face in what is an obvious attempt to cover a smile.

"This isn't funny."

His eyes flare, pupils dilating before returning to normal. "Agreed. Far from funny. We were just about to get to the good part."

Heat jumps to my cheeks in an instant, but Steel doesn't see because there's still someone banging on the door and he's gone to check who it is.

If that's room service, I'm gonna cut someone.

Steel quickly looks through the peephole and then doesn't hesitate to throw open the door. He's shoved aside quickly, and I jump to my feet, immediately on the defense.

It's only right before Sable plows into me that I realize there's no threat.

"Don't you ever do that to me again. You hear me?"

I pat Sable's back awkwardly as she squeezes me to death. "Okay?"

The room starts to fill with familiar angel-borns, but I'm distracted by a sniffle. Forcing space between us, I look into Sable's face. Tears have collected in her crystal gaze. One spills over and slides down her cheek.

"Sable? I'm here. I'm all right," I assure her.

"I know. I know. I'm just . . ." Finally releasing me, she wipes her eyes. "Just promise me you won't do that again, Emberly. I was terrified when I learned you and the others snuck away like that. I will always have your back. Angel-borns stick together, we don't—" Cutting herself off, she glances out the window while she collects herself. I didn't realize that she . . . cared so much.

I give her hand a squeeze. "I hear you. It won't happen again. I promise. And, I'm sorry."

Her smile is watery, but she nods, accepting my apology.

"Out of the way! You're not the only one who wants a piece of that hot little thing."

Sable's knocked to the side when Sterling rushes past her and picks me up. She throws an annoyed glare in his direction which softens almost instantly. No one can resist Sterling.

"Yo, sis! You're still alive!"

"I'm happy to see you too," I laugh. "Now put me down." He sets me gently on the ground after two more spins. "And I'm not your sister."

"Not yet," he says and then winks at me.

Steel, who's talking to Deacon behind Sterling starts to choke on nothing and Deacon hits him on the back a couple of times.

I shoot Sterling a look. "Not funny."

"Was too."

"Best friends should get first hug privileges, not last." Ash has to push her way through several large angel-borns to reach me. She takes my face between her hands when she does. Her gaze bounces around my face and then runs up and down my body. "I'm so glad you're all right."

Now my smile is watery. "Me too," I admit. "Where's everyone else?" I ask as I scan the group for Greyson and Nova. I would have thought Tinkle would be here for sure, parading as a fancy poodle or something.

"Couldn't all fit in the chopper. Grey and Nova pulled

the short straws," Sterling answers for her instead. "There's a few Neph outside standing guard at the door, and the pilot is waiting for us."

"And let me guess, Tinkle didn't want to come without Nova?" That doesn't surprise me, but I still roll my eyes.

Ash and Sterling exchange a quick look, then glance at Steel, whose face instantly hardens.

"He didn't return to you?" he asks, looking back and forth between his brother and Ash.

"No. We thought he was still with you. But if he's not, where is he?" Ash asks.

Steel's lips press into a hard line as his gaze finds mine. A sinking feeling has already started in my stomach and only grows with each second that passes. And by the time a half-dozen have ticked by, I'm not sure I want to hear his explanation.

37

"What do you mean you left him behind?"

Nova marches toward Steel with murder sparking in her green eyes.

"It wasn't like that, Nova."

Her pointed nail sinks into his shirt when she pokes him in the chest. "You said he'd be fine. You said you'd protect him."

We're on an airplane getting ready to fly over the Atlantic, straight to the Elders' compound. After Steel and Deacon retrieved the orb and stashed it in some sort of box that concealed its power, the helicopter took all of us to a private airport in upstate New York.

They weren't taking any chances with me this time. When we landed, an eight-person team of trained Nephilim marched forward and escorted me directly onto the jet. My babysitters-slash-bodyguards are currently stationed in front of every possible exit, as if I'm going to try to jump ship mid-air or something.

I mean, I could if I wanted to. Having wings rocks.

Reuniting with Greyson and Nova was joyful right up until Nova asked where Tinkle was.

"The last time I saw Tinkle, he was dive-bombing a couple of Forsaken as a pigeon. I told the idiot to shift into a dragon and barbecue the lot, but he didn't listen to me. He was yelling about small packages reigning down the hottest fire or something. I was knocked clean out and came to in the cell in Whitehold. I just assumed he'd escaped and returned to you."

I keep my mouth shut. I was gutted when I learned my little friend was missing, and spent the entire ride from Mont-Tremblant to the airstrip in New York fretting over him. I'm having a hard time not blaming Steel as well, so I know where Nova is coming from.

"You know what happens when you assume?"

Steel rolls his tongue over his bottom teeth, pushing out his lower lip. "Seriously, Nova?"

"It was true when we were six, and it's still true today," she says, but removes her finger from his chest and turns, slouching onto the bench seat next to me.

Sometimes it's easy to forget how long the two of them have known each other. Silver's taunts about their romantic involvement rise up, whispering through my mind, but they are easy to push aside. In truth, Nova and Steel act much more like siblings than two individuals with a romantic history.

"We'll figure something out when we get to the compound in Farafra. Right now, everyone take a seat," Sable orders.

Steel glances at Nova and then at Ash. He gives me a lingering look, but he doesn't say anything before striding toward the front of the plane and finding a seat near his brothers at an oval table.

This aircraft is ridiculous. It rivals a luxury hotel inside —only with low ceilings. Although, it hardly matters, because a transparent four-foot panel runs the length of the cabin, letting the mid-day sunshine straight in.

There are two bedrooms, a full bathroom and stocked kitchen. And that's only what I noticed on the way in. I haven't explored the front end of the plane yet.

Nova nudges me with her elbow. "How are you doing? Really?"

Ash leans forward to hear my response. I lift my gaze to Nova, shaking my head slowly and whisper, "The things that happened in that place." I have to bite my lip to keep the tears from forming.

Nova's perfect cupid's bow mouth downturns. There hasn't been time yet to fill them all in on the details from the last week of my life. They don't know about the group of humans I found or what happened to them. They don't know Steel was turned into a Forsaken and that I used my power to bring him back. They don't know about Thorne, or that Seraphim even existed.

The truth is going to come out. I'm not hiding anything —there simply hasn't been time to update the group yet. The Nephilims' first priority is securing Steel and my safety and getting us locked down in the Council's compound. Then the questions will come. It's wishful thinking to hope I'll only have to recount everything once.

The plane's engine starts, and an angel-born pops into existence in the aisle in front of us. I let out a yip of surprise. He's dressed in all-black tactical gear like the rest of my Neph babysitters. Without acknowledging us, he presses a hand to the communication device wrapped around his ear and says, "We're clear."

Flying should in no way be frightening to me, but my stomach dips when we shoot down the runway and take off. I've never been on a plane before, but I try not to let that show. Once we level off, the pilot announces over a speaker that our total travel time will be a whopping twenty hours, with one re-fueling stop when we reach land on the other side of the ocean.

We're only an hour into the flight when Sable comes up to me, tapping my shoulder. I'm sitting at a table with Sterling, Greyson, Nova, and Ash, munching on cheese and nuts. We're all laughing at Sterling's failed attempts to throw grapes into the air and catch them in his mouth.

Sable tips her head to the side, where Deacon and Steel wait behind me. "We need to talk."

Easing out of the seat, I follow Sable and the guys into the plane's private conference room.

"What's up?" I ask after I've dropped into one of the padded leather seats. Steel takes the one beside me and Deacon and Sable find their own seats on the opposite side of an oblong table.

"We have Malachi on the line. We want to hear as much of your story as you can recount while it's still fresh." Sable leans forward, propping her elbows on the table in front of her. Her hands fold under her chin. "I know you two are probably exhausted and need a good solid rest, and I'd like you to do just that when we're done here. But it will be tremendously helpful if you can tell us as much as possible right now. With enough information, the Council might be able to mount an attack on this Whitehold before we even touch down at the base."

I wasn't looking forward to this, but I'm ready . . . kinda .
. . sorta.

"Who's Malachi?" I ask.

"The cherub Elder."

"He leads the Council," Steel adds with a curled lip. "In
an unofficial capacity, of course. Officially, all the Elders
have equal power."

"Steel," Deacon warns.

"Common knowledge, man. I'm not saying anything that
everyone already doesn't know."

Sable clears her throat. "Remember we talked about all
the different Elders?"

"In my defense, I didn't think I'd actually be meeting
them, so . . ." I trail off when Sable's mouth tightens and eyes
narrow at the reminder of our deception. "Um, how about
you give me a quick refresher? Please?"

"The other members and their lines are," she takes a
breath and then spits them all out at once. "Draven of the
thrones, Zara of the dominions, Sorcha of the virtues, Lyra
of the powers, Arien of the rulers, and Riven of the
archangels."

Yeah, I'm not going to remember that, but I paste on a
smile anyway. "Thanks."

"We're just meeting with Malachi right now. He'll fill in
the rest of the Council until we can talk to them in person."

"How are we—"

Deacon grabs a remote on the ledge behind him and hits
a button, revealing a screen in the wall. Immediately, it
flickers to life. The image of a man from the chest up fills
the display. He's looking down, seemingly writing something while he waits for us.

"Never mind," I mumble.

His head lifts. Gray eyes instantly connect with mine. It's creepy. And what throws me for another loop is he's old. Not in a decrepit "Grandpa's-gonna-die-any-day-now" way. More of an attractive "don't-you-know-I'm-Brad-Pitt-and-I-only-get-better-looking-with-age" kind of way.

It's just . . . shocking. I've never seen a Nephilim look older than mid-thirties. This man looks like he could be in his early fifties. Although guessing his actual age would be impossible.

"This must be the elusive Emberly."

His eyes crinkle in the corners when he smiles. His full head of black hair is only peppered with gray near his temples.

"I wish this could have waited until we were face to face, but from the reports I've received, time is somewhat of the essence."

I gulp. Despite his smile, the authoritative vibe this guy throws off is strong. Even via teleconference. I imagine being in his presence is going to be that much more intimidating.

"Yes . . . sir?"

He chuckles. "None of that. Call me Kai. And please, start from the very beginning."

38

*I*t takes a solid two hours with minimal interruptions to recall everything from the last week. I don't spare a smidgen of detail. Steel jumps in here and there when they ask about his experiences. Now it's all out on the table. They know about Thorne and his claims that I'm descended from a seraph. About the orb and the hellhounds called barghest. I describe as much as I can remember about Whitehold and its infrastructure. I tell them about the humans and Seraphim. They even know about my dreamscaping. And finally, Steel and I tag-team the part about how he merged with a Fallen and became a Forsaken until I blasted him with enough pure angel-fire to burn the Fallen out of him.

I pay extra attention to Malachi's reaction throughout, trying to see through the cracks in his façade. I have a pretty good nose for detecting frauds—if I don't count Thorne, that is—so when I'm finished I've determined there's either a lot the Council didn't know about or he's a very good liar. Both options are disturbing in different ways.

The room is silent. Malachi's hands are steepled in front of his mouth while he considers everything. Sable's eyes are wide and even Deacon looks a bit shaken.

Taking a deep breath, Malachi sits back in his chair, folding his arms across his chest before speaking.

"So in a nutshell, there's a seraph Fallen we didn't know about who has a super-powered kid, but she probably died when she tried to merge with you. Steel spent an hour as a Forsaken, there's a secret enemy compound we didn't know about, and there are magic stones that can manipulate the known rules that govern this world and the other?"

I shrug a single shoulder. "I guess those are the highlights."

"And you've learned some pretty impressive things about yourself as well."

Another shrug.

Pressing his lips together, he inhales and exhales through his nose. "All right."

A beat goes by. Then another.

Um. That's it?

Steel leans forward, settling his forearms on the table. He's moved ever so slightly closer to me throughout the last couple hours. His thigh rubs against mine whenever one of us moves. It's . . . nice. Comforting.

"So what happens now?" He takes the words right out of my mouth.

Mirroring Steel, Malachi sits forward.

"Now, I brief the rest of the Council." He turns his gaze to Sable. "Make sure to get as much information about the location of that compound as you can. I'll need it as soon as possible."

Sable's eyes flick to Steel. He gives a single nod.

"Give me a map and I'll show you the area. I'll probably be able to pinpoint it within a fifty-mile radius."

"Good," Malachi says. "Emberly, I'm looking forward to meeting you in person." He reaches forward and the screen goes black.

Alrighty then.

"Steel, can you please stay with Deacon and figure out that location? I'll get Emberly settled into one of the staterooms. She may not have very much time to rest when we get to Egypt."

"Sure." He swivels in his seat to watch me rise and follow Sable. "Em?" I'm halfway out the door when he calls for me. I look over my shoulder at him. "I'll see you soon, okay?"

My brow furrows. That's an odd thing to say.

"Great." I throw him a thumbs-up because apparently I'm the world's biggest weirdo. Turning, I scurry after Sable, not wanting to see Steel's reaction. His chuckle dogs me as the door latches with a click.

The plane is quiet. Everyone is doing their own thing. The only one who even looks up as we pass is Greyson.

"Where you headed?" he asks.

"I'm going to show Emberly the stateroom so she can sleep."

Greyson unfolds from his seat, setting aside the crossword he was working on. "I'll take her."

"You sure?"

"You guys," I say, "I'm cool heading back there on my own."

"Naw, it's okay. I've got this." He tips his head and says, "This way."

Sable throws a wave and heads back toward the conference room to rejoin Deacon and Steel.

There are two doors at the back of the plane. When we reach them, Grey loiters for a moment, and I wait patiently. We both know I didn't need an escort back here.

"Emberly, I'm really glad you're all right."

"Yeah, me too." I offer Greyson a smile, not quite sure what's going on.

He shifts his weight from foot to foot, looking unsure. I'm not used to seeing him like this. If there's anything the Durand family has in spades, it's confidence.

"Is something wrong?" I ask.

"Yes. No. Not really. It's just . . ." He plows a hand through his hair. "This is my fault. I can't tell you how sorry I am."

I blink back at him.

"What do you mean? You don't have anything to apologize for."

He fidgets with his hands, his eyes downcast. "Yes, I do. It was *my* idea to go after Steel. You never would have ended up in that place if we'd only gone to someone with authority first. Thinking we could handle this on our own was stupid. *I* was stupid."

I'm not really a touchy-feely kinda girl, but I lay a hand on Grey's shoulder, hoping to offer him some comfort.

"Grey." I wait until he lifts his gaze and then give his shoulder a squeeze before letting my hand drop. "We all made that decision together. Just because you brought it up first doesn't mean that everything that went wrong after is your fault. Silver was gunning for me. If she hadn't taken me then, she would have found a way eventually."

Greyson's eyes harden when I mention his sister's name. "If I ever see her again, I'm going to kill her."

Whoa. I mean, I get it. Silver has done plenty to earn her

brother's scorn, but Greyson's not bloodthirsty. Concern furrows my brow.

"There's something you need to know about Silver." I pause for a moment, unsure how to proceed. "She's not a Fallen."

His head tilts and mouth pinches. "I know. She's a Forsaken."

I'm going about this all wrong.

"No, I mean she's still in there. As in, it's still your sister, kinda. The Fallen that tried to possess her never took over. Or at least not fully." Pulling my bottom lip into my mouth, I bite down, debating if I should tell him she might be able to be restored. He should know, but there's a solid chance it's going to give him false hope. Sucking in a breath, I release it slowly before going on. "I might be able to bring her back."

Greyson is already shaking his head. "No. That's not possible. She's gone."

"That's what I thought about Steel too."

I take a few short minutes to give Greyson a high-level recap of what happened to Steel and how I was able to restore him.

"If it was possible with Steel, it may be with Silver as well," I finish.

His face is washed in awe. "Emberly, that type of power is . . . unbelievable." He takes a few seconds to let it set in, and then a line appears between his eyes. "Have you already told the Council?"

I nod. "I just told Malachi."

He presses his lips together and the crease between his eyes deepens. "I guess it was unavoidable."

"You think I should have lied about it?" I'm surprised.

"No, no, it's just . . . that's a powerful ability."

I shrug. "It may have been a one-off."

"I guess time will tell."

I sway a little when the plane bounces from turbulence.

"Shoot, you need to rest. I'm sorry. The room is right through here." He points at the door to my left. "We can talk later. I'll make sure you won't be bothered until we need to get ready to land."

"Unless you hear something about Tinkle. I'll expect one of you to wake me for that."

The ghost of a smile settles on his face. It's not much, but it's something. I know he's carrying guilt he shouldn't, and this news about Silver will be a lot to digest. "Yeah, for sure. Now get some rest."

"Will do."

Greyson leaves, and I turn the handle and enter the room carefully. Keeping the lights off, I slip off my borrowed sneakers and slide between the covers. The sheets feel like clouds, soft and cool. It's been several days since I've slept in an actual bed. Three, I think, but I'm not even sure. I've become soft at the academy and crave a real mattress now.

I release a small moan of pleasure when my head drops to the pillow. The buzz of the plane's engine along with the rhythmic rocking lulls me to sleep almost immediately.

It must be hours later when I finally wake because my body feels refreshed. Refreshed and toasty warm.

Especially my back.

And my neck.

Warm puffs of hair tickle the short hairs at my nape and I come fully awake.

Citrus. Pine. Sugar.

Steel's cuddled behind me. Arm thrown over my waist. Chest flush against my spine. Face half-buried in my hair. Lips only a whisper away from my neck.

Mmm. Spooning is nice.

I should leave. I'm going to leave. Any second now I'm going to slide out of this bed and get up.

"Your thinking is waking me up. So stop." Steel's sleep-heavy timbre sounds like gravel and grit and sends a shiver up my spine. Tightening his arm, he drags me even closer, nuzzling the back of my neck and releasing a contented hum.

It may be my imagination, but the slashes on either side of my spine where my wings release tingle.

The thought crosses my mind that maybe I should just snuggle in and enjoy the moment, but the longer I'm awake, the more reality sinks in, the more I think about that line we almost crossed in the hotel in Mont-Tremblant, and the more I realize how much I need clarity right now rather than our usual melee of mixed signals.

Steel's breathing has leveled out again, and I think he must have fallen back asleep. I gingerly grasp the wrist lying against my stomach and lift his arm. I've only raised his hand a few inches when a growl comes from his chest.

Shaking off my hold, his hand snakes over my ribs and clamps down.

"What are you doing here, Steel?"

"I told you I'd see you soon. Had to keep my promise."

This guy.

"Steel. Let me up." My voice is firm and full of fake displeasure.

He grumbles something into my hair.

"What?"

"Dreamt about this for days. Need it."

"Dreamt? You're still having dreams about me?"

My body stiffens as my muscles seize. He mentioned his dreams to me before, but wouldn't elaborate.

"Not one of *those* dreams. I didn't mean it in a literal way." Groaning, his hand slides away as he rolls onto his back.

Flipping, I push to my knees and stare down at him. He rubs his face, not looking half as refreshed as I feel.

"Steel, tell me about the dreams. The real ones. The ones you mentioned when we were looking for Blaze and Aurora." I'm speaking softly, but my tone doesn't leave room for argument. It's time, and I want to know everything.

Steel peels his hand from his face and shoves himself to a seated position, his back resting against the headboard.

He's completely nude. At least from the waist up. The covers hide the rest of him.

"Why are you naked?" I squawk. "Did you honestly climb into bed with me with no clothes?"

Steel didn't just step over the line, he leapt over it . . . in the buff.

He looks down at himself, as if just now noticing his bareness. "I'm not naked. Here, look."

He starts to lift the covers off himself, and I tumble from the bed in my last attempt to shield my face. Steel's dark chuckle fills the small space. He rustles around and then calls to me.

"Come on back up. I'm covered now."

I peek over the top of the bed, my gaze landing on Steel in the darkened room. His long-sleeved shirt is back in place and he's also wearing a pair of jeans. Most likely one of his brothers', because they look a little tight—not that I mind. I drag my eyes from his lower half and meet his gaze.

"Since you're not going to let me sleep anymore," he says. "We should talk."

Clearing my throat, I lower myself back to the bed. Legs crossed as I face him.

Leaning over, he flicks a switch and a lamp bolted to the wall turns on. The bulb is dim, but with our Neph eyesight, it's more than enough light to see by.

"Your dreams," I prompt.

"Right."

Steel rubs the back of his neck, looking nervous. It's not a look I see on him often, but I find it oddly endearing. Leaning forward, I brush my fingers over the top of his hand, wanting him to know I'm a safe person for him to talk to.

"Before I start, I want you to know that I'm not sure what any of this means, or how it's even possible. I haven't told anyone else." He gives me a pointed look that I take to mean he'd like this conversation to stay between us.

I nod my acceptance and it seems as if a drop of tension leaves his body.

"The visions started before we ever met. I've told you that part before. They weren't clear at first. Just snippets of an ethereal being. I found myself looking forward to the night in hopes I'd have another visit from this beautiful enchantress." My cheeks warm, knowing that he's talking about me. "The nights I dreamt about her—about you—I'd wake and the visions would fade. Holding onto them was like trying to keep water cupped in my hands. They'd linger for a moment, but then details would slip through my fingers.

"And then one day, we met. And I didn't know it was you who visited me at night. I only knew I felt something for you that I didn't want. A liability I couldn't afford."

Steel stares at the blank wall across from us as the confession pours from his mouth. I try to ignore the prick of sadness his words cause.

"The day you morphed, when you saved me from the Forsaken in the alley, I thought I was dreaming. You were as real to me that day as you were when I was sleeping. My golden siren. It was only after I kissed you that I realized the truth. That it was you all along. That you were flesh and blood along with beauty incarnate and that . . ." Steel pauses. His chest heaves, but he forces himself to meet my eyes. "That terrified me like almost nothing in this world ever has. My desire for you was a palpable thing and so I did what I could to destroy it."

He took a good shot at it. Looking back at those days, I can still feel the hurt and rejection I'd experienced with a single glance.

My mouth is dry, and a lump lodges in my throat. "But . . . why?"

He shoves a hand through his hair, but I know this time that the frustration is directed at himself.

"Stupidity mostly. I thought I was protecting my family by staying away from you. I thought I was protecting myself. But it wasn't only that. After your first morph, the dreams started to change. They got dark. I'd lose you in thick fog. You'd cry out for me to save you. And then you'd cry out for me to . . . to kill you. Eventually I convinced myself staying away—pushing you away—would also protect you."

I cross my arms, an involuntary move to protect myself.

He doesn't mean it, but these words pick at scars that haven't fully healed.

Seeing my rigid stance, Steel plows on. "You have to understand, these dreams—nightmares really—didn't just scare me, they terrified me on a physical level. They were so real, I'd wake from them in cold sweats. Vomiting at times when I dreamt of hurting you."

"How would you hurt me?"

"When you begged for me to kill you, sometimes I'd look down and my hands would be covered in blood. Your blood. I'd have buried a dagger in your gut. And the look in your eyes when that happened . . ." Steel's body is reacting from just talking about these visions. His breaths release in quick puffs and small beads of sweat form on his brow.

Concern for Steel overrides my wounds. "Hey, look at me." His gaze reluctantly swings to mine. "I'm right here. You haven't physically hurt me. You would never do that."

"That's not all. In the last few weeks, it wasn't just the two of us in these visions. After I stabbed you, someone would come and take you from me." He pauses, clearly not wanting to say the next part. "It was Thorne. That's how I recognized him at Whitehold."

I search for an explanation, coming up with one quickly. "I told you about Thorne when I pulled you and everyone else into that dreamscape. Your mind must have formed an image of him from my description. Our brains do a lot of wacky things when we're sleeping."

He shakes his head. "No. Thorne first appeared weeks before you were even taken. I saw him in my dreams after I left the academy on my hunt for Silver."

I want to dismiss Steel's dreams because they're so disturbing, but how can I ignore that he first laid eyes on me and then Thorne before he actually met us? Could this be a dormant power of his? To be able to see glimpses of the future?

"Is there some sort of angel ability that could explain what's happening to you?"

"Not one that I know of, or even one that I've researched since it all started happening. You're the only Nephilim in existence that I know of who can manipulate the unconscious mind."

"Could I somehow be doing it without realizing?"

"I suppose it's possible. But how would you have known to reach out to me before we even met? I was having dreams about you in your gilded armor and wings long before we ever plucked you off those downtown streets."

There has to be an explanation. Something like this can't be explained away by coincidence.

"Could they be prophetic?"

"That's exactly what I'm afraid of. And separating myself from you seemed like the safest option at the time."

It hits me like a blow.

"That's why you left Seraph Academy? To get away from me?"

"Not only that, but in part, yes."

This is a lot to process. I blink back at Steel, confused over my own feelings.

"I don't want to let fear rule me anymore, Emberly." Reaching forward, Steel brushes the tips of his fingers over my cheek, smudging the wetness I didn't even realize was there. "I was so wrong before. So very wrong. And for that I'll most likely spend my lifetime trying to earn your forgiveness."

With gentle hands, he coaxes me closer until I'm resting

in his arms. My tears are soaked up by the soft material of his shirt as he rubs a hand up and down my spine.

"Emberly," he whispers. His head rests atop mine, as mine rests on his chest. "You are like a flame that's ignited the darkness inside me. You've illuminated those shadowed places I buried from the world. You're breaking down my walls and lighting up my life in a way I never knew was possible."

Those words. He's killing me slowly with them, but it's a death I'll gladly embrace. My eyes grow heavy, and I drift off to sleep, this time to the steady thump of Steel's heart.

39

"Did the Council of Elders have slaves?"

Sable shoots me a startled look as she descends the stairs next to me. "After what was done to our people for generations? No, never."

"Then how in the world did they build pyramids?"

I knew we were traveling to Egypt, but I had no idea I'd be stepping into an alternate civilization when we got here. The compound is located in an area of Egypt called Farafra that's known for its hot springs—of course—and was basically in the middle of nowhere. I didn't get a great look at it from aboard the plane. The Nephilim had devised a way to camouflage the whole multi-structure compound from the air with mirrors. I didn't understand even a bit of the engineering when Greyson tried to explain it. Now, as I step into the hot, dry Middle Eastern day and descend the stairs to the airstrip, the entire compound sprawls out in front of me—including two pyramids.

"Oh. That's actually an interesting story. I'll let Raziel tell you all about it. He oversaw its construction over two millennia ago."

I release a low whistle. Dude is old.

Just then, a high-pitched scream sails through the air. Jolting, I snap my gaze up to search for the threat when a small person rams into my stomach. Thin arms with a surprising amount of strength wrap around me and squeeze.

Aurora's blue-black head of straight hair gleams in the light. I look around for help, only to see Blaze's arms wrapped around Steel in a similar fashion. Steel ruffles Blaze's hair.

"I was so worried for you," Aurora says with her face buried in my middle.

"Hey, look at me." She raises her cherub face. Large blue eyes blink rapidly to keep tears from falling. "I'm here. I'm all right."

"Did you meet the one who's like you?"

My eyebrows pleat together. "Do you mean Thorne?"

Her head bobs.

"I did. But how do you know about him?"

"The monsters were talking about him in the caves. They said he was like you."

"Oh."

"Please don't tell anyone I knew though, okay? It's a secret."

When I nod, Aurora drops her arms from around me. I catch Blaze send a concerned look toward his sister, but he wipes it away quickly.

Something is going on here. Why didn't Aurora tell us about Thorne months ago?

Steel saunters over carrying Blaze under one arm. The

little boy is squirming to free himself, but it's no use. He's not getting out of that hold until his older brother feels like it.

"You have an admirer who wants to say hello," Steel tells me.

"Dude. Not cool," Blaze complains.

I do my best to keep the smile off my face, not wanting to embarrass the boy any worse than he already is.

"Hey, Blaze. You been keeping the Elders on their toes?"

The grin that splits his face is one hundred percent wicked and two hundred percent Sterling.

"You know it."

"We're not allowed into the Council's meeting room anymore," Aurora says.

Steel's eyebrows shoot up. "Were you ever allowed in there?"

"Well . . . no," she admits.

Steel chuckles and then pretends he's going to drop Blaze, and another yelp comes out of him. He punches his older brother in the arm when his feet are on solid ground, but there's no fire in the move.

Aurora launches herself at Steel, whispering something secretive in his ear when he picks her up.

"Hey, younglings," Greyson says as he joins our small group. "Where are Mom and Dad? I'd have thought they'd be waiting at the bottom of the plane to ring Steel's neck the moment he arrived."

The smiles on both the small twin's faces fall, and they exchange a somber look. Blaze tilts his head in question, and Aurora gives him a small nod.

I swear, those two can communicate without words. Or maybe it's just a twin thing?

"They're in a meeting," Blaze finally explains. "Emberly and Steel are supposed to go straight there when they arrive." He lowers his voice, eyes shifting back and forth. "But we aren't supposed to know that."

"Aren't supposed to know what?" Sterling asks, holding out his fist to Blaze for a greeting while swooping low and popping a kiss on Aurora's cheek.

"Steel. Emberly. Can you please come over here?" Sable calls.

Sable is standing on the edge of the tarmac next to a woman dressed in a blue and pink floral dress. The long skirt billows in the wind, tangling around her calves. A thin layer of sand blows over her leather sandals.

Sweating in the cozy, oversized clothes from the hotel, I'm instantly jealous.

"Steel, Emberly, this is Sorcha, the virtue Elder."

Her eyes are covered by black-tinted shades. Her hair is braided down her back, a single dark plait with a hint of red. A streak of white runs from her right temple and weaves throughout the braid.

Not knowing what to do when meeting an Elder in person, I do the worst possible thing. I dip into a little curtsey. "Nice to meet you, your . . . Supreme Highness?"

Steel makes a choking sound and only dips his head in acknowledgement.

Oh my gosh. Why? I'd trade my fire powers for invisibility any day.

"Oh goodness, dear. None of that." She has a slight Irish accent that starts to put me at ease. "Please call me Your Majesty. Supreme Highness is so formal."

Umm.

Her lips curve at the corners. I don't know what to do.

Sable comes to my rescue. "She's joking. You can refer to all the Elders by their first names."

A full smile breaks over Sorcha's face. She's beautiful, but the smile highlights a few of the fine lines and wrinkles absent from the rest of the angel-born. They contrast with the youthful smattering of light freckles on the bridge of her nose.

"Sorry. I couldn't help it. Supreme Highness does have a nice ring though." Her quiet chuckle is warm and so I relax a bit. "In all seriousness, though. We have to go. There's a . . . situation that needs immediate attention. I'm so sorry we can't let you rest before jumping into the fray."

"We understand." Sable speaks for all of us.

"Come." Sorcha motions us forward. We walk through a stone archway that opens up to a pedestrian street of packed sand. She sets a quick pace as we breeze past several square buildings, nondescript except for the giant sand-colored bricks they're made from. It's soon clear we're headed toward the larger of the two pyramids.

"We sent troops to Whitehold while you were in the air. The place is deserted," Sorcha tells us. "We're trying to collect as much intel as possible, but the early reports are that it's pretty cleaned out."

"Is that what the Council wants to discuss with us?" I ask. Sorcha exchanges a look with Sable, who then casts Steel a worried glance. Something is definitely up.

"It's Silver. She's here."

40

I'm still trying to swallow the realization that Silver is here when Sorcha pushes open the ten-foot-high double doors to the Council's meeting room.

There weren't any windows when we marched down the halls—because we're in a pyramid—and there still aren't any when we enter the inner sanctum.

A group of people are seated at the long rectangular table in the middle of the room when we enter. I recognize Steel's parents, Laurent and Eloise, first.

Eloise springs from her seat and hurries toward her son as Sable and Sorcha find a place at the table. Grabbing his face between her hands, Eloise's gaze bounces over his features before sweeping his body for injuries. Seemingly satisfied, she tugs him into a quick but fierce hug. She lets go and moves to the side, allowing Laurent to step forward and pull Steel into a quick one-armed embrace.

I'm watching the father and son duo when Eloise picks up my hand. Holding it between both of hers, she leans forward and kisses me on the cheek.

"I'm so glad to see you are safe. We were all so worried."

I can't talk over the sudden ball lodged in my throat, so I simply bob my head.

"And what you did for Steel." Tears start to collect in her crystalline eyes. "We'll never be able to repay you."

"Oh, no. That's not—I mean there's no need—"

"Please, everyone sit."

I recognize that voice. Malachi stands at the far end of the table, eyes already on me when I spot him. He gives me a quick nod before addressing the entire room. "We have several important matters to discuss, so please forgive these quick introductions. Emberly, everyone here has been updated. You know Deacon and the Durands."

Deacon winks from one of the seats closest to me. He must have booked it off the plane and come directly here.

"But this is the rest of the Council."

As he rattles off names, each of the Elders nods once in my direction. I immediately forget who is who under the pressure of all their stares.

When he's finished with introductions, Malachi gestures toward the remaining seats. I hesitate for a moment, unsure exactly where to go, when Steel takes my hand and tugs me forward.

As we pass his parents, I catch his mom smile out of the corner of my eye and my cheeks heat.

I was kidnapped, imprisoned, almost possessed by a Fallen, escaped from a secret enemy stronghold, and flown across the world—all in the last week—and what ruffles me is holding my boyfriend's hand in front of his mom.

Oy.

Steel isn't officially my boyfriend, but the guy did tell me I was the flame that ignited the darkness inside him, so I'm pretty confident that means we're making it official.

Oh, gosh. I hope that's what it means.

The comfort of his warm, calloused fingers also boosts my confidence a half-notch. A warm fuzzy feeling blossoms in my heart when he refuses to release my hand when we both sit.

Deacon cocks an eyebrow at us from across the table, but I pretend not to notice.

"Emberly. Steel. I want to start out by letting you know that you wouldn't normally be here for a meeting like this."

It's hard not to prickle after a comment like that. It must show because Malachi goes on to say, "Simply because you are novices—if only in the technical sense, of course. You've proven yourselves highly capable in battle, but there's a particular reason you were asked here today. About an hour ago, the Forsaken known formally as Silver Durand walked out of the desert and up to our compound."

If nothing else, the girl's got guts.

"She claims to have some time-sensitive material about the Forsaken and Fallen's plans that she's willing to give up . . . on the condition she's restored to her previous condition as a Nephilim."

In other words, if I can blast the Fallen out of her, she'll flip sides.

My gaze drifts to Eloise and Laurent. This is their daughter we're talking about. They're sitting perfectly still. Too still.

It seems as if the whole room is waiting for me to say something, but I can't offer much but the truth. "I don't know how I did it."

"Would you be willing to try again?" Malachi pushes.

My eyes find their way to Steel's parents again. They watch me carefully. "There's a very good chance I'll end up killing her in the process," I confess. They need to know that. "I thought that's what I'd done to Steel. Are you willing to take that risk?" And then I sway my gaze to Malachi. "Is Silver cool with that?"

"It's our understanding that she's been fully apprised of what happened to Steel. Most likely she talked to firsthand witnesses herself. She claims to have been unconscious when the event took place, but even so, we believe she's aware of the possible consequences."

That's not good enough for me, especially since Silver is already in the driver's seat. Yes, as a Forsaken she isn't the same girl she once was, but I'm now more sure than ever that what she'd claimed was true—that she'd somehow overcome the Fallen that had intended to take over her body.

"If there's a chance we can get our daughter back," Laurent voices, "we want to take it."

"I'm willing to try, but I have a condition of my own. I want to talk to Silver first."

After spending so much time in the spectrum world with Silver, it's jarring to see her in the mortal one. Her fragile beauty is striking. Her skin is pale but glows as the picture of health. A slight blush tints her cheeks, and her hair hangs down her back in a sleek sheet, every strand perfectly in place rather than the greasy, matted mess I'm used to. Her teal eyes sway this way and that as she surveys the nondescript room she's trapped in.

She doesn't look like a feral killing machine anymore, but rather a sedate fairy-tale princess come to life. The only hint she gives of being anything but perfectly relaxed on the other side of the one-way mirror, is the rapid tapping of her pinky finger on the metal table her hands are chained to.

"Are you ready?" Malachi asks.

I glance around the small, crowded room. Half the Council is here. Eloise and Laurent stand closest to the mirror. Eloise has her hands pressed against it and her eyes trained on her daughter. Sable stands to my left and Steel's at my back. He's not touching me, but I can feel his presence.

I take a deep breath. "Yeah. I'm good to go." That wasn't convincing at all.

"Are you sure you don't want me to go in there with you?" Steel says. I glance over my shoulder to see him nod toward his sister, seated sedately on the other side of the glass.

"Yeah. Things tend to get a bit explosive between the two of you. I want to keep things as chill as possible."

A frown tugs at his mouth. Before following Malachi into the antechamber connected to the interrogation room, I lay a hand on Steel's bicep and squeeze gently. It doesn't do much to dispel the worry fogging his gaze, but it's all I can offer at the moment.

Malachi turns to me when it's just the two of us. "Whenever you're ready, Emberly. Just give us the signal when you're done." There are microphones in the walls of the room beyond, so the peanut gallery will be able to hear every word we say once I join Silver.

"Thanks." I offer him a waning smile, turn the knob and

step into the room. The door behind me drifts shut, the lock clicking back into place.

Silver's hearing is excellent, perhaps even better than mine, so she no doubt heard me in the antechamber before I even stepped foot into this room. She takes her time before acknowledging my presence. It's not until I sit on the other side of the table that her gaze meanders in my direction.

She considers me with a cat-like demeanor—seemingly uninterested, but secretly ready to attack at any moment. It puts me even more on edge. "They expect you to do your fire mojo in this room? How . . . odd."

"No. I'm not here to use angel-fire on you."

Her eyes flare and narrow before settling back into a bored expression. "I won't tell them anything more than I already have until I'm a Nephilim again. Run along." She flicks her hand at me in a shooing motion, her gaze wandering off me and over the seams of the room.

I tamp my irritation down.

"I'm not going to attempt to restore you until I know why you even want this. And that you also understand the possible outcomes. One of which is you'll end up a pile of ash on the ground."

With an "oh, you're still here" sigh, she locks gazes with me. "I'm well aware of what your unchecked powers can do. I saw the carnage you left at Whitehold. I'm operating off a working theory that your angel-fire won't hurt me."

"You're willing to stake your life on a theory?"

"What concern of yours is it if I am?"

"There are still people out there who care whether you live or die."

Silver turns her head toward the two-way mirror and I follow her gaze with my own. On this side, we only see our reflections. Silver stares at a point between the two of us as if she's looking directly into someone else's eyes.

"I figured you'd be back there, Brother. Not letting her out of your sight anymore, hmm? Probably a good idea. A few more days with Thorne and I think she may have been lost to you forever."

Oh no she didn't.

I slap my hand on the table to get her attention, but the loud bang doesn't even make her flinch.

"Are Mommy and Daddy back there with you?" she asks with a wicked grin.

"Silver," I snap. "I'm not agreeing to anything until we have this conversation."

With another sigh, she swings her head back and pins me with a glare. "Yes, I realize there's a greater chance you'll end up barbecuing me than actually restoring me. Yes, I will take the chance anyway. Is that good? Can we get on with it already? These bracelets," she holds up the cuffs shackling her to the metal table, "are starting to chafe."

I sit back in my seat only half-satisfied.

"Why do you want to do this?"

A dark look settles on her face. "You won't ever be able to understand my motivations."

I return her look with a fierce one of my own. "Make an effort to explain, or this isn't going to happen."

Lifting her top lip, she hisses at me, revealing a tiny piece of the monster that lives inside. It takes her a minute, but she eventually gets control of herself and the bored mask settles over her features once again. She starts inspecting one of her pointed nails.

"Maybe I want to be with my family again?"

"Lie. Try again." I cross my arms over my chest and

slouch more comfortably into my seat, letting her know I'm willing to wait her out.

"What do you know about Forsaken?" she asks, eyes still on her nails.

"That they look like nasty corpses in the spirit realm."

She rolls her eyes.

"Is that all?"

I flick my gaze to the mirror, even though I know I won't be able to see anyone. Where is this going?

"That's a pretty broad question. Want to narrow it down so we can get to the point?"

"You're like Nephilim Barbie, aren't you? Pretty to look at with a hollow head."

"You really want to spend time trading insults right now?"

"There are worse ways to pass the time."

"Fine. I'll play along. Forsaken are the result of what happens when an angel-born or a willing human merges with a Fallen. When they merge, the Fallen takes over autonomy of the host's body." I incline my head in her direction. "Usually. We've recently learned that's not always the case. After they merge, a Forsaken is created. Forsaken absorb the power of the host, but not the individual abilities like shifting or casting or control of the elements. They can travel unfettered between the spirit realm and mortal world, just like a Nephilim, but their true character is revealed in the spirit realm, which is why they're so fugly there.

"Forsaken are also confined to the dark in each world because—just like the vampire myths they helped create— the sun will burn them. Oh, and also like a vampire, they have a taste for blood. Major 'ew' factor, by the way."

Leaning forward I rest my arms on the shiny metal table. "How's that? Did I hit the major highlights? Or are you going to further enlighten me?"

She slow claps. The chains hanging down from her cuffs clank together with the movement. "Congratulations. Looks like you have the gist."

"So, I'll repeat. Why do you want to be restored to a Nephilim?"

"Because I want to shed the limitations of a Forsaken. And of course I'd like to be able to tan up a bit as well. Pasty is too hard of a look to pull off."

I ignore the snark, my mind whirling on her real reasons. "You want your angel-born powers and to be able to walk unfettered in the daylight. To what end?"

"My own, of course. If you think I'm going to look out for anyone but myself, you're mistaken." She dips her chin and cranes her head slowly toward the mirror. Her eyes thin to slits as she gazes past her reflection. "I've only ever been able to rely on myself anyway."

That jab probably found purchase in Steel's and his parents' hearts.

"How are we going to know anything you tell us is the truth?"

That's really for the Council to worry about, but we need a subject change. It works. After she cracks her neck, Silver's posture returns to lazy indifference and she goes back to staring at her nails.

"I have no skin in the game. After I'm turned back into a Nephilim, my old crew isn't going to want me anymore." She means Thorne and whatever is left of his army. "I don't have a problem with the angel-born. I'm happy to part with some secrets as long as they agree to let me go my own way after."

I lift my eyebrows. Malachi didn't mention Silver's release being part of her conditions as well. I wonder if the Durands knew about that? Well, if they didn't before, they do now.

Sucking my bottom lip into my mouth, I run my teeth over it as I consider the situation. The Council must think Silver has a great deal of knowledge of Thorne's agenda to ever agree to something like this. All he revealed to me were general ideas and vague hints at the future he wanted to create, in which Fallen and Forsaken rule humans and aren't trapped in either realm. If Silver could provide the Council with information on how to thwart his plans, and she accepted the risks, trying to restore her would be worth it. But if I fail, Steel's whole family will experience losing her all over again.

I wave once at the mirror, giving the signal I'm done, and push back from my seat. I'm striding the short distance to the door when Silver speaks.

"Well? Have I passed the test?"

The door buzzes and the lock disengages. Grasping the handle, I glance at her over my shoulder. She regards me with a hooded gaze.

"With flying colors."

41

One of Silver's demands is that Steel be with me when I turn her back. I'm not sure exactly why, but it's not something I'm opposed to. In fact, I'm glad he's here. I'm jittery as I pace in the large training room roughly the size of a basketball court. Finally out of the hotel sweats, I'm in a pair of ripped skinny jeans, tank top, and chunky heeled combat boots. Fashionable, yet functional. But who really cares because I'll be phasing to the spectrum world as soon as they bring Silver in.

I agreed to this arrangement without protest, but it doesn't feel right. I could kill Silver so easily. I may not like her, but the thought of killing someone outside of a battle feels too close to murder for me.

I shake out my hands then clench them into fists.

"Hey, relax." Steel comes up behind me, placing his hands on my shoulders and kneading the tense muscles. "It's going to be all right."

Mmmm. That feels nice.

"You don't know that," I argue. "And how can you be so calm right now?"

"Want to know a secret?" he whispers in my ear, doing an effective job distracting me. "I'm not."

Craning my neck to the side, I catch his eye. His face is blank, but there's a restlessness behind his gaze I can see if I search deep enough.

A door slams open across from us and in walks Silver with two Nephilim guards. Her hands are bound behind her back as she struts forward, looking more like she's on a catwalk than possibly marching to her own death.

"Should we go out and give you guys a few more moments," she asks. "You look cozy."

Steel's hands slide off me, and he steps away. His expression hardens as he crosses his arms over his chest and stares Silver down.

"So, how are we doing this thing? Should I stand up against the wall so you can blast me with your lightning bolts? Lie down so I don't hurt my pretty face when I fall?"

I can't help but wonder if her snark is an attempt to cover her own nerves. If so, she's doing a better job than me. I'm jumpy and jittery and all out of sorts.

I close my eyes and phase into the spectrum world, confident the rest will follow suit. It's not even a minute before Steel, the two bodyguards, and Silver appear in the fortified room with me.

Silver curls her lip, showing me one of her sharp fangs. There's the girl I got to know over the last week.

In order to use my angel-fire, I have to morph. I take a deep breath and close my eyes, centering myself like Thorne taught me. It's not long before heated energy flows through my body.

I stoke the flames until the intensity reaches its peak, and I let it release. The change washes over me like a tidal wave. My wings unfurl and armor molds itself to my body.

What seemed like an impossibility only a few weeks ago is now a reality. I can control my transformation.

Steel stares at me, something like awe shining in his eyes. I have to tamp down the desire to preen.

"Whenever you're ready," flows a voice over the speakers. The Elders, as well as Steel's parents, are watching us on video from another room.

"They need to leave. Or at least step behind me," I say, pointing to Silver's guards.

"I don't think that would be a good idea," one of them says.

I look to a camera in the corner of the room. "There's no way I'm unleashing pure angel-fire with them standing so close to her."

"Zander. Onyx. Leave the room."

The guard who spoke up opens his mouth to argue, but then just shakes his head, gesturing to the other to stand down. After they leave, I nod to Steel and he moves to the back corner of the room.

"Are you really going to leave these on me?" Half turning, Silver shakes her bound wrists.

"Did you really think we'd let you out of them?" Steel asks.

She hisses at him.

"If all goes well, we'll take them off after," I explain. "Or they'll burn up with the rest of your body. Either way, they won't be an issue for very long."

Closing my eyes once again, I focus my power. This time, I funnel it into my arms and down to my palms as I begin to form a ball of energized angel-fire between my hands.

This is not how it happened before, but I was in the heat of the moment fighting for my life. I can't recreate those conditions, so I'm doing my best.

It's boiling in the room, but that's not what causes sweat to break out on my brow and trickle down my hairline. My arms shake as the ball grows in power, but instinct tells me it's still not enough.

As I force myself to create even more power, I open my eyes. Flames lick my skin and I smile because now I'm getting somewhere.

Tendrils of fatigue worm into my muscles, but I can't stop now. I won't stop. I only get one shot at this, and if I do it wrong, Steel and his parents will have to watch their loved one burn alive.

With that thought I reach deeper and the blaze between my hands turns a green color. The power blows my hair back like a gust of air.

Lifting my gaze off the angel-fire, I locate Silver. She's still standing on the other side of the room, her back pressed up against the wall, arms still secured behind her back.

Even though she's trying to hide it, she's frightened. It's clear from the wild look in her eyes and her body language. She might bolt at any moment.

And . . . I like it.

A deep sense of satisfaction burns in my chest, fueled by her fear. I'm intoxicated by the knowledge that with a flick of my wrist, I could end her. That my power cannot be contained. It's a wild and potent thing that only I can control. I could tear the world down and rebuild it in my own image with the energy coursing through my veins. There isn't a creature alive who could stop me. And . . .

What am I thinking?

This is not like before. This is not like me.

The ball of angel-fire between my hands shrinks under the weight of my confusion.

"Steady." Steel's voice snaps me out of my downward spiral. "You were almost there."

Shaking off the foreign feelings, my eyes stay locked on the concentrated energy I hold between my hands.

Only one shot, I think again as the ball regains its size and color.

Throwing everything I have and everything I am into the angel-fire, I release it toward Silver with a scream that comes from the depths of my soul.

It blasts straight at her, and at the last moment she tries to duck out of the way, but it's too late. Smacking right into her chest, the flames overtake her instantaneously.

I push even more power into the blaze and then my body gives out, having spent all my energy on that one blast.

Steel's right there with me. He drops to a crouch, positioning himself in front of me to block any blowback from the blast.

Silver remains standing as if the angel-fire won't let her do any less. Her back bows, and her head snaps skyward in a silent scream. Her handcuffs crack, and her arms fly out to either side. Agony is written all over her face and body.

I can still see her through the flames. They haven't consumed her yet, but as I watch, the ends of her hair start to catch fire.

"Steel, move!" I yell, stumbling to my feet. "It's not enough, I've got to hit her again."

I have no idea how I know, but it's true.

Steel's gaze lasers on mine, saturated with doubt. I don't have time to convince him.

He tries to stop me as I sprint toward Silver, but his hands skim off my armor. Plunging into the flames, I set my palms over Silver's heart and shoot every last drop of angel-fire I have left into her chest.

Silver detonates like a bomb. I'm flung back and slam into Steel. We both hit the ground and slide about ten feet, but quickly wrangle ourselves up again.

The flames enveloping Silver burn white and gold. A dark substance leaks from her eyes, ears and mouth. It trickles at first, but soon pours from all three. Darkness starts to leak from her very skin and a shadowy cast of Silver forms in front of her, mirroring her stance. Just like what happened with Steel.

I slap my hands over my ears, remembering what comes next. Steel only follows my lead when the first high-pitched screech leaves her body. When it reaches a level to shatter glass, the shadow in front of her explodes in a cloud of ash and Silver drops to the floor.

Steel and I exchange a panicked glance before rushing to Silver. There are scorch marks on the ground beneath her and the wall, but it's clear that it worked. Besides the fact that she isn't a pile of cinders, her skin has darkened to match the bronze look of the rest of her family and her hair —besides the singed ends—is glossy and clean.

Silver isn't a Forsaken any longer.

With a cough, her lids flutter open, revealing the same teal eyes as her brother's. They now hold a soft vulnerability I've never witnessed in her before. Her gaze bounces from

Steel to me and back again as we hover over her prone form.

"I'm alive." Her chin trembles and eyes glisten with unshed tears.

The smile that breaks over my face is genuine. "Yes, you are."

Steel tries to help her sit up, but she jerks out of his grasp. Anger hardens her features. "Don't touch me," she snaps at him.

Steel flinches but backs off. "We should phase back."

We all take a moment to do so, and then Silver wobbles to her feet without accepting help from either of us. The door to the gym flies open, smashing back against the wall, and Eloise shoots through. Her cheeks are covered in tears as she runs to Silver and throws her arms around her daughter.

Silver stiffens and doesn't move to embrace her mother, but Eloise either doesn't notice or doesn't care.

Laurent enters a moment later with the rest of the Council. I step back to let the family have their moment, even if it is a super awkward one. For as overjoyed Eloise and Laurent are to have their daughter back, Silver only appears agitated.

A presence hovers next to me. One of the Elders stands to my right. I think it's Zara, the dominion Elder.

Her hair is sheered into a chin-length bob, longer in the front and shorter in the back. She's tall, even for an angelborn female—probably around six-six. Her eyes are hooded and light gray, the combination just shy of unsettling. There isn't a wrinkle on her face; instead, her age shows in the grace of her movements and the sharpness of her gaze.

"You realize, this changes everything."

The words sink into my gut and sour. Floating my gaze past the Durand family, I catch the rest of the Elders standing in a bunch. Their focus not on the reunion in front of them, but on me.

What have I done?

42

I don't know why I feel compelled to talk to Silver, but I can't get it out of my head. It's been two days since I blasted her with enough angel-fire to burn whatever remnants of the Fallen were left in her. She's been questioned multiple times by the Council and is being kept under lock and key.

She refuses to see Steel, but has spent time with Greyson and Sterling, who came back from their visits saying she seemed withdrawn and stoic—a far cry from the older sister they remember from their childhood or even the snarky Forsaken she once was. Eloise and Laurent have hardly left her side, but the youngest set of twins haven't been to see her yet.

Word of her transformation was supposed to be kept hidden, but from the unabashed stares of the angel-born at the compound, it's clear the news leaked. Just this morning a woman stopped me in the halls and shoved pictures of her daughter in front of my face, begging me to turn her back into a Nephilim. I mumbled apologies and condolences and fled as soon as I could.

I don't regret what I did for Silver, but I should have thought through the consequences of my actions beforehand. If word continues to spread, Nephilim from around the globe will want their loved ones restored to them. I don't fault them for that, but I still don't know enough about what actually happened with Steel and Silver to know if it's something I can do over and over again. I used angel-fire against so many other Forsaken in the arena at White-hold, and they had all burnt to ash.

You realize, this changes everything.

When I finally had the time alone to ask Steel about his experience as a Forsaken, he didn't have the answers I was looking for. When Legion took control of Steel's body, his awareness had been pushed into darkness. He admitted he couldn't remember much.

My working hypothesis is that I can only help Forsaken who've retained some of their autonomy after the merge, but I need more information about how often that actually happens. Which means I need to talk to Silver.

I tiptoe down the corridor. The chilled stone beneath my feet makes me wish I'd thrown on some sandals. The winter in Egypt is nowhere near the frigid temperatures of Colorado or Canada, but the air still carries a snap of cold, especially at night.

I was focused more on staying quiet than my attire when I snuck out of the room I share with Ash. The Council won't let anyone but themselves and family see Silver—something I'm more than a bit peeved about—so nighttime is my best chance to slip in and see her. Ash would never turn me in, but I want her to have plausible deniability if I get caught.

I come to a corner and press my back to the wall to peer around the edge. When I see the coast is clear, I resume my hurried shuffles. The compound never fully shuts down. Activity occurs around-the-clock, which helps my plans this evening. No one is going to think too much of me padding through the guest suite hallway at night. But surveillance is twenty-four hours a day and I'd rather not run into anyone. My cover story, in case I get stopped, is that I'm looking for food.

Up ahead, Silver's door comes into view. It's easy to identify because there's a giant Nephilim standing in front of it. Dressed in fatigues, his beefy arms are crossed over his chest as he stands with his feet shoulder-width apart. He has a wicked curved sword hanging at his hip and guns holstered under each arm. As I approach, his whole persona screams "Don't even try because if you do I'll rip your arms from their sockets and use them to beat you to death."

My throat dries when I stop in front of him. He looks down his nose at me. I'm no shrinking wallflower, but I hesitate. This guy might have a clean foot of height on me.

My grand plan is to talk my way past this giant. If that doesn't work, I'm going to have to knock him out and drag his body into the supply closet down the hall. Thorne showed me some pretty effective ways to put someone temporarily down, a few of which he even tried out on me. I didn't enjoy those experiences. I hope it doesn't come to that, but this door is the only way in or out of the rooms beyond. I already checked the exterior of the rectangular visitors' dorm, and the windows into Silver's rooms are sealed.

The Council has her locked up tightly in their own version of a gilded cage. I can't imagine she's taking it any better than I did.

"So . . ." I begin. "Malachi sent me to check on Silver."

Lie. Big, fat lie.

The guard takes me in from top to bottom, his eyebrow lifting when he gets to my bare feet. I'm in leggings and an oversized t-shirt, but lack of shoes when conducting official business is kinda weird. Total rookie mistake right there.

"Is that so?" he drawls.

"Yes," I say and then clear my throat. "They're worried about some of the effects after the procedure I performed on her. You know, the one that turned her from a Forsaken back into a Nephilim." I wait a beat, hoping to spot a spark of interest, but go on when he remains a statue. "I need to phase into the spirit realm to check her aura."

That sounds convincing-ish. Admittedly, lying isn't my forte. I'm much better at fleeing and hiding, but I dug deep for that performance and think I kind of nailed it.

"I don't think so. Move along."

I wrinkle my nose, annoyed. "Listen, I need to have a little chat with her, okay? You can let me in, or I'm going to let myself in."

He immediately pulls his sword from its sheath.

Oh, shoot.

I stumble back a step just as the door flies open.

"What's going on?" Eloise peeks around the body blocking her view and sees me. "Emberly, what are you doing here?"

The first tingles of a headache start. I bring my hand to my temple to rub the spot, my shoulders slumping. I could have taken the large Neph—maybe—but there's no way I'm going to try to knock out Steel's mom.

"I need to talk to Silver."

Eloise nudges the guard over and steps into the hall.

"Yes, of course. Why haven't you come sooner?"

I raise my eyebrows, feeling my forehead pleat. Seriously?

"The Council won't let anyone else see her."

Eloise blinks back at me, confusion darkening her features. "That's silly. Come on in."

She motions me forward, but the large angel-born raises his weapon and bars my entry. "Move aside, Adom."

"Apologies, Mrs. Durand, but I can't do that." He doesn't look apologetic at all.

Eloise's eyes snap with irritation. "This girl has saved four out of my six children in the last several months alone. If that doesn't make her an honorary member of my family, I don't know what will. If I say she can see my daughter, she can see my daughter. And if you have a problem with that, you'll have two of us to go up against." Her tone doesn't leave any room for argument. Even I'm a tad intimidated.

The guard shifts his weight, his gaze bouncing from Eloise to me and back again. Finally he lowers his weapon and steps back. "I'll be reporting this to the Council."

"You do that," Eloise says as she motions me forward again. This time Adom's large form sways out of the way so I can pass.

They've put Silver into one of the apartment guest quarters. We enter a dimly lit room with seating and a kitchenette in the corner. There's a door on either side of the room, most likely leading to bedrooms and bathrooms.

"Is everything all right, Emberly?" Eloise asks.

It's only then I realize I'm wringing my hands. I stop the motion, forcing my arms down at my sides. "I'm just worried . . ."

"About how you did what you did and how you're going to do it again?"

I nod.

"I'm not surprised. There's quite a buzz going around the compound. Let me get Silver for you. She's . . ." Eloise takes a moment to search for the right words. "Still adjusting to the transformation. It may be good for both of you to talk, though."

Eloise goes to one of the doors and knocks softly before letting herself in. After only a minute she emerges.

"You're welcome to go in. She's still awake." Tipping her head in the direction of the door she says, "I'm going to head back to sleep. Feel free to let yourself out when you're finished, dear."

With a soft smile she pads to the other side of the room. I crack open the door to Silver's room and there's only darkness. I push it open farther, widening the gap enough so I can enter.

Silver sits in a chair and stares out her window. She doesn't bother turning toward me, so I stand awkwardly for several moments before deciding to take a seat in front of the window as well. She still doesn't acknowledge my presence, even after I've lowered myself into the chair next to her.

I'm the one who sought Silver out, but now that I'm right next to her, words escape me. I glance out the window, not seeing anything of interest that may be holding her attention.

"It's different than I thought it would be." Her voice isn't loud, but it's still jarring in the silence.

I swivel my gaze back to her. The moonlight brushes her face, creating a ghostly pallor against her now-golden skin. "I used to think my childhood memories were so clear, but now I wonder . . ."

I can't exactly tell if that's the end of her sentence, or if there is more she was about to say.

"How's it different?"

"There are more . . ." She struggles for a moment to gather her thoughts into words. "More layers than I remember."

"Layers to what?"

"People mostly. But also, myself. Life is simpler as a Forsaken. Desires run dark and focused. And now there's just . . . more."

I don't fully grasp what she's saying, but I suppose having never been a Forsaken myself, comparing the two states of being would be difficult. Expecting someone who lived as a monster for over ten years to adjust in a few days isn't realistic.

Shifting, she finally turns her head to look at me. "I was wondering when you'd find your way here."

"The Council hasn't made it easy."

"I didn't imagine they would. But the warrior who can slay dozens of foes with a single blast of power wouldn't let something small like permission stop her."

"That's a bit of an overstatement."

"Is it though? Did you stop to count the casualties you left behind at Whitehold? Because I did." The first flash of real emotion sparks behind her eyes as they flare before returning to their demure state.

"If you saw what I did to so many Fallen and Forsaken, why would you take the chance? I could have killed you the other day. Almost did."

A solid six inches of hair was burnt off the ends during her transformation. It's freshly cut now and falls just below her shoulders.

"I heard what happened to Steel. I figured if you could do it for him, you could do the same for me. The Fallen rattling around inside me these last ten years had become rather annoying. It's nice to only have to juggle my own thoughts." Her tone is almost bored. But that answer is too simple. Too canned.

"That can't be it," I press. "Did you know it would work for you because of your . . . condition." I don't know what else to call it. "Are there many other Forsaken like you?"

"That's what you really want to know, isn't it? How many other Forsaken are like I was? If that's the reason why you were able to turn me back?"

I consider her for a moment. I can't think of a reason to lie. "Yes. I want to understand why I can do what I can do. How I can do it."

She lifts her hands, palms up. "How can any angel-born do what they do? Are you not a product of your parentage? A mix of abilities inherited from the ones before you?"

She's being purposefully obtuse. "You know that's not what I'm asking."

"I don't know the number." She turns her gaze back out the window. "I've met a few over the years, but not many. I don't have the answers you're searching for. Did I think I had a better chance of surviving because of my . . . condition?" Her eyebrows lift on the last word, and the corner of her mouth quirks. "Sure. Did I know for certain it would work? No." I can't help but feel I'm missing something. "I guess to figure out the answers you're looking for, you're just going to have to fry a few more Forsaken."

I grind my teeth. Forsaken or Nephilim, Silver is still a difficult person.

"Is there anything useful you can tell me then?" I sit back in the chair, deflated.

"You should have sided with Thorne. This won't end well for you."

Whoa. Where did that come from?

"Why would you say that?"

"It's the truth. The Nephilim have no idea what's coming for them. If they did, they'd turn you over to Thorne themselves."

Frustration slips toward fear. What is she talking about?

"Why would they want to do that?"

"It's what's best for everyone. You'll see. I imagine before this is all over you might be running toward him yourself."

This visit is churning up more questions and uncertainty than answers and confirmations.

"Do you regret being turned back then?" It's not what I came here to ask, but I suddenly want to know.

"This is always who I was meant to be."

That's not really an answer. We both fall silent.

"Why are you still wearing that?" Her finger taps the milky stone on my bracelet. The one Thorne gave me.

It's a good question. I forgot about it mostly, but realized yesterday that it wasn't fused to my wrist anymore. Maybe phasing back into the mortal realm had broken whatever enchantment kept me from removing it? I probably should have tossed it by now. Or at the very least given it over to the Council to study. But despite everything, I believed

Thorne when he said it was simply a protection against Fallen. I've gone to take it off several times and always stopped myself.

"It's pretty." Silver isn't the only one who can give stupid answers.

"I'll bet Steel loves that you're wearing charms given to you by another man."

I shake my head. I'm not going to verbally spar with her just for funsies. "I'll let you get your rest," I say instead.

Rising, I pad back to the door. I'm about to turn the knob when I glance over my shoulder at Silver. Her gaze is once again fixed on the nothing out the window.

"Do you think you'll ever forgive Steel for what he did?"

"So he told you then?"

"Yes."

She makes a sound in her chest that might be a laugh. "If someday someone you love—someone you care about in a way that transcends reason and understanding—betrays you, then you can come and ask me that question and I'll give you an answer."

"A simple 'no' would have worked as well."

Her shoulders lift in a shrug. I slip out of Silver's apartment with a new heaviness in my heart.

I sneak back into my room and pad to the bathroom, closing the door quietly behind me. I fill a paper cup with water. Thorne's bracelet catches my eye in the mirror's reflection.

I don't want Silver's comments about the piece of jewelry or Thorne to bother me, but they do. Setting the cup of water down on the counter, I slide the gold cuff over my wrist.

I'll give it to the Council in the morning. It belongs in whatever vault they're keeping both of the orbs in anyway. I don't need protection from the Fallen anymore.

My fingers linger on the warm metal as it sits innocently on the counter in front of me. I'm hesitant to part with it, but that's silly. I release the bracelet, and a small wave of dizziness sweeps over me. I slap my hand against the wall to steady myself. Something thumps in the other room.

"What? Who?" I hear Ash call.

Blinking to clear my thoughts, I catch my reflection and something flashes red in my eyes.

"Emberly, are you in there?" Ash is standing right outside the door.

I step toward the mirror, checking my eyes, but there's nothing there.

"Emberly?" Ash calls softly again.

Shaking off the feeling of wrongness, I down the cup of water and open the door. I turn off the lights as I slip back into the room.

"Yeah. I just got a little dizzy. I need a good night's sleep. Sorry I woke you."

Her head tilts as she regards me.

"You sure you're okay? You look a little pale."

I smile, hoping the forced levity will calm her down. "I'm always pale. I just need some rest."

"Yeah, okay. I guess that could be it." She rubs her eyes, and I pull back the covers of my bed as she climbs back into her own. My wrist feels odd without the bracelet, but I tell myself to ignore it. I just got used to having it there over the last week, that's all.

Sliding between the sheets, my body is heavy with fatigue. I must be more tired than I thought. My head hits the pillow, and as I drift off, a husky chuckle vibrates in my mind. My brain sparks with concern, but my body doesn't follow suit. I can't rouse myself as a heavy weight pulls me under and I'm asleep within moments.

43

The world shakes, and I crack an eyelid.

"—told you I can't wake her."

An alarm sounds. An ice pick straight to my brain. I seal my lids again.

"It's going off again. We need to get her up." That's Greyson.

"Sterling, go grab some water from the bathroom," Nova says. "See if that wakes her."

Water sounds nice. I'm parched.

I try to pull myself together, but it's not happening. Did someone weigh down my limbs with cement?

A door slams against a wall, the sound loud over the pulsing alarm.

"She won't wake up. I was going to throw some water on her." Sterling is the worst.

"Turn the shower on. Cold water only." Steel's here. Maybe he can make the noise stop. I can't do much more than cringe as the ice pick digs deeper into my brain.

"Last chance, Em. You going to wake up?" he asks.

I can't so much as moan.

Dizziness becomes my world as I'm hefted into the air. I'm able to pry my lids open a sliver to see Steel looking down at me as he walks me to the bathroom. His mouth is tight and brow pinched. He looks concerned. I would be too if I could string two thoughts together right now. My mind is like a scrambled egg.

Opening the glass door, Steel steps right into the shower, positioning me directly under the spray.

The water feels like needles hitting my skin, but it's just what I need to groggily lift my head.

"What's going on?"

Steel releases a breath and places a kiss on my forehead. "Thank goodness," he whispers, then yells, "She's awake!" over his shoulder.

"Can you stand?"

"I'm not sure," I admit.

Steel slowly lowers me to the ground. With an arm still around me, he turns the shower off. Both of us drip chilled water onto the tiled floor.

My legs are shaky, but I wake more with each passing moment. Brushing a clump of wet hair off of my face, I tilt my head up. The alarm has stopped, but the pounding in my head hasn't.

"What's going on?" I ask again.

"That's what we need to figure out. Come on." He leads me back into the bathroom. Grabbing a towel off the rack, he wraps it around my shoulders before ushering me into the room.

Nova and Sterling are seated on Ash's bed, the one

closest to the door. Greyson paces in front of the window next to Ash.

"Em. What was that?" he demands.

"I was . . . tired?" How can I explain something I don't understand myself.

"Let's go to my parents' room. Blaze and Aurora will be there too. It's best we stay together," Steel suggests.

The alarm starts again. Through each burst the sound grows in intensity before fading, only to start again.

"It's the compound's alarm. Something's up, but we're not sure what," Nova says.

Ash pulls open the dresser, yanking out clothes, and then herds Greyson toward the door. "I've got her clothes. She can change in the Durands' room. Let's go."

We leave in a cluster. I'm almost mowed down by an angel-born the second I step out the door. There are shouts in the distance, but I can only make out a few words here and there.

In under three minutes we've traversed the building and barge into the Durands' sitting room. Eloise spins toward us. It looks like she was pacing a hole into the floor.

"Oh, thank goodness," she says.

Blaze and Aurora are seated on the couch, unusually quiet. That freaks me out a bit.

"Your father has already left for the Council meeting room. We received a call telling us to stay put, but he didn't listen." Catching sight of me, she stops. "Emberly, why are you soaking wet?"

I drip puddles onto the floor.

"They couldn't wake me up?"

Her face twists in confusion as Ash pushes me toward a

closed door. Throwing it open, she plants the clothes she grabbed in my hands and shoves me in. I dress as fast as I can, now realizing how hard it is to get out of wet leggings. I toss the soggy clothes into the bathroom once I've changed into a similar outfit, and rejoin the group.

"Come on," Steel says the moment the door clicks shut behind me. He's pulled on a fresh shirt, but his jeans are still wet. "You, me, and Greyson are going to look for Dad. The others are staying put with my mom."

Nova waves her cell phone in the air. "If you forget to call and update us, I'm going to cut off your—" Her gaze dart to Eloise. "Umm, just don't forget."

Grabbing my hand, Steel pulls me back into the hallway. Greyson isn't far behind. We sprint out of the building and onto the street. There are even more Nephilim running in different directions here. Setting our eyes on the large pyramid, we set off.

Pain slams into my skull when the alarms go off another time. I miss a step, but Steel catches my arm and rights me before I face-plant.

"The sirens," I say by way of an explanation.

His face is tight, but he nods.

It isn't long before we bust through the door of the pyramid. Steel takes the lead, guiding us through the maze of corridors to the belly of the structure where the Council hosts their official meetings. He shoves the mammoth doors open when we get there.

My guess is that normally, three novice angel-borns bursting into the Council's meeting room wouldn't go unnoticed, but this morning it does. No one so much as turns to tell us to leave as we storm into the room.

From a quick scan of the area, it looks like every Elder is

present. Besides them, there are at least two dozen other Nephilim in the space, including Sable, Deacon, and Laurent. The angel-born are separated into small groups. It appears that the Elders are issuing orders to different angel-line factions.

Suddenly, Malachi's voice booms above the rest. "We have visuals in London."

He talks into an earpiece and a moment later a screen flashes to life behind him. The display shows an aerial view of parliament and Big Ben. Fire pours from the windows on the left side of the historic landmark, the part farthest from the famous clock tower.

Another screen flicks on and it shows a ground shot of Piccadilly Circus. The displays that usually light up the area are blank; swarms of people run every which way.

The next screen shows Trafalgar Square. The giant lion statues are smashed to bits, but this area is free of humans.

One image after another pops up, revealing different parts of downtown London. A few areas remained untouched, but much of the scenes show destruction.

People running. Bridges collapsed. Fires exploding.

"What is happening?" Greyson asks next to me.

I shake my head, even though I know he's not talking to me.

"Steel. Grey. Is your mother safe? Your siblings?" Laurent joins us, but I don't take my eyes off the displays on the far wall. I can't.

"Yes, they're fine," Greyson says.

"Where's Silver?" Steel asks, and I wrench my gaze from the displays to see Laurent answer with a frown and a quick shake of his head.

What does *that* mean?

"What's causing all this?" As soon as the words leave my mouth, I catch a blur on one of the screens out of the corner of my eye.

Wait, it's not a blur. It's an all-too-familiar sight.

"A shadow beast," I whisper. I can hear the horror in my own voice. Shadow beasts are only Fallen, but they're exponentially more terrifying in this form. You can't see their bodies in order to know how to fight back or defend yourself. The scars that riddle my body are from years of their attacks. "Are these cameras broadcasting from the spirit realm?"

I shouldn't have bothered to ask; I already know the answer.

"No."

The room is silent as we all watch the events in London unfold.

It happens only here or there, but dark shadows fly in and out of the cameras' view, causing fires and smashing cars, statues, and small structures.

"What are those?" Draven, the thrones Elder asks.

"They're Fallen," I answer when no one speaks up.

"Dear, that's not what the Fallen look like," Sorcha says gently.

"That's exactly what they look like when I half-phase into the spirit realm."

"Not possible," someone says, but I don't bother answering because I'm staring after Sable as she bolts from the room, her cell phone pressed against her ear. Deacon watches her go but doesn't follow.

The room erupts into a chorus of voices once again.

"Get as many powers gathered as possible, send them straight to the city center."

"Check with every academy, see if they can spare any staff."

"Find out where else this is happening, then report back."

My head pounds. I'm not sure if the Elders believe me about the shadow beasts, but the longer I watch the screens, the more sure I am that's what they are.

Somehow, someway, the Fallen have punched through the veil between the mortal and spectrum worlds and are staging an invasion. And I know down to the very fibers of my being, this was Thorne's plan all along. We just weren't fast enough to stop him.

Something drops out of the sky and lands on my head. With a squawk I bat at it, but it dissolves in a shower of sparkles before I make contact.

"Tinkle?"

"Why'd you have to swat at me?" He stands on the table in his preferred flying squirrel form, tapping his foot in annoyance. "I've gone to a lot of trouble for you and the thanks I get is a backhand?"

"Tinkle! Oh my gosh. Where have you been?"

"Getting help. Of course."

"What help?"

I look around as if something magical is going to appear before my eyes.

It doesn't.

"Not here yet. I'm faster." He pushes his little furry chest out in pride.

Someone gasps, and my eyes snap back to the screens.

"St. Paul's Cathedral just exploded."

"Tinkle, do you know what's going on?"

His nose scrunches. "Very bad things."

Tremors begin to shake the room. Nephilim trade startled glances with each other as the vibrations intensify.

The doors to the room don't simply fly open—they splinter as gusts of smoke-laced air swirls through. We all duck for cover.

Steel shoves me down and under the table, using his body as a barrier between me and whatever is about to come through that doorway. Several others shelter around us.

We're under attack. What other explanation is there?

Something strides into the room. Thumping steps pound in my ears and chest. The ground shivers with each footfall.

Ducking under Steel's arm, I spot feet wrapped in golden sandals coming toward us.

I suck in a breath as the table above us is thrown in the air. It smashes against the wall of screens.

Screams sound and I'm worried someone is hurt, but all thoughts are knocked out of my mind when I take in the being in front of me.

He towers at least eight feet tall and is covered from neck to toe in gold-plated armor. Three sets of wings trail behind him like a tiered cape, each feather gilded.

A sword is sheathed at his waist and a dagger fused to his right thigh. His form is masculine, but the perfection of his features has no earthly equal. His head is unprotected and a river of white-blond hair flows to just above his shoulders. There's fire in his gaze as he scans the room.

There's no mistaking what this being is. An angel.

Wood snaps in the back of the room. I manage to tear my eyes away long enough to watch Malachi stumble to his feet in the rubble.

His eyes betray his fear, even if his voice does not.

"Who are you?" he asks.

The angel's golden eyes continue to roam until they land on me, and stick.

"Camiel. Her father."

EPILOGUE
THORNE

From my perch on top of the London Eye, I watch the city burn. Across the Thames, smoke spirals up from the charred remains of Westminster. Somehow the clock tower at its end—Big Ben—has escaped destruction.

I'll have to do something about that.

Upriver, the flames that engulf the dome of St. Paul's Cathedral spike high in the morning sky. Dust clouds bloom from boroughs across London as the Fallen wreak havoc on the populace.

I wasn't convinced she could pull this off, but I should have known better. Events had gone down exactly as we'd planned, and when I received the signal that the orbs' powers had been combined, I unleashed the Fallen on the mortal world.

The impossible has been achieved. We've taken the first step toward rebalancing the world.

Standing on top of the observation wheel's highest glass carriage, the wind pulls at my wings. The air is scented with smoke and stale water from the river below. I survey the victory unfolding before me with an odd sense of detachment. Years of plotting and planning and hiding and sacrificing have finally come to fruition. But all I feel is . . . nothing.

I thought in this moment, I'd feel something, if even just a sense of achievement, but if anything the yawning emptiness inside only grows a bit more after each monument to human greatness is razed.

Odd.

I wonder if sharing this moment with another—if Emberly had chosen to remain at my side instead of returning to my enemies—would have made this triumph more complete.

A frown pulls at my lips. I honestly don't know.

I crouch then spring into the air, spread my wings and glide over the Thames toward Buckingham Palace. On my order, it remains untouched. It seemed like a waste to have to build a palace of my own when there's a perfectly good one already standing.

The blurred forms of Fallen dart back and forth below. They are only smudges of darkness to a mortal eye, but soon they'll be able to fully manifest in this world.

Touching down in St. James Park, I stride toward the laureled gates of the palace. Human guards with rifles stand three deep in front of the fence. They point their weapons at me as I draw near.

The side of my mouth kicks up in a half-grin. This next part is going to be fun.

I stoke the power running through my veins, casting a sphere of angel-fire between my palms. Fear blooms in the humans' eyes as the fire grows in shape and intensity.

Someone shouts commands, but before they're able to get a round fired, I chuck the angel-fire. It explodes against the gates, blowing them wide open and sending people flying in all directions.

Bullets whiz through the air, but I deflect them easily with my wings.

With my gaze fixed on the palace, I force my mind to focus on what comes next. London is only the appetizer. When I'm finished with the meal, I'll have devoured the whole world.

ANGELIC CLASSIFICATION
IN ORDER OF SPHERE

Angelic Spheres – The nine classes of angels are divided equally into one of three spheres. Each sphere has related roles and responsibilities and it's believed—but not proven —that the most powerful angels are from the first sphere with decreasing power down to the third.

Seraphim – Literally translated as, "burning ones," seraphim are the highest angelic class and considered the most powerful. Part of the first sphere of angels, these supernatural beings are said to have six wings and protect the throne of their Creator. There are no known Nephilim from the seraphim line, because not a single seraph angel rebelled and therefore there are no seraph Fallen.

Known Descendants – Emberly & Thorne

Cherubim – Part of the first sphere of angels, cherubim are the highest angelic class that rebelled. The Nephilim of this line can typically shift into one of three different forms in the spirit realm: a lion, an eagle, or a bovine. It's very rare for a Nephilim to be able to shift into two or all three of these forms.

Known Descendants – Steel, Greyson, Sterling, Aurora, Blaze, Eloise, Laurent, Silver, & Malachi (Cherub Elder)

Thrones – The thrones are part of the first sphere and are said to be natural protectors. Nephilim of this line can manipulate and build wards to protect the academies and compounds from supernatural enemies by pulling on energy contained in underground springs.

Known Descendants – Deacon & Draven (Throne Elder)

Dominions – Part of the second sphere of angels, Dominions regulate the duties of the lower angels as well as govern the laws of the universe. Dominions are considered to be divinely beautiful with feathered wings of various colors. The Nephilim of this line value friendship, family, and loyalty and tend to be the peacemakers of the angel-born world.

Known Descendants – Ash & Zara (Dominion Elder)

Virtues – These angels are known for their signs and miracles. Part of the second sphere, they ensure everything is acting the way it should, from gravity keeping the planets in orbit, to the grass growing. Nephilim of this line can control natural elements in the mortal world, but their abilities are more powerful in the spirit realm.

Known Descendant – Sorcha (Virtue Elder)

Powers – Part of the second sphere, these angels are considered the warriors of the angel hierarchy. As such, they are always on the frontlines of battle. They are known to be single-minded and focused on their cause. Nephilim of this line are skilled in combat and have a knack for military strategy. They are able to manifest wings in the spirit realm.

Known Descendants – Nova & Lyra (Power Elder)

Rulers – As part of the third sphere, these angels guide and protect territories and groups of people. They preside over the classes of angels and carry out orders given to them by the upper spheres. They are said to be inspirational to angels and humankind. Nephilim of this line tend to manage and govern different bodies of angel-born. Their natural talents veer toward shepherding and their powers manifest as defensive rather than offensive.

Known Descendants – Sable & Arien (Ruler Elder)

Archangels – These angels are common in mortal lore. Part of the third sphere, they appear more frequently in the mortal world than other classes of angels—with the exception of the angel class. Tasked with the protection of humanity, they sometimes appear as mortals in order to influence politics, military matters, and commerce in their assigned region. Nephilim of this line are skilled chameleons. They have the easiest time blending in with humans and many of them work as Keepers.

Known Descendant – Riven (Archangel Elder)

Angels – Perceived as the lowest order of celestial beings, angels—sometimes called "plain angels" or "guardian angels"—belong to the third sphere. Their primary duties are as messengers and personal guards. Nephilim of this line are believed to have been murdered over two millennia ago. As a result of their weak powers, Forsaken and Fallen targeted this line for elimination. Not much is known of what their powers and abilities were.

Known Descendants – No known living descendants

GLOSSARY

Angel – A winged supernatural being who protects both mortal and spirit realms from Fallen and Forsaken.

Angel-born – The common name for Nephilim. An elite race of supernatural warriors born of human females and male Fallen, and their descendants. They have varying powers and abilities based on their Fallen ancestor's angel class. They are stronger, faster, and their senses more enhanced than humans.

Barghest – A serpentine, dog-like creature most commonly known as a hellhound. Barghest have elongated muzzles and their bodies are covered in scales. Several rows of spikes protrude along their spines and a tuff of needle-like hair crowns their heads. They exist only in the spirit realm and are known to be highly aggressive, only trainable through the use of Enochian commands.

A fabled supernatural being that acts as a protector for angel-born. Nephilim tell their children fairy tales about these creatures, but their existence has never been confirmed.

Celestial – A fabled supernatural being that acts as a protector for angel-born. Nephilim tell their children fairy tales about these creatures, but their existence has never been confirmed.

Council of Elders – Comprised of the oldest Nephilim in each of the seven existing angelic lines: cherub, throne, dominion, virtue, power, ruler, and archangel. They are the closest thing to a ruling body the Nephilim have, yet—unless there is a global threat—their normal duties are to act as judges to help settle disputes between angel-born.

Elder's Compound – A highly protected stronghold where the Elders of each Nephilim line are based, which consists of several buildings including lodging for over three hundred occupants, training centers, a vault for cherished Nephilim artifacts, and two pyramids. The compound is located in an area of Egypt called Farafra that's known for its hot springs.

Fallen – Angels who rebelled and were banished to Earth as punishment. They retained their strength, immortality, and wings, but lost their class specific angelic powers. They are unable to access the mortal world.

Forsaken – Fallen who have merged with a Nephilim—or willing human—and taken on the form of their host's body.

They are able to travel between each realm unencumbered. Their appearance is hideous in the spirit realm, reflecting their true nature. Forsaken thirst for blood—although it's not their primary source of sustenance—and are unable to withstand the sunlight in either realm.

Keeper – Nephilim tasked with monitoring and collecting information about the human race.

Mortal World/Realm – The dimension on Earth where humans reside.

Nephilim – The proper name for angel-born.

Phasing – When a Nephilim, Forsaken, or angel travels from the mortal world to the spirit realm or back again.

Seraph Academy – One of nine secret academies around the world devoted to the education and training of Nephilim children. Nephilim youth attend the academies from age eight until twenty, at which time they are considered fully trained. Seraph Academy is located in the Colorado Mountains near the town of Glenwood Springs.

Spectrum World – What Emberly calls the spirit realm.

Spirit Gem – Small gems or stones of different colors that originate from the spirit realm and have various uses and properties. Some examples include concealing powers, amplifying natural abilities, creating shields, controlling objects or people, or forcing people into or out of the spirit realm. It is believed that there are yet undiscovered varieties of gems still hidden in the spirit realm. The orbs in the Council of Elders vault are both large spirit gems. Until recently, the Nephilim were not aware of their existence.

Spirit Realm – The plane of existence that can only be accessed by supernatural beings. The spectrum of colors differ in this realm and sound can be seen as ripples through the air. Angels spend the majority of their time in the spirit realm warring with Fallen for control of territories. Nephilim's angelic powers activate in this realm.

The Great Revolt – When the Nephilim rose up against the Forsaken and Fallen who had enslaved and used them as vessels for Fallen.

The White Kingdom – Also known as "Whitehold" this fortress is located in the Laurentian Mountains of Quebec, Canada. This stronghold was the primary training ground for Fallen and Forsaken and ruled by Thorne and the seraph angel, Seraphim. It remained a secret from the Nephilim for hundreds of years, but since its discovery it has been abandoned.

PLEASE WRITE A REVIEW

amazon   good**reads**

Reviews are the lifeblood of authors and your opinion will help others decide to read my books. If you want to see more from me, please leave a review.

Will you please write a review?
http://review.ForgingDarkness.com

Thank you for your help!

~ *Julie*

FALLEN LEGACIES BOOK 3
UNLEASHING FIRE

"And when the halflings' numbers grew, they realized they had the power to overcome the evil that stalked them. And a great revolt shook the earth and all of its inhabitants. The creators no longer ruled their creations, and so the beasts sought to wipe them from existence."

- Book of Seraph, Chapter 18, Verse 28

A clay pot smashed against the packed earthen floor at Ambrosine's feet, sending shards in all directions. It was a wedding gift from her older sister, lovingly formed and hand-painted, but she didn't give it a second glance as she shoved cured meats and vegetables into a woven pack. Her hands shook, making her movements clumsy and sending other once-treasured items scattering around the room.

As panic clawed at her gut and marched up toward her chest, bursts of painted lights appeared in her peripheral vision.

She needed to pull herself together. This wasn't the time to let terror take hold.

Slinging the bag packed full of food and essentials over her shoulder, she closed her eyes and allowed herself one deep, drawn-out breath to get herself under control. As the air hissed out of her lungs, her son's sweet cry filled the silent room.

Rushing to the fur pallet on the floor, Ambrosine scooped up her infant and secured him across her chest with a bleached piece of fabric. His cherubic face scrunched and reddened as his soft protests continued. He was most likely hungry, but there wasn't time to do anything about that.

Swaying back and forth, she tried to coax the baby back to sleep while she scanned the sparse dwelling for anything else they might need.

"Don't worry, Nikias. Your father will be back soon, and we'll go to a safe place. We're going to find a magical land flowing with milk and honey, someplace we will never be discovered and can live without fear." Her soothing words were meant more for her own soul than the infant in her arms, but hearing his mother's voice seemed to placate the babe and his cries turned to happy coos. "That's right my dear, we won't have to fight the monsters anymore. You'll grow to be happy and not know a day of sadness."

Shadows overtook the light that had been streaming into the room, chilling the temperature. Ambrosine gasped and clutched Nikias closer to her breast. She snapped her gaze to the beast of a man filling the doorway and sagged in relief. She'd recognize her husband's silhouette anywhere.

"Nikandros, you startled me."

Rushing into the room, he grabbed a pack in the corner

and turned to his wife. Blood covered the left side of his face and trickled down his neck in a steady stream.

"You're hurt!"

Bending to plant a quick kiss on his son's head, he straightened and wasted no time grabbing his wife's hand.

"It looks worse than it is. Shallow cuts sometimes bleed the most." He wasn't telling her anything she didn't already know. Yet seeing her husband covered in blood was still enough to give her heart a shock.

Staring into the turquoise eyes of her love, she nodded her understanding.

"They've found us," he explained as he hurried her out the door and into the light of day. "We haven't a moment to spare."

"Yes, we must go." A bolt of sadness shot through her. Another home left behind, this time more suddenly than the last. They usually had more notice—time enough to pull together their meager belongings and set out before the monsters arrived, but this time had been different. Their enemies had descended without warning, giving them hardly any time to react.

Pressing her son to her chest, she pumped her legs to keep up with Nikandros's long gait as he led them through the labyrinth of tented homes in the makeshift settlement their community had established.

At least they still had their friends and loved ones. At least they still had their family. People were more important than possessions anyway.

"Are we meeting the others in the mountains, or have they already moved on to the next location?" Escape strategies were always the first thing decided on when they settled in a new land.

Nikandros remained quiet as he pulled her along, his gaze scanning, eyes wide and alert.

Her heart had not fully settled since the first call of the horn announcing danger an hour before, but her husband's behavior caused veins of dread to slither over her skin and bury in her center.

"Nik," Ambrosine implored weakly, suddenly terrified to hear him speak.

His hand tightened on hers as they crested the last foothill before the mountain range. Spotting the path to their designated hiding place—a cave hidden under a stone ledge, impossible to see from above—he turned his face to her at last. Grief danced in his gaze, and he pressed his lips into a firm line as he shook his head once.

"None remain but us." The words were delivered in a deadened voice that didn't match the emotion splashed across his face.

"No, that can't be." She stumbled over a small rock, but he easily righted her. Her heart was too heavy to fully process his words. "They can't be all gone. We can't be the last of our kind."

Her pace slowed as her mind struggled to believe that they'd lost everyone close to them. Her parents, siblings, nieces and nephews, lifelong friends. All because of something they'd been born into. Something they had no control over.

"Ambrosine." Nikandros's sharp tone startled her. "We must reach a safe haven or we will meet the same fate."

Her throat was clogged with emotion, so she returned his command with a sharp, silent nod. Now was not the time to mourn.

A familiar jut of rocks came into view and the sweet tang of relief washed over her. Salvation lay before them.

Just as the beginning of a smile touched the corners of her lips, the ground shook beneath them, throwing both of them to the ground. She twisted to avoid falling on her son, but all the wrong places took the brunt of the impact. The side of her head and left shoulder smashed into the unforgiving earth, and her ankle and knee both twisted at unnatural angles.

Nikandros was on his feet a moment later, yanking her up. But her body betrayed her and she fell back with a cry.

"Come, my love." He tugged on her arms. "We must hurry."

Realization sank like a heavy stone in her gut. She slung the cloth strap that held her son over her injured shoulder and pushed the precious bundle toward her husband.

"Take him," she ordered.

Nikandros obeyed without delay, deftly pulling the sling over his head and adjusting the material before reaching once again for his wife.

"No!" Ambrosine slapped his hands away. "Go, now!"

He shook his head. "I won't leave you. I can carry you both."

Another tremor shook the ground, and a fissure appeared on the mountain crest to their left. They both knew they had no more time. The heavens were warring; any moment they would be discovered and turned into prey.

"You will let me go, or you will be responsible for killing us all," she yelled. "I'm no use to them like this. You can come back for me when the threat has passed."

It was a lie neither of them believed. Yes, her broken

body wouldn't be of any use to the monsters, but there would be nothing left of her for him to find later. At least nothing living.

"My heart . . ." Wetness trickled down Nikandros's face. It both broke her heart and frightened her to the core. She'd never seen her husband cry before. "I cannot live this existence without you."

"You can, and you will. For Nikias." She steeled herself for what must be said next. Surely the words would rip both their souls to shreds. "You will leave now, or I will never forgive you."

Pain sliced across her husband's face, but even still, he didn't heed her demands. With one last look at her husband and her precious baby, she closed her eyes and did the only thing she could think to force his compliance. She heard her husband's tortured cry a split-second before brightness burst behind her lids.

When she snapped open her eyes, the world was awash in colors more beautiful than words could describe. She took a deep breath, settled in the knowledge that with their son strapped to his chest, Nikandros wouldn't be able to follow her here—and waited for her end.

Continue Emberly and Steel's epic story at
www.UnleashingFire.com

ACKNOWLEDGMENTS

The lion's share of the acknowledgements in this book belong to you, the reader! I'm so humbled by the overflowing of excitement for this series. The beautiful social media posts, super cute *Fallen Legacies* Funko POPs, and all the comments, posts, and messages I received, prove that you have fallen in love with Emberly and the whole *Fallen Legacies* gang! Heart hands to all of you who take the time to interact with me on social media and share your love for this series!

As you probably noticed, the cast of *Fallen Legacies* characters is rather lengthy. An extra special "thanks," with puppies and sprinkles on top, goes to the members of my Facebook reader group, Julie's Warriors, who helped with the majority of the names for the Council of Elders when my name well ran dry. And especially to Sarah Barnhart, who suggested the name Thorne, for my mysterious and morally ambiguous *Forging Darkness* villain. If you are into interacting with other urban fantasy book lovers, you should join the Warrior's clan and check us out! We talk books, host special author takeovers, and bookish give-aways are a regular occurrence.

To round out my list of acknowledgements, I have to thank my amazing (and amazingly patient) editor, Rebecca, of Rebecca Faith Editorial, Inc. She hung in there with me when I struggled to wrangle *Forging Darkness* into submission. Through doubts, tears, highs and lows she was (and continues to be) one of the biggest cheerleaders for this series. I know the story would not shine as brightly without her help. Steel would also like to thank her for her undying love, devotion, and insistence that he has it in him to win over Emberly's heart.

GET UPDATES FROM JULIE
JOIN MY NEWSLETTER

Please consider joining my exclusive email newsletter. You'll be notified as new books are available, get exclusive bonus scenes, previews, ridiculous videos, and you'll be eligible for special giveaways. Occasionally, you will see puppies. 🐾

Sign up for snarky funsies:
JulieHallAuthor.com/newsletter

I respect your privacy. No spam.
Unsubscribe anytime. 🤍

JOIN THE FAN CLUB
ON FACEBOOK

If you love my books, get involved and get exclusive sneak peeks before anyone else. Sometimes I even give out free puppies (#jokingnotjoking).

You'll get to know other passionate readers like you, and you'll get to know me better too! It'll be fun!

Join the Fan Club on Facebook:
facebook.com/groups/juliehall

See you in there!

~ Julie

ABOUT THE AUTHOR
JULIE HALL

My name is Julie Hall and I'm a *USA Today* bestselling, multiple award-winning author. I read and write YA paranormal / fantasy novels, love doodle dogs and drink Red Bull, but not necessarily in that order.

My daughter says my super power is sleeping all day and writing all night . . . and well, she wouldn't be wrong.

I believe novels are best enjoyed in community. As such, I want to hear from you! Please connect with me as I regularly give out sneak peeks, deleted scenes, prizes, and other freebies to my friends and newsletter subscribers.

Visit my website:
JulieHallAuthor.com

Get my other books:
amazon.com/author/julieghall

Join the Fan Club:
facebook.com/groups/juliehall

Get exclusive updates by email:
JulieHallAuthor.com/newsletter

Connect with me on:

f facebook.com/JulieHallAuthor
BB bookbub.com/authors/julie-hall-7c80af95-5dda-449a-8130-
  3e219d5b00ee
g goodreads.com/JulieHallAuthor
O instagram.com/Julie.Hall.Author
▶ youtube.com/JulieHallAuthor

BOOKS BY JULIE HALL

FALLEN LEGACIES SERIES

Stealing Embers (Fallen Legacies Book 1)

www.StealingEmbers.com

Forging Darkness (Fallen Legacies Book 2)

www.ForgingDarkness.com

Unleashing Fire (Fallen Legacies Book 3)

www.UnleashingFire.com

LIFE AFTER SERIES

Huntress (Life After Book 1)

www.HuntressBook.com

Warfare (Life After Book 2)

www.WarfareBook.com

Dominion (Life After Book 3)

www.DominionBook.com

Logan (A Life After Companion Story)

www.LoganBook.com

Life After - The Complete Series (Books 1-4)

www.LifeAfterSet.com

AUDIOBOOKS BY JULIE HALL

My books are also available on Audible!

http://Audio.JulieHallAuthor.com

CPSIA information can be obtained
at www.ICGtesting.com
Printed in the USA
BVHW031307270321
603578BV00007B/95